EMPIRE O⟨...⟩

THE COLLEC⟨...⟩ ⟨...⟩RIES

RED MERCURY

NEPTUNE RISING

TITAN'S FIRE

This collection first published 2015

Cover image and text copyright Rod Gillies

ISBN-13: 978-1507738962

ISBN-10: 150773896X

For anyone who likes a bit of clank

RED MERCURY

ROD GILLIES

Thanks for giving
this a go.
I hope you enjoy it.

Rod Gillies

The pilot pulled the gas mask over his head, hauling on the straps until the rubber seal pinched at the skin of his face. Probably too tight, he thought, but he wasn't risking a lungful of poison. Not now, not as they approached the crater.

Satisfied with the fit of his mask, he flicked a switch on the control panel, activating warning lights throughout the airship, signalling the crew and their passenger to don their own protective equipment.

Alerted by the flashing lamp, the man crammed uncomfortably into the observation turret pulled his eyes from the viewfinder. He slipped the canvas and rubber breathing apparatus over his head, his hands shaking. The level of devastation below was like nothing he had ever seen, terrifying and exciting in equal measure.

Mask secure, he returned his gaze to the ground, cranking the handle on the box camera at regular intervals, documenting the scene. The force of the blast wave must have been incredible. Even from this altitude, the trees were flattened as far as he could see, strewn out in arcs across the blackened earth, their scorched trunks stripped of lesser branches.

The crater itself was enormous, perhaps five hundred yards across, an almost perfect bowl shape scooped from the frozen ground.

Of the buildings that had stood here previously, nothing remained. The village of Tunguska and its inhabitants were gone, vaporised in the first instant of the explosion. The observer smiled to himself as he continued his photography. The General would be pleased.

*

The sky over the shipyard was a bright cloudless blue, winter sunlight glinting off the gentle waves beyond the breakwater. A pleasant change from the Lake District's usual weather. Anderson couldn't recall a single visit during the last year when it hadn't been pouring with rain.

A whole year, almost to the day, since the project had been given the nod by the Admiralty. Twelve months of training the crew in Southampton, punctuated by regular rail journeys north to Barrow to check on the great steel skeleton as it took shape.

"Lovely day for it..."

Anderson turned to see the squat frame of his chief engineer bustling along the quay.

"It certainly is Mr Dixon. A good omen I think."

"Here's hoping." DIxon frowned. "Sunny skies won't mean much if she springs a leak."

The man was a born pessimist, thought Anderson, his glass not so much half-empty as broken. As Dixon put it, "Always assume the worst, that way you'll only ever be pleasantly surprised." Still, that healthy paranoia meant the chief now knew every seam, valve and rivet of his new charge even better than the shipyard workers who had put her together. Whilst Dixon's outlook was bleak in the extreme, there wasn't a better engineer in all the Royal Navy.

"Stow that chatter Chief. I don't want you spooking the crew."

Dixon straightened his shoulders. "Aye aye sir. Chatter stowed." His mouth, however, retained its downward cast.

"Cheer up man. You've seen even more of her than I have. You know she'll do us proud."

Anderson looked up the slipway towards the assembly shed. There, just visible in an interior darkened by the contrast with the low sun, he could make out the bow of his new command – Her Majesty's Submersible *Nautica*, the first submarine vessel to enter Imperial service.

For years the Royal Navy had concentrated on the building of dreadnoughts at the expense of all else. Most of the top brass shared a dismissive attitude towards submersibles. The whole idea of waging undersea warfare was seen as "damned difficult and damned unsporting."

But concerns about naval fair play were of little import to the Germans. Britannia was supposed to rule the waves, yet the Hun was now the unchallenged master of the ocean's depths. This simply wouldn't do, and so the Empire's cadre of naval engineers had quietly turned their attention to submersibles. *Nautica* was the result – a prototype designed to sail further, faster, and deeper than any other vessel.

Anderson pulled at the chain of his fob watch and flicked the dented casing open. The timepiece was nearly twenty years old now and the intervals it could sustain between winding were becoming shorter. He supposed he really ought to consider a replacement but the watch had been a gift from his wife to mark his first commission and he was fond of its familiar heft.

He raised his hand, signalling to the workers waiting at the top of the ramp. The men swung their sledgehammers and knocked out the last two support posts beneath the submersible's bow. With a harsh metallic screech, the vessel began its progress down the greased slipway towards the water. The thick links of rusted chain dragging behind were designed to stop her picking up too much momentum, but the submersible had still reached a fair old speed as she slid past Anderson and Dixon.

The vessel's rounded bow struck the water with a sharp slap, sending a wave surging out into the calm of the channel. *Nautica* slid forward, lowering herself into the water. Her front half disappeared beneath the swell for a moment before she laboured to the surface, finally free from the cradle which had held her since the first ribs of her keel were laid.

At least she floats, thought Anderson, that's a start.

"Isn't she a beauty?" Dixon's grin was somewhat out of keeping with his usual demeanour.

"That she is Chief."

In truth, *Nautica* would never win any medals for her looks. She wallowed in the water as she was hauled in, an ungainly tube of wooden planking, riveted plates and hoops of steel. Sixty feet from bow to stern, and thirteen feet in diameter, her stubby cigar shape was broken only by the bulbous glass dome of her bridge and the steering fins at her stern.

"Seems a shame not to have a band though", grumbled the engineer. "Don't seem proper without some kind of celebration."

Dixon was right. But no band, no ceremony, and above all, no reporters – that had been the decision. The Admiralty wanted the launch of *Nautica* to be kept as quiet as her construction. Ostensibly to prevent alerting the Germans to Imperial ambition, Anderson suspected the secrecy was also a way of avoiding any public embarrassment if the new vessel should prove less than watertight.

The men ran the gangway out from the quay and Anderson walked down its steep gradient, stepping onto the hull of his new command for the first time. His officers and crew clambered aboard behind him, excited to see their boat finally afloat. Their short training dives to the bottom of the Solent in the Navy's single bathysphere had whetted their appetites. To a man they were keen to get *Nautica* underwater where she belonged.

"Right chaps," Anderson called to his assembled officers. "I want her fuelled, provisioned and ready to sail within the hour."

"Aye aye sir," they chorused.

The officers dispersed amongst the crew, setting men to the work.

Anderson made his way through the activity, heading for the forward hatch. A good crew, he thought. And they should be. He had picked them himself, given a free hand to select the best men in each specialty.

He had also made sure they were all unmarried, or like himself, widowers without children. He figured it was for the best, especially in light of the orders he had received from London the previous evening.

*

The bitter cold seeped into Jones' extremities. At least the deadening chill helped take his mind off the constant motion. It was a small blessing, but he'd take it.

With the airship now side-on to the gusting wind, the gondola swung back and forth beneath the gasbag, Jones' stomach rebelling with every lurch. He steadied himself and felt the vibration through the plates of the hull – the engines straining to keep the craft on course. He was sure the airship was flying through winds well beyond what its manufacturers might have advised, but there wasn't much he could do about that. For the last three hours he'd done little more than peer out of the window into the night, trying to keep his supper down.

He was unused to feeling so powerless, and it filled him with frustration. It would have been a different matter on a boat, whatever the weather. He'd been aboard many a race yacht pitched and tossed as badly, or worse, but had never felt so apprehensive. He was a strong swimmer, after all, but he couldn't fly.

Jones regarded the man seated in the pilot's chair. He wondered if the airman would look quite so chipper if the tables were turned and they were out in the choppy Solent rather than amongst the storm clouds.

Wing Commander Wilberforce certainly appeared to be enjoying the flight, whooping and grinning with each plunge of the craft as he wrestled with the controls.

"Ha!" roared Wilberforce as the airship took another broadside gust. "This is my kind of flying. Better than a boring old jaunt over Surrey, eh?" He smiled at Jones. "How are you enjoying the flight Major?"

"Positively delightful." Jones swallowed as the aircraft dropped, sending his stomach bumping against his ribs. "Will the delightfulness be continuing for much longer?"

"How the bloody hell should I know? I only point the thing where I'm told. Hold on a moment..." Wilberforce flicked open the speaking tube.

"Navvy!" he bellowed. "How much longer? Our passengers are anxious to disembark." He drummed his fingers on the control column.

"Burrows!" he shouted again. "Are you asleep back there? Have you got any bloody idea where we are?"

A voice crackled from the tube. "Yes sir. Right on course sir. Ten minutes to destination sir."

"You're not working from that blasted abacus thing again?"

"No sir. Double-checked by hand sir."

Wilberforce flicked the tube shut. "There you go Major. The lad's altogether too keen on that new-fangled Babbage thing, but he can plot a course. I'll grant him that."

Jones nodded and turned from the flight deck. He headed back down the narrow corridor, shoulders thumping the bulkhead on one side and then the other as the gondola swung. Ten more minutes and then we can throw ourselves into the night from a perfectly serviceable aircraft. Bloody madness. He had seen quite enough of the insides of airships during the long journey from London to Aberdeen and then on to Finland, but that didn't mean he wanted to jump out of this one.

Three men sat on the low benches in the rear compartment. Fitzgerald and Webster looked miserable, exhaling clouds of frozen breath, occasionally stamping one foot and then the other to keep their blood circulating. The compartment's third occupant, Kowalski, was fast asleep, seemingly oblivious to the cold, head resting against the fuselage, his snoring audible over the engine's thrum.

"Ten minutes, gentlemen" said Jones making for the packs piled up between the benches. "Time we were properly attired."

"Dressing for dinner, are we?" asked Webster.

"Naturally. Perhaps you could wake our transatlantic cousin? We wouldn't want him to be late to the party."

Kowalski came awake with a grunt as Webster shook his shoulder. He took a look round through gritty eyes and rolled his shoulders.

"We finally getting out of this tin can of yours?"

"Not mine Captain, Her Majesty's."

"Heh. My apologies. We colonials ain't always the best at remembering the niceties."

"Don't worry. The niceties are not why you're here."

Jones saw the look Kowalski gave him – the man wasn't stupid. Jones could read the question in his eyes – why was he here? He would find out soon enough. For now it was enough that Kowalski was the only one of them who'd ever dropped from an airship before.

The men shuffled around the compartment, pulling first the metal wing assemblies and then the bulky packs onto their shoulders. They took turns hauling on each other's straps, fastening the buckles tight.

Jones double-checked their inventory. All had knives and pistols strapped to their belts and Kowalski had a repeating carbine tied across the top of his pack. Alongside rations and cold weather gear, the packs were stuffed with bundles of explosive, fuses and timers. Manufacturers' marks and identifying insignia had been carefully removed from every item which wasn't genuine Soviet issue.

"Everyone ready?" Jones asked.

"Ready to get killed maybe..." Never the cheeriest of fellows, Fitzgerald looked distinctly unhappy. "This is bloody ridiculous Major. Webster and I spend all our time behind desks. We've never done anything like this before."

Behind him, Webster nodded, his round face similarly troubled.

"If it's any consolation, neither have I," said Jones. "However, the Captain here has dropped dozens of times and lived to tell the tale."

"Bully for him," snorted Webster. "Surely there are whole squadrons of dragoons specially trained for this sort of thing?"

"You know there are. But few who could be mobilised in time, and fewer still who speak Russian. You heard the Duke. We were the best he could muster." Jones looked hard at his fellow Englishmen. "Now are we going to jump out of this bloody thing, or am I going to have to throw you out one after the other?"

Webster's bluster evaporated in a blown-out sigh. "Very well. Let's get it over and done with." He shuffled towards the large bulkhead door at the rear of the compartment.

Fitzgerald held Jones' stare for a long moment before his shoulders too slumped in defeat.

"Alright Major, you win. But if I make it to the ground in one piece, I demand one of those fancy cigarettes of yours as a reward."

"Fitz, I'll tell you what – if we both make it down alive, you can have the whole damned case."

*

Three nights before, sitting in the Duke of Buckingham's office in Whitehall, Jones had harboured many of the same reservations as Fitzgerald and Webster.

Hanson, the Duke's advisor, had welcomed them as they filed into the high-ceilinged room. "Gentlemen, thank you for joining us at such short notice this evening. I do hope you were not overly inconvenienced."

Jones' summons had arrived, in the hands of a junior officer, as he was sitting down to dinner with his aging aunt and uncle at their home in

Richmond. Whilst they kept an excellent table, their conversation was generally dreadful and Jones had jumped at the opportunity to escape. Many a time over the next few days he was to find himself wishing he had stayed in Richmond and finished his soup. But then you didn't volunteer for Buckingham's Special Operations Division if you wanted a quiet life.

Buckingham himself sat behind an antique desk before a wall dominated by an enormous oil painting. A Gainsborough, if Jones remembered correctly, but not a good one. The old man pulled himself erect and negotiated his way round the desk, leaning heavily on his cane.

"Let us begin," he said. His moustache bristled as he spat words like machine gun bullets. "I've got a job for you lot. A rescue mission. With an added helping of demolition."

He introduced the gathered men to one another. "This is Fitzgerald, and Webster − specialists from my Russian section. This disreputable-looking chap is Major Jones, on secondment from the Queen's Guards."

Webster thrust his podgy hand out. "Delighted to make your acquaintance old chap," he said, pumping Jones' arm up and down. "Heard a lot about you."

Fitzgerald said nothing, offering only a nod as he and Jones shared a short, firm handshake.

The Duke indicated his other guest with the tip of his cane. "And this is John Kowalski, from Florida. A Captain in the infamous Free Fleet..."

Webster and Fitzgerald stared with undisguised curiosity. Kowalski gave them a casual fingertip salute in response, barely acknowledging their presence. Jones assumed you got used to curious looks when people discovered you were a mercenary. The Floridian's sharp-eyed gaze spent more time fixed on Jones. Not a challenge − rather an appraisal, the measured assessment of one professional by another.

The men settled themselves and Buckingham pulled a photograph from a folio of documents and tossed it onto the large mahogany table. The sepia image showed a balding man, perhaps sixty years old, with thick round glasses and a goatee beard.

"Our man is here," said the Duke, tapping on an unrolled map of Russia's northern provinces. "Kovdor Mine. Just outside Murmansk. Middle of bloody nowhere."

"Who is he sir?" asked Fitzgerald.

"Scientist. Jewish chap. Alexei Eisenstein. You chaps have to get him and his daughter out of there."

"Won't the Russians have something to say about that?"

"Yes, I imagine they would. If they knew anything about it. Which can't happen. Small team of men. Got to be in and out before the comrades realise."

Hanson spoke up. "Stealth and discretion are essential. If it became apparent that Imperial agents were blundering around inside Russia then I daresay Lenin and his chums would be less than impressed."

Buckingham leaned over the table. "Germany and France seem set upon a collision course. Damned idiots. If it happens, we'll have no option but to honour our treaties and support the French. Now, we could have counted on Tsar Nicholas. But since the bloody Bolsheviks took over?"

The Duke harrumphed into his moustache. "The whole thing is up in the air. The Soviets might make for uncomfortable allies, what with all that socialism claptrap of theirs, but we can't afford to push them into the arms of the Kaiser."

Webster looked up from the map.

"I can appreciate the need for discretion, but why us? I mean, why Fitzgerald and I?" He indicated the other men round the table. "The Major I know, if only by reputation, and I'm sure Captain Kowalski is capable enough. But Fitzgerald and I are bureaucrats, bloody paper-shufflers, if you'll excuse my French. Granted, we did some sneaking around when we were young, but that was nearly ten years ago." He patted at the paunch barely contained within his waistcoat. "I can't climb the stairs without getting out of breath nowadays, never mind a rope, or God forbid, a wall."

Buckingham raised his cane, waving it in Webster's direction. "I don't see you with one of these yet. You'll manage."

"Local knowledge could be the key to all this," said Hanson. "Granted, it's some time since either of you were out in the field, but there's not an Englishmen alive who's spent as long in northern Russia as you two."

Webster and Fitzgerald glanced at one another, clearly unhappy.

"Chin up chaps," said Buckingham. "You'll have old Jonesy leading your little excursion. What you may lack in recent field experience, he makes up for in droves. And we're lucky enough the Captain here was available at short notice. I'm sure he can be guaranteed to supply any required muscle..." The Duke jabbed the cane at Kowalski. "That's the word you colonials use, I believe?"

"Something like that, Your Lordship."

"We are short on time, and short on people. Hence retaining the services of Captain Kowalski, as well as pulling you men in."

"Interrupted a damned good dinner doing it too," put in Jones.

The Duke arched an eyebrow. "I thought you were awfully quiet. I assume you have some questions?"

Jones slipped his hand into his jacket and took out his cigarette case. He opened it and removed one of the slim, white cylinders, rolling it backwards and forwards between his thumb and forefinger. Eventually he looked up at the Duke.

"Only the obvious one. This Eisenstein chap, what's he working on?"

"Now Major," said Hanson. "Let's just say there are certain details you don't need to be acquainted with in order to carry out your duties."

"My experience in the field is regularly to the contrary." Jones lit his cigarette and blew out a cloud of fragrant smoke. "I find being in full possession of the facts often makes it easier to get the job done."

"As I said, there are things you don't need to know. Now moving on –"

"I just wondered, if it might have something to do with Red Mercury?"

Hanson's eyes narrowed. "How could you possibly know that?"

"Well, let's say I heard Murmansk is a good place for digging up uranium ore. And you've already told us we're going to infiltrate a mine. And let's say I also heard uranium is a key ingredient in this Red Mercury stuff which everyone seems to be excited about."

Jones took another draw on his cigarette before continuing. "As to how I heard these things? Let's say there are certain details you don't need to be acquainted with in order to carry out *your* duties."

"That's quite enough." The Duke cut. "Hanson, I think these men have heard enough to make further secretiveness pointless. Tell them."

Hanson looked fit to burst, but made do with a glare at Jones before speaking. "The Soviets are extracting and purifying uranium for conversion into Red Mercury. Current methods are painfully slow – in five years, the mine has produced no more than four ounces of the stuff. Our man Eisenstein has perfected a new process that will allow them to do things much more efficiently." He tapped his finger on the photograph of the scientist. "The Professor wants out. He contacted us a week ago, through channels you most definitely do not need to be acquainted with." This last comment was accompanied by another sharp look at Jones.

"Why? And why now?" asked Jones.

"Eisenstein is no Bolshevik. His wife was held in a labour camp to ensure his loyalty. She died last month. His daughter works with him at the mine, and he will not leave Russia without her. The longer we leave it, the more likely the Soviets will move her somewhere else as they did with his wife. Leverage, you see."

The Duke spoke up once again. "The head man in Murmansk is no fool. Met him once, at a summit in Warsaw. Gorev – great brute of a chap. Handshake like a vice. Very bright though, and ambitious too."

"Done well for himself since the revolution," said Hanson. "Runs the Committee of Scientific Advancement. Favourite of Lenin's apparently."

Jones ground his cigarette into the ashtray. "From what I hear, Comrade Lenin's favour can wax and wane – just ask poor old Trotsky. How do we to get into Russia?"

"Whoa there," put in Kowalski. "Slow up a little. Still a bunch of things I need to get straight. What does this here Red Mercury stuff do?"

Hanson hesitated, glancing at the Duke who nodded for him to continue. "Red Mercury is a deadly poison, but one that does not need to be touched or inhaled. It can sicken and kill from a distance. Beyond these immediate unsavoury properties, if prepared correctly it can be used to make bombs which explode with astonishing force."

"Like nitro-glycerine then, but poisonous?"

"Red Mercury makes Mister Nobel's concoction look positively harmless. A one-pound bomb could destroy the entire city of London and poison its ruins for a hundred years."

Silence descended as the assembled men pondered this information. Eventually the Duke spoke.

"Those four ounces? The Bolshies used them in a test two months ago. Blew a bloody great hole in Siberia. They've got the know-how, and now they're on the verge of being able to produce Red Mercury in quantity." Buckingham shook his head. "If the Soviets build more of these bombs, a conflict between France and Germany will be immaterial, a petty little sideshow. With such a weapon, Communist Russia would sweep across Europe and Great Britain unchallenged. Captain, I doubt even your United States could stand against her."

"Not my United States, Your Lordship. I'm Floridian. But I get the gist."

"We have to get Eisenstein and his daughter out. And put a serious dent in the operation of that damned mine." Buckingham looked at each of his guests in turn. "This is obviously a mission for volunteers. You're free to leave now if you wish. Time to decide – in or out?"

Jones nodded. "Whilst I figure they'd struggle to get an airship close, I don't fancy the thought of the Bolshies sneaking a bomb up the Thames on some tatty steamer. I'm in."

Webster and Fitzgerald looked at each other for a moment before they too nodded their agreement.

"I go where the Fleet tells me," shrugged Kowalski. "Just so long as you keep paying the bills."

"Very well gentlemen," said Hanson. "If you could follow me, we have a railway special waiting at Victoria. You're off to the aerodrome at Farnborough – first stop, Aberdeen. We'll finish briefing you up there."

The Duke wished them luck as they filed out, but he motioned to Jones as he brought up the rear. "Hang on a moment Major..."

Buckingham let the others continue after Hanson down the corridor. He closed the door and turned to Jones, a frown fixed in place.

"Sorry David, but I haven't been totally honest with you. Things are not as simple as they may appear..."

*

"Five minutes!" Wilberforce's voice crackled from the speaking tube.

Kowalski stood by the hatch as the three Englishmen shuffled into line. Webster looked terrified, Fitzgerald angry. Jones was impassive as ever. Kowalski wondered if the man ever got flustered. Perhaps what they were about to do might crack the Major's composure.

"Gentlemen," he said. "When it's your turn to drop, you'll take a large step forward with your arms crossed over your chest. Clear?"

All three nodded. Kowalski had drummed the procedure into them umpteen times in the last few days. He reckoned they could all repeat his lines without even thinking. But this time it was no drill.

"You count to ten. No more. No less. Then you pull the cord and your wings will deploy. If your wings don't deploy, don't panic. Reach round to your back and pull the rope handle. Can you all feel the rope?"

The men all checked and nodded once more.

"Follow the wing-lamps of the man ahead of you. Adjust your body position like we practiced. Make sure you ain't bunching up on the man ahead, or falling too far behind."

He resisted the urge to smile as he recalled the 'practice' he had taken them through over the last few days in a selection of spartan military accommodations, first in northern Scotland and then Finland. The three Englishmen, lying on their stomachs across mess room chairs, attempting to keep their arms and legs stretched out, rocking backwards or forwards as he shouted directions. He'd made no attempt to teach them how to make calculations from their altitude and descent speed gauges. Np point complicating things. Instead he'd come up with the much simpler plan of them following him and watching his wing lamps.

"As we approach the ground, I'll activate my props. My wing-lamps will change to red. When you see the lamps of the man ahead of you change, count to five and then throw your chest lever." He summarised, drumming the points home. "Count to ten, pull the cord. Red light, count to five and throw the lever. That's all you need to remember gents. After that, it's a cakewalk."

He figured they knew he was lying, but there wasn't much he could do about it. Aerial dragoons trained for months before their first drop. Kowalski had done his best to get them ready. He hoped it was adequate preparation for a night drop through unfriendly skies.

He'd done what he'd been paid for. The rest was up to them.

*

Burrows entered the compartment and pointed past the assembled men. They parted to let him through. The navigator clipped his safety line to a bracket and grasped the wheel on the bulkhead door.

"Ready?"

"As we'll ever be, Mr Burrows," said Jones.

The airman turned the wheel and pulled the door inwards. The wind hurled itself in through the widening gap, lowering the temperature in the compartment even further. Kowalski pulled his leather facemask down and adjusted the fit of his goggles. Jones and the others did the same. Preparation over, they waited amidst the noise and cold, trying to avoid contemplating what was to come.

"Ready..." came the voice from the tube.

Wilberforce's amplified tones crackled their way through the countdown. Burrows displayed the numbers with his fingers.

"Five..."

Kowalski shuffled forwards to the edge of the door.

"Four..."

He tugged one last time on the straps of his harness.

"Three..."

He crossed his arms over his chest, Burrows keeping him steady in the doorway with a firm grip.

"Two..."

He took a last glance back and nodded to the men behind him.

"One!"

Without a pause Kowalski tipped headfirst into the darkness.

Webster hesitated only a moment and followed, although less gracefully than Kowalski. Fitzgerald stood unmoving. Burrows pulled at the reluctant man's shoulder, hauling him forward.

Jones gave him a push from behind. "Get out the bloody door!"

Fitzgerald turned, eyes wide behind his goggles. Jones prepared himself to shove the man through the opening, but Fitzgerald saw the intent and made up his own mind. He grabbed the sides of the hatch and threw himself into the night.

Jones paused for a moment, still astonished he was really going to go through with this. He was roused by Burrows thrusting a small, oilskin-wrapped package into his hand. Jones looked at it stupidly then stuffed it into his pocket. He nodded his thanks to the airman and jumped.

He tumbled in the air, catching a vague glimpse of the airship's bulk before it was swallowed into blackness. The wind's fierce blast forced its way through the fabric of his clothing and facemask, producing a chill like ice splinters where it found skin.

Jones tried to concentrate on his count, distracted by his racing heartbeat as he plummeted through the night. Reaching ten, he pushed his arm down against the rush of air, hunting for the flailing release cord. The cable slipped from his grasp at first, causing him a moment of sick panic. But on his second attempt, he grabbed hold and pulled. With a sudden jerk, the wings deployed from the assembly on his back. He felt a flood of relief course through him as his rate of descent began to slow.

Definitely slower, but still fast enough to break every bone in his body when he hit the ground. Craning his head to the side, he checked his props. There, barely visible in the darkness, the blades mounted halfway down the metal wings were spinning furiously, exactly as they were designed to do. The props would build pressure in his chest box as he fell, pressure which would be converted into motive power when he threw the lever, reversing the direction of the props' rotation, creating lift and slowing his descent.

The theory was simple, and in practice it came down to one key element – throwing the lever at the right moment. Too soon and you would not have built up enough pressure, causing gravity to rudely reassert itself before you were safely down. Too late and you would have plenty of pressure but not enough time before you smashed headlong into the ground. As Kowalski had wryly informed them, falling never hurt anybody – abrupt deceleration was what you really had to worry about.

Jones searched the sky below for his fellows and soon spotted a pair of green lights beneath him and off to the left – Fitzgerald. After a moment he made out another two lights further down, to the right this time – Webster. Finally, far beneath him, leading the descent, the final pair – Kowalski. Thank God the night was clear, otherwise they would never have been able to see one another. But there they all were, wings safely deployed.

He watched Webster's lights drifting right, bringing him into line with Kowalski. Fitzgerald was moving too, but with more seesawing, overcompensating first one way and then the other. Jones rolled his shoulders a little, and watched the lights below him shift. He straightened up and moved back a touch, finding the right balance between the shrieking wind and the forward momentum given him by his wings.

Surprised at how stable he felt, Jones realised he was almost enjoying the sensation. He wondered how it would feel to try this in daylight, to see the panorama of the earth spread out below. And maybe somewhere warmer he thought, the biting slipstream continuing to stab its way through his multiple layers.

Below him the lowest set of lights changed to red. Jones began counting to himself and, sure enough, on five, Webster's wing-lamps changed colour. Another five and Fitzgerald's also turned crimson.

After making his own count, Jones threw the lever on the chest box. With a screech of shifting gears, his props began their counter-rotation. His harness jerked tighter, driving the breath from his lungs.

They flew in close formation now and Jones could make out the shadowy outlines of wings and men in the glow from the thin crescent moon. In the same faint, silvery light he began taking note of the surroundings, rather than simply concentrating on the lamps of the men below. They were falling, more and more slowly, towards a snow-covered waste dotted with patches of darker forest. Away to the north, perhaps ten miles or so, a faint cluster of lights could only be Murmansk.

Kowalski's wing-lamps began slipping to the left and the three Englishmen followed with varying degrees of grace. The Floridian was leading them towards a field near one of the small clusters of trees. Jones hoped the snow was deep, and soft.

The last few moments were a blur. Although rationally he knew his rate of descent had reduced dramatically, the white ground still appeared to be approaching at a terrifying rush. Remembering his training, he lifted his head and arms to swing his body almost vertical. He pushed his legs out before him, feet together – nothing to do now but brace for impact.

He thumped hard into the snow, his landing burying him deep in the drift. Lying there, staring up at the dark sky above, he wiggled his fingers and toes in turn, then gingerly moved his arms and legs. Delighted, and not a little amazed, to find himself whole and undamaged, he pulled the mask and goggles from his face and let out a long breath.

He unclipped his harness and struggled to his feet. He detached the wing assembly and chest box from the rest of his pack and tossed them aside. He withdrew an electrical lamp from the pack and flashed it briefly to each of the four points of the compass.

First to lumber out of the snow towards his signal was Webster, almost breathless with excitement. "Quite astonishing, eh Major?" he panted, face flushed and eyes gleaming. "Once I realised I wasn't going to die immediately, I found that most invigorating."

"Here's hoping Fitz felt the same, I practically had to push him out."

"Poor dear. I thought he was looking a little green around the gills."

They both turned as Kowalski and Fitzgerald trudged out of the darkness together.

"Everybody alright?" asked the Floridian.

"Quite well," said Webster. "Keen to have another go, actually..."

"Reckoned you'd get the hang of it."

Fitzgerald offered them a sour look. "I swear, if I ever have to do something like that again, I'll kill myself first."

"Cheer up Fitz," said Jones, "Let's get into the trees for a bit of cover. And then you can have that smoke I owe you."

"Ah yes," said Fitzgerald, perking up at the thought. "I do believe you owe me the whole case."

"Don't push your luck. I nearly had to toss you out the door..."

"That you did. Let's call it quits with the one."

The four men gathered their gear and headed towards the trees.

*

They moved north through the snow-covered countryside, staying inside the cover provided by patches of woodland wherever possible. Whilst the uneven ground between the pines made for difficult going, none of them complained. Although it was hard work concentrating on their footing between the trees, it was infinitely preferable to the apprehension they all felt in the pit of the stomach when forced to cross patches of open ground. Despite their fear, they encountered no signs of life. The land around them seemed frozen solid in a deep winter sleep.

Hours passed during which the sky brightened as much as it would at this time of year. The pale sun limped up over the horizon, bringing a little light but no warmth. Jones didn't mind. Despite the bitter chill in the air, he found himself sweating profusely. His thighs burned with the effort of dragging his legs through the knee-high snow. At least the terrain they traversed was reasonably flat. He wasn't sure they would have managed if there had been any hills to contend with.

They took turns leading the way, the first man in line forcing a path for the others. It was exhausting work out in front and he and Kowalski ended up taking the lion's share of the lead as the other two struggled. Despite stopping at regular intervals in the patches of forest to recover their strength, their progress was torturous. Surely it couldn't be far now, Jones thought, his eyes fixed on the next line of trees.

Moving into cover past the first few trunks, he slipped his pack from his shoulders and sank to the ground. He leaned back against a dark, moss-covered pine. Fitzgerald and Webster shuffled up and collapsed in ungainly fashion, both of them wheezing badly.

"Good Lord," groaned Webster. "I'm in worse bloody shape than I thought. I sound like a set of broken bagpipes. Got to do something about this midriff of mine." He removed his pack and flopped back full length into the snow. "Mind you, at least my extra layer helps me keep warm. I don't know how a gangly rake like you can stand it Fitz."

"Don't you worry about me old boy. All I need is a smoke every now and again. Nothing like it for warding off the chill." He cast a dark look towards Jones. "Although goodness knows when we'll be allowed one..."

"Funny," said Webster. "Never developed a taste for tobacco myself. Plenty of other vices of course."

"Talking of smoke," said Kowalski. "I can see some rising above the trees ahead."

"Murmansk I hope," replied Jones. "Unless we are spectacularly lost and have arrived somewhere else."

"Major, there ain't anyplace else to arrive at."

"Let's take a look, just to be sure." Jones got to his feet. "Fitz, Webster – you two stay here with the equipment. Get some food inside you. No fire, no noise, and sorry Fitz, still no smoke. The Captain and I shall head forward to get the lie of the land."

The men on the ground nodded, clearly relieved at the prospect of a decent rest. Jones and Kowalski left them and pressed on.

Without discussion, the pair began moving more carefully, checking their footing with every step, slipping silently through the woods. One would head forward then pause, pressed against a tree, whilst the other moved past him. Jones considered the natural pattern he and Kowalski had fallen into – it was a pleasure to work with a fellow professional.

At the edge of the trees, they dropped to the ground and crawled the last few feet. From their vantage point under the firs they looked out over the bleak approaches to Murmansk.

The wood at their backs stood on a small rise above a rough track of frozen, rutted mud. This sorry excuse for a road ran about half a mile to their left before disappearing between more trees. In the opposite direction, it curved round to the north to meet a metal-framed bridge. Two guards stood at the near end of the bridge, hands tucked into their armpits, trying to keep warm.

Across the river, the town squatted – a dismal collection of ramshackle sheds, dilapidated warehouses and ugly brick factories with towering chimneys. Tattered red flags snapped in the wind and plumes of steam billowed from vents and grilles, mixing with the chimney smoke to form a grim smog. Where the river met the waters of the Kola Sound, cargo ships moored at the dockside beneath a forest of cranes.

With a mechanical groan and a great hiss of steam, a tractor emerged from one of the riverfront warehouses directly opposite them. It ground its way along the road dragging a heavily-laden sledge towards the docks. The observers spotted men in greatcoats and furred hats, somehow insignificant against the leaden backdrop of grey buildings. The tiny figures trudged the streets, hunched up against the cold, trailing little puffs of frozen breath as if they too were steam-driven.

"Welcome to the workers' paradise..." said Jones.

"Honestly Major, it don't seem much different from the less salubrious parts of London I've seen. Or New York, for that matter."

"Careful now Captain. You're beginning to sound like a Bolshevik."

"Heh. No danger of that. I'm all for free enterprise. And I can't abide the vodka the Reds all drink. I'm a bourbon man through and through." Kowalski stiffened, head to one side, listening. "What's that?"

Jones heard it too, and then felt vibration in the ground beneath him.

"We're about to have company."

Off to their left came the rumble of heavy machinery over a slow rhythmic thump. The sound grew louder as its source approached, coming into view where the path emerged from the trees. Striding down the track, its massive steel feet crunching through the frozen mud, a mechanical walker led a column of soldiers.

The walker's metal bulk towered over the men marching behind. Its body was a steel cube, ten feet square and studded with rivets and grilles, the forward panel dominated by a short, fat cannon barrel, like some kind of ugly snout. Above the gun, a slatted viewport allowed the pilot within to see where he was headed. Gears grumbled round on its flanks and pistons expanded and contracted with sharp squeals of steam, propelling the vehicle forward in an unstoppable gait.

Watching the walker lurch along the track, Jones dreaded to think how it would feel to be shaken back and forth inside the two-legged behemoth. Mind you, it would be a sight warmer in there than it was for the soldiers trudging in its wake.

The company was made up of a hundred men or so, lined up in ranks of four. Their boots and greatcoats were filthy and their marching was out of step over the broken track, but they held their heads high and carried their weapons with assurance. These were no raw conscripts.

"That's a lot of soldiers," whispered Kowalski. "And they're all heading in the same direction as us."

"Hardly surprising. Murmansk is a barracks town for the Red Army."

"And we're going to stroll right on in there?" Kowalski looked aghast.

"Every week hundreds of men arrive and depart by land, air and sea. Who's likely to notice four strangers? It's perfect."

"Major, you have a damned funny idea of perfection. Figure the Fleet should have charged that Duke of yours something extra for all this..."

They lay in silence as the line of troops filed past. The dull thump of the walker's heavy feet turned to harsh metallic clangs as the column moved onto the bridge. When the last rank of soldiers had marched past their position, Jones and Kowalski shuffled back into the trees.

*

They moved west through the woods, seeking an unobtrusive point to join the track. After half an hour's careful, quiet walking, they found the perfect spot where the trees stood right alongside the rutted road.

They shrugged out of their snowsuits to reveal Red Army uniforms beneath. Jones sported the shoulder boards and decorations of a Major, Kowalski a Captain, and Webster and Fitzgerald both wore the rank of Sergeant. Their packs delivered up olive green greatcoats and fur hats with red star insignia to complete the outfits. However, as they finished getting changed, Jones realised something was still missing.

"Mud," he said. "We need some mud. Those soldiers were filthy. I don't want to end up in some gulag because of a pristine jacket."

Fitzgerald stamped his foot. "We'll have to soften this up then, and I don't think a fire is a good idea."

"Definitely not a good idea, but perhaps the comrades may have helped us with their little parade earlier..."

Jones checked the road was empty in both directions and stepped from the woods. Sure enough, within a few yards he found what he was looking for. There, where the walker's steps had cracked through the surface ice, lay a dark patch of dirty water, not quite refrozen. He waved the others out and they took turns to stamp through the filthy liquid, spattering their uniforms. Within a minute or two their clothes looked more lived-in, if not quite as bedraggled as the men they had seen earlier.

"Right," said Jones. "Follow my lead, and Russian only from now on."

They trudged up the track toward the bridge under the gaze of the two guards. The soldiers appeared neither suspicious nor particularly alert, but Jones saw Kowalski adjust his grip on his carbine all the same.

"Relax Captain," he whispered. "New faces all the time, remember."

He pulled a cigarette from his case and held it up as they approached the guards, calling out in fluent Russian. "Comrade Corporal, do you have a match? Or even better, perhaps any vodka?"

The corporal smiled and pulled off one of his gloves. He fished a squashed box of matches from his pocket. "No vodka unfortunately, Comrade Major, but at least I can supply with you a light."

"Thank you," said Jones, taking the proffered box. He struck a match and lit his cigarette, hands cupped around the flame. "I am to report to the Comrade General when I arrive. Where would I find him?"

"The General spends most of his time out at the mine. This time of year, the only way out there is the train. Next one is tomorrow morning."

"Very well. And the Cheka office?"

A flicker of distaste crossed the soldier's face, but the emotion was quickly hidden. Nobody wanted to fall foul of the Soviet secret police. He turned and pointed over the bridge. "Straight up the road. Keep going until you reach the square."

"Thank you again Comrade. For the light, and for the directions. Shame about the vodka..." Jones gave the guard a salute and marched on.

The others followed him over the bridge. Gaps between the girders offered glimpses of the turbulent brown water below, dotted with chunks of ice churning their way downstream. The river was the reason for Murmansk's existence – its fierce current kept the Kola Sound free of sea ice, even in the depths of winter, making the town the primary supply port for the whole of northern Russia.

Safely away from the guards, Kowalski spoke. "Nice work Major."

"Our game of charades is only just beginning," said Jones.

Across the bridge they entered the town, the road hemmed in by the high brick walls of factories and warehouses. The buildings were arranged in haphazard fashion, tight alleyways cutting between them at odd angles. Founded only ten years previously, Murmansk was clearly the result of a rush of unplanned construction.

Through every doorway and dirty window pane they saw signs of military preparation. In workshop after workshop, men scuttled around, lit by the dull glow of forges and the sharp spray of sparks, feeding the voracious appetites of the machinery with coal and steel. In one building they spied a half-assembled walker standing tall and naked, awaiting its armoured plating. The next warehouse was filled to bursting with bundles of rifles and stacks of shells. The town overflowed with the sights and sounds of fearsome industry.

"Our friend Ivan is getting ready for war," muttered Fitzgerald.

"It's the same all across Europe," replied Jones. "The difference is we all know who we're going to be fighting. Ivan hasn't decided yet."

The road up from the river was full of workers and men in uniform, stomping here and there, nobody dawdling in the cold. The infiltrators were forced to stand aside along with everyone else to let large steam tractors rumble past, their massive wheels standing taller than a man. Amongst all the hurly-burly, nobody paid the four of them the least notice, except for the odd salute directed at Jones whenever a soldier spotted his collar pips.

As they approached the centre of the town, they encountered a group of men in patched and filthy clothing. This squad of unfortunates shuffled down the muddy street, their steps hampered by the shackles connecting each man to his neighbour. Painfully thin, with shaved heads and sunken eyes, they appeared a battalion of the walking dead.

Jones grabbed the arm of a passing soldier and indicated the wretched parade. "Who are they?"

"Who knows? Poor bastards did something to upset the Cheka. Next thing they know, they're digging in shifts out at the mine." The man shook his head and moved on.

Jones watched the pitiful band file past, perhaps thirty men in all. At their rear marched a Russian sergeant, shouting and aiming the occasional kick at the prisoners to keep them moving. Jones would have dearly loved to give the overseer a kick of his own. He saw his own anger reflected in Kowalski's dark gaze.

"Now is not the time, Comrade Captain," he said, turning and leading the others up the road.

As they reached the bustling main square a dark shadow overtook them, the throb of engines drifting down from above. Murmansk's residents were used to the sight of airships, but even so, soldiers and workers stopped in the street to stare and point at this aerial monster. The dark grey bulk of the huge dirigible moved over the town, its ribbed gas envelope blocking out the sun. At an altitude of only a hundred feet or so, it flew low enough that those on the ground could make out figures at the bridge windows and the stubby cannon barrels poking from the gunports down the gondola's flanks.

One of the really big ones, thought Jones. A Tupolev surely – almost as big as the German Zeppelins. Heading for the air marshalling yards to the north of the town, no doubt. From there the Soviet airships ranged out, supplying and protecting the isolated mining and drilling operations scattered across the islands of the Arctic. He knew the top brass in Whitehall were concerned at the growing capability of Soviet aeronautic forces – one more reason everyone worried which way Russia might turn in the event of war. If it wasn't the German navy, it was Soviet airships – it seemed the days of unrivalled Imperial power were at an end.

The enormous airship droned out of sight and movement across the square resumed, pedestrians once again dropping their heads against the wind. Jones and his men dodged between horse-drawn sledges and rumbling tractors, crossing the open space and heading for a narrow street on the opposite side.

At the square's corner, their way into the alley was blocked by a group of uniformed men, gathered around a commotion. Two men clad in black leather trenchcoats kicked at a young soldier curled into a ball on the ground, his hands held up around in his head in a feeble attempt at protection. The spectators looked on in sullen silence, wincing in sympathy as the blows rained in on their unfortunate comrade. One or two muttered their displeasure, but none looked ready to intervene.

The grizzled old soldier in front of Jones turned away, unable to watch as another kick thumped into the helpless man. His eyes shone with tears but lit up with sudden hope when he spotted Jones' insignia.

"Major, you have to help." He clutched at Jones' sleeve. "My brother's son. He did nothing wrong. He was just lucky at the card table. Now these pigs are sober, they want their money back. Please..."

Other soldiers around them grumbled their agreement, looking to the senior officer now in their midst to take action. Damn it, thought Jones –

the last thing they needed now was to draw attention. But the older man's voice grew more desperate and Jones found himself at the centre of an expanding circle of expectant stares. He would have to do something. Walking away now would be worse than taking action.

He shoved his way through the soldiers. "That's enough Comrades."

The two Chekists turned, their anger at the interruption fading to a dull simmer of resentment as they took in Jones' rank.

"This man interfered with the work of the Cheka —"

"As am I," snapped Jones. "Will I receive similar treatment? Whatever work you were about, it is finished."

He glared at the pair and they backed away. The old soldier pushed forward and helped the injured youth climb unsteadily to his feet.

"What is going on here?" rose a voice from the edge of the crowd.

The onlookers parted to reveal a tall figure. This man too was clad in the trademark dark coat of the Cheka, but leant an even more sinister aspect by the black patch over his left eye. A livid scar emerged from beneath the patch and ran down his cheek, pulling the corner of his mouth up in a cruel half-smile.

The two policemen snapped to attention as the newcomer stepped into the circle of soldiers. He turned his head, his single eye working over the crowd, fixing on each face in turn as if filing it away for later identification. None of the assembly met his gaze, instead developing an interest in the hard-packed snow beneath their feet. Soldiers on the fringes of the crowd began to slink away as unobtrusively as they could.

The new arrival settled his attention on Jones. "A problem Major?"

"A trivial matter. Nothing to concern yourself with."

"A trivial matter, eh?" The officer turned to his men. "Well?"

The pair shared a look. "The Major is correct..." said the first.

"It was nothing. A misunderstanding," said the other.

They shifted uncomfortably under the one-eyed man's stare but said nothing more. The Cheka officer turned back to Jones.

"The matter does seem to be settled. For the moment." The man raised his voice. "This gathering will disperse. Immediately."

The Chekist stepped up close to Jones.

"I will speak with my men. Perhaps you and I will talk again?"

"I look forward to it."

The uninjured side of the officer's face formed a brief, cold smile. He turned on his heel and marched off, subordinates in tow.

Fitzgerald sidled up to Jones. "Excellent stuff Major. Perhaps you could have picked a more public place for your little performance?"

"Probably not." Much as Fitzgerald's tone irked, Jones couldn't disagree with the sentiment. "Let's go before anything else happens."

As they entered the alley, they passed the old soldier tending to his nephew, wiping at his bloodied face with a dirty rag. The veteran nodded gratefully at Jones before returning his attention to the younger man.

Jones counted junctions and turned left at the appropriate corner, hoping Hanson's maps had been correct. Sure enough, they came to a rail yard full of freight cars. The far side of the snow-covered space was taken up by an open-sided shed. Its roof sheltered a large black locomotive, two passenger cars and a half-dozen coal trucks attached behind.

Across the yard from the engine shed, beyond the static rolling stock, stood a dilapidated wooden hut. Its low roof slumped under its burden of snow, icicles hanging from the broken guttering. Jones gathered his men in the lee of one of the cars and indicated the tatty building.

"Our accommodation..."

"Shabby lodgings in normal circumstances," said Webster. "But if it gets me out of the cold, it's as good as the bloody Ritz."

Kowalski nodded. "Amen to that."

"How do we know it's empty?" asked Fitzgerald.

"It's the old telegraph office. The Bolshies built another one in the centre of the town and Hanson's contacts swear this one is never used. But you're right, we can't be sure. Someone will have to go and check. Captain Kowalski, if you would be so kind?"

"My pleasure, Major."

"Quietly, if you don't mind."

"Well obviously."

*

Kowalski climbed onto the low wooden deck in front of the hut. He moved to the padlocked door, testing each board before trusting it with his weight. He raised a gloved hand and rubbed a clean patch on the filthy window pane. The hut appeared to be unoccupied.

He checked around, scanning the yard and the street beyond for any signs of movement. Confident he was unobserved, he drew his pistol. He also pulled a six-inch brass tube from his pocket. He screwed the piece of metal carefully onto the barrel of the gun.

The attachment was a new development from the Fleet's gunnery workshops. Whilst it ruined the balance of the weapon, and brought its effective range down to a matter of feet, it also dramatically reduced the noise of firing the pistol, making it almost silent. Just the thing for a secret mission he'd argued when Jones had raised concerns about taking along a piece of non-Soviet equipment. They had struck a compromise with Kowalski filing off the maker's mark.

He raised the pistol and fired. The noise of the punctured padlock clattering to the planks was louder than the muffled pop of the shot itself. He gathered up the remains of the lock and eased open the door.

The room held a wooden table and chairs and a small iron stove. One wall was taken up by a bureau desk covered in a jumble of wiring and telegraph gear. The layer of dust over the furniture implied the hut had been unused for some time. He checked the smaller room to the rear, confirming it too was empty. He lowered the blind over the window in there, and the one in the main room. He returned to the door and signalled to Jones and the others that all was clear.

"Nice little contraption you have there," said Webster when they were all inside. "We hardly heard the shot at all."

Kowalski held up the suppressor. "You folks are mighty proud of your Imperial ingenuity, but us colonials have a trick or two up our sleeves."

"You certainly do Captain. Most impressive." Webster turned to Jones. "Well Major, what now?"

"Everyone needs to get some food and some sleep. We're all dead on our feet, but we've got a few hours in which to get some rest. In the morning that train will be carrying an extra four passengers."

"And I suppose we'll be disguised as miners will we?" Fitzgerald shook his head. "Seems I neglected to pack my pickaxe."

"I'll work something out Fitz. I promise to let you know when I do."

Fitzgerald glowered, but said no more.

They risked lighting the small stove, figuring any wisps of smoke from the hut's chimney would be invisible against Murmansk's general smog. Webster got a brew on and handed round mugs of scalding tea. Kowalski grimaced – the Brits and their damned tea. He wished they'd brought some coffee along. All the same, the drink was hot. He cupped it in his hands and moved as close to the stove as he could without catching fire.

"Now that is exactly what Momma Kowalski's little boy needs."

"Missing your Florida sun, Captain?" asked Webster.

"You have no idea. Florida boys ain't built for the snow, even ones with a Russian mother. First time I've felt warm since we left London. Hell, it might even be colder here than when we stopped over in Aberdeen."

This brought smiles from the Englishmen.

"Russian parents?" asked Fitzgerald.

"Momma. My Pappa's Polish. They headed west when some Prince or somesuch cleared them off their land. Went to England first, but then took the boat to the States and ended up down in Florida. They're still there to this day, enjoying the sun."

Webster arranged his bedding on the floor. "Sunshine feels like a distant memory. This Florida of yours sounds most agreeable."

"It is. Well, if you can avoid the flies and the 'gators, that is. The coasts and the towns are all pretty gentrified nowadays, but the interior? It still ain't much more than swamp."

"Makes one wonder why your neighbours to the north spent so long trying to reclaim the territory."

"Well, they sure talked a lot. But in all honesty, they didn't try that hard, and certainly not after the Fleet started proving itself useful."

"Ah yes, the Americans paid for your little excursion into Cuba."

"Ain't sure I'd describe it quite like that. But at least it was warm..."

In truth, Cuba had been a hot, steaming cesspit. And dangerous too. His first mission after signing up with the Fleet, he'd dropped into the jungle to help snuff out the Cuban revolution. He'd seen plenty more jungles since, all over south America.

Despite all his travels, this had been his first trip across the Atlantic, and definitely his first anywhere in such luxurious style. But damned if acting as security for a trade delegation from Miami wasn't the single most boring assignment he had ever received. He'd just begun wishing for a little less afternoon tea and a little more excitement when the telegram had arrived, instructing him to report to Whitehall.

Jones finished his tea and stood, interrupting Kowalski's thoughts.

"It'll be getting dark soon. Get some sleep. I'll take first watch."

Kowalski lay down beside the others, shuffling in as close to the stove as he dared. "What about you?" he asked once he was settled. "Or don't you officer types need sleep?"

"I've always believed I'll get more than enough sleep when I'm dead."

"Heh. Careful what you wish for Major."

Kowalski rolled over and pulled his blanket up around his chin.

*

Jones waited until the breathing of the three men on the floor fell into regular patterns. When he was sure they were all asleep he took a wooden box from his pack and crept over to the cluttered desk.

He tugged on the cable running down the wall. The rusty nails securing it came free easily from the damp wood. He cut the cable and pared the covering off the ends, revealing the metal beneath. He twisted the bare wire around the screws protruding from the box's rear. He spun the wing nuts, securing the connections before turning the unit upright.

The top of the box was taken up by a metal plate and the spring-loaded hammer switch of a telegraph transmitter. Running along the front face, above a collection of brass switches and dials, was a line of wheels, like a stack of coins viewed side-on. Around their edges, the wheels were stamped with a succession of tiny letters and numbers.

He checked on the sleeping forms of his companions once more then flicked the rightmost of the unit's switches. There, at the limits of his hearing, he made out the faint clicking and whirring of the gears and rods as they began to turn and shift inside the box. Jones gave a sigh of relief. He had worried the box's innards might have been damaged during the drop from the airship.

Settling himself in his chair, he turned the brass dials from one setting to the next. On his third adjustment the silver wheels along the front clicked around, displaying a row of letters. Got you, he thought, with a tight smile of satisfaction.

He hunched over the telegraph, peering at the messages scrolling across the tumbler wheels, absorbing the information coming in and out of Murmansk. With the flick of one switch he could release the message to continue on its way. With another he could hold the telegram from its onward journey, or even reply to it himself.

As he read through the messages, he silently blessed the boffins beavering away at Bletchley Park, Buckingham's residence outside London. Jones had visited the workshops there and had come away both baffled and impressed by what he had seen. He wondered what the Russian and German High Commands would say if they knew Buckingham's men were regularly intercepting telegraph traffic from across Europe and deciphering it using these automated machines. More to the point, what might the French think of it? Buckingham set little value on treaties and alliances – as far as the old man was concerned, anyone's messages were fair game.

After two hours checking on the intermittent messages, Jones was confident the Russians were still unaware of their presence. Or if they did know, they were keeping it awfully quiet. He straightened up, stretching his back and stifling a yawn – time for a rest.

He took a bundle of old wiring from the heap on the desk and dumped it on top of the newer equipment, concealing it from view. He shook Kowalski awake.

"I've been thinking…" he said once the Floridian had come to his senses. "I want to head into town and see what we can find out."

"Risky…"

Jones gave a snort. "No more so than this whole bloody enterprise."

"Fair enough."

"Right. Two hours kip for me. Your turn on watch."

Kowalski glanced towards the others. Jones spotted the look.

"They haven't done this sort of thing for some time now Captain. I think we can leave them to their beauty sleep. I'm sure the lovely maidens of Murmansk would agree those two need it more than we do."

"Heh. Undoubtedly Major, but if you've got any of those lovely maidens hidden away, it's damned unsporting of you not to have shared."

Jones smiled as he arranged his blanket on the floor. "I didn't want to wake you, and the young lady in question had to rush off. The next one that happens along? You can have her all to yourself."

"I'll hold you to that. My Momma would be delighted if I brought home a nice polite Russian girl."

"Well let's keep our eyes out for a suitable prospect, shall we? I should hate to disappoint the good Mrs Kowalski."

Jones lay his head on his pack and closed his eyes. He had long ago picked up the soldier's habit of grabbing snatches of sleep whenever the opportunity presented itself.

One could never sure when the next chance would arrive.

*

Bleary-eyed from their all too brief rest, the party stashed their equipment in the smaller room and prepared to head into the evening.

"I still don't see why we're taking this risk," complained Fitzgerald. "Especially after that nonsense in the square earlier. Or why we're going back out in the cold before we absolutely have to."

"Firstly," said Jones, "I want to see if we can pick up any loose talk about the train, the mine, this chap Eisenstein, or even the blasted weather – anything that might help get the job done. Secondly, I don't know about you chaps, but I could do with a drink. And thirdly, and perhaps most importantly, I can't face being stuck in here with you whining all night Fitz."

"Now hang on just a bloody minute," said Fitzgerald. "All I'm doing is trying to work out what's going on. Not easy with you playing your cards so close to your chest."

"Meaning what, exactly?"

"Meaning I think you have no idea how we're going to get aboard that train, and even if you did, you wouldn't tell us until morning."

"Probably not," answered Jones, unwilling to reveal he had formed a plan whilst the others had slept. It wasn't a good plan, but it would do.

"Just as you have no intention of telling us how you'll get us away from here in the unlikely event of us actually pulling this Professor out."

Jones' gaze grew hard. "Definitely not."

"Good God, but you're a cold bastard..."

"Maybe. But it keeps me alive, and I won't apologise to you for it." Jones stepped close, his face only inches from Fitzgerald's. "You'll know exactly what I want you to know, exactly when I want you to know it, and not before. That way, if you're caught, you can't tell them a damned thing, no matter what they do to you."

Fitzgerald fell silent, cowed by Jones' harsh logic.

"You know how this works Fitz. I have to play it like this. There's more at stake here than just our lives."

Fitzgerald slumped, his anger spent. "Seems you win again Major. Let's go and get that drink. But you're bloody well buying."

"Done," nodded Jones. "But I am worried I seem to be spending my entire time bribing you with drinks and cigarettes..." He tried to make the comment a joke, but was unable to keep the edge from his voice.

"I knew a girl like that in Cuba," put in Kowalski.

All four men laughed, releasing the tension.

"Funny that," said Webster. "She sounds similar to one in Berlin."

"Really? Do tell..."

The Floridian put his arm around the shorter Englishman's shoulders as they moved outside into the freezing air. Quietly comparing notes, the pair led the way as the group made for the dim lights of the street beyond the ranks of freight cars.

*

Jones had found himself in some dubious hostelries in his time, but this basement dive was surely down there with the worst of them. The room was packed with a heaving mass of soldiers in varying states of inebriation, a cacophony of shouts, laughter and singing filling the space under the low ceiling beams. Faces everywhere were flushed from a combination of gutrot vodka and the stifling heat spewing from a huge iron stove. The floor was a sucking quagmire of inches-deep mud with only the odd plank here and there to provide more solid footing.

The combined smell of drunken sweat, stale beer and rough tobacco was enough to bring tears to the eyes. Jones' nose wrinkled further as he caught other odours suggesting that not all the patrons were bothering to stagger outside when they felt the call of nature.

There was no bar counter as such, simply a couple of wooden railway sleepers spanning the gap between two barrels. Behind this makeshift servery stood a burly barman in a filthy apron, arms crossed, surveying the crowd with a threatening scowl. Jones knew the type – poacher turned gamekeeper, fists itching for a sign of trouble, eager for a scrap.

When they had barged their way through the crowd, the barman grunted in reply to their order, thumping down a bottle and four dirty glasses before scooping up Jones' coins with his meaty hand. As they turned from the bar, a nearby table of men had lurched to their feet and headed for the door. Jones and the others won the scramble for the vacant seats, and now huddled together in the cramped wooden booth.

They tipped their drinks back. Webster turned crimson and began coughing and spluttering, and Fitzgerald and Kowalski smothered coughs of their own. Jones sucked air over his teeth. The vodka was rough, but the peppery burn in the back of the throat was almost welcome after the walk through the frozen streets.

"Major," said Kowalski. "You bring us to the nicest places."

"I aim to please, Comrade Captain."

Jones topped up all four glasses then shoved the stopper back into the bottle. "That's your lot my friends, make it last."

"Don't worry about that," said Webster, recovering his breath. He raised his drink to the light and peered at the clear liquid. "I think a second glass of this would kill me. It's not exactly The Famous Grouse is it? Or even a Bell's."

Jones frowned. "A Red Army sergeant discussing the finer points of a good Scotch? A little out of character, don't you think?"

Webster blanched. "Sorry Major."

"No harm done. But think harder before you speak. That goes for all of you. Listen more than you talk." The others nodded, faces serious.

"Spread out," said Jones. "Buy your new friends a couple of drinks. But don't go overboard. You're supposed to be poorly-paid soldiers. Find out anything you can about the train or the mine."

Jones looked to each man in turn. "Be back at the freight yard in two hours. Anyone who doesn't make the rendezvous – you're on your own."

Fitzgerald shuffled in his seat. "And what if you're the one who doesn't make it back?"

"I'm touched by your concern. Still worried about your ride home?"

"Who wouldn't be? I don't want to be stuck here because you were too bloody pig-headed to tell us before you got yourself killed."

Jones considered for a moment and then relented. "From tomorrow, for the next three nights, our friend Wilberforce will have his airship waiting beyond the ridge to the north of the mine. He'll arrive at midnight each night and stay for two hours. If he doesn't see the signal, he leaves."

"What's the signal?" put in Webster.

"A flare or a fire, a mile to the south of where we want picked up."

Webster frowned. "Why not pick us up at the flare?"

"Because although the place should be deserted, I don't think Wilberforce fancies inadvertently dropping in on any wandering Bolshies having a campfire sing-song."

"Ah, yes. One sees his point."

"And what happens after the third night?" asked Fitzgerald.

"After three nights, that's it. If you still want out of Russia, you walk."

Kowalski lifted his glass. "Here's to us all catching our ride. I've had enough walking in the snow to last a lifetime."

All four clinked their drinks together and took a sip, even Webster. Toast complete, Jones pushed his chair back and stood.

"See you all in a couple of hours Comrades."

*

Kowalski made his way round the crowded bar, observing its patrons. In the corner near the stove, he spotted a likely prospect. The Russian sergeant was flushed and a little tipsy, but wasn't roaring drunk. Even better, he was moving back and forth between two different groups of soldiers. Perfect. If Kowalski engaged him in conversation, neither group would pay much attention. He'd bump the man the next time he passed. Buying a drink by way of apology would serve as a good introduction.

Before he could act on his plan he felt a hand on his arm.

"I need you outside." Jones' face was serious. "Now."

The two men squeezed through the throng. They climbed the creaking steps to street level, grateful for the fresh air, pleased to be out of the bar's fug. It had started to snow whilst they had been inside. Fat, heavy flakes now swirled through the patches of lamplight.

They marched off down the street, Jones setting a brisk pace. Kowalski took a good look around, checking they were alone.

"What's the story Major?" he asked, dropping back into English for the first time since they had left the freight yard.

"We need to get back to the hut, sharpish."

"Why?"

"I'll explain later. I need to think."

Kowalski was doing some thinking himself – thinking perhaps Fitzgerald was right, Jones did keep his cards too close to his chest. Still, the man hadn't got them killed just yet, and that counted for a lot in Kowalski's book.

He loosened the flap on his holster and scanned the street for any sign of observation or pursuit. Jones was clearly worried about something, and the Major didn't strike him as the type to worry easily. Kowalski decided he would worry too, even if he had no idea what he was supposed to be concerned about.

*

The freight yard looked as deserted as before, but Jones still waited a good five minutes, watching from the dark pools of shadow between the flickering streetlamps. Only when he was sure no welcoming committee awaited did they proceed towards the hut. Once inside, he moved quickly to the desk and swept the jumble of wires away from the telegraph unit. He turned a dial and the silver wheels immediately shifted alignment in a flurry of clicks.

"Telegram from the Queen?" asked Kowalski.

"I'm not quite old enough to be getting one of those yet. Keep an eye out would you?"

Jones turned from Kowalski's frown and scrolled quickly through the telegraph's stored messages. At this time of night, communication traffic was light and it didn't take long to find what he was looking for. The message out of Cheka headquarters had only been sent in the last few minutes. They might have a bit of time after all. He tapped out a reply on the spring-loaded switch and flicked the machine to transmit.

He abandoned the desk, and rummaged through the stowed gear. By the light of the small electric lamp he transferred items from one pack to another. Satisfied, he straightened up, offering a smile in response to Kowalski's bemused expression.

"That will have to do." He hefted a bulging pack onto each shoulder and made for the door. "I'm off out again. Shan't be long."

"And I suppose I stay here?"

"Yes please."

"Whatever you say Major..."

Jones ventured into the night.

*

The fire was out, but the stove was still warm to the touch. Kowalski discovered he could perch on it and still see into the yard through the gap in the blind. He waited for Jones to return, the heat in the metal working its way through his various layers. Twice now this little stove had made him warm and happy. Kowalski thought he might have found true love.

At the faint crunch of a footfall in the snow outside, he abandoned his cosy seat and padded across the room to stand behind the door. He raised his pistol.

"Kowalski..." came Jones' whisper. "It's me. All in all, I'd rather you didn't shoot me."

The Englishman slipped inside, brushing snow from his shoulders. The two packs were nowhere to be seen.

"All set outside. Time to arrange a surprise in here."

Jones put the carbine on the table and began fiddling with the weapon. Kowalski returned to his perch on the stove.

"Major, I hate to sound like Fitz, but is there any chance you could give me a single clue as to what the hell is going on?"

"You won't be in the dark much longer, I promise. Here, take this." Jones tossed him a roll of wire and gestured towards the other room. "Run this through and climb out the window. Wait for me outside."

Once they were both out in the cold, Jones eased the window back down, leaving a small gap for the wire. They moved out into the darkness of the yard, playing out the cable behind them, heading for a group of freight cars about thirty feet away. Dropping to their knees, the two men crawled beneath a rail truck.

Squeezed in beside Jones, Kowalski found they had a good view round the side of the hut, back toward the streetlights at the edge of the yard. Jones lay alongside the packs he had obviously stowed here earlier, clutching the wire running from the hut.

As Kowalski hunkered down, Jones handed him another length of cable. "On my signal, give this a tug. There's a good chap."

Kowalski got as comfortable as he could on the gravel between the rail tracks. Settled, he turned his head and whispered.

"I figure from all this you're expecting company?"

"Well deduced. Unless I'm very much mistaken, the place will shortly be crawling with our Russian friends."

"The others got caught?"

"Caught. Or something else."

Lying on the freezing ground in the middle of hostile territory, apparently waiting for half the Red Army to show up, Kowalski was in no mood for mysterious hints.

"Spill the beans Major. What did you read on that machine?"

Before Jones could answer, the night's quiet was shattered by shouts and the pounding of feet, all over the top of a dreadful mechanical racket.

The shapes of men with guns materialised between the freight cars. Behind them, lurching out of the shadows with clanking, squealing steps, appeared the formidable bulk of a walker.

The walker stomped between the rail trucks, towering over the yard, snow swirling around its metal frame. It crunched to a halt, turning its armoured body with a growl of revolving gears. Its blunt cannon pointed straight at the hut which Jones and Kowalski had so recently vacated.

A searchlight blazed out, casting long shadows from the soldiers surrounding the building. Where light struck snow, it reflected up, hard and bright. The yard became a monochrome world of dazzling white and inky, dangerous blacks.

An amplified voice echoed across the space, crackling in heavily-accented English. "Come out. Immediately."

"They ain't messing about," said Kowalski. "What now?"

"What else? We pick a fight."

Jones gave his wire a sharp yank.

The harsh chatter of the carbine burst from the hut, the tug on the wire having activated the trigger mechanism. Jones had wedged the weapon in place, aimed towards the window and the yard beyond. The glass shattered, blasted to fragments by the sudden fusillade from within. The surrounding soldiers threw themselves to the ground or sought cover behind the trucks.

After a moment of disarray, the Russians returned fire – the crack of rifles joined by the sharp repeating bark of the walker's cannon. The hut visibly shook under the impact of hundreds of bullets, snow sliding from the trembling roof tiles.

"Jesus," said Kowalski. "I'm glad we ain't in there."

"But hopefully our Bolshevik friends are convinced we still are," Jones replied. "Give that wire a tug."

Kowalski pulled and the night erupted in noise and flame.

The explosives blew the dilapidated building into matchwood. The blast knocked the Russians from their feet and showered them with debris. A hot wave of air rolled out, its warmth reaching the two men beneath the freight car as clumps of soil and chunks of wood clattered back to earth. A fat, greasy fireball boiled into the sky and it became clear the hut was gone, replaced with a burning pile of rubble.

That poor little stove, thought Kowalski.

"Haul in the cable," said Jones.

They pulled in the wires as the Russians began picking themselves up. Confused soldiers staggered around in the smoke attempting to shake off the concussion of the blast. One man, greatcoat on fire and arms flailing, was pushed back down and rolled in the snow by his fellows. From the hatch atop the walker, an officer yelled panicked orders which were duly ignored by his stunned troops. The prone figures nearest the wreckage remained still, either unconscious or dead.

Jones tugged at Kowalski's arm. "Let's go..."

Dragging their packs, they squeezed out from under the rail car. They picked their way round the fringes of the yard, keeping in the shadows of the trucks cast by the fire. The engine shed beckoned and the pair made for its shelter. They crossed the tracks in front of the locomotive's curved snowplough and put the dark bulk of the engine between themselves and the soldiers at the yard's centre.

Jones ignored the footplate and the passenger cars, leading them down the train towards the coal trucks at the rear. He clambered up onto the last of them and peered over the side.

"Hop up Captain. Here's our ride."

"Nothing warmer?" asked Kowalski as he climbed aboard. The hopper was a metal box designed to swing over and dump its cargo of coal. Currently empty, it was about five feet deep, and filthy.

"Not exactly the Orient Express, is it?" said Jones.

"You can say that again. Webster would be appalled."

"A little dust never hurt anyone. And it definitely beats walking."

"There is that," said Kowalski, slumping down, using his pack as a seat. "Now, you really need to tell me what the hell is going on."

"Tired of my mysterious ways?"

"Heh. Now there's an understatement."

"Very well," said Jones, shifting to get comfortable. "We were betrayed to the Russians. By one of the men we brought with us."

Kowalski stared at him, speechless.

"Information has been leaking to Russia for some time. Buckingham narrowed the problem down to two intelligence sections."

"Webster's and Fitzgerald's?"

A nod. "When this business with Eisenstein arose, the Duke couldn't risk any news reaching the Russians before we arrived. He reckoned if we took them along it would keep our mission secret, and eventually the turncoat would reveal himself. Two birds, one stone – that sort of thing."

"So you still don't know which of them it is?"

"No. The telegraph message I intercepted used a codename."

"And where do I fit into this picture?"

"You're here as the only man I can trust." Jones shrugged. "I'm sorry I haven't brought you up to speed sooner. But I couldn't risk you behaving differently towards our fellow travellers. It was important our traitor believed he remained unsuspected."

"So getting a drink and gathering information? That was all baloney?"

"I was giving our turncoat the opportunity to contact his police chums. With us safely dead, the Cheka should follow the orders I sent them. We tag along as stowaways, hopefully identifying our man, and getting us into the mine facility." He offered a half-smile. "Two birds, one stone."

"Just like that?"

"It's an unorthodox plan, but it's the best I could come up with."

Kowalski tipped his head back and rested it on the cold steel of the truck. "Major, it ain't unorthodox, it's unbelievable."

*

Commander Baburin, the head of the Murmansk branch of the Cheka, slipped a fingertip under his eye patch and rubbed at the scar tissue beneath. He closed his good eye and leaned back in his chair, taking a draw of his cigarette and taking stock of his conflicting emotions.

It appeared he had captured a ring of Imperial saboteurs bent on the destruction of one of the country's most important scientific endeavours. However, the fact remained the infiltrators had penetrated to the heart of his jurisdiction without him being any the wiser. And he himself had seemingly spoken with the ringleader earlier in the day. Intolerable.

Rather than providing his ticket out of this frozen purgatory, he had worried this turn of events would see him moved onward to a gulag cell somewhere even colder. Thankfully, it seemed his Moscow superiors were taking a positive view of Baburin's most recent communiqué.

Perhaps his achievement would be brought to the attention of Felix himself, the wily old head of the Cheka. Baburin stubbed out his smoke and picked up the telegraph message, barely suppressing the smile twitching at the corner of his mouth.

Your captive is who he claims to be. Allow him to make his way home. Take the others to the General for interrogation and then send them on to Moscow. Well done Comrade Commander.

The Englishman was ushered in. Baburin waved him towards a chair and indicated for the guard to remove the captive's shackles.

"My apologies for doubting you Comrade, but I'm sure you understand my need to verify your credentials."

The man visibly relaxed. "Of course. Perhaps now you can get me a drink? Some brandy, or a whisky. Anything but vodka."

Baburin disliked the tone of command, but decided he would humour the Englishman. He had, after all, given Baburin's career a significant boost this evening.

The occasion called for something special. He pulled a bottle of whisky from his desk drawer and poured two measures of the amber liquid. Earlier in the month the liquor had been confiscated from a steamer captain. The smuggling of decadent luxuries could be an expensive business – the enterprising sailor had lost cargo, boat and freedom in short order.

"How are you to return to England?" asked Baburin as he handed over the drink. "Our superiors are keen for you to resume your former duties."

The Englishman took a sip, sighing in contentment. "Midnight airship. Picking up to the north of the mine."

Baburin nodded. "We will take you out to the mine later this morning. The General will want to debrief you in person, and I'm sure he will want to speak to your compatriots."

Baburin was relishing the moment when he revealed the captured spies to the General. Gorev treated the secret police and its Commander with disdain, resenting the control the Cheka's Commisars exercised over his officers. Baburin could have cabled the army man with the news, but had decided to deliver the information in person. It promised to be a most satisfying morning. He raised his glass.

"Later tonight you will be on your way home, the sole survivor of a failed mission."

"Not before you've captured Jones and the mercenary. If I return to London claiming they're dead, I can't very well afford for them to turn up alive and well. I need to see them in chains. Or in coffins."

"I am awaiting news, although I don't foresee a problem. I sent twenty men and a walker."

"Don't underestimate them. They're both extremely capable."

The conversation was interrupted by a knock at the door. A mousy secretary snuck in, note in hand. Baburin took it and dismissed her with a backhanded wave. He raised an eyebrow as he read.

"Not that capable after all. Your friends are dead."

"You're sure of this?"

"My men moved in and there was an exchange of fire. The building exploded. Nobody came out." Baburin passed the note across the desk. "A shame we now only have one Imperial spy to interrogate, but at least your tale will contain a greater element of truth."

The Englishman shook his head. "Jones took on a whole platoon and a walker? Typical – bravery and stupidity in equal measure."

Baburin chuckled and hoisted his drink in a toast. "Long may such Imperial stupidity continue, eh Comrade Webster?"

The traitor smiled and lifted his own glass. "I'll drink to that."

*

Dawn broke and the train became the focus of increasing activity. The tramp of feet and shouted orders echoed under the engine shed's roof. Jones and Kowalski heard the sounds of the locomotive being prepared for service – the shovelling of coal and the rising hiss of steam pressure.

Whenever voices or footsteps sounded near their end of the train, they crouched as low as they could in the steel hopper, unconsciously holding their breath.

Despite their unspoken fears, the closest they came to discovery was when a passing soldier threw his cigarette butt into their truck. The glowing ember sailed unannounced over the side and landed between them. They shared nervous smiles after the smoker had stomped off.

They listened now to the arrival of a whole troop of men. The marching feet came to a ragged halt and the doors on the passenger cars clattered open. Soldiers boarding for the change of security detail at the mine, thought Jones. He resisted the urge to peer over the truck's lip to catch a glimpse of any other passengers. He was desperate to see if he could recognise either Fitzgerald or Webster, but the risk of being spotted was too great. Identifying the traitor would have to wait.

Of course, they might not even be on the train. It was a fair assumption the two men would be taken out to the mine for the General's attention, but it was by no means a certainty. Jones clamped down hard on this line of thinking. No use in second-guessing himself now. Nothing he could do about it. They would be aboard or they would not – only time would tell.

A long shrill whistle sounded from the locomotive. The note faded away and the train jerked into motion.

"Thank God," said Kowalski. "I was starting to go a little crazy."

"Don't get too excited. It's still an hour's journey to the mine and it's going to be bloody cold."

"Nothing new there..."

Kowalski couldn't have been more wrong. The journey introduced them to a new level of cold, unlike anything they had experienced so far.

The train picked up speed and the wind whistled into the open truck, chilling the two stowaways to the bone. They pulled the flaps of their fur hats close about their faces and crouched against the forward wall of the hopper seeking what little shelter it afforded. Any small desire either man harboured to see the passing countryside was overwhelmed by the awful thought of lifting his head and exposing his face to the bitter wind.

They huddled together for meagre comfort as time stretched out in a haze of cold and cramp. Jones' teeth chattered, set vibrating by the combination of chill and the truck's vibration. He felt like he had been stuck in this freezing metal coffin for an eternity. To make things worse, snow began to fall from the leaden sky, adding damp to their misery.

At last, just as he was beginning to drift off into a numb state of shock, Jones felt the vibration ease. The bite of the wind began to ebb. The train was finally slowing down. He flexed his frozen joints.

"Here we are. Time to risk a little look."

Avoiding any sudden movement they raised their heads, a fraction of an inch at a time, until they could just see over the side of their truck.

The train was rolling on at barely more than walking pace. Ahead, and opening now to allow their passage, was a gate of thick planks bound with iron. It provided the only access through a rough stone wall crowned with spikes, running off in either direction. Jones was relieved at the lack of watchtowers. It had been his primary worry, that a guard with a raised vantage point would glance down and spot the two infiltrators crouched in the coal truck. The guards on the gate were safely on the ground, unable to see over the high sides of the hopper.

Outside the wall, to the right of the rail tracks, a work party of shaven-headed prisoners leaned on shovels and picks, stealing a respite from their digging as their overseers turned to watch the train roll in. The pit they were covering over with soil was deep, but Jones and Kowalski could still see the thin frozen limbs of the corpses reaching up to the sky from beneath the dirt. The two men in the coal truck looked at each other, eyes cold and hard. Without words they agreed, someone would pay for this.

Beyond the gate the rails curved round in a wide spiral descending into a natural bowl-shaped depression. The tracks went on to form a circular loop half a mile in diameter, running through clusters of cranes, loading towers and low wooden buildings. Within the space enclosed by the rails, conveyor belt systems climbed from heaps of earth, and huge shovel-tractors spewed steam and smoke as they trundled back and forth.

Across from the gate, in the hill above the station platform, Jones saw a pair of huge steel doors hanging open to reveal a tunnel heading back into the rock. The laboratories, he thought, remembering the smuggled layouts Hanson had shown them days earlier. That was where they would find the Professor and his daughter.

At the centre of the depression, towering over all else, four pylons rose. Mounted between them on enormous gears was a steel cylinder, forty feet in diameter, its surface covered with a tangled network of pipes and vents. The cylinder's base tapered to a point in tiers of jagged metallic teeth. The mouth of the mine itself gaped below, a perfectly round hole matching the proportions of the fearsome drill and disappearing straight down, its black void contrasting starkly with the snow-covered ground.

They dropped back into concealment as their truck approached the gate. Jones suspected no noise would carry over the rhythm of the wheels but he still waited until they were past the guards before he spoke.

"When the train stops we'll need to hop out and get into cover."

Kowalski pushed his gloved hands into his armpits. "Long as we ain't in this icebox a moment longer than we need to be, it's fine by me."

The train rumbled round the spiral, descending into the bowl through the falling snow. With a long hiss of steam and the squeal of brakes, the locomotive slowed. The train came to a halt with the two passenger cars lined up alongside the station platform – the coal trucks stretched out behind amidst the boilers, pipes and cranes.

Amidst the banging of doors and the shouting of the officers, the passenger cars emptied. Jones moved to the other side of the truck, away from the activity. After a quick check, he clambered up and over. His stiff knees complained as they absorbed the impact with the icy ground.

Kowalski joined him and, staying low, they moved away from the train into the cover of a twisted forest of piping and valves. They sought shelter beside a large steel boiler, its girth concealing them from the tunnel entrance – the surrounding jumble of pipes and machinery preventing casual discovery from other directions.

The boiler's riveted plates were piping hot and both men pressed their backs up against it. The boiler's fierce heat slowly drove the numbing cold from their torsos, and after a few minutes even their fingers and toes began tingling back into life.

"Now we're thawed out, we should prepare some surprises..." Jones patted the pack by his side. "Time to distribute the presents we brought with us from England. How are you with gift deliveries?"

Kowalski raised his hand and adopted a solemn tone. "Neither snow, nor rain, nor gloom of night shall stay this courier from the completion of his appointed rounds..."

Jones stared at him, baffled.

"Got an Uncle in the Postal Service..." said Kowalski. Jones appeared none-the-wiser. "Heh. I'll explain over a beer later. What's the plan?"

"We split up," said Jones, relieved the conversation was back on steadier ground. "I'll head around the outside and put a charge on anything that looks expensive. We meet up back here."

"What do you want me to do?"

"See that bloody great drill thing?" Jones nodded towards the centre of the tracks. "I thought we might break it. Think you could manage that?"

"Breaking things is what you're paying me for," said Kowalski with a smile. "What kind of timing do you want on the fuses?"

Jones checked his watch. "Let's start the party at noon. Gives us three hours to find the Eisensteins."

"These Soviet timers you insisted on – they ain't the best. Over three hours we'll end up with a big spread."

"A spread will be fine. Keeps things lively. As the Bolshies respond to one blast, another will knock them sideways."

Jones stood and hoisted his pack. "I'll see you on the other side..."

*

"Good morning Comrade General," said Baburin.

Gorev lifted his head from a desk strewn with technical drawings and paper scribbled with equations. The man was something of a contradiction. With his bulky frame and bulging muscles, he certainly didn't look like a scientist. Baburin knew the soldier spent as much time in the gymnasium as he did in his laboratories.

The General's lip curled. "What are you doing here?"

"A matter of state security."

"Isn't it always? What is it this time? Another ship's captain and his unlicensed alcohol?"

"Forgive me, perhaps I should have gone straight to the Comrade Director in Moscow, rather than interrupting your, ah, mathematics..." Gorev's eyes narrowed. Baburin continued before he could speak. "But as military governor of the region, you should know I have captured a band of Imperialist agents, bent on damaging your precious enterprise."

Baburin felt a fierce satisfaction at the look on the General's face. This moment was worth all the sneering he'd put up with from the senior officer. The Army and the Cheka rarely saw eye to eye, but the General was an extreme case. He showed little interest in political security, even allowing Jews and other undesirables to work on his project, despite Baburin's objections. Objections which now looked all too valid.

"You have these men in custody?" The arrogance was gone from the General's tone, faded along with blood from his face. The shock of a threat to his endeavours had cut through his confidence.

"One captured, another two dead. Thanks to a Chekist agent, a hero of the people."

"Their objective?"

"To sabotage your efforts here at the mine, and to spirit away their man on the inside."

"What man? What are you talking about?" Gorev looked close to panic now. Imperial agents were one thing, but a security issue within his own staff was another matter entirely – a matter for the Cheka.

"The Jew. Eisenstein. He is an Imperialist traitor."

"You have proof of all this?"

Of course I have proof, Baburin wanted to scream. But much as he had the upper hand over the Army man at the moment, it wouldn't be wise to push too hard. Gorev was a powerful man, both physically and politically. If the mood took him, the General could break Baburin in either fashion.

"I brought the two Englishmen with me. I assumed you would wish to speak with them."

"You assume correctly." The General got to his feet. "I will summon Eisenstein too. If what you say is correct then he must face the consequences of his betrayal." He drummed his fingers on the desk. "I cannot afford to execute him, regardless of his crimes. It would not do to waste such a mind…"

His cold stare fixed on Baburin's face and he smiled. "Perhaps he will watch as his daughter loses an eye."

Baburin winced, resisting the urge to rub at his scar. "Or she could provide some entertainment for your soldiers?"

The General nodded. "Crude and unsophisticated, but perhaps effective. We shall see how he reacts when confronted with the failure of the Imperial saboteurs. If he begs for mercy, an eye. If he is defiant, the troops." He paused for a moment. "Good work Comrade Commander."

That must have hurt, thought Baburin. He couldn't recall the last time Gorev had accorded him or his rank any respect. He could almost feel the warmth of a new posting in Moscow.

*

Charges set and pack considerably lighter, Jones cut across the mine workings and made for the train. He headed for the locomotive at its front and pulled himself up onto the footplate.

The cab's forward wall was a mass of gauges, valves and levers. The open hatch of the firebox gaped beneath the control panel, glowing coals visible within. Before this welcome heat an engineer perched on an upturned bucket, warming his hands. The man looked up at his visitor, face streaked black beneath his filthy cap.

"Good morning Comrade," said Jones. "Do you mind if I borrow some of your warmth?"

The engineer waved him in. "Help yourself. Plenty to go round."

Jones removed his gloves, rubbing his hands together before the firebox. "You must have the only warm job in the whole of Russia."

"Maybe…" The engineer shrugged. "A sight too warm when we have to get moving. Nothing beats the chill like shovelling coal."

"I don't envy you that…" Jones lifted his gaze to take in the controls. "But I do envy you driving this magnificent machine. How you remember which lever does what is beyond me."

"Ah, it's not so difficult." The man tapped the side of his nose and leaned forward conspiratorially. "We railwaymen like to make it look complicated, you know." He barked out a laugh. "Keeps us in a job."

"Just like soldiering. We make it look harder than it really is."

Jones pulled out his cigarette case and offered it to the other man. The engineer took one then lifted a pair of tongs. He plucked a glowing coal from the firebox so they could light their smokes. He tossed the ember back and sat, puffing in obvious pleasure.

"These are good. Better than the usual muck we get round here."

"I'm lucky. A friend in Moscow keeps me in decent tobacco."

"Very lucky, to have friends such as those," said the engineer, taking another deep draw.

Jones indicated the banks of levers and switches. "If I promise not to reveal your secrets, would you tell me how you drive this thing?"

The engineer smiled. "Like I said, it's simple really..."

Ten minutes and another cigarette later, Jones climbed down from the footplate and headed for his rendezvous with Kowalski.

*

The two men walked along the station platform through the falling snow. A huddle of soldiers clustered around a glowing brazier, a couple of the men looking up from the flames as they passed.

Kowalski resisted the nervous urge to whistle. He had always believed it was vastly over-rated as a marker of innocence, convinced guards the world over were sent to special training schools where they were taught to be doubly-suspicious of anyone whistling. Besides, the only Russian tune he could think was Tchaikovsky's 1812, which wasn't exactly whistling material.

Climbing the steps from the platform, they came to a broad paved area in front of the tunnel. A pair of steel doors, fully ten feet high, stood open at the entrance to the underground complex. Jones gave the solitary guard a nod as they approached. The Russian returned a lacklustre salute, more interested in shuffling around trying to stay warm than in the comings and goings of senior officers.

They passed through the entrance, into the side of the hill. The tunnel was round, clearly bored out by some smaller sibling of the giant drill outside. Kowalski was surprised to find the walls dry – he had been expecting some kind of dank hole. They marched down the slight slope for about fifty feet before bulkhead doors began punctuating the rock on either side. Electric lamps dangled from the roof's curve, gradually taking over illumination duties from the weak light filtering in from outside. The sickly sodium glare of the floodlights shone down over a mix of soldiers and civilians, bustling this way and that through the complex.

"A regular rabbit warren," said Kowalski. "You know where the Professor and his daughter are?"

"They have offices on the fifth level. Here's hoping they're both hard at work this morning..."

Two hundred feet in, the tunnel opened up into a wider space, criss-crossed with the metal struts and cabling of an elevator system. Thick metal poles, slick with grease, formed two shafts for the passenger cages and their counterweights. These central cores were surrounded by a framework of girders anchored to the rock walls. A wooden staircase spiralled down between the struts and disappeared into the darkness. As Jones and Kowalski waited, the cables sang and a large counterweight block sailed downwards – one of the elevators was on its way up.

The cage arrived and the concertina gate opened with a metallic crash. A man in grey overalls emerged, hauling a trolley cart laden with rock samples. He didn't offer the pair a second glance as he wheeled his load towards the tunnel.

The infiltrators stepped into the elevator cage and pulled the gate shut. Jones moved the lever to select the fifth level. Kowalski looked down and immediately wished he hadn't. Beneath the soles of his boots and the thin metal strips of the mesh floor, isolated girders caught occasional patches of light. The steel struts framed a deep, square darkness that seemed to descend into infinity.

Kowalski felt a moment of sickening vertigo and clutched at the railing. Ridiculous – he couldn't be scared of heights. He jumped out of God-damned airships for a living. Somehow this was different though – a cramped and claustrophobic abyss, unlike the wide, rushing freedom of a drop. The elevator jerked into action and began its shuddering descent. Kowalski's fingers clenched on the rail, knuckles white.

"How far down does this thing go?" he asked, unsure if he wanted to know the answer.

"Seven levels..."

The first floor slid past in splash of light. Twenty, maybe thirty feet between floors, reckoned Kowalski, doing calculations in his head. Couple of hundred feet in total? Barely a fraction of the altitudes he'd cheerfully dropped from.

Annoyed and amused with himself in equal measure, he eased his grip on the rail. He took deep breaths, silently counting the floors as they passed. The thump of his pulse slowed, but he resisted any urge to look down again.

*

The elevator juddered to a halt. Jones and Kowalski stepped from the cage. They found themselves in a semi-circular chamber hewn from the bare rock, its straight side taken up by the steel framework of the elevator shaft at their backs. In the centre of the curved rock facing them was a heavy metal door, a match for those on the upper levels. Jones peered through the thick glass of the door's porthole.

"One guard," he said. "I'll do the talking, but get that pop gun of yours ready, just in case..."

Kowalski attached the brass suppressor cylinder to the barrel of his pistol. When the Floridian nodded in readiness, Jones spun the lock and the heavy door swung inwards.

The pair ducked through the hatchway and entered the corridor beyond. The air was warmer and the walls were smooth and finished, unlike the rough stone of the rest of the complex. The surfaces were painted too, an institutional shade of magnolia, although it appeared dazzling white at first as their eyes adjusted to the stronger lighting.

The long corridor ran straight ahead, wooden doors to either side, frosted glass panels painted with numbers and names. Only the lack of windows and the soldier sitting behind a desk suggested this was anything other than a normal office building.

The guard looked up as they entered, frowning as he took in their dishevelled uniforms. Clearly this area of the facility was not often frequented by men who had spent the night in a coal truck. Nonetheless, he stood and offered a salute, despite their appearance.

"Comrade Major, Comrade Captain, what can I do for you?"

Jones returned the salute. "The General wishes to speak with Professor Eisenstein. We have been sent to escort him upstairs."

"The Jew?" The guard frowned. "They have already taken him..."

Jones thought fast. "Typical. They collected the wrong Eisenstein." He gave the guard a rueful smile. "They were supposed to bring the daughter. If they've already taken the Professor then we shall make do with the girl. Where is she?"

"The girl? Not sure I'd call her that. Not to her face anyway." The soldier jerked a thumb over this shoulder. "She's in her office. But I'll need to see your passes before I can let you through."

Jones gave an apologetic shrug. "We don't have any yet. We just arrived and the General sent us straight down here." He indicated his dirty uniform. "Didn't even give us time to change."

"Forgive me Comrade Major, but I will have to check. It will only take a moment." The guard reached for the telephone on the desk.

Jones winced, silently cursing the man's dedication to his duty. "Captain..." he said, taking a step to the side.

There was a muffled crack and a small round hole appeared in the guard's pale forehead. The soldier crumpled to the floor, lifeless. Kowalski stuffed his pistol back into his greatcoat and went to lift the body.

"Some folks are just too damned keen on following orders."

"Quite. What shall we do with him?"

Kowalski indicated a nearby door, 'Fire' labelled across it in bright red Cyrillic lettering.

"Perfect," said Jones, grabbing the dead man's feet.

They were almost there, the body slung between them, when a door opened further up the corridor. A young man in a dark suit emerged, a sheaf of papers in hand. Engrossed in the text, he began walking down the hall towards them. Kowalski fumbled for his pistol, but the man didn't look up from his reading as stopped at the next office down, knocked once and entered.

"Scientists..." breathed Jones. "Oblivious to the real world."

"I ain't complaining," said Kowalski.

They stuffed the corpse in amongst the fire-fighting equipment.

Jones pulled the dead man's weapon from its holster and pocketed it. He straightened up from the body and the Russian's head rolled back. Jones' eyes locked with the guard's frozen stare.

"Sorry about that old chap," he said as he pulled the door closed.

*

The office was two-thirds of the way down the corridor. The frosted glass panel in the door read 'Dr M Eisenstein'.

"Doctor, huh? And a Professor for a Pappa? Smart family."

"Let's introduce ourselves shall we?"

Jones gave the glass a rap with his knuckles and turned the handle without waiting for a response.

The office was small and cramped, an impression magnified by the heaps of books and papers piled on every surface. The walls were taken up with overflowing bookshelves and blackboards covered in a chalked scrawl of equations and diagrams. Behind a cluttered desk sat a woman, her long dark hair pulled messily back in a loose ponytail. She turned to look at the visitors, leaping to her feet when she spotted the uniforms.

Kowalski wouldn't exactly have described her as beautiful, but she was certainly striking. He would have placed a sizeable wager there and then on her having a wonderful smile. However, it became immediately apparent there was no hope of seeing it at the moment.

"What are you doing in here?" she snapped. "Where is my father? What have you done with him?"

"Please..." said Jones. "There is no need to shout."

"No need to shout?" If anything, the volume rose. "You had no need to drag my father off like some criminal. Where is he?" The woman looked like she was winding up to go on like this for some time.

"For God's sake…" Jones hissed in English. "Keep your voice down."

Shocked into silence, she stared at them, conflicting expressions of suspicion and hope chasing one another across her face.

"Who are you?" she asked in heavily-accented English, her tone quieter but no softer.

Before Jones could answer, there came a sharp knock at the door, a fist rapping on the glass panel. Kowalski drew his pistol and the woman's eyes widened at sight of the gun. He gave her what he hoped was a reassuring wink and shifted the weapon behind his back.

Jones yanked the door open. "Yes?"

Arm raised mid-knock, the civilian outside seemed taken aback. He licked his lips and smoothed a hand over his hair. He took in the two soldiers and lifted himself up on tiptoes to peer over their shoulders.

"Comrade Doctor, is all well? I heard shouting."

The woman paused. Her eyes flicked to Kowalski's pistol.

"Go back to your office Comrade Nevsky. I was trying to find where these brutes have taken my father."

The man in the doorway grimaced. "Be careful Maria. You would do well to distance yourself from the old man now. His opinions have already placed you in a questionable position." He puffed out his chest. "If you wish, I could go to the General directly on your behalf. Then you would not have to speak with these more junior officers."

"I can deal with this myself. And I shall not be distancing myself from my father either. Not for Party favour, nor for any other reason."

The man's lip curled. "Such an attitude could cost you dearly. You would do well to remember that when your father, ah, retires —"

Kowalski watched the woman draw breath and narrow her eyes, clearly preparing to tear strips from Nevsky. Just what they didn't need – a shouting match. Jones must have seen the same.

"Thank you for your concern Comrade. I'm sure the doctor appreciates it. Now, on your way."

Jones ushered the man out and closed the door in face. Nevsky's shadow was visible through the frosted glass as he stood outside, clearly deliberating if he should object to being manhandled out. After a moment, he turned and moved off.

"Poor Nevsky..." The woman shook her head. "If only his scientific ability matched his ambition. There is one man who would not be sorry if my father were to disappear."

"That's why we're here ma'am," said Kowalski. "To help you and the Professor in your vanishing act."

"You will forgive me if I don't believe you straight away. There was to be a token of proof..."

Jones fished into a pocket and removed a small package wrapped in oilskin. He untied the string and handed it over. The doctor took the parcel from his hand, fingers trembling as she unwrapped its cover.

Kowalski whispered to Jones. "More secrets Major? If I didn't know you better, this would hurt my feelings."

The woman pulled out a small black book from the folds of oilskin and held it up, tears welling in her eyes. "You know what this is?"

"Your mother's diary," said Jones. "Your father sent it to us."

"I must admit I never thought I'd see it again."

"Well, I'm not sorry to disappoint you Doctor Eisenstein."

Her face broke into a broad smile. Bingo, thought Kowalski, he'd have won that bet. He stepped forward and swept his fur hat from his head, offering the woman a small bow.

"Pleased to make your acquaintance ma'am. Captain John Kowalski, of the Floridian Free Fleet. I am at your service."

Jones rolled his eyes. "And I'm Major David Jones. I work for the British government."

"How did you get here?" Her gaze flicked between them. "Into Russia? Into the mine?"

"A long story that will have to wait. We're have a tight itinerary. You need to take us to your father's laboratory. I want to ensure none of his research survives what's going to happen here."

"What is going to happen here?"

Jones' voice matched his stare, cold and hard. "Fire and blood."

"Not all the people working here are like Nevsky. Many of them have doubts over what Bolshevism has become, they —"

"We don't have time for an ideological debate Doctor. Personally I couldn't care less how Russia chooses to govern itself. But this bomb of yours is monstrous. It must be stopped, whatever the cost."

"This bomb of mine?" Maria bristled. "How dare you? You think I had a choice to work on this?"

"Of course not. But you do now."

Jones' words sank in and the anger in her eyes burned itself out.

"I hate to remind everyone…" said Kowalski into the silence. "The clock is ticking and we still need to find the Professor."

"The Professor, and our traitor," replied Jones.

"Traitor?" Maria looked bewildered. "What traitor?"

"Another part of that long story. It too will have to wait." Jones drew the dead guard's pistol. "Can you shoot?"

Maria's spark returned as she took the gun. "Of course I can." She checked the magazine then closed it with an expert flick of the wrist. "I fought in the revolution – back when Communism was worth fighting for."

She tucked the pistol into the back of her belt and opened the door.

"Follow me," she called over her shoulder as she strode out.

Kowalski turned to Jones, a broad grin on his face.

"She's a firecracker, ain't she?"

*

"How are we going to find the old man?"

Jones stopped at the guard desk and lifted the telephone. "Why don't we call someone and ask?"

"You're kidding, right?"

"Nobody will think twice if we ask where we should report to. And it's a safe bet wherever we find the General, we find the Professor."

"And Fitzgerald and Webster. And a whole heap of trigger-happy Reds too, no doubt."

As if on cue, the bulkhead door at the end of the hallway swung open and four Russian soldiers filed through. Their leader, a slab-faced sergeant, marched up to the desk and began to speak. Jones, playing for time, held the telephone speaker to his ear as if listening and raised an imperious finger in a silent command for the man to wait.

"Yes. Very clear, Comrade General," said Jones into the mouthpiece. "I will arrange it." He hung the speaker back on its cradle.

The sergeant pointed. "I am to take this woman for questioning."

Jones grabbed Maria's upper arm as the man spoke. Seemingly making sure she wouldn't flee, in reality he was stopping her reaching for the pistol at the small of her back. She glared at him. He returned her stare and gave a slight shake of his head. The three of them, armed only with pistols which none of them even had drawn, would be seriously outgunned if it came to a firefight against men with carbines. They needed to talk rather than shoot their way out of this one.

"Sergeant, I'm glad you've arrived. Your orders have changed. You are to detain the traitor Nevsky."

"Comrade Nevsky? A traitor?"

"Indeed. Shocking, I know. A Party man through and through – revealed as an enemy of the people." Jones leaned forward and lowered his voice. "Seems he has been selling information to the Germans."

The sergeant's face hardened. "Where is the bastard?"

"Still in his office, unaware his treachery has been discovered. You are to hold him there until the General arrives. Tell him nothing while he waits. Let him sweat, wondering how much we know."

"Perhaps my boys and I will soften him up a little in advance." The sergeant gestured to Maria, still held in Jones' grip. "And what of her?"

"The Captain and I will deal with the Doctor. Where is the General? He needs to know what is happening."

"Level three – the observation chamber."

"Very good. Carry on."

The soldier snapped off a salute and waved the rest of his squad past. The four Russians marched off down the hallway. Jones, Kowalski and Maria made for the elevator.

"Quick thinking," said Kowalski as they stepped into the cage.

"Best I could come up with at short notice. I almost feel sorry for that Nevsky chap though."

"To hell with him," spat Maria. "Nevsky reported my father to the Cheka last year. That Baburin pig locked him up. Spent three days questioning him. All because my father had spotted a mistake in Nevsky's calculations. The bastard deserves whatever he gets."

"Heh. Hope I never get on your wrong side Doc," said Kowalski.

She gave him a fierce smile. "Best you do not Captain. Especially now the Major has given me a pistol."

*

Fitzgerald found himself thinking of Moscow, assuming once they were finished with him here, he would be shipped south.

Before the revolution he had visited the city many times, as both diplomat and spy. He thought of the views across the river and the ornate chapel opposite the Kremlin. This time there would be no sightseeing. He would be lucky to see anything but the inside of a cell.

The bruises he had suffered so far would be nothing compared with the treatment he'd receive at the hands of the torturers in the Russian capital. Fitzgerald knew what awaited him in the Soviet cells – mind-altering drugs which made opium look like a little pick-me-up, along with the skilled application of violence.

He would tell them everything – he knew it. It was inevitable, although his self-respect would demand he resist them as long as he could. And then, when they were sure he could tell them no more, there would be a walk in the forest, a single bullet, and an unmarked grave.

He turned his wrists, trying to reduce the chafing from his manacles, something he supposed he would have to get used to. He was chained to one of the seats placed around the long table. A single lamp hung above, casting a dim light over the room's centre. The only other illumination came through the observation windows – a full wall of glass.

Beyond the glass partition, a mass of pipes, valves, conveyor belts and pumps made up the ore refinery. Men clad in clumsy protective suits tended the machines. Their helmets and air flasks, coupled with the green tinge lent everything by the glass, made them look like deep sea divers.

Fitzgerald worked his tongue around his dry mouth, wincing as he prodded at puffed lips and loose teeth. He lifted his head and glowered at the man across the table.

"You certainly had me fooled, Webster," he croaked. "I'd never have had you pegged as a Bolshevik. Too interested in the finer things in life to be a man of the people."

"And that's the problem Fitz, don't you see it? You think the ordinary people don't deserve the finer things in life." Webster gave him a wry smile. "Actually it's more than that. Your lot think the ordinary people are incapable of appreciating them."

"Your lot? My family are farmers from Staffordshire. Hardly the bloody aristocracy."

"They own the land which others work for their benefit – a privileged class who control the means of production." Webster shook his head. "You can't see it. That's the whole problem with capitalism."

"Whereas this…" Fitzgerald jerked his head, indicating the mine, Murmansk, the whole of Russia beyond the room. "This is utopia?"

"Of course not. Not yet. But it will be Fitz, it will be."

"Good God. You don't really believe all that radiant future claptrap?"

"Why not? It's no different from your faith in British Imperialism. At least my vision of the future is one of equity and justice. At least –"

Webster's political lecture was interrupted by the opening of the chamber's steel door. A soldier stepped through, followed by the black-clad policemen who had brought them on the train. Last to enter was a tall, thickset man in the uniform of a Soviet General.

Webster leapt to his feet, eager to impress. Fitzgerald watched the traitor suck in his stomach as he offered his hand in greeting.

"Pleased to meet you Comrade General."

Gorev's huge hand swallowed up Webster's podgy fingers. "The pleasure is mine. I am told without your intervention the Imperial saboteurs could have disrupted my work and kidnapped my scientists. You have done Russia a great service."

Webster's eyes shone. "Anything for the good of the cause. It is an honour to serve the people, even in secret."

The military man nodded, but Fitzgerald thought he looked uncomfortable with Webster's zeal. The cold gaze swung round.

"And this one? He is one of the saboteurs?"

"The only one left alive," said Baburin.

Gorev loomed over Fitzgerald. He stared straight back determined not to let the man see his fear.

"Look at him Comrades," said Gorev. "Defiant – despite his chains, despite his bruises. That stiff upper lip the British seem to value so highly." He clapped Fitzgerald on the shoulder. "Your bravery will serve you well in the cells of the Lubyanka."

The metal door swung open once more and an old man was bundled into the room. Fitzgerald recognised Eisenstein from the photograph he had seen in Buckingham's office. With a jolt he realised the meeting with the Duke had occurred only four nights previously. It felt like an eternity ago – a different lifetime.

The scientist recovered from his jostling. He brushed at his ill-fitting suit and adjusted his spectacles. He peered round at the assembled men, eyes widening as he recognised Baburin.

"What is the meaning of this?"

The General gave a wave of command and the scientist was shoved towards the table. Eisenstein lowered himself into a chair, taking in Fitzgerald's bruises with a nervous glance. Baburin sat beside Webster.

Gorev sat at the head of the table, back to the observation windows. With his broad shoulders framed against the otherwordly glow from the refinery, he leaned forward, fingers steepled beneath his chin.

"Well Comrades, now we are all together, what shall we talk about?"

*

Sergeant Volikov took in the shocked faces of his squad then looked back to Nevsky. He crouched, checking the crumpled figure on the floor, but already knew it was pointless. They had all heard the sickening crack as the scientist's head struck the edge of the desk on his way down.

"Damn it. I didn't even hit him that hard."

His men shared wide-eyed looks. The soldiers' obvious fear was a stark, sober contrast to their previous glee at being able to push around one of the uppity scientists for a change.

"Look at you lot," Volikov growled as he got to his feet. "A set of quivering women. What's the matter? Never seen a corpse before?"

"But the General..." said one. "He wanted to question him..."

"He did. Won't get any answers out of him now though, will he?"

The squad remained silent, staring at the dead man.

"Look, it's simple..." said Volikov. "Comrade Professor Nevsky tried to resist. There was a struggle, and an unfortunate accident. That's all." He stared at each man in turn. "Isn't that right?"

The soldiers gave wary nods, clearly unconvinced. Gorev had a notorious temper and little patience with those who made mistakes.

"You're like a bunch of frightened children." Volikov's own apprehension fuelled his irritation. "How often do the damned Cheka tell us a man died resisting arrest? This happens all the time." He gave the body a kick. "Who cares anyway? Bastard traitor. Got what he deserved."

Not just a traitor, a damned nuisance too. Imagine keeling over and dying like that. No backbone, thought Volikov. Well, not any more anyway. He knew he'd catch some trouble for this. His men too. But really, who would worry too much about the death of a German spy?

"Come on lads. Worst case, we end up with a few days of latrine duty." He slapped the youngest man on the shoulder. "Can't make Boris here smell any worse."

Weak smiles greeted the attempt at humour. Volikov shook his head at them pushed past them, out into the hallway.

Scattered heads peeked out from offices down the corridor – scientists disturbed from their work by the noise of the brief struggle. Look at them, he thought – all spectacles and brains, not a real man amongst them. He glared at the faces, his brows lowered in an intimidating frown perfected through years of practice on parade ground and battlefield. One by one the heads ducked back inside, doors closing. Whatever was happening to the unfortunate Nevsky, it was clearly none of their business.

He turned back to his squad, still clustered around the dead man.

"I'm off to make a report. You lot, stay here." He rolled his eyes at the sight of their pale faces. "Don't let him escape, eh?"

Volikov stomped off down the passage toward the guard station at the elevators. They had one of those telephones there, he remembered. He braced himself to speak with the General.

*

The laboratories on level four were guarded in similar fashion to the offices below, but the soldier on duty recognised Maria and waved her, Jones and Kowalski through.

The walls here were formed of large panes of glass set in riveted metal frames, allowing a view into each of the research chambers. The trio made their way down the passage and Jones and Kowalski took in the contents of the rooms – steel tanks stencilled with Cyrillic warning signs, shelf after shelf of rock samples, and long bench tables cluttered with beakers, bell-jars and gas burners.

In one of the larger chambers a huge machine generated what could only be described as captive lightning. A shimmering, writhing electric charge squirmed in the air between two copper poles. Even through the glass they could hear the hiss and crackle of the raw current.

Kowalski stopped to stare, transfixed by the flickering, ever-changing shape of the harsh blue electricity. It was a moment before he noticed the man inside the chamber, standing calmly only inches from the writhing stream of energy. The scientist turned his head towards the observers, eyes invisible behind the black glass of his protective goggles. He raised a gloved hand in greeting then returned to his experiment, jotting notes in his journal.

"What does it do?" asked Kowalksi.

"My father's new process," answered Maria, pride in her voice. "A way to electrically separate the different types of ore. It doesn't work perfectly yet, but it is beautiful."

"That it is Doc."

"Deadly too. The charge in there could burn you to a cinder."

"Seems to be a lot of that round here. Don't you science folks ever build things that won't kill everyone?"

Maria glared at him. "Rich, coming from a soldier."

She strode off, halting at the next chamber.

"My father's laboratory," she said as she swung the door open.

The walls were covered with generators and coils of electrical equipment, no doubt connected to the lightning display next door. A long bench rand the centre of the room, its surface laid with an elaborate arrangement of scientific apparatus – glass jars and tubes, burners and ceramic bowls. Kowalski pointed at one particular piece of equipment.

"I won't pretend to have a clue what all this stuff does, but I'll be damned if that don't look like an accordion."

Maria gave him a withering look.

"It's a bellows of some sort I think," said Jones with a smile.

"Looks like you could get a decent tune out of it."

"You're welcome to try, but first we'll get some charges set, shall we?"

The two men set to work as the doctor kept watch. Within a few minutes they had rigged their remaining bundles of dynamite. Charges in place, the trio marched back through the laboratory complex, nodding to the guard as they made for the elevators.

*

Level three was unlike the other floors they had visited. The lift cage did not arrive in a lobby area here, but directly into a large pump room, its walls crowded with piping and studded with gauges and control valves. The ceiling was higher here too, allowing a gantry walkway to run round the walls. Two metal doors broke up the tangle of pipes.

"Where now?" asked Jones.

"The observation chamber..." said Maria, pointing to the door on the right. "The other leads to the dressing room."

"Dressing room?"

"Protective equipment for the workers. The air in the refinery is poisonous, full of Red Mercury dust. A lungful of it and you're dead in a matter of hours – an unpleasant way to go."

They crossed the open space towards the right hand door. All three drew their weapons.

"No time for a fancy plan," said Jones. "We go in as if we're escorting our prisoner. They're expecting someone to bring the doctor in. We should have a few seconds before they realise something's not right. Make your first shots count."

"That's it?" asked Kowalski.

"As I said, nothing fancy." Jones turned to Maria. "When the shooting starts, find some cover." She made to protest but Jones continued. "Cover first. Then you can do as much shooting as you like."

Mollified, the woman nodded.

Jones reached for the door. "Ready..."

The air was suddenly filled with the screaming wail of an emergency klaxon, the noise reflected and magnified by the harsh metallic surfaces of the room. The clatter of booted feet was added to the cacophony as soldiers poured onto the gantry above.

The trio raised their pistols, but it was already too late. A half-dozen soldiers now stood around the walkway, carbines trained on the exposed figures below. Starting a shooting match now would be suicide.

The klaxon cut out abruptly, leaving their ears ringing in the sudden silence. Jones gave the others a grim look and threw his pistol to the floor. He raised his hands in surrender, and after a moment Kowalski and Maria did the same.

The noise of the door behind them prompted them to turn. A bulky uniformed figure stepped through the portal. He looked down at Maria and smiled. The expression went nowhere near his eyes.

"Doctor Eisenstein, so glad you could join us." He looked at the others. "And you brought guests too..."

He stood back and gestured to the door.

"Come and join us. Make yourselves comfortable. I am very much looking forward to making your acquaintance."

*

"You told me these two were dead, Comrade Commander," said Gorev. "They look remarkably healthy to me, no?"

Baburin shifted in his chair. He lifted a hand and rubbed at the scar down his cheek. "Apparently so. I can only apologise..."

"No harm done. We have them now." Gorev gave a thin smile. "Thanks to my security detail."

The Cheka officer winced, but remained silent.

Jones and Kowalski sat at the table, wrists bound with rope, an armed guard standing behind them. Maria sat with her father, eyes downcast. Fitzgerald, still shackled to his chair, looked haunted, sunken into himself – his final hope of rescue crushed.

Webster had been astonished at first, goggling at Jones and Kowalski as if he'd seen a pair of ghosts. He had recovered his poise soon enough as the fact of their capture sank in. He now grinned at the two men across the table, his piggy eyes twinkling.

The sight of the man filled Jones with disgust. He followed the traitor with a cold stare as Webster got to his feet and walked over to the prisoners' equipment, piled up on the bench at the side of the room.

"Ah, here it is," he said. He held up Kowalski's brass pistol suppressor. "General, if you don't mind, I'll be taking this clever little contraption – a memento of my fallen compatriots."

"If you need a demonstration..." said Kowalski. "I'd happily oblige."

"I'm sure you would Captain, but no thank you." Webster regarded Jones. "You're very quiet Major. Nothing to say?"

"I'm imagining ways to make you pay for selling us to the enemy."

"Has the Queen declared war recently? Maybe I missed it – I have been out of the country. But I don't believe Russia can be officially described as the enemy yet, can she?" Webster smirked. "Besides, I haven't sold anyone or anything. I'm not doing this for anything as vulgar as money. You're as bad as old Fitz, always assuming the basest motives."

"You serve a higher purpose, I suppose?"

"As much as you do. At least I've thought about my choices, rather than just doing as I was told, like a little boy playing soldiers."

The General cut in. "Much as I hate to interrupt this touching reunion, there are other matters to attend to." Gorev turned to Baburin and indicated the captives. "Comrade Commander, prepare yourself for a trip to Moscow. You will accompany the saboteurs on their journey south."

"Yes Comrade General."

Gorev went on. "You will travel in style, gentlemen. We shall arrange for one of our airships to take you, rather than the train. Much faster that way. In Moscow you will properly enjoy the, ah, hospitality of the Cheka. You will discover how Russia deals with spies and –"

"General?" Webster's interruption carried a note of urgency and they all turned to look at him. He stood at the bench of captured equipment, but now held one of the packs in his hand.

"Take whatever you want," snapped Gorev. "I have more important things to deal with…"

"No General, you misunderstand. Commander Baburin, the explosion at the rail yard – how large was it?"

Damn it, thought Jones. He had hoped for longer.

"How large?" The Cheka officer scowled. "Large enough to destroy the building and kill seven of my men. Is that large enough?"

Webster frowned. "No Comrade. Not big enough by half." He turned to the General. "We were carrying four packs between us. Packs stuffed with dynamite charges and timing fuses." He hefted the bag. "These are nearly empty. And if the explosives were not destroyed at the rail yard…"

Gorev understood at once. He stormed over to Jones and hoisted him up by the lapels. "What have you done with the other charges?"

"I don't know what you're talking about."

The General dropped Jones back into his seat and struck him across the face. The backhanded slap echoed round the chamber.

"Where are the explosives?"

Jones worked his jaw before answering. "You'll find out soon enough."

This cool response tipped Gorev over the edge. His face turned crimson and twisted in an animal grimace. He drew his pistol and shoved the barrel into Jones' face, forcing his head back.

"Where are they?" Veins stood out in Gorev's neck.

"Go ahead," grunted Jones. "Shoot me."

Gorev appeared to give the invitation serious consideration, grinding the gun against Jones' cheekbone, his knuckles white on the grip. Abruptly he withdrew the weapon and turned away.

"No." The tone was quiet again, but infinitely more dangerous. "Not yet. But someone else shall pay for your lack of co-operation."

Gorev stalked round the table and raised the pistol again, pressing the weapon against the back of Fitzgerald's skull. He looked down at the bound man and then back to Jones.

"Once more, where are the explosives?"

Fitzgerald looked up, his face bruised and battered, shoulders hunched beneath Gorev's menacing bulk. Jones made to speak but the other man gave an almost imperceptible shake of his head. Jones felt a hot flush of shame that he had ever doubted Fitzgerald's loyalty.

"I doubt Jones will talk," put in Webster. "Too wedded to his damned duty." He shrugged. "We English can be pig-headed like that I'm afraid."

Gorev didn't shift his gaze from Jones as he responded. "You may well be right. But I cannot have the Major think me a man of idle threats."

The shot was incredibly loud.

Blood sprayed across the table. Fitzgerald's upper half slumped forward, his head impacting wetly on the wood, concealing his ruined face from view. The shot's echoes faded away into stunned silence.

"I'll kill you for that..." Jones spoke through gritted teeth, his eyes fixed on Fitzgerald's still form. "If it's the last thing I do, I'll kill you."

Gorev holstered his weapon. "Words Major. That is all you have. And yet you refuse to say the words which could save your comrades..."

He moved to stand behind Maria's chair and placed his hand on her shoulder. She visibly shuddered at the touch. The reaction seemed to please Gorev. He rubbed a lock of her hair between his fingers as he went on, continuing to stare at Jones.

"Perhaps Comrade Webster is right and your sense of duty will keep you silent." He smiled. "But I wonder if you also suffer from a misplaced sense of chivalry..."

Balling his fist in her hair, Gorev hauled Maria from her seat. She screamed as he dragged her across the chamber. Ignoring her shrieks, Gorev pinned her against a support pillar, shifting his hand to cover her mouth. His captive silenced, he stretched out his other hand, palm up, towards the guard.

"Your knife, Comrade," he said.

The soldier handed over the blade and Gorev raised it to Maria's face. She squirmed, eyes wide above the iron grip of his hand. She grasped his arm to try and prise it away, but the General was too strong for her.

The Professor rose, attempting to go to his daughter's aid, but the guard stepped in, blocking his path. The soldier swung the butt of his carbine into the old man's side and Eisenstein collapsed into his chair.

Heedless of the Professor's moans, Gorev tilted the knife from side to side before the terrified woman's face. The pale green light from the refinery winked on the blade's edge.

"The explosives Major. Or the doctor becomes a Cyclops, like my friend Baburin..."

*

Kowalski could scarcely believe this was happening – first Fitzgerald and now Maria. He stared over the table at Jones. The Englishman's face remained impassive. He'd clearly let them all die if it meant stopping the Reds in their tracks. Someone had to do something.

"Wait," he said. "Leave the Doc out of this."

The General turned his head. "You have something you wish to say?"

Kowalski's eyes flicked between Jones, the slumped mess of Fitzgerald, and the helpless woman.

"General, let me deal with this," said Webster, still pale after Fitzgerald's sudden execution. "I have a feeling the Captain might be more reasonable than my stubborn compatriot."

Gorev nodded. "Go ahead Comrade, but my patience grows short."

"There's quite a difference between these two. Jones here, he's a patriot, misguided but loyal – a dog that can't see his master's faults. He would never consciously betray his superiors."

The traitor turned from Jones and clapped his hand down on Kowalski's shoulder. "But this one? He's a different beast altogether. A soldier of fortune – he owes no loyalty except to the highest bidder."

Baburin was outraged. "You're suggesting we pay this saboteur?"

Webster waved the Cheka commander to silence.

"Sometimes one should adopt the methods of one's adversaries. What do you say Captain? Do you still believe in capitalism? Could we come to some arrangement?"

Kowalski looked at Jones over the table. The Englishman glared back, his hands balling into fists. "Kowalski..." he growled.

"Now now Major," said Webster, clearly enjoying himself. "Leave the Captain to make his own decisions. All in the spirit of free enterprise, eh?"

Kowalski lifted his hands, displaying the rope round his wrists. "Hardly free. More like blackmail." He paused, not daring to catch Jones' eye again. "But I don't want to end up like old Fitz. Go on, I'm listening."

"Judas," spat Jones. "Is this what it comes to? Every man for himself?"

Kowalski hung his head, unwilling to respond. Webster however, was only too happy to speak. "But that's what capitalism always comes down to. That's why the system will always fail in the end. That's why –"

"Enough politics," snarled Gorev. "The explosives..."

"Ah yes. Quite right." Webster turned back to Kowalski. "Well Captain, here is the deal, as I think you colonials might put it. Help us, and we'll let you live. Who knows? We might even let you leave. Simply show us where you and Jones planted your little bombs."

Kowalski raised his head, holding Jones' black stare. "Him? He didn't place any of the charges himself. Typical officer – left me to do the work. I got my hands all dirty whilst he had a smoke."

Kowalski saw the spark of realisation in Jones' eyes as he spoke the lie. Thank God, he thought, finally the man gets it. He went on, injecting a note of bitterness into his voice. "The British ain't paying me nearly enough to die for them. I'll show you where the damned explosives are."

Webster smiled in triumph. "See Comrade Baburin. Sometimes capitalism does have its uses."

The General released his grip on Maria and pushed the woman back into her seat. "You should thank him," he said to her. "His mercenary nature has saved your pretty face. For the moment."

But Maria was clearly in no mood to be grateful to a turncoat. She glared at Kowalski with undiluted revulsion. Ouch, he thought, if looks could kill, he'd be six feet under at least.

Gorev continued. "Baburin, take him. Recover the explosives. If you think he is lying at any point, feel free to encourage him as you see fit." He thumbed the edge of the knife. "The removal of a finger or two can provide a great deal of motivation."

The Cheka commander hauled Kowalski from his chair and bundled him towards the door.

*

Baburin marched Kowalski across the pump room. The soldier on guard snapped to attention when the Cheka officer spoke.

"We are to escort this prisoner to the surface. If he attempts to escape, shoot him."

Kowalski could feel the carbine's aim as an itch between his shoulder blades as they stood waiting for the elevator.

"I'm going to need these free," he said, raising his bound hands. "Unless you want to defuse the charges yourself. Tricky business, fiddling with explosives. Ain't sure I'd want to try it with one eye..."

Baburin glowered at Kowalski, but nodded to the soldier. The Cheka man covered Kowalski with his pistol as the guard drew his knife and sliced through the ropes.

Kowalski rubbed his wrists as the elevator cage arrived, fingers tingling as his circulation returned. The guard slid open the gate and entered the lift, backing into the corner, carbine at the ready for any sign of trouble. Baburin took the other corner and Kowalski stood between them, sliding the concertina gate shut at the Cheka officer's instruction.

"Take us up," ordered Baburin and the guard threw the lever. The cage shuddered and began its ascent.

"The big one ain't on the surface," said Kowalski over the racket.

"Where is it then?" demanded Baburin.

Kowalski raised a finger. "On the roof of the cage..."

Both men looked up and Kowalski seized his chance. He swung his arms up and out, the edges of his hands chopping into the exposed throats of the Russians. He felt the crunch of cartlidge as his right hand connected with the guard's neck. Gasping for breath through a crushed larynx, the soldier collapsed.

The other blow was less successful. Kowalski's left hand struck Baburin on the side of his neck rather than full in the throat. The thump stunned the Cheka officer momentarily but left him very much alive.

Baburin brought his gun round and Kowalski grabbed for it, throwing himself at the Russian. The pistol fired, the bullet tugging at Kowalski's sleeve as it flew wide. The noise of the shot reverberated through the girders of the elevator shaft and echoed back from the rock walls. With both hands clamped on the Russian's wrist, Kowalski battered the man's hand against the railing. Baburin gave a grunt of pain and the gun tumbled away. It clattered on the metal mesh then bounced between the bars of the cage and into the void.

The Cheka man swung his head forward with savage force. Kowalski staggered back, eyes streaming with tears and blood pouring from his nose. He stumbled over the dead guard and dropped to his knees. He shook his head stupidly, trying to regain his senses.

Before he could recover, Baburin was on him, hands locking around his throat. Kowalski flailed, clawing at the choke-hold, slumping as Baburin's weight bore down. The Russian's face twisted in animal effort, spattered with blood, single eye burning with fury.

Kowalski's lungs burned, his vision darkening around the edges as the Russian pushed him back on top of the lifeless guard. His scrabbling fingers closed around the hilt of the knife in the dead soldier's belt. Summoning his last reserves of strength, he pulled the blade free and slashed it across Baburin's thigh.

The Russian roared and released his stranglehold, clutching instead at his wounded leg. Kowalski sucked in a huge lungful of air and boosted himself to his feet. He swung his hand round in a wide arc. The strike was clumsy but carried the weight of desperation, smashing aside an upraised arm. The knife plunged to the hilt in the side of the Russian's neck.

The Cheka commander swayed, his eye locked on Kowalski. His hand came up and he pawed weakly at the weapon lodged beneath his ear. Still staring, he gave a single bloody cough and keeled over.

Kowalski fumbled for the control lever, halting the elevator's progress. Suspended between levels in the twilight gloom, he sank to the floor beside the dead Russians, sucking down painful, grateful breaths.

*

Gorev used the telephone to summon two soldiers to remove Fitzgerald's corpse. The chamber's occupants watched in silence as the body was hauled out, the dead man's heels dragging across the concrete floor. The blood spatter across the table remained, an ugly testament to what had occurred.

"You have accomplished nothing Major..." said the General once the body was removed. He gestured to the observation windows, to the workers in their protective clothing, now filing out of the refinery. "Another shift finished. Another load of ore purified. Another step completed in our development of the most powerful weapon the world has ever seen." In the green light cast from the windows, Gorev's smile looked demonic. "A slow process, but it cannot be stopped."

"And once you have it?"

"Then Russia cannot be stopped either. For too long the other powers have looked down their noses at us, thinking us the backward child of Europe. No longer." He clenched his fist. "With this power, and the will to use it, we will take our rightful place."

In Gorev's gleaming eyes, Jones spotted the truth. "You mean you will take your rightful place, don't you? This isn't about Russia at all."

"And why should I not be rewarded for helping my country?" The General's tone grew more strident. "The people of Russia crave a strong hand. That is why they suffered under the Tsars for so long. That is why they flocked to the red flag of Vladimir Ilyich in the revolution – not because they were true believers in Communism, simply because the Romanovs had grown weak."

Gorev appeared to remember he had an audience. His eyes flicked towards the guard and Webster. "Of course..." he went on in a more reasonable voice. "All I want is to serve the Party for the glory of Mother Russia, in whatever capacity my country requires."

"How very noble of you."

"No less noble than your vain quest to stop us. It is a shame your hired hand proved unreliable."

Jones bit his tongue, holding back the response he so dearly wanted to throw in the General's face. He had no idea what Kowalski had planned, but out of here, on the move, the Floridian surely stood a better chance of making his escape. And if not, at least Jones was confident Kowalski wouldn't be helping the Soviets find the explosives.

Very shortly, the charges would be going off and work at Kovdor would come to an abrupt, explosive halt. He could live with that. Not that he would of course, unless they could get out of here in the next hour.

He avoided Gorev's gaze, somehow nervous the other man might be able to read his mind. His eyes fixed on the bloody stain on the table, unable to stop himself following its pattern.

"Just think..." said the General, noting the direction of Jones' stare, "If you had been willing to co-operate in the first place, your companion would still be alive."

Jones was thinking of little else, but he'd be damned if his guilt would be a source of amusement for the Russian. He glared back at Gorev.

"We both know that's nonsense. We're dead men regardless. You may have convinced Kowalski otherwise, but I know we're all Moscow-bound."

"Don't worry. Any unpleasantness you suffer in the capital will be short-lived." He turned to the Eisensteins. "Unlike the unpleasantness you two will experience here."

"Do with me as you will," stammered the professor. "But please —"

"Please don't hurt your daughter?" Gorev snorted. "Don't be naive, Professor. Don't you see? I have to hurt your daughter."

Eisenstein crumpled. "I'm sorry..." he whispered to Maria.

She took her father's hand. "Don't give him the satisfaction."

"What did you expect Professor?" said Gorev. "You are a traitor to your country and a personal embarrassment to me. And yet you remain too valuable to our efforts for me to kill you." He narrowed his eyes. "With your wife no longer with us, I will turn my attention to the remainder of your family to keep you motivated. And to punish you for –"

The General's tirade was interrupted by a sharp tapping from the other side of the room. The chambers' occupants turned to see a lone figure standing beyond the green glass. He was clad in a protective suit of heavy canvas and rubber, his face obscured by the metal bell of his helmet. The man smacked repeatedly on the glass with his gloved hand.

"What is this idiot doing?" The General stalked toward the window.

The figure was waving now, gesturing wildly, repeatedly pointing at the floor in an exaggerated fashion. Gorev stood before the glass, staring at the gesticulating man, anger taking over from curiosity. "Go and see what the fool wants," he snarled at the guard.

As the soldier moved towards the door, Webster looked away from the scene beyond the window and caught Jones mouthing instructions at the Professor and Maria. Struck with sudden realisation, the traitor shouted a warning to the General.

Gorev turned at the noise, frowning as first Jones and then the Eisensteins tipped their chairs to the floor. Then the chamber was flooded with light and heat and the locomotive roar of an explosion.

The chamber's bulkhead door blew inward, torn from its hinges by the blast. Propelled by a ball of flame, the panel tumbled end over end, sparks rising where it struck the floor. The guard had an instant to spot the approaching chunk of steel – enough time for him to realise what was happening, but not enough to even raise his hands. The door hurtled into his body, smashing him aside before crashing to a halt against the wall.

The echoes of the blast faded away. There was a moment of silence then the air was ruptured by the piercing howl of the emergency klaxon.

*

All around the ruined doorway, the walls were cracked and scorched. Ruptured piping, blackened and twisted, spewed clouds of steam. Scattered clumps of burning wreckage were strewn across the chamber, creating a thick atmosphere of acrid smoke.

Jones fought his way to his knees amidst the remnants of his broken chair. Clumsy with dizziness, ears ringing from the explosion, he struggled to push himself up with his bound hands. He shook his head, but the movement sent his vision swimming in and out of focus. Of Webster, and the Eisensteins, he could see nothing through the smoke, but he spotted Gorev slumped against the observation windows. The Russian had a deep cut across his forehead. Blood streamed down his face.

As Jones watched, Gorev's fingers twitched and his head lifted. With a grunt of effort, the man hauled himself to his feet. Jones tried to match the movement, but his limbs refused to respond.

The Russian leaned against the window. He blinked, bleary eyes tracking across the room, goggling at the carnage. His stare sharpened into angry focus as it fastened onto Jones.

Gorev lurched into motion, limping forward, staggering one way and then the other. He fumbled at the holster on his hip, evil intent written plainly across his bloodied face.

Jones' legs remained stubbornly useless. He tipped himself forward and crawled, scrabbling at the floor. The advancing Russian managed to extricate his pistol. The weapon came up, wobbling in his grip. The gun fired, but the shot was wild, flying over Jones' head.

Jones' searching fingers closed around the leather strap of the guard's carbine. He hauled the weapon into his hands. He raised the gun, bound hands clumsy, his head still spinning. He squinted along the barrel and tightened his finger on the trigger. Bullets spat from the carbine's swaying barrel, the recoil playing havoc with Jones' aim. Despite the wayward spray of fire, two of the scattered shots found their mark.

The first bullet caught Gorev in the chest, thumping him back a step. The Russian looked down stupidly at the blood spreading across the front of his uniform. His head came up in time for another bullet to take him beneath the chin. The projectile blasted through the back of his skull in a spray of blood and bone.

The General dropped like a felled tree.

*

Still clad in the protective clothing of a refinery worker, but minus the brass helmet, Kowalski barged his way into the observation chamber, pushing through the twisted remnants of the doorway.

He stepped over the broken body of the guard, to where Maria and the Professor were helping Jones to his feet. They were all dazed and perhaps a little scorched in places but he was relieved to find they seemed at least half alive. Unlike the General. Gorev's body lay full-length on the floor, a puddle of blood spreading from the back of his head.

"Good shooting Major. Sorry I couldn't be more help, but I definitely had a ringside seat."

"Oh, I think you did more than enough." Jones wiggled a finger in his ear. "Are you quite sure you used enough explosives?"

"No time to tailor things. I liberated a charge from the laboratory."

"Good thinking." Jones appeared to notice the state of Kowalski's face for the first time. "Good grief. What happened to you?"

"Don't you worry none, I'll be fine. You should see the other guy..."

Maria eyed his injuries and winced. "Captain, I owe you an apology. I should never have doubted you."

"Perhaps I can escort you to dinner once we're out of here?" Kowalski smiled, although the movement sent pain shooting through his throbbing nose. "Reckon that's the least you could do..."

Jones interrupted the exchange. "Let's concentrate on our escape before we start arranging our social calendars. Where's Webster?"

The Professor pointed to a prone figure. "Your spy has taken a knock to the head. But he is alive, I think."

"We'll soon see about that," growled Kowalski.

"I want him alive," said Jones. "We're taking him back to London."

"You've got to be kidding me Major. We've already got two civilians in tow, and now you want to take prisoners?"

"I can look after myself," put in Maria. "And my father if I have to."

"The Doctor is right." Jones began gathering up their bags. "Besides, this isn't up for debate. Webster comes home so he can tell us how much information he's passed on, and the names of his contacts in England." He continued, talking over Kowalski's objections. "No time to argue. I'm surprised that siren hasn't summoned half the soldiers in Russia by now."

Kowalski was distracted from the issue of Webster. "Heh. They'll be a while yet. Those charges we placed in the laboratory?"

"What about them?"

"I sent a couple upstairs."

*

Three levels above, Sergeant Volikov bellowed over the klaxon's wail, trying to bring some kind of order to the chaos around the elevator shaft.

He had been a hundred feet up the tunnel, halfway to the exit, when the blast set the rocks shaking around him. He'd been lucky – suffering little more than a sprinkling of dust. Unlike these poor bastards, he thought, spotting a hand poking from beneath the rubble.

The explosion's flash and roar had been followed by the rumble and crash of falling machinery. Watching helpless as a group of men went down beneath tumbling metalwork, Volikov had offered up a most un-Communist prayer of thanks he hadn't been caught in the carnage. He ran back down the tunnel gathering men as he went. He took charge of the scene in the absence of any more senior officers.

"You!" he yelled at a group of soldiers. "Stop gawping and get those bodies out..." He grabbed another man. "Fetch some engineers, and some bloody crowbars or something." He pointed at the twisted girders and scorched wood blocking access to the shaft. "We need to get all this shit cleared out of the way. Understand?"

The soldier nodded dumbly before turning and running up the tunnel. Volikov shook his head at the stunned faces of the younger men around him. Bloody children. This was nothing compared with a real battlefield.

He raised his voice again, shoving confused soldiers into action, sparing no curses and delivering kicks and thumps here and there to get them moving. He figured a few blows and some harsh language would be nothing compared with what the General would do to them all if stayed stuck down that hole for much longer.

*

Jones and Kowalski stood at the elevator station, peering up into the dark. Clangs and crashes and muffled shouts echoed down, accompanied by the occasional tumbling girder or splintered plank of wood. The beams of the elevator shafts themselves were twisted out of shape, and whole sections of the wooden stairway had been swept away by the impact of debris from above. Jones doubted they would have visitors any time soon.

"Good work Captain. Although it does rather beg the question of how we're going to get out of here."

Kowalski looked crestfallen. "It seemed a swell idea at the time."

"I'm sure it did."

"Maybe there's a back stair?"

"A tradesman's entrance? If so, you'd have thought we'd be knee-deep in angry Bolshies by now. I don't recall seeing any on Hanson's plans, but let's check with the Professor and the good Doctor."

They returned to the observation chamber where the two scientists stood watch over a groggy Webster. Eisenstein and his daughter were silent as Jones explained the situation, and both shook their heads gravely at mention of other stairs.

"Only one way in or out..." said the Professor. "For security."

Webster chipped in at that point, a sickly smile playing across his features. "Trapped here after all eh? It's only a matter of time until the soldiers get through, and then this little caper of yours will be over..."

"Oh do be quiet," said Jones. "It is only a matter of time. But not in the way you think." He checked his watch. "If we don't find a way out of here in the next hour or so, then it really will all be over – soldiers or no." He gestured towards the windows. "The mine, the refinery, the whole kit and caboodle, is going to end up in quite a mess. You do remember how much explosive we brought with us, don't you?"

Webster swallowed nervously and didn't reply. Good, thought Jones. The situation had not improved, but at least he'd wiped the smile off that bastard's face. Now Webster looked as worried as the rest of them. The rest of them that is, except for Professor Eisenstein, whose face suddenly lit up with new-found hope.

"The refinery!" he exclaimed. "That's it!"

They all stared at him.

"The ore for the refinery. The conveyor belt..."

Maria picked up on her father's excitement. "Which leads directly from the mine shaft..."

She turned to the others.

"Which has a ladder to the surface!"

*

Made clumsy by the heavy canvas and rubber of the protective suits they now wore, the five of them shuffled across the refinery floor.

Jones had been surprised the view through the thick glass of his helmet was not cast in shades of green, but the peculiar colour had been the result of the tinted observation windows rather than any particular lighting within the factory itself. However, whilst his vision was fine, his other senses were all dulled within the cocoon of the suit.

He could hear little inside the helmet beyond his own breathing and the faint hiss from the compression flask on his back. The air it supplied had a metallic taste and a rubber smell, an unpleasant combination.

Webster turned and cast a sullen look through his own visor. Jones waved him forward with his pistol. At first the turncoat had refused to don the suit, or enter the refinery, proclaiming he would not be taken back to England to face the hangman's noose. Jones had made the traitor's choices abundantly — an immediate bullet now, or a chance to convince Buckingham to let him live.

For a moment Jones had thought the other man might choose to die there and then, a Hero of the People. But Webster's last dregs of courage slipped away in the face of the harsh reality of the pistol's muzzle. No point choosing the romantic ideal of dying a martyr for the revolution if there was nobody around to witness the act.

Now, hustled forward, Webster scrambled to join the others on the plates of the conveyor system. Kowalski covered the prisoner as Jones climbed up in turn. Clambering to his feet, Jones waved them along the belt towards the dark tunnel from which it emerged.

Maria took the lead, ducking down and crawling into the space. Her father followed, stiff beneath the twin burdens of protective clothing and age. Then came Kowalski, glancing back regularly to check on Webster. Jones crawled at the rear, doing his best to keep his weapon trained on the traitor's back.

Helmets and air flasks bumped and scraped along the low ceiling of the tunnel. Their electric headlamps illuminated the dust stirred by their passage. The ore swirled in the beams – a blizzard of golden snow. Deadly stuff, Jones reminded himself, no matter how pretty it looked.

The walls and ceilings abruptly opened out and they found themselves blinking in a dim twilight. They clambered down from the conveyor belt and perched on a thin ledge – no more than three feet wide, running the circumference of the shaft. This circular platform had to be where the massive drill engine paused during its return to the surface, depositing its cargo scoured from the depths of the earth.

Checking Kowalski had Webster covered, Jones peered over the edge. The weak light from above allowed him to see the walls continue down perhaps twenty feet before all was swallowed by inky blackness.

"How deep?" he shouted to Maria. His voice boomed incredibly loud inside his helmet, but he knew she would barely be able to hear him through her own headgear.

"A thousand feet," she yelled back. "Straight down."

The doctor grabbed Jones' arm and pointed with her gloved hand. There, fixed into the cold rock, were the first rungs of a metal ladder. Jones tipped his head back and followed their course. The ladder rose above them, climbing towards a pale circle of daylight.

*

It felt like the climb was taking forever. Above Kowalski, the Professor was struggling to match Maria's pace up the rungs. The old man kept stopping to catch his breath, forcing Kowalski to wait beneath. But with any luck, this might be the last such halt. Looking up, he watched Maria disappear over the lip of the shaft, only fifteen feet or so above where the Professor rested.

Kowalski leaned back further and the massive drill unit suspended above came into view. Its concentric rings of cruel teeth descended to a sharp point seemingly aimed straight down at the insignificant figures clambering up the great shaft.

He thought of the explosive charges strapped to the machine's supporting pylons. When they blew, the drill would collapse, plugging the mine permanently – and most spectacularly. Kowalski wanted to see the results of his demolition efforts, but preferably from a distance. They couldn't hang around down here, no matter how tired the old man was.

He lifted his hand, set to tap the Professor's ankle to prompt him into motion, but the elderly scientist began to haul himself up once more without encouragement. Kowalski gave a grunt of respect. Fair play to the old man, he was holding up pretty well, all things considered.

Before he resumed his own ascent, Kowalski checked on Jones and Webster. The gaping dark below did its best to make him vomit. As before in the elevator, the enclosed space and yawning depth filled him with a cold dread. He tried to keep his gaze fixed on the men on the ladder rather than letting it stray further out towards the beckoning void.

The two Englishmen were twenty feet below him on the rungs, about halfway up from the conveyor belt ledge. They were making poor time, even worse than the Professor. Webster wasn't in great shape – Kowalski remembered how badly he'd struggled on their trek from the airship drop, right back at the start of this crazy adventure. And Jones wouldn't want to get too close to the traitor's feet. You didn't stray within kicking distance of a man with nothing to lose.

Kowalski turned back to his climb. The slow pace frustrated him once again, but finally Eisenstein was clambering over the top. Reinvigorated at the prospect of getting out of the mine and out of his helmet, Kowalski practically scampered up the last few rungs. He crawled out onto the snowy ground and flopped onto his back.

Grey cloud filled his vision and the sun was nowhere to be seen, but he thought the sky looked pretty-much perfect – a hell of a lot better than being stuck down that God-damned hole.

He pulled himself to his feet and took a quick look around. Other than Maria and her father, nothing moved within the area enclosed by the rail tracks. The steam-shovels and tractors were still, their drivers no doubt pulled away to deal with the trouble in the complex.

Over by the tunnel entrance, men scurried back and forth as black smoke curled out between the doors. It gave Kowalski a nice warm feeling to see the fruits of his labour.

Webster appeared at the shaft's rim. The traitor hauled himself up and shambled away from ladder, hunched over, obviously gasping for breath. As Webster wheezed, Jones too appeared over the edge.

The sudden noise of an explosion brought Kowalski swinging round. Even muffled to a hollow crump by his helmet, the sound was unmistakeable. Beyond the towering drill, smoke billowed into the sky and a tongue of flame bloomed within one of the clusters of piping. The first of the Russian timers had finished its ticking.

Kowalski and the two scientists stood transfixed as a huge cylindrical boiler, weakened by shrapnel from the first blast, split in half, rivets popping like firecrackers. With a roar of escaping pressure, the boiler ripped itself apart in a spectacular burst of steam and flying metal.

*

Webster straightened up to see the others all facing away, distracted by the explosions. If he wanted to avoid the noose, this was his chance – his only chance.

He lunged towards Jones – the man still down on his hands and knees, crawling off the ladder. Head lowered, his vision limited by the brass helmet, Jones was oblivious to Webster's approach.

With a desperate glee Webster stamped his booted foot down on Jones' gun hand. He felt bones crack even through his heavy sole. Jones reared back and the pistol dropped from his shattered grasp. He tumbled onto his side, clutching at his injured hand.

Webster gritted his teeth and channelled all his rage and fear into his kick. He caught Jones full in the ribs and battered him back towards the mineshaft. Webster relished the sight as Jones slipped over the edge, clawing at the earth with his good hand.

Webster leaned out, eager to watch his adversary plummeting into the dark. Instead he felt a surge of frustration. Rather than falling, Jones hung above oblivion, fist locked around the top rung of the ladder. Legs flailing, scrabbling for purchase, Jones' hold was precarious, but for the moment at least he was very much alive.

The man had the lives of a cat, seethed Webster. Still, Jones would be fully occupied for the next few seconds at least. Webster bent for the pistol – time for the mercenary to receive his comeuppance.

As if feeling the weight of Webster's thoughts, Kowalski turned back from the explosions. His eyes went wide at the sight of the gun in Webster's fist. The Floridian must have realised Webster had the upper hand, but he went for his carbine all the same. Webster had to admire the man's ambition.

He pulled the trigger and relished the sight of Kowalski going down hard. Shocked at the pistol's sharp report, the Eisensteins turned. The woman dropped to her knees beside Kowalski, her anguished cry audible even through Webster's helmet. Cry all you like dearie, he thought. You and your father won't be far behind.

But first Jones. The man still hung there, arm twisted, helmet and air flask bashing on the rock as he tried to swing onto the ladder. Webster grinned as he moved his foot over the gloved hand clutching the rung. Why waste good ammunition? Time to break those other fingers.

Something thumped into his shoulder – a hammer blow sending him stumbling. He dropped the gun and clutched at the wound. He reeled as the initial shock of impact was replaced with the beginnings of a dreadful pain. He lifted his gaze to see the woman, still kneeling beside Kowalski, her pistol raised.

Webster lifted his hand to ward off the shot he knew was coming. The gesture was futile. The bullet smacked wetly into his chest, lifting him off his feet and tossing him backwards into the abyss.

He plunged silently into the dark, the grey circle of sky dwindling above as the icy cold spread through his body.

*

Over the waves of agony from his crushed fingers, Jones could feel his other hand losing its grip. He swung his injured arm again, trying to turn and get his feet to the rungs, but the pain of the attempted movement foiled him once more. That bastard Webster might well have sailed past a moment ago, but Jones knew he would shortly follow.

It seemed unfair somehow for it to end like this. A bullet he could have taken, indeed he'd invited one from Gorev earlier. To be gunned down by the enemy, to fall in combat, that was how he'd always expected things to turn out. But falling down a bloody great hole? That was just damned embarrassing.

A hand grasped his arm through the suit's thick fabric, easing the strain on his shrieking muscles. His unseen saviour pulled at him – not enough to lift him, but enough that he finally got turned and got his feet on the rungs.

Summoning his last reserves of strength, Jones pushed up with his legs. Another hand grabbed at the back of his belt. Hauled from above, he slowly, painfully, clambered out of the shaft to collapse on the ground.

God, but the earth beneath him felt good.

*

Lights danced behind Kowalski's eyelids. A female voice calling his name filtered through the noise reverberating in his head. His gathered his scattered thoughts and willed his eyes to open. The light set off fireworks of pain inside his skull and he let out a groan.

Maria gasped and pulled Kowalski close. He struggled to make sense of what was going on, but when he finally realised, he returned the embrace. Every cloud, he thought, winking up at Jones over her shoulder. The Englishman rolled his eyes.

Kowalski reluctantly eased himself from Maria's grasp and took a look around. He sat propped against the wheel of an enormous steam-shovel, the vehicle idle between the slag heaps. The others must have carried him here from the top of the shaft. Or, more accurately, Maria and her father must have carried him. Jones looked about done in, wincing as the Professor wrapped a strip of fabric around his hand.

"What happened?"

Jones grimaced. "I got my fingers broken and you managed to get yourself shot."

With his free hand, Jones lifted Kowalski's helmet, showing off the large dent in the brass, the deformed slug of a bullet at its centre.

"That explains the noise." Kowalski shook his head, ears still ringing. "I thought someone had smacked me with a bell. Where's Webster?"

"Got on the wrong side of the Doctor. She sent him packing." Jones gestured back towards the mineshaft. "Much as I wanted to take him back to London, I have to admit I'm glad to see the back of him."

Kowalski turned Maria so he could see her face. "Are you alright?"

She stared at him with a mix of guilt and pride. Kowalski looked in her eyes and saw it all – the conviction that she had done the right thing conflicting with the hot shame that came from killing.

"You did good Doc. Way I see it, you saved the hangman some rope."

Another explosion ripped through the track-side machinery, off to their left this time. A ball of flame curled skyward.

"That's our cue," said Jones. "We've a train to catch..."

"A train? You said we had an airship coming?"

"Surely you don't believe every story you hear over a drink?"

*

Jones climbed onto the locomotive's footplate. The engineer stood with his back to him, transfixed by the chaos around the tunnel mouth.

Soldiers staggered from the complex, soot-covered and coughing up smoke. Other men unwound fire hoses and donned clumsy breathing apparatus. Thus clad, the fire fighters hauled their equipment toward the entrance. Clearly all was not well inside.

Another blast erupted nearby, blowing apart some sort of pumping station. The engineer jumped at the sudden noise, and then cringed at the clatter of falling debris on the roof of his cab. He jumped even higher when Jones tapped him on the shoulder.

"Apologies my friend," said Jones. "I didn't mean to startle you."

"Comrade Major, you scared the shit out of me." The man waved at the carnage. "What the hell is going on?"

"Saboteurs. We need to move your train so they don't get it as well..."

The engineer tossed his cigarette out into the snow and tugged his hat down. "Right. Let's get the old girl warmed up."

He tapped at a couple of the gauges and nodded to himself. He pulled at a lever, and tightened a valve, then turned to Jones. "Won't take long. She just needs stoked up. Don't suppose you'd give me a hand?"

"No problem. But let's get the cars disconnected..."

Jones hopped down from the footplate, keeping the train between him and any eyes on the tunnel side. The engineer leaned out of the cab and shouted after him.

"Don't you want to move the cars too?"

Jones ignored the question and beckoned the man to join him. The railwayman frowned but climbed down all the same. Jones led him past the coal tender. Together they pulled out the heavy pin which attached the locomotive to the rest of the train.

"I still don't see why we couldn't move it all."

"Because we only need the locomotive..." Jones raised his pistol. "Sorry Comrade. You shouldn't have told me how to drive her."

Kowalski and the two scientists materialised from their hiding place. Jones spoke to the Floridian.

"Captain, I was just explaining to our friend here about the German saboteurs." He tipped Kowalski a wink. "Perhaps you could keep an eye on him whilst I get the engine ready to depart?"

"Jahwohl," deadpanned Kowalski in a truly terrible German accent. He pulled the carbine from his shoulder.

"Hande hoch!" he ordered. "Bitte?" he added in an uncertain tone.

Jones winced at Kowalski's pronunciation and clambered aboard the locomotive. He checked the firebox and threw three shovelfuls of coal inside. He waved the two scientists aboard and signalled to Kowalski.

The Floridian raised his weapon, peering down the barrel at the railwayman. "Run!" he barked.

The unfortunate engineer needed no further encouragement. He bolted off into the heart of the mine workings. The man sprinted, ducking left and right, desperate to avoid the hail of bullets he clearly expected to come after him. No bullets flew though – Kowalski ignored his departure and climbed aboard the engine.

Jones handed him the shovel and moved to the controls. Kowalski looked unimpressed. "Figure this is what Webster would have called an inequitable distribution of labour."

"Perhaps. But it seems that whilst anyone can shovel, only one of us knows how to drive."

With a long-suffering sigh Kowalski moved into position between coal tender and firebox, shovel at the ready.

"Get us moving Major."

Jones opened the throttle, releasing pressure into the pistons. The locomotive began to inch forward. The train's departure went unnoticed as further explosions ripped through the buildings around the mine.

Speed steadily increasing, the engine climbed the spiral gradient around the side of the depression, giving its four passengers a grandstand view of the unfolding chaos below. Multiple fires now blazed and thick black smoke spewed out, mingling with the billows of escaping vapour from a hundred broken pipes and ruined boilers. The circular bowl of Kovdor was a roiling cauldron of steam.

In a white-hot flash, the first of the charges under the central drill unit detonated. With a metallic groan, audible even over the rest of the destruction, one of the tall pylons supporting the massive cylinder buckled. The huge mechanical monster listed to the side, the remaining supports bending and cracking under the unstable burden.

The second charge exploded and the damaged structure could take no more. The support struts snapped and the drill unit came crashing down. Its jagged rings of metallic teeth flew apart as the steel cylinder shed its skin of plating and pipework.

The roar of the machinery's collapse echoed round the bowl of the mine. The shriek of steam pressure escaping from its shattered innards was like the death wail of some dreadful creature from prehistory.

The guards at the railway gate stood and gawped as the entire mine facility blew itself apart in a frenzy of steam and fire. Surging out of the clouds of smoke, the black apparition of the locomotive was on them before they could react. Barely a shout was raised as the engine thundered past. The vicious snowplough blade smashed through the gates and the train rumbled into the snow.

Clear of the mine, Jones looked back. He shared a fierce smile of satisfaction with Kowalski as they surveyed the destruction in their wake.

Now all they had to do was get out of Russia.

*

The Captain watched his men array themselves around the yard. The telegraph message from Kovdor had been garbled, but there seemed to have been an accident at the mine. Then someone, somehow, had managed to steal the damned train.

Probably some poor bastards the Cheka had hauled out there to scrabble in the dirt – most likely couldn't take it any longer. Took advantage of the confusion, killed their guards, and hijacked the train. He couldn't really blame them – working at the mine must be like hell on earth. But orders were orders, and his were to round up the escapees. If they were lucky, they'd get sent back out to the mine again. If they were unlucky, well, the next thing they'd be digging would be their graves.

From his vantage point up in the walker's hatch, he was the first to spot the locomotive as it crested the hill on the outskirts of town. Ducking his head down he ordered the pilot to move. From the cramped seat within the cab the man nodded, adjusting his goggles and turning back to his controls and the narrow viewport. With a crunch of gears the walker lumbered forward, positioning itself astride the railway tracks.

The Captain called down to his men below and they formed lines on either side of the rails, ready to surround the engine. Satisfied with the deployment, he looked up to the approaching locomotive once again.

He frowned. The black engine was much closer than he had expected, almost into the yard already. Now the walker was still, he could make out the roar and rumble of the locomotive's approach. With the sound came the sick realisation of how quickly the oncoming train was travelling. He yelled down into the cab.

"Get us off the tracks!"

The walker jolted into motion, the pilot hauling desperately at the drive levers. The Captain peered out of the hatch and watched the engine's thundering approach in horrified fascination. The walker lifted a clumsy foot. Too slow, thought the officer. Too slow.

The locomotive sped between the ranks of soldiers, some too shocked to react, some quick enough to raise their weapons and snap off useless shots at the impervious engine.

The snowplough blade caught the walker across the legs, slicing clean through the first and twisting the other beneath it. The steel box of the walker's body was hoisted into the air before the round black frontplate of the train smashed into it. Despite the heavy armour, the cab's frame crumpled, crushing the pilot to a pulp and pinning the Captain's legs between twisted plating. With his top half hanging helplessly out of the hatch, he began to scream. The engine ploughed on, the wreckage of the walker impaled on its front.

Belching smoke and steam, shedding chunks of debris, the train roared through the engine shed, smashing aside the buffers which marked the end of the line. Off the rails now, the locomotive thumped and bounced on the uneven ground. With a screech of tortured metal, it tipped over onto its side, but still it slid on, ploughing up a jagged trench in the frozen earth.

Finally, with an almighty crunch, the runaway train struck the high brick wall of a warehouse at the yard's edge. There, fifty feet beyond the end of the line, it came to rest, spent, the ruin of the walker and the front half of its boiler embedded in the building.

After the cacophony of the crash, relative silence fell, broken only by the tumbling of displaced bricks and the hiss of steam leaking from the engine's fatal wounds.

The soldiers ran towards the wreckage through the engine shed, following the path of destruction. Arriving at the train's final resting place they stood stunned, mouths hanging open as they took in the carnage.

Jones and Kowalski's last two bundles of dynamite contained enough force to convert the locomotive's footplate and cab into shards of metallic shrapnel, propelled outward by an expanding ball of flame. The deadly hail cut a bloody swathe through the squad of soldiers. The handful of men who survived the first blast were felled by a second, larger wave of explosions as the munitions piled in the warehouse began to go up.

The noise and heat was ferocious. Stacked artillery shells, huge round bombs for the airships, and box after box of bullets and hand grenades – all of them exploding, one after the other, in a dreadful chain reaction.

*

Two miles back down the tracks, the escapees paused in their trudge through the snow. They raised their heads as the sound of the huge blasts rolled out across the frozen countryside.

Kowalski turned a quizzical look on Jones. "We didn't put that many charges on the train. Someone start a war without letting us know?"

An enormous fireball ballooned up into the sky above the trees which masked their view of the town.

"Whatever it is, it should prove an excellent diversion," said Jones. "Come on, the river can't be far."

They slogged on through the snow, their march accompanied by the regular beat of explosions and the rapid tattoo of exploding machine gun ammunition. They reached the river without seeing a soul, and turning east, they followed the turbulent waters towards the town.

Murmansk was in chaos. Panicked officers and factory foremen yelled conflicting instructions at groups of men. Thick oily smoke surged upwards from the direction of the rail yards, the sure sign of a major fire taking hold. Alarm bells and klaxons added to the general din and confusion, punctuated by the booming reports of more shells going off.

They slipped through the pandemonium on the streets unchallenged. Dodging between the rushing squads of men and the great rumbling tractors, they worked their way steadily along the waterfront, heading for the docks and the forest of cranes along the quay.

"Planning a boat trip Major?" said Kowalski.

"Something like that."

"Have to warn you, I get real seasick."

"I hope we won't be out there long enough for you to need your sea legs." Jones halted, peering down at a small steam launch. "This will do. And no crew about to repel our boarding party."

Jones limped down the steps and clambered aboard the vessel. He made his way forward and disappeared into the wheelhouse. The others followed and Kowalski helped first Maria and her father traverse the gap between the steps and the boat.

Jones poked his head out from the cabin. "Let's get her running. Shouldn't take long. Be a good chap and prime the kerosene..." He indicated a rusted pump handle at the stern then turned to the Russian scientists. "Take a seat. We'll be on our way in no time."

The Eisensteins slumped onto the bench at the side of the deck and Kowalski moved aft.

He grumbled to himself as he yanked the fuel pump up and down – if it wasn't shovelling coal, it was pumping kerosene. The mechanism screeched in protest and his muscles echoed the complaint. This had been the longest day of his life, and he now found himself aching in places he hadn't known he possessed.

"Good show," shouted Jones eventually. "That should do it."

Kowalski stopped pumping and leaned heavily on the handle. He had barely recovered his breath when an indignant voice echoed down from the wharf above.

"What are you doing?"

He looked up into the furious bearded face of a Russian sailor. The man could be nothing else, clad as he was in a donkey jacket, waterproof galoshes, and a woollen hat. The seaman stood at the top of the steps, a large wooden crate in his arms.

Kowalski smiled at the irate sailor. "Relax Comrade. We're just borrowing it. We'll bring it back safely."

"The hell you will." The sailor's face darkened further. "Bloody Army. Think you can do anything you damn well please. I'll find someone to sort this out..."

Enough, thought Kowalski. He whipped his carbine round off his shoulder. "Down you come. Quietly now."

Rather than complying with the instruction, the sailor tossed his crate towards the boat. Kowalski ducked out of the way and the tumbling box smashed across the deck. He brought his gun up again, but the sailor had seized his chance. The man was gone, out of sight beyond the edge of the wharf above. Out of sight maybe, but Kowalski could hear him just fine, shouting the alarm.

"Major!" yelled Kowalski. "We need to go. Right now."

To Jones' credit he didn't ask why, but immediately threw the launch's throttle fully open and jumped to the forward rope, knife in hand. Pulling his own blade from his belt, Kowalski sliced through the aft cable. Jones returned to the helm and the vessel puttered away from its mooring.

Kowalski ran to the wheelhouse. "Doesn't this thing go any faster?"

"It seems not. Why the sudden departure?"

Kowalski gestured back towards the wharf where a group of onlookers clustered. The boat's angry owner shoved his way to the front of the crowd, tugging at the sleeve of an army officer. The soldier peered across the widening gap between launch and dock. Kowalski snapped off a salute, willing to try anything to buy them a little more time. The baffled soldier gave a half-hearted salute in response, clearly struggling to make sense out of the ranting of the enraged sailor.

Shouting and pointing toward the stolen boat, the seaman continued his tirade, and eventually the message got through. The officer began shouting himself and raised his pistol at the boat, now fifty feet away.

"Get down," called Kowalski.

The shot's flat crack echoed over the water. The bullet smacked into the wheelhouse's wooden lintel.

"Be glad he doesn't have a carbine," said Jones.

"He doesn't. But I think his friends might..."

The officer was now flanked on the quay by a dozen men, all swinging their weapons up to their shoulders. Kowalski hoisted his own and pulled the trigger. The onlookers on the quay scattered at the harsh clatter of the gun, civilians and dockworkers diving for cover.

The soldiers, however, stood their ground, and bullets flew in both directions across the water. Facing twelve carbines, Kowalski was seriously outgunned and was quickly forced to duck down as enemy fire started thumping into the boat.

The windows in the wheelhouse shattered, adding flying glass to the storm of splinters which engulfed them. Maria and her father lay prone on the planking, sprayed with debris but out of the direct line of fire.

Kowalski prostrated himself beside the wheelhouse, occasionally holding his carbine above his head and sending haphazard shots in the general direction of the shore. A shard of glass struck his forehead and splinteres peppered his face and hands, but somehow no bullets found their mark.

The relentless fusillade from the shore poured bullets into the wheelhouse. Jones stayed crouched within as the projectiles ploughed through the flimsy structure. Kowalski was amazed to see the Englishman keep his hands on the controls despite the onslaught, one pushed forward on the throttle lever, the other clutching the helm, keeping the launch fixed to a vaguely straight course away from the quay.

Kowalski had had about enough – of the day, of the country, and most of all, of being shot at. He raised his weapon again and sprayed fire blindly towards the quay, finger clamped on the trigger.

He bellowed over the barking of the guns. "Stop. Shooting. At. Me."

With a click, his carbine fell silent, its circular magazine empty.

"God damn it!"

He tossed the useless weapon over the side. Why did the other guys never run dry? He hunkered down, hands over his head.

Slowly but surely, the boat pulled away and the hail of fire diminished. Eventually, when they were about two hundred yards out into the Sound, the firing stopped altogether.

Kowalski pulled himself to his feet and made to check on the others. After finding Maria and her father shaken but unhurt, Kowalski moved to the wheelhouse. He found Jones standing, eyes wide, poking his finger through one of the holes which riddled the planking.

"You alright Major?"

Jones blinked and looked down at himself, absently brushing broken glass and fragments of wood from his clothing.

"Yes..." he said. "I think I am."

Kowalski glanced back to the dock where uniformed figures continued to point at the escaping vessel. "It won't take long for them to get a boat out after us. And it ain't likely to be any slower than this one."

Jones tore his glazed eyes from the holes in the planks. He gave a shake of his head and seemed to come back to his senses.

"I rather hope our little boating trip is almost over."

"I don't see any of your dreadnoughts out here. If you've got any other tricks up your sleeve, this would be a swell time to play them."

Jones looked over Kowalski's shoulder and gave a tired smile. He clapped the Floridian's arm reassuringly.

"Cheer up Captain. Here's our ride..."

*

Anderson rubbed at his unshaven face with both hands and massaged his aching eyes. He had been watching Murmansk's waterfront through the glass of his periscope since first light. They had arrived the previous night and taken advantage of the darkness to spend some time on the surface replenishing their air flasks. But now *Nautica* was back where she belonged, lurking twenty feet below the gentle swell, half a mile offshore, well away from the obvious routes in and out of port.

He had spotted the black smoke curling into the sky from the other side of the town and wondered if it had anything to do with his mission. Whatever was going on, it had caused a sudden flurry of activity throughout the parts of Murmansk he could see.

Made nervous by all the movement ashore, he called the crew to action stations, although to give them their due, they couldn't have been any more alert. Four days submerged in an untested vessel, penetrating foreign waters – it certainly served to keep the men on their toes.

"Hold on," he muttered under his breath. "What's this?"

He clicked the handle on the periscope. The lens head twenty feet above smoothly substituted one set of optics for another. The panoramic view changed to a closer, magnified image.

Anderson refocused and turned the periscope, tracking in on the small boat now pulling away from the shore. He winced as he watched the soldiers on the wharf open up with their weapons. He couldn't see what was happening aboard the craft, and of course he couldn't hear the shots, but he dreaded to imagine the pounding the boat's crew were taking.

"Our passengers are on their way," he called. "Prepare to take us up."

He watched the little boat slowly pull out of range of the guns. Time for *Nautica* to make an appearance.

"Blow the tanks. Take us up. Half ahead."

Compressed air hissed through the vessel's piping as the ballast tanks were pumped dry. The submersible's screw began to turn, pushing her forward and up. Anderson adjusted his footing to compensate for the incline of the deck.

Nautica broke the surface in a boiling spray a dozen yards in front of the launch. Streams of water ran from her back and a weak but welcome sunlight flooded through the glass dome. Squinting, Anderson realised this was the first time his vessel had ever surfaced in daylight. He reached for the speaking tube.

"Mister Dixon," he said. "Get our passengers aboard..."

*

The launch bobbed in the water alongside the submersible, tiny in comparison. Dixon's men tossed grappling hooks and pulled the little boat in, tugging it tight against *Nautica*'s flank.

The boat's occupants hauled themselves up the rope ladder and Dixon got his first proper look at them. The old man and the woman appeared exhausted. Sympathy for their condition overtook Dixon's initial shock at seeing a female come aboard. He ushered the pair towards the hatch and turned to the next arrivals.

If he'd thought the first couple looked a state, well, he didn't know what to make of these two. Their faces were drawn and haggard beneath cuts, bruises and dried blood. They leaned on each other as they crossed the deck, like nothing so much as a pair of bilge-rat drunks who had found themselves on the losing side of a tavern brawl.

But as they lurched forward, Dixon revised his opinion. He reckoned it was the Bolshies who'd found themselves on the wrong end of things today. Despite their bedraggled appearance, there was something dangerous about these men, a look in their eyes suggesting they were not to be trifled with. They had a hardness about them, the sort of men he'd want at his side in any kind of a tussle. He offered the pair a salute.

"Welcome aboard. Captain Anderson is waiting on the bridge."

The two men nodded and limped towards the hatch. As the first of the pair descended the stairs to the companionway below, the other looked up towards the shore and the town.

"I shan't be sorry to see the back of this place."

"Looks a little cold for me sir."

"Oh, it got plenty hot enough..."

Dixon followed him, sealing the hatch before making his way along the cramped companionway. The new arrivals stood in the control room, wrapped in blankets, tired eyes working their way across the banks of controls and taking in the glass dome overhead.

"Everything secure topside?" asked Anderson.

"Aye sir. Hatches shut."

"Flood the tanks. Make our depth thirty feet."

"Aye aye sir," chorused the crewmen around the bridge.

The passengers watched the water creep up the glass overhead. None of them looked too happy as the waves washed over the dome's crest and the weak daylight faded away.

"Welcome aboard the *Nautica*." Anderson thrust his hand out in welcome. "Major Jones I presume?"

Jones introduced his companions in a round of handshakes. The old man began asking questions in his broken English, clearly fascinated by the submersible and curious about its operation.

"Relax Professor," said Anderson. "We have four days sailing ahead of us. Plenty of time to explain how everything works." He paused. "If I'm allowed to tell you anything at all. I'll take your guidance on that Major."

"Professor Eisenstein and his daughter have given up everything to help us against the Communists. They are, without a doubt, some of the Empire's bravest friends."

Anderson nodded gravely. "Very well, I will see Mister Dixon here gives them both a guided tour as soon as they've been fed and watered." He spotted Dixon's look. "Problem Chief?"

Dixon felt his face flush. "It's only... begging your pardon, sir. But, well, it's frightful bad luck, sir. Having a woman aboard."

"Good grief man. What would you suggest? We can't exactly put her back ashore, can we?"

"I'd like to see anyone try," said Kowalski. "The Doc here don't take kindly to being told what to do". He slipped his arm round the woman's shoulders. "Besides, this little lady has been a regular good luck charm for me since I first met her..."

The woman rolled her eyes, but Dixon noticed she made no attempt to shrug off the arm.

"What a load of old tosh," put in Jones. "You've almost been killed umpteen times in the last few hours."

"Heh. Exactly Major. Almost been killed. Almost."

Anderson smiled with the others then called to the helmsman.

"Set course for home. Full steam ahead."

*

Sat in his office overlooking Lubyanka Square, Comrade Director Felix Dzerzhinsky of the Committee for State Security reached once more for the closely-typed pages of the report.

Scowling, he flicked through the document. Repeated reading did nothing to improve its contents. His most reliable investigators had been despatched to Murmansk to unravel the sequence of events, but even they seemed unable to verify the important details. That the mine at Kovdor had been targeted by saboteurs was beyond doubt, but what these mysterious men were said to have accomplished seemed beyond belief.

A handful of agents appeared to have destroyed the entire facility. Not to mention half the Red Army's arsenal. And had they really assassinated so many high-ranking officers and scientists, along with the local head of the Cheka itself?

Dzerzhinsky's brain whirled with questions, none of them satisfied by the report in his hands. Putting his own questions aside, he knew Vladimir Ilyich was livid, demanding an answer to the largest question of all – who had dared launch this attack against Russia's most secret project?

At least there Dzerzhinsky felt he could provide the Comrade Chairman with an answer. He had a report of the infiltrators speaking German, but more importantly there were dozens of witnesses who swore the escaping spies had been picked up by a submersible. One of the Kaiser's damned u-boats prowling within Russian territorial waters – outrageous.

What had possessed the Germans to commit such an open act of aggression? He had always had Bismarck pegged as a more wily and subtle opponent than this clumsy move suggested.

Regardless of the reasons, the Kaiser and his Iron Chancellor had made a mistake this time – and with Europe on the brink of war, and Lenin spitting blood in his rage, this mistake might very well prove fatal.

***

Neptune Rising

Rod Gillies

Windward Passage, off Hispaniola

The boy clutched the stern rail and stared back at the ships. He blinked, determined not to cry – not in front of these last remaining members of the crew.

On his father's orders he had been dragged unceremoniously from the bridge – out of the wheelhouse, down into the depths of the vessel, through companionways packed tight with grim-faced men preparing for battle. Ignoring his protests and ineffective blows, the sailors had bundled him into the launch. The boat cast off and steamed away at once, her boiler stoked to bursting, paddles thrashing at the water, seeking safety in the gathering night.

Smoke and fire erupted from a dozen broad muzzles, followed a split-second later by the booming concussion. Distracted from his anger, the boy thrilled at the power and noise of the cannon, imagining the incendiary shells ripping an arc through the sky.

The reply, when it came, crushed his excitement. The full immensity of the English dreadnought became suddenly apparent as the thunder flash of her broadside rippled down her length. Three times the size of his father's vessel, carrying four times as many guns, the warship was massive. And beyond her size, she was possessed of all the fearsome efficiency the Royal Navy instilled in its men.

One relentless fusillade followed another, the dreadnought's gunners quickly finding their range. Rounds thumped into the target with merciless accuracy. At first there were scattered shots in response, but these dwindled as flames blossomed on board. The English shells rained in and the ship the boy had called home was reduced to a slowly-sinking bonfire.

The one-sided battle receded in the launch's wake. The boy resisted the urge to look away until long after the fire's glow was extinguished.

Not old enough to fight, but old enough to want to, Jack Rackham burned with shame as he sailed away into the darkness.

*

Ypres

The star shell burst over No Man's Land and began its descent, a phosphorous glare painting the landscape in stark flickers of white.

The men stopped crawling and pushed themselves into the mud. All veterans of the trenches, they buried their faces in the crooks of their arms, attempting to stop tell-tale clouds of breath forming in the cold air – a tactic learned from bitter lessons handed out by German snipers.

Jones found it ironic the weapons that scared him most were not the giant war machines that stalked the trench-scarred battlefields – you could see them coming. What brought him out in a clammy sweat was the thought of his face coming into focus in the telescopic sight on some Mauser rifle. You'd never know. Might not even hear the shot. Although granted, it would at least be mercifully swift.

No shots came this time though, and as the star shell spluttered out its last light, Jones and his men were plunged back into darkness and relative safety. He lay in the sucking cold of the mud, waiting for his eyes to adjust. Eventually able to distinguish his surroundings once more, even if only in shades of darkest grey, he waved the men forward.

After an exhausting hour slithering on their bellies, punctuated by frozen moments of phosphor-lit fear, the four men reached their destination. The ruined observation post was long-since abandoned, the collapsed trenches it had served relegated to No Man's Land months before as the front line shifted back and forth. Jones wasn't sure which side had built the shelter in the first place. Not that it mattered. Any port in a storm and all that. The soldiers squeezed into the cramped confines of the squat building, glad to be out of the quagmire.

"Not long now boys," said Jones. "We'll wait for daylight, then in and out, and back for lunch."

His companions nodded, eyes wide in filthy faces.

Carson, Wills and Sergeant Mackenzie had all volunteered for the mission. Jones wondered if they were regretting it now as the sick tension built up. He'd never ask of course, not the done thing. There were clear expectations of the officer class – a stiff upper lip and snappy one-liners in the face of danger. Never mind the exhausting nausea which affected him every bit as much as his men.

Jones rolled his aching shoulders and shifted, trying to get comfortable. He leaned back and regarded the lightening sky through the rotten timbers of the roof. The next thing he knew, he was snapping awake at a touch on his shoulder.

"Fritz is moving," whispered Mackenzie.

Jones flicked the clasp on his pocket watch and frowned down at the luminous dots around its face. He had dozed for twenty minutes.

"You looked like you needed the kip Major."

He gave the Scotsman a grateful nod and raised his head to peer through the observation slit. He could see nothing, but his ears picked up the rumble of engines and the tramp of feet. Mackenzie was right, somewhere out there an army was stirring.

As dawn broke, the German guns opened fire. The synchronised thunder followed long seconds later by the hollow crumps of explosions in the distance as the shells fell back to earth. After ten minutes of sustained fire, the artillery fell abruptly silent, its clamour replaced with shouted orders and the noise of massed infantry on the move.

Jones couldn't help but feel a little sorry for the Germans as the first ghostly figures moved past them in the dim light. Even if the British hadn't already known about this particular assault, the artillery fire would have done little damage to the deeply-fortified positions, serving no purpose other than to warn the boys of the Queen's Guards the Hun was on his way. Why did the army chiefs on both sides still insist on throwing away the element of surprise like this? Conventional military wisdom, supposed Jones. Something his current mission had little to do with.

The press of troops heading for the British lines grew thicker. Riflemen led the advance, picking their way through the barbed wire. Behind came pairs of men managing the heavier weapons, one man carrying a box of ammunition, the next struggling under the unwieldy burden of a Spandau machine gun and its tripod mounting. Once within range of the enemy, the fearsome gun would be braced into place, its hand-cranked mechanism capable of blasting out a hundred rounds in less than a minute.

Here and there across the battlefield, the infantry made space for the ugly box shapes of land-tanks. The riveted metal beasts rumbled alongside the soldiers, growling out clouds of dirty smoke, the thick links of their treads cutting new ruts into the mud.

Behind the men and armoured vehicles lumbered the enormous frame of a four-legged walker. The articulated toe plates of its feet adjusted to the uneven terrain as it lurched past the concealed observers, shaking the ground, pistons expanding and contracting with each ponderous step. Atop the wide platform of the walker's deck, wreathed in wisps of expelled steam, figures scurried back and forth, preparing carbines and mortars to unleash a deadly hail into the British trenches.

No regular soldier on either side envied the men who rode the walkers, despite their elevated position and heavy armaments. The steel monsters always drew fire in any battle – magnets for artillery and aerial bombardment, resulting in terrible casualties amongst the crews. The walkers were damned impressive in a parade, and Jones knew the top brass revelled in their mechanical power, but he had seen too many of the contraptions blown to shrapnel when a round punctured their boilers.

The dawn's light filtered through the clouds, and the full scale of the offensive became clear. Jones lost count as wave after wave of men and machinery rolled past his position. The Hun wasn't messing around here – this was a serious push. Just as well it was no surprise. Poor old Fritz was in for a rough time. The Guards had been bracing for the attack for over a month, thanks to the talkative German officers who had ordered their schnapps from a waiter whose ears belonged to England.

The infiltrators lay concealed in the abandoned outpost until the last of the advancing troops filed past. As the first barks of gunfire echoed from the battle now being joined to the west, Jones stood, stretching the knots out of his muscles.

In the growing light he took in his men's appearance – all, like himself, dressed in German uniforms. Pulling the clothing from the enemy corpses scattered across No Man's Land had been one of the mission's more unpleasant preparatory tasks.

"Right chaps," he said, taking a bloodstained bandage from his pocket and tying it around his head. "Sooner we get this over and done with, the sooner we can get out of this ridiculous clobber."

*

Kramer turned from the map table and watched as the wounded officer was helped into the command bunker. The man's uniform was filthy, as was the garb of the private who supported him.

Major Von Stalhein grimaced at the state of the new arrivals. Typical aristocrat, thought Kramer, more concerned with a bit of mud than the information the man apparently bore.

The injured soldier attempted a salute, swaying on his feet. Kramer pulled out a chair. "Take a seat Captain. We have plenty to spare."

The wounded man settled into the canvas chair. He blinked, casting tired eyes around the bunker. "Where is everyone?" he asked.

"All who could be spared are at the front," snapped Von Stalhein.

"We have thrown everything into this offensive," said Kramer. "When the gas alarm sounded, I sent the others to the shelters. The Major here has been reduced to making his own coffee."

Von Stalhein scowled and Kramer allowed himself a smile. He did enjoy twisting the tail of his stuck-up subordinate. "Perhaps you could go and rustle up a mug for the Captain? He looks like he could do with it."

The Major stared back, clearly aghast at the suggestion. Kramer held his gaze until Von Stalhein offered a grudging salute and stomped from the room. Kramer returned his attention to the seated man.

"So my friend, what is this message that is so important?"

The soldier bent forward, fumbling in his leather pack. When he straightened, the dazed expression was gone, replaced with a grim determination. The hand came out of the bag holding a pistol.

"Queen Victoria sends her regards."

Kramer was stunned, as much at hearing English spoken within his command post as at the sudden appearance of the weapon. His faculties deserted him, his ability to think, to react, replaced with a lonely thought echoing round in his head: how could he have been taken in by such a simple ruse? By the time he gathered his wits, he had already been disarmed by the man's companion.

The Englishman gave a weary smile and reached up to pull the bandage from his head. He spoke to his compatriot. "Watch him."

Kramer seethed as the imposter tucked away his weapon and began scouring the command post, moving methodically round the room, grabbing handfuls of papers from the tables and stuffing them into his bag. He paused before the wireless desk, contemplating the stacks of radio equipment – a baffling collection knobs and switches.

He lifted a wooden box, its front studded with dials. With a jerk, he tugged the cables from the device's rear and pulled it clear. Kramer winced. He had hoped the Englishman wouldn't grasp the box's significance. Whatever happened, they could not be allowed to take the cipher machine. He took a step forward.

The gun butt smashed between his shoulder blades and he crumpled to the floor in agony. The figure looming over him turned the carbine, bringing the muzzle back round to point into Kramer's face.

"Dinnae bother..." came the accented growl.

"Mackenzie," snapped the Englishman, distracted from his looting. "That's enough."

The soldier stepped back, frowning at the reprimand.

Kramer hauled himself to his feet, pain shooting across the muscles of his back. "There is no honour in this..." he said, finally finding his voice.

The man glared across the bunker. "You lost all honour when you dropped the gas shells, Colonel."

The words struck Kramer like a slap in the face. He had argued with High Command not to deploy the poison gas. It was a coward's weapon, and an ineffective one at that. But his superiors were desperate to break the deadlock of the trenches and he had been over-ruled.

"You cannot claim any moral high-ground," he said. "You deployed gas this very morning..."

The Englishman's expression switched from anger to amusement. He pulled a metal canteen from his pack and tossed it onto the map table, sending the carefully arranged formation markers tumbling.

"Only a little flask of the stuff. A whiff under your detector pipe, and you all went scuttling for cover. Like cockroaches."

Despite himself, Kramer was impressed. "You came prepared..."

"We had plenty of time to get ready. We've known about your offensive for some time." The Englishman smiled at Kramer's reaction, although the eyes remained cold. "Our lines are all set to give your men the appropriate reception."

Two soldiers burst into the command post. Kramer's heart lurched in hope, only to have it dashed as he spotted the slumped form they dragged between them. They dropped the body and made their report.

"Nobody around. All hiding from the gas," said the first man.

"But we found this one in the galley..." said the other, gesturing to the corpse. "He picked a fight. He lost."

So Von Stalhein died with honour, thought Kramer. Perhaps he had underestimated the man after all.

The English officer returned his attention to Kramer. "Right then Colonel. Time to take a walk. You're coming with us."

Von Stalhein's body drew Kramer's eye. How ironic – the arrogant fool providing the honourable example. He drew himself erect and gave a firm shake of his head.

"I cannot allow you to kidnap me."

The Englishman stared at him, a measure of respect in his dark gaze.

"We thought you might say that..."

He drew a curiously-shaped pistol, different to the one he had brandished earlier. He adjusted a dial mounted above the grip and a high-pitched whine began to emerge from the gun. The man's companions traded nervous looks and backed away as their leader raised the pistol.

Kramer mastered his nerves. Whatever this exotic weapon was, one death was very much like another. He pulled himself to attention, glaring at the man who had hoodwinked him.

"Get on with it."

The Englishman pulled the trigger.

*

The lightning's blue crackle faded away, leaving the soldiers blinking at the after-images dancing around their vision. Jones nudged the fallen German with his foot. Little curls of smoke rose from scorched patches on the man's uniform.

"Still alive?" asked Mackenzie.

"And sleeping soundly for the next six hours, if this contraption has done its job," said Jones. "Mind you, he'll wake up with a hangover that would kill a horse." He tucked the electrical pistol away and turned to Carson and Wills. "Go and find a stretcher. I'll be buggered if I'm lugging him all the way back by myself. Mackenzie, help me set the explosives."

The Sergeant fished into his pack and pulled out a string bag bulging with shiny black spheres. "Fifteen minutes?" he asked.

"Ten," said Jones. No point risking a stray guard stumbling on the scene. The whole point of the exercise was to leave the wreckage of the bunker safely on top of any evidence the command post had been ransacked and the Colonel kidnapped.

They turned the clockwork timers on the compact demolition charges, starting them ticking quietly. The pair moved round the room, depositing explosives at each of the chamber's support pillars. As the final charges were placed, Carson and Wills returned with a stretcher. Kramer was strapped tightly into its canvas bed.

All four men pulled gas masks over their heads, Jones fitting another over the face of the unconscious German. Each man took a handle of the stretcher and they slipped out of the bunker and away into the trenches.

They encountered only scattered guards as they negotiated their way through the muddy warren. It seemed Kramer really had thrown the bulk of his men into the assault on Ypres. The remaining Germans eyed the party through their masks with little interest – just one more wounded man on his way to the charnel house of the medical tents.

Reaching the point where they had slipped into the trenches earlier, the British soldiers waited. After what seemed an eternity, the flat reports of the demolition charges echoed behind them, the noise accompanied by a faint tremor rippling through the ground. A moment later the klaxons sounded, mixed with shouts of alarm as the Germans discovered the damage inflicted on their command post.

Banking on the distraction providing cover for the final stretch of their escape, Jones and his men hauled their unconscious captive up and over the side. Hoisting the stretcher between them, they stumbled over the uneven ground of No Man's Land towards the distant sound of battle.

Away from the German lines, Jones cast his mask aside, grateful to be free of the heavy canvas hood. His men did the same.

"Not far to the tunnel now..." he said.

Being dressed in the uniform of the enemy made their return to Imperial lines somewhat complicated. There seemed little point in making it all the way back after this foolhardy exercise, only to be shot by their own sentries. The tunnel had been a key element in the plan.

Imperial sappers had gone to work with their drilling machines – rotating rings of iron teeth gouging at the earth, the soil liquefied by hot steam and piped back out to the surface. The resulting passage stretched for a mile, stopping just shy of the deeply-sown mines both sides had peppered across No Man's Land to prevent subterranean assault.

The tunnel's low ceiling had looked set to collapse at any moment and the seeping groundwater made it like crawling through a sewer. But now, his nerves jangling, twitching at every crack of gunfire, Jones longed to reach the welcoming safety of the underground passage.

The gunfire and explosions marking the German assault grew steadily in volume as the party stumbled onwards. As they scrambled up the last ridge before the tunnel's entrance, the sounds of battle were complemented by the drone of engines from the skies above.

The bulk of an airship emerged from the low cloud, the props mounted along the gondola's side tearing swirling holes in the vapour. Engines rumbling, the airship slid down out of the murk until it loomed above them, the dark tan of its gasbag making for an ominous contrast with the red, white and blue markings on the tail fins. The men stared up as the long doors on the underside of the gondola cracked open.

"Get down!" shouted Jones.

They dived for cover, scattering as the bombs began to fall.

*

Jones stormed into Brigadier Gourlay's office and tossed the hand onto his superior's desk. The appendage was whole enough, if a little dirty, but the wrist ended in a ragged stump with an inch of white bone protruding from the torn flesh.

Gourlay frowned, leaning forward to give the offending article a poke with the tip of his pen. He looked up at Jones, an eyebrow raised.

"There is a limit to my indulgence you know..."

"The only piece left of Colonel Kramer," said Jones. "Thanks to those blithering idiots in the Aeronautic Corps."

Gourlay cursed and leaned back in his chair, rubbing at his temples. "You actually had him? Buckingham's crackpot scheme worked?"

Jones pulled out a cigarette and struck a match, willing his hands to stop shaking long enough for him to get his smoke alight. He slumped into a canvas chair and blew a stream of smoke towards the ceiling.

"All credit to the old man," he said around the side of his cigarette, "the plan worked a charm."

"Your friend Kramer might disagree," said Gourlay, nodding towards the grisly remnant on his blotting pad. "What happened?"

"Two minutes from the damned tunnel and one of our own airships dropped a tonne of explosives on top of us. Blew the Colonel to bits, and sent Mackenzie flying. Broke his bloody leg. Rest of us had to carry him."

"Lucky you weren't all killed."

"Don't feel very lucky. All that effort, and for what? A handful of files and the gubbins from some wireless..."

"You're determined to be miserable, aren't you?" said Gourlay. "The Bletchley lot will be delighted to get their grubby paws on that souvenir of yours. They've been in the dark for months since the codes changed. Now they'll be able to read Fritz's love letters again."

"Not quite the same as having a genuine Kraut Colonel to question though, is it?" Jones gave a bitter smile. "I'd love to see the Duke's face when someone tells him what happened."

"You can tell him yourself. He's next door."

"Buckingham? He's here?"

"Arrived just after you left last night. Wanted to see you as soon as you returned." He waved towards the door. "Off you trot. Best run along and see what the old man wants."

Jones pulled himself up. He left the Brigadier prodding at the severed hand and made his way to the next office along the corridor, knocking once before pushing open the door.

The Duke of Buckingham turned from a bundle of papers. His penetrating gaze gave Jones' dishevelled appearance the once-over. Appraising the goods, thought Jones sourly. Checking I'm still in one piece, checking I'm still useful.

"Glad you're back. Got a job for you." The Duke spoke in his usual brisk style – short, sharp phrases delivered through his moustache like machine gun bullets flying from an ambush position.

"Don't you want to hear about the last one?"

"Already heard. Bloody annoying, but can't be helped."

"Can't be helped? God Almighty," Jones wiped his hand down his face. "You don't seem bothered one of our own airships wasted months of planning. And almost killed me and my men into the bargain."

The Duke regarded him from beneath a low frown. "And if I indulged my irritation, would it alter the outcome?" He shook his head. "Besides, you obtained the cipher machine."

"But lost the Colonel..."

Buckingham waved the comment aside. "We have another problem. In the Caribbean."

Jones snorted. "We have enough problems right here."

"We do indeed. But they'll only get worse if this affair isn't sorted. Dreadful business." The old man got to his feet and shuffled round the table, leaning heavily on his cane. He pointed at the cigarette in Jones' hand. "Give me one of those, would you?"

Jones pulled the metal case from his pocket, popped it open and let the old man extract a cigarette. Buckingham took the proffered matchbox and lit up, sucking in a lungful of blue smoke. Jones dragged a chair over and dropped into it, suddenly exhausted, the tension of the last twenty-four hours catching up with him in a rush of weariness and nerves.

Resignation washed over him, coupled with more than a little trepidation – here we go again.

"What's going on? And what has it got to do with me?"

Buckingham stared at him for a long moment before speaking. Jones could tell something must be seriously amiss. Normally the old man relished this moment, the grand unveiling of his latest scheme.

But the usual glint in the eye was absent. Jones had never seen the Duke's expression so grave.

"I'm sorry David," said Buckingham. "I have some bad news..."

*

Havana

"Welcome to the Protectorate of Cuba."

The customs official refolded the travel documents and handed them back across the desk. Jones nodded his thanks and tucked the passport and visa into his jacket. He moved past the counter and crossed the marble floor of the aerodrome's first class terminal. Passing through the revolving door, he made his way out into the baking Cuban sunshine. The heat was like a physical obstacle, stopping him in his tracks.

The attendant at the rank of automobiles stepped forward with a tug at the brim of his cap. "Cab *senor*?"

"*Si, gracias.*" Jones didn't know much Spanish, but he knew enough to be polite.

The man pulled open the rear door of the first vehicle in line and Jones climbed in, taking a seat beneath the striped canopy. The cab driver turned to look at his passenger.

"No bag?" he asked in accented English.

"The airship company will send my trunk along."

The driver smiled broadly. Jones supposed hauling luggage around in this heat was nobody's idea of fun. The driver's grin widened further when Jones gave him the address. The Cuban turned to his controls, opening valves and pushing forward on the drive levers. With a crunch of gears and a sharp squeal from the boiler, the cab moved off.

As they puttered away from the aerodrome, Jones glanced back to see the airship's bulk looming over the terminal building and its flanking palm trees. His journey across the Atlantic in the massive dirigible had been most civilised. He was going to miss the food.

He quickly realised he would miss the cool winds of higher altitudes even more. The breeze created by the cab's motion proved all too brief. The vehicle settled into the heavy flow of traffic and slowed to little more than walking pace. The air closed in again, thick and heavy.

The palm-lined road was filled with steam tractors, horse-drawn carts, and cabs like Jones' own. Mechanised bicycles zipped here and there between the vehicles, the only conveyance able to move in anything other than intermittent bursts. Jones' driver seemed determined to compete for every inch of road, and they jerked forward in fits and starts. The other drivers were just as aggressive, engine noises and the braying of horse and donkey almost drowned out in a cacophony of shouted curses and angry blasts on horn and whistle.

Jones tapped the driver on the shoulder. "Is it always like this?" he called over the din.

"No *senor*. Is much better since the Yankees build the new road."

Jones plucked his hat from his head and fanned himself with it. He closed his eyes and tried to ignore the noise as the cab jolted on.

The congestion eased as they reached the outskirts of Havana. Most of the heavier vehicles turned off the main road, making for the industrial quarter, its factories and mills marked by a forest of towering chimneys spewing steam and grimy smoke into the sky. The cab continued on towards the city itself.

The road became a broad boulevard running between a frontage of tall, brightly-painted buildings and the sea wall. Across the waters of the bay, a fortress squatted atop the cliffs, whitewashed walls gleaming beneath the red, white and blue of a limp Stars and Stripes.

The cab stuttered to a halt before an imposing three-storey building set back from the road behind a well-kept hedge. The driver hustled round to get the door but Jones was already out of the automobile, gazing up at the ornate frontage of cream and white stonework. Wrought iron balconies faced the sea from the upper floors and gilded lettering above the doorway proclaimed the establishment to be the Mirador Hotel.

Jones pulled a dollar bill from his wallet and handed it over. The driver's grin reappeared.

"Enjoy your stay *senor*. Don't let the Mirador tire you out..."

The man jumped back into his cab and the vehicle pushed its way out into the flow of traffic, earning a chorus of angry toots and whistle blasts.

Jones stood for a moment taking in Havana's riot of colour – the pinks and yellows and creams of the buildings, the white glare of the sand beyond the road, and the bright blue of the water and the sky above. It made for quite a change from the relentless grey of Ypres. Warmer too, he thought, tipping back his hat and dabbing a handkerchief at beads of sweat. Turning from the shorefront vista, he climbed the steps of the terrace, heading for what he hoped would be the pleasant shade of the hotel foyer.

The air inside the lobby was indeed wonderfully cool, kept circulating over the checkerboard tiling of the floor by a brace of wooden fans. The soft tick-tick-tick of the fans revolving overhead was the only sound. Jones' ding of the reception desk bell echoed round the space.

A young man in a white shirt and black waistcoat appeared through the door behind the desk. He welcomed Jones with an efficient smile and flipped open the register.

"It seems very quiet…" said Jones as he filled in his details.

"Actually, we are fully booked at the moment sir," replied the receptionist with only the merest hint of an accent to his English. "However, most guests enjoy a *siesta* during the heat of the afternoon."

"Now that sounds a fine idea."

Despite his restful crossing of the Atlantic, Jones still felt bone-tired. It would take more than a few nights to catch up on the sleep he'd missed over his months in the trenches.

"You shall find things much livelier in the evening. Might I suggest you join us later for a drink and dinner?"

*

Jones awoke to the noise of other guests stirring and the murmur of conversation floating up past his window from the hotel's central courtyard. He stepped out onto his balcony and watched the sky darken over the water, moving through rich shades of blue and purple before the first stars winked into existence. He checked his watch and returned to his room. Time to get ready.

After dragging a razor across his traveller's stubble, he took a light suit from his trunk, turning it this way and that to check the linen material wasn't too crushed.

The bellboy had offered to unpack his things for him earlier, but Jones had waved him away. He had never liked anyone fussing around him, had never felt the need to employ a "gentleman's gentleman", unlike so many of his friends. It had made him something of an oddity in the circles he had moved in before the war – this stubborn insistence on doing everything for himself. There had been gossip about his finances of course, but he didn't care. He could certainly afford the staff – his father's investments had left him very comfortable on the money front – but the thought of having servants at his beck and call simply didn't sit right.

Dressed, he made for the stairs, entering the lobby as a raucous group of young men piled through the front doors. They threw hats and coats at the cloakroom attendant and made for the salon, clearly looking to continue what must have been an afternoon of drinking. Jones thought one or two of them looked like they were already in a state of fairly advanced refreshment.

He followed them through into the bar, concerned he was about to wade into some drunken watering hole. A drink would be fine, but he was in no mood to sit amidst the noisy carousing of others. Thankfully, he spotted the group of rakes being ushered through to some private space, the *maitre d'* obviously keen to ensure the young bucks did not disrupt the rather more civilised atmosphere of the main bar.

The salon was filled with high-backed chairs and ornamental palms. Dark wood trim and burgundy leather offered a handsome contrast to the glitter of the gaslight chandelier reflecting from the bottles and mirrors behind the bar. The strains of a string quartet drifted from a phonograph in the corner, a background for the general hum of conviviality permeating the room. Most of the seating was occupied, the clientele a mix of gentlemen in suits, and ladies bedecked in what Jones could only assume were the latest fashions. His knowledge in this area was limited – his time in France hadn't included any Parisian shopping excursions.

He took a high stool at the bar. "Whisky," he ordered, "with ice."

The barman prepared the drink, using a hand pick to chip chunks of ice from the block melting slowly on the back bar. Jones thanked the man and lifted the glass, relishing the chinking sound of the ice as he swirled the bourbon round. Not real whisky of course but, by God, it would do.

He savoured the sweet smoky burn of the spirit and regarded his reflection in the bar mirror. Gaunt – that was how his dear aunt in Richmond would have described him, no doubt prior to insisting he had a nice hot bowl of soup. But despite his drawn and pale face, here he was, very much alive, enjoying a snifter amongst the dandies of Havana.

A fortnight ago, he had been knee-deep in blood-stained mud, creeping into the heart of the German lines, half-expecting not to see another sunrise. The lads of the Queen's Guards would be green with envy if they could see him now. He hoisted the glass in a silent toast to the boys. Wish you were here gents, or at least not back there.

He watched the crowd in the mirror as he sipped at his drink. At some of the tables business deals were clearly being conducted – earnest conversations concluded with hearty handshakes and orders for champagne. But observing the room, Jones realised other, more subtle, business was also underway throughout the salon. Every now and again one of the young ladies – and he noticed now they were all young – would whisper in the ear of her male companion and stand, leading him away by the hand through a door at the rear of the room. The departure was sometimes accompanied by nudges and knowing looks from the man's fellows, but more often than not, went unremarked.

Jones was momentarily shocked, and then amused at his own reaction. If the lads would have been jealous before, they'd be doubly-so now. These thoughts were interrupted by a presence at his elbow. He turned and found himself looking into a pair of dark brown eyes.

The woman was striking, her penetrating gaze and sharp cheekbones framed by a tumble of black curls. She was clad in emerald silk, the dress shimmering under the light of the chandelier, the figure beneath it either a natural wonder or a marvel of corsetry.

"You must be *Senor* Jones..." she said, the slight Hispanic accent lending an exotic tinge to his most humdrum of surnames. "Our English gentleman visitor."

Jones pushed himself to his feet, bending his head to brush his lips on the back of the proffered hand. "I am indeed," he said as he straightened, "but I am afraid you have the advantage of me."

The dark eyes flashed. "Be careful I do not make use of it, eh *senor*?"

Unsure how to respond, Jones made do with a polite smile.

"Forgive me." She placed her hand on his arm. "I could not resist. My name is Isabella De La Vega. I am the proprietor of the Mirador."

"Then allow me to offer my compliments. From what I have experienced thus far, your establishment is of the highest quality."

"Thank you *senor*. We do try to make our guests comfortable. I hope you will enjoy your stay." She leaned forward, adopting a conspiratorial tone. "Now tell me, what brings you so far from home?"

"I'm a journalist," said Jones, dropping into the story he had agreed with Buckingham. "The Times wants articles from areas of the world untouched by the war. Something to lighten the cares of our readers." He gestured to indicate their surroundings. "I was lucky enough to bag a jaunt to Cuba and the Antilles."

De La Vega tipped her head to the side and regarded him intently. "Such tired eyes. They do not look like the eyes of a writer."

Jones felt his face flush under her appraisal, once again finding himself at a loss for a response. He was saved from the awkward moment by a loud interruption.

"Son of a bitch! I should have known..."

A tall, broad-shouldered man strode through the bar towards them, arms thrown wide. The smile across his features was a mirror of Jones' own. The pair shook hands warmly before Jones returned his attention to the woman at his side.

"My apologies, my friend and I have not seen one another for nigh-on two years. May I introduce Captain John Kowalski? Captain, this is –"

"Oh we've met," said Kowalski. He offered the woman a bow. "How are you doing Isabella? Did you miss me?"

Her eyes narrowed, but the tone stayed light. "Havana is not the same when the sailors of the Free Fleet are not in town."

"Heh. Seems to me the Major here was doing his best to keep you entertained –" Kowalski stopped at Jones' pained expression. "What?"

De La Vega turned to Jones, a twinkle in her eye. She lowered her voice. "Don't worry *Major*, your secret is safe with me." She waved a hand and the barman hurried over. "I shall leave you two gentlemen to get reacquainted. Samuel here will look after you. If there's anything else you require, you only have to ask."

With a swish of her skirts the hotel's owner departed. Both men watched her move off, winding her way between the tables. She stopped occasionally to speak with one or other of her guests, a hand on a shoulder here, a tilt of the head and flirtatious laughter there, clearly in her element as she worked the room.

Kowalski clapped Jones on the back. "Hardly in the country and you're already mixed up with the most formidable woman in Cuba. Quick work Major."

Jones rolled his eyes. "We were just talking. Anyway, I have a bone to pick with you..." He indicated their surroundings. "What sort of place is this to arrange a meeting? It's a damned bordello."

"A damned good one too. And that's the point. Isabella wasn't lying – she really will keep your secret. Places like this have to keep secrets. It's how they make money. It's how they survive."

Jones considered this statement. Perhaps the Floridian had a point.

"Besides," continued Kowalski, "if I'd known I was meeting such a miserable old Puritan, I'd have picked someplace else. Like maybe a Temperance House?"

Jones returned the smile. "Well, perhaps you'll allow this Puritan to buy you a drink?"

"Major, I thought you'd never ask."

*

As ever, the Mirador's kitchen provided an excellent dinner. Kowalski relished his stays here, even more so when he could bill the not-inconsiderable expense to one of the Fleet's clients. Food and drink always tasted better when someone else was picking up the tab.

He finished the last tender morsel of his steak and pushed his plate to the side. "Should have guessed a cryptic telegram from headquarters would see me running into you again. What's his Lordship wanting blown up this time?"

"He's a Duke," said Jones, dabbing at the corners of his mouth before folding his napkin and placing it on his sideplate.

"His Dukeship then. All I know is his idea of a good time involves other folks getting shot at."

"Not us. Not this time." Jones paused. "Well, not if all goes to plan."

"Heh. And how often does that happen?"

Kowalski pulled two long cigars from his inside pocket and clipped the end off one. He offered the other to the Englishman.

"I'll stick to these," said Jones, holding up his cigarette case.

"Havana's finest," said Kowalski. "Cost a damn fortune. You don't know what you're missing."

Both men lit their respective smokes. After taking a few deep puffs, Kowalski regarded the glowing red tip of his cigar, rolling it to and fro and watching the vapours curl upwards before they were swept round, dissolving in the revolutions of the fan blades overhead.

"So, back to this plan which ain't going to see me get shot at..."

The Englishman looked over his shoulder, surveying the dining room. They had asked for some privacy on moving through from the bar and had been seated in a quiet corner of the opulent dining room. The waiters, bustling around in their black waistcoats and long white aprons, were being kept busy by the other patrons. Seemingly satisfied they couldn't be overheard, Jones leaned forward.

"Have you ever been to Tortuga?"

Kowalski coughed on his cigar smoke. "You're kidding, right?"

"I wish I was. I need to take a look at this infamous den of iniquity. And you're coming with me."

Kowalski realised now why the telegram from the Admiral had contained so few details regarding his new assignment. His superior had known what sort of response he would have received.

"There's some decidedly unsavoury characters on Tortuga. Not one of them I'd like to tangle with."

"Jack Rackham?"

"The worst of the lot. A direct descendant of the original Calico Jack and Anne Bonney. Or so he claims. A nasty piece of work and no mistake."

"You've met him?"

"Seen him once. From a distance. I hear it's the safest way."

"How so?"

"They call themselves a democracy over there – got a constitution and everything. Around five years back, Rackham gets himself elected and then hangs each and every man who'd stood against him. One man, one vote – just so long as Calico Jack is the one man in question." Kowalski grimaced. "Best head back to London, Major. Go tell his Lordship to leave Rackham and his pirates well alone."

"And that's been the policy of the Floridian government, and your neighbours to the north, for far too long."

"They don't attack our shipping. They know better."

"So you'll cheerfully look the other way while they plunder the ships of other nations..."

"Damn it Major. It ain't like that. It'd take half the Free Fleet to clear out that hornets' nest. It just ain't worth it." Kowalski shook his head. Didn't the British have more important things to worry about? "What's the problem? They don't go after anything flying a red duster neither."

"Until five weeks ago..." Jones ground his cigarette into the ashtray. "That's when they took the *Milford*, a merchantman out of Bristol. Stole her cargo and used her for target practice. One man survived just long enough to tell the Consul what happened."

Kowalski frowned. He'd heard nothing of this. Jones went on.

"Since then another three British ships have gone missing in the area. No mayday messages. No reports of bad weather. The Admiralty is convinced Rackham and his band of cut-throats are responsible."

"Four ships in five weeks? If it is Rackham, he's not messing around."

"Quite. And why those ships? That's the question. Other British vessels have passed unmolested."

"Any connection between them?"

"Not really. All out of different ports – India, Hong Kong, Jamaica." Jones' brow furrowed. "The only common denominator? All four were carrying arms destined for France."

The pair fell silent as the waiter arrived to clear their dishes from the table. They waved away the dessert menus and Jones waited until their server was well out of earshot before he spoke again.

"With the Royal Navy tied up keeping u-boats out of the Atlantic, we can't spare the ships to come over here and teach Rackham a lesson." He shrugged. "Not that we would of course. The Americans wouldn't appreciate a squadron of dreadnoughts throwing its weight around on this side of the pond. Caribbean is *their* ocean apparently. If we ever hope to get them into the war on our side, we can't afford to upset them."

"But if your navy ain't coming, why are you here?"

"Reconnaissance. I'm here to take a look at Tortuga with you. Between us we have to work out how much it would cost."

A cold knot formed in Kowalski's stomach. "To do what?"

"Her Majesty's government will be securing the services of the Free Fleet, and any of the smaller Floridian mercenary corps which may be required in support. We're going to wipe out Tortuga's little infestation."

"Ain't going to be cheap Major. If it can be done at all."

"We cannot allow any interference with ships coming through Panama. Nor can we allow Rackham's antics to encourage other miscreants by going unpunished." Jones frowned, a distant look on his face. "It's bloody awful in France at the moment. With Lenin and his chums sitting firmly on the fence, the Kaiser's free to fling everything at us. You won't read it in the newspapers of course, but if we start losing supply ships, it could tip the balance."

"That bad, huh?"

Jones' battle-weary eyes gave Kowalski his answer.

"So why did Buckingham send you? No offence Major, but this sounds like a job for a sailor, not a foot-slogger."

"Two reasons. Firstly, it seems I have a personal relationship with a highly-regarded officer of the Free Fleet..." He raised his glass. "That's you by the way. In case you didn't recognise the description."

Kowalski returned the toast. "I'm flattered."

"You should be. I didn't recognise it either."

"Heh. And the other reason?"

Jones' smile faltered. He tipped his head back, draining his whisky. He stared into the empty glass for a long moment before lifting his face to meet Kowalski's gaze.

"Buckingham knew I would insist on coming. The captain of the *Milford* was my brother."

*

The next morning they met for a walk along the Malecon, the wide promenade dividing Havana from the azure waters of the bay. Although the sun was shining, it had not yet heated the air to unbearable levels and a pleasant breeze rolled in over the beach. Well-dressed men and parasol-toting ladies strolled up and down, taking the morning air. Kowalski missed no opportunity to tip his hat to the prettier of the women, earning him a few flirtatious giggles from behind gloved hands, and no end of scandalised tutting from matronly chaperones.

"How's Maria?" asked Jones.

Kowalski had the decency to look sheepish. "She's up in Boston, working at the Technological Institute. She's busy. We write one another."

"Please give her my regards in your next letter. Lovely young woman. She'll make some lucky man in Massachusetts very happy I'm sure."

Kowalski scowled and stomped off ahead. Jones smiled to himself before lengthening his stride to catch up. As they approached the harbour, he spotted a dark shape, barely visible in the water offshore.

"What's the wreck?" he asked.

"The *USS Maine*. Can't see much just now, but at low tide her funnels and upper deck come clean out of the water."

"Why hasn't she been broken up for scrap?"

A whole dreadnought's worth of steel, just lying there, practically sitting on the beach – the salvage would have been easy. With stalemate in France, every spare piece of metal in England was being harvested for the war effort. Jones' aunt and uncle were still bemoaning the loss of the railings from their garden wall.

"Don't let any Yankees hear that kind of talk," said Kowalski. "Three hundred sailors died when the Reds blew her up. It's a shrine for them."

"Sentimental claptrap. And a waste of good steel."

"Ain't how the Americans feel about it, although I reckon most Cubans might agree. The wreck's a nasty reminder of history round here. If the *Maine* hadn't gone down, the occupation might never have happened. The Americans were mighty unimpressed at her sinking – she was the pride of their fleet at the time." Kowalski stared out at the wreck and gave a wry smile. "Only ten years ago, and the whole class is obsolete. Her sister ships are lined up in the breaker yards over at Guantanamo.

Seems it's fine for the Cubans to demolish dreadnoughts after all – just as long as the Yankees are paying for the privilege."

They walked on, the brightly-painted hotels and grand houses giving way to the duller stonework and plain wood of shipping offices, carpenters' workshops and chandlers' stores. Steamships and barges lay moored at every quay, tall freight elevators carrying pallets of cargo up and down between the seagoing vessels and their airship counterparts anchored above. Barrels of oil from the Gulf Coast, sugar from the plantations of Jamaica, coal and ore from the mines of central and southern America – every day the produce of half the world passed through Havana's bustling harbour and airyards.

They turned away from the seafront and Jones followed his guide down a cobbled alley, the buildings on either side leaning in overhead, the balconies almost touching. The narrow thoroughfares away from the front were packed with people and the pair rubbed shoulders with merchants, sailors and stevedores as they squeezed through the crowds. Gangs of street urchins ran barefoot through the throng prompting a warning from Kowalski to keep a weather-eye open for pickpockets.

After a few hundred yards, Kowalski stopped and pulled Jones into a doorway, a temporary refuge from the press of people. He indicated a tired-looking tavern on the other side of the street, its sagging timbers broken up by grimy windows, impenetrable to the eye.

"Delightful," said Jones. "You're sure this is the best place?"

Kowalski nodded. "It don't look like much. And in truth, it ain't. But this is where the smuggler captains do their drinking. We need a boat, and a man at the helm who knows the waters and can keep his mouth shut. This is where we'll find him."

*

The walls of the bar were stained a dirty brown. A thick haze of smoke hung in the air, as much a permanent fixture of the place as the leather-faced men whose cigars produced it.

Conversation at the tables around the bar's perimeter died away as the two men entered. Kowalski felt the cold appraisal of the assembly pass over him before the patrons returned to their drinks and muted discussions. Checked over, and dismissed as no immediate threat, the pair made their way towards the counter at the rear of the room. The barman abandoned his newspaper and shuffled over.

"What can I get you gen'men?" The accent was a thick Southern American drawl. Mississippi, thought Kowalski.

"Whisky," he said, counting five dollar bills onto the bar top. "And some information."

The grizzled bartender eyed the money, his tongue slipping out to run over cracked lips. "The drink ain't no problem..." He reached down and pulled glasses and a bottle from beneath the counter. He poured out two measures. "The other part? Kind of depends, don't it."

"I just need a recommendation is all," said Kowalski. "My friend and I are looking to take a fishing trip. But someplace more interesting than the usual spots. You know a boat that might be available?"

"Maybe's I do," said the man, scratching at his unshaven chin. "This trip of yours... I guess it might be going off the beaten track. Looking for a secluded cove or somesuch?"

"Something like that." Kowalski placed another dollar onto the pile.

The barman swept up the money, folding it and tucking it away. He padded from behind the bar and over to a table. He bent to whisper in the ear of one of his customers then returned with the man in tow.

"This here is Luis. He might be able to help you folks out."

The bartender went back to the counter and his newspaper, leaving Kowalski and Jones regarding Luis. The sailor was short and scrawny, the sleeves of his filthy shirt rolled up to reveal forearms covered in tattoos. Dark hair and a week's stubble framed a weatherbeaten face. The Cuban smiled, revealing a row of gold-capped teeth.

"*Senors*, you are looking for a boat?"

"You have one?" asked Kowalski.

"A most excellent one." Luis eyed the glasses on the bar. "Let us discuss the qualities of my vessel over a drink."

He waved over the barman and ordered rum. The drink arrived and the sailor crossed his arms, staring at Kowalski, who duly tossed a coin onto the bar top. Luis flashed a golden smile and lifted his glass, leading the way to an empty table situated away from the other customers.

They sat, and Luis raised his drink in a salute. Kowalski and Jones both took sips, whilst the Cuban drained the amber liquid in one and smacked the glass back down on the table. He wiped his mouth.

"You plan a fishing trip? One you want to keep private thinks Luis."

Kowalski leaned forward. "Very private. My friend and I are keen to avoid any undue attention."

The sailor grinned at them both, metalwork gleaming. "And this is why you need Luis. Nobody knows these waters as well as he." The eyes narrowed. "But Luis has drink to buy and women to rent. These things are not cheap. And neither is Luis..."

Kowalski pulled out a wad of money and peeled off fifty dollars.

Luis looked from the pile of bills to Kowalski. "The cargo you are moving. It is valuable?"

"Valuable to us. It's just me and my friend here."

The sailor jerked his thumb in Jones' direction. "This friend of yours does not have much to say."

Jones stayed silent, sticking to the plan of letting Kowalski do the talking. American accents were commonplace, they didn't need the extra attention his English tones would generate.

"He's a newspaperman," said Kowalski. "Writes more than he talks. He's planning a story about our destination."

A sly glint appeared in the Cuban's eyes. "*Si, si.* Your destination. Luis thinks you would not have left this detail until last if it was not the most important part of the arrangement. The most expensive part perhaps..."

"You already have fifty dollars."

"Enough for Luis to take you many places. But not all places, no."

Kowalski paused. Here we go.

"Tortuga," he said. "We're heading for Tortuga."

The Cuban blanched, eyes darting round to see if any of the other patrons had overheard. "*Madre de Dios...*" he muttered, wiping his hand through the grimy sweat on his forehead.

Much the same reaction as my own, thought Kowalski. He pulled the wad of money out once more and counted another fifty dollars out.

"There'll be a hundred more when we're safely back in Havana." The sailor stared down at the bills, golden teeth chewing at his lower lip as Kowalski continued. "You'll take us to the northern shore and drop us someplace quiet. You'll wait twenty-four hours and then we'll all sail away again." He patted a hand on the pile of notes. "Come on Luis. I'm sure you know a sweet little beach that would suit us just fine."

Kowalski watched the internal struggle between greed and fear play itself out behind the sailor's eyes. Greed won.

"Another hundred now," snapped Luis. "And another two hundred when we return. Luis will not do this foolish thing for any less."

The Cuban sat back, folding his tattooed arms across his chest. Kowalski shifted his attention to Jones who gave a curt nod. Kowalski shrugged, turned back to the sailor and handed over the extra money.

"You should be glad my friend here is so free with his currency."

The gold-toothed grin remained conspicuously absent as the sailor stuffed the bills away.

"Tomorrow morning *senors*," he said. "Sunrise. You meet Luis at the end of the old pier. It takes all day to make the crossing. You go ashore at dusk. That way we avoid the watchers." He scowled at the pair opposite. "But Luis will not wait a night and a day in that place. He sails the following dawn. With or without his passengers."

Kowalski stared over the table. "You don't want to cross me Luis. Worse things can happen than not getting your extra two hundred."

The Cuban recoiled from the look. "*Si, senor*," he mumbled.

Jones and Kowalski got to their feet. As they made for the door, Luis called after them, his bravado returning, no doubt boosted by the feel of the bank notes in his pocket. "*Hombres*! You don't finish your drinks?"

Kowalski shook his head in reply and pulled the door open. He watched the Cuban pick up each glass, draining them in turn before beckoning the bartender over. Kowalski sighed as he followed Jones out into the street. He hoped Luis wouldn't try to drink a full two hundred dollars worth of liquor before morning.

*

The next stop on their tour of Havana was in an altogether more prosperous district of the city. They strolled through the cobbled expanse of a broad square, past the gurgling dolphins of its fountain and into a wide tree-lined boulevard. Art galleries, clothing boutiques and restaurants ran down either side of the street, and rather than sailors and merchants, the pedestrian traffic was made up of society ladies and well-scrubbed houseboys toting their mistresses' acquisitions.

Kowalski led Jones to a small storefront set back from the road beneath a shady colonnade. The shelves in the windows were draped with intricate timepieces, both classic pocket watches and the newer models designed to be worn on the wrist.

The Floridian pushed open the door and a brass bell jangled cheerfully on its spring. A voice called through from the back shop.

"One moment please..."

Jones surveyed the cabinets lining the walls. Behind the glass, dozens of watches and clocks glittered. Many had been designed to reveal the complicated innards of the mechanisms, as if their maker deemed the jewels and precious metals of their casings merely a decorative addition to the beautiful functionality of the gears and levers themselves. Much as he appreciated the fine craftsmanship on display, Jones was about to ask why they were here when a small bespectacled man bustled through the rear door, rubbing his hands with an oil-stained cloth.

"My apologies, *senors*. I was —" He broke off as he recognised Kowalski. "John! It is good to see you."

The Floridian shook the man's hand. "Been too long, Ramon." He gestured towards Jones. "This is Major David Jones, from London. Major, let me introduce Ramon Cuervo, the finest watchmaker in the world."

The man tutted at Kowalski, wagging a long finger at him before shaking hands with Jones.

"The Captain has always been one for the exaggeration. Pay him no heed." A playful gleam appeared in the eyes behind the thick spectacles. "I'll settle for being the best outside of Switzerland."

"Heh. Don't believe a word of it. False modesty. Ramon has been supplying the Free Fleet for as long as we've been in business."

As he waved the compliment aside, Cuervo's eyes alighted on Jones' watch chain. "I recognise those links," he said with a note of excitement. "A Cartwright, if I am not mistaken. May I?"

Jones pulled the timepiece from his pocket, handing it across to the watchmaker. The man ran his thin fingers over the smooth casing and popped the catch. He peered down at the face and hands through his half-moon spectacles.

"Ahh," he breathed in appreciation. "The Portsmouth. The waterproof model. A lovely piece." He frowned. "A little scratched..."

"It's travelled some," said Jones. "And been through the odd scrape."

Cuervo returned the watch. "Somewhat like yourself, I would imagine. Especially if you are a friend of the Captain here."

"You got that right," said Kowalski. "And I reckon the Major would appreciate a look at the special merchandise."

Jones gave the watchmaker a polite smile, unsure what the fuss was about. "Your timepieces must be very fine to generate such enthusiasm."

The other men shared a look and Kowalski laughed. "Ramon don't make us anything as mundane as clocks. He has a sideline in an altogether different area. His, ah, hobby."

The watchmaker moved to his front door, locking it and placing a 'Closed' card in the window. He ushered his visitors past the counter and into the cramped workshop at the rear of the store. The wooden shelving was stacked with small boxes filled to overflowing with springs, cogs, scraps of metal and a hundred different lengths of thin brass screws. Cuervo reached up to one of the boxes, pulled it aside and fumbled with something at the rear of the shelf. With a click, a section of shelving swung back, revealing a steep set of wooden steps heading downwards.

The trio descended. At the base of the stairs, the watchmaker flicked a switch, bathing the cellar in bright light from an electric lamp affixed to the centre of the ceiling. Jones stared at the merchandise on display.

Kowalski slapped him on the back. "A regular Aladdin's cave, eh Major? And a little more our style than clocks."

The cases mounted round the walls displayed the most diverse collection of weaponry Jones had ever seen. A quick survey revealed different calibres of pistols, rifles, shotguns and carbines. Other, more unusual items hung alongside the guns – swords, crossbows, throwing knives and harpoons amongst them. Grenades of all shapes and sizes were stacked in neat pyramids – small black spheres the size of cricket balls alongside heavier canister charges. Jones even spotted a weapon similar in design to the electrical pistol he had used in France – supposedly still top secret, the latest development from Buckingham's workshops at Bletchley.

Bloody hell, he thought, we could fight a whole damned war with just the stuff in this room.

Kowalski stood beside Cuervo, a broad grin fixed in place. "Ramon, I want you to fix up the Major with whatever he takes a shine to. My treat."

Jones snorted. His treat indeed. As if any bills wouldn't eventually find their way back to London in the extortionate fees the Admiralty would end up paying to hire the Fleet.

But he moved over to the cabinets all the same, drawn in by the intriguing arsenal on display. One device in particular had already caught his eye and he wanted to examine it further.

After all, it couldn't hurt to have a little look...

*

"Well Major, here's to a successful fishing expedition."

Jones clinked his glass against Kowalski's. The salon was still quiet at this stage of the evening, the pair having enjoyed an early dinner with a view to getting a good night's sleep before their dawn departure.

"How's the new toy?" asked Kowalski.

Jones couldn't help but smile as he patted the mechanism running down his right forearm beneath the sleeve of his jacket.

"I must admit I've been amusing myself with it all afternoon. Most fun I've had in months. How did you get on with the rest of the gear?"

"Packed and ready. I doubt we'll need half of it, but it don't hurt to be prepared."

Jones raised his glass again. "Amen to that."

Kowalski's gaze slipped beyond Jones' shoulder. "Look out Major, I think you've been targeted..."

Jones turned to see Isabella De La Vega approaching, her eyes fixed on him, a smile playing at the corners of her mouth. Her hair cascaded over bare shoulders, the ruby dangling at the end of her necklace contriving to draw the eye downward to the ample charms revealed by the low neckline of her black dress.

Caught up in appreciation of the sight as she progressed across the room it was some time before Jones noticed the uniformed man following at her shoulder. He was perhaps fifty, bushy white sideburns sprouting from either side of a broad face, the stiff collar of his shirt pushing up into the weighty folds of his chin.

"Good evening *Senor* Jones," said De La Vega. She nodded coolly at Kowalski. "Captain."

"Heh. Charming as ever Isabella," said the Floridian.

The woman ignored him, speaking once again to Jones. "Allow me to introduce Commodore Silas Culpepper of the United States Navy, head of the military here in the Cuban Protectorate." The men shook hands. "The gallant Commodore protects us from the perils of Communism..."

The American frowned. "Which is no matter for levity, madam." He returned his attention to Jones. "So you're the newspaperman?"

Jones glanced at Isabella. Her eyes sparkled with mischief.

"David Jones, of the Times. Delighted to make your acquaintance."

"And what drags a reporter away from the war? One would assume Europe has more than its share of stories still to be told."

"Sometimes people like to hear something other than war stories."

"My girls would certainly agree with you there *senor*," put in Isabella. "Such tales become quite tiresome after a while. Sailors in particular will talk of little else. As if they have a, how do you say it? A one-track mind."

Culpepper's face coloured and Jones had to smother a smile.

"Perhaps you will allow me to visit your headquarters?" he asked.

"To what purpose?"

"I feel certain our readers would be interested in how the American administration runs its occupation of the island."

Culpepper's eyes narrowed at the phrasing. "There is no *occupation* Mister Jones. I can assure you, aside from all but a small handful of malcontents, the Cubans are very happy my troops and ships are here."

"A handful? I had heard the rebel movement was on the increase."

"And there we have a perfect illustration of the dangers of an unfettered press. A baseless exaggeration of the facts. Our presence here is no different from you British being in Gibraltar or Hong Kong." Culpepper gave Kowalski a sideways look. "Take care your opinions are not coloured by the questionable company you keep. These secessionists are always keen to paint the United States in a bad light."

Silent before now, Kowalski spoke up. "It's a pleasure to meet you too Commodore. Your reputation precedes you."

Neither man made any attempt to instigate a handshake.

"As does yours Captain. I noted your arrival in Havana with interest. I like to keep appraised of the movements of you mercenary types."

"By my reckoning, you wouldn't even be in Cuba if us mercenary types hadn't been around to sort things out for you a few years back..."

Culpepper scowled. "A course of action I opposed at the time."

"Ah. Still rankles then, that you needed us folks to help you out?"

With a visible effort the American controlled his temper. "Tell me Captain, how long do intend to stay in Cuba?"

"You'd have to ask my employer." Kowalski jerked a thumb towards Jones. "After all, I'm just the hired help."

Culpepper glowered at the Floridian then turned to Jones once more.

"You will excuse me. I have another engagement. Contact my office. They will arrange a suitable time for your visit and our interview. In the meantime, try not to let your acquaintance lead you too far astray."

The American bowed to Isabella and strode from the salon.

"So that's the infamous Commodore Culpepper..." said Kowalski.

De La Vega placed her hand on Jones' arm. "My apologies *senor*. He heard we had a reporter staying and insisted on an introduction."

"And when a gentleman like that insists," said Jones, "I imagine it's difficult to refuse."

A spark of anger flickered in her eyes. "The *senor* is no gentleman. And it is impossible to refuse any of his demands, be they for introductions, money or, ah, entertainment."

"He takes bribes?"

Isabella smiled at Jones' surprise. "This is Cuba *senor*. Everyone takes bribes. The mark of a gentleman is how he asks for the money."

"Heh. In London, I believe they judge a gentleman by how he treats a lady. Ain't that right Major?"

"Really?" Isabella fixed on Jones. "And how would you treat me?"

Jones struglled for an appropriate rejoinder. What was it about this damned woman that made it so difficult for him to talk?

Kowalski gave an exaggerated yawn. "I'm going to hit the sack," he said. "Don't let this one keep you up too late Major."

He bowed in the face of Isabella's withering glare and tipped Jones a wink. "Good night folks. I'll leave you to it."

He ambled away, leaving Jones and Isabella at the bar.

"You don't like him very much, do you?" said Jones.

She turned to face him. "Neither would you *senor*. Not if his Free Fleet had murdered your brother."

Jones felt the dull ache of his own grief pull at him. "Your brother?"

"A fighter in the Revolution. At least he wanted to be. He was only a boy." She gestured towards the door through which Kowalski had departed. "And they came here and killed him. For money."

"At the behest of the Americans..." said Jones.

"You are a loyal man. More loyal than he deserves."

"I owe him more than loyalty. He's saved my life. More than once."

"These newspapers of yours must be a dangerous business. You will have to explain that to me at some point." She leaned forward, lowering her voice. "Along with the truth of why you are really in Cuba... Major."

"I fear if I failed to cultivate my air of mystery, I would not receive quite as much of your attention."

The smile this time was genuine. "Come with me," she said, taking his arm and steering him towards the glass doors of the balcony.

"We shall look out at Havana and you will tell me of London, and the way English gentlemen treat their ladies..."

*

The twinkling gas lamps of Havana's waterfront curved away on either side of the hotel, the water beyond the sea wall reflecting the silver glow of the quarter moon. Jones found himself neglecting the view in favour of the woman at his side. She stood, hands on the railing, eyes closed, face tilted upwards, breathing in the night air. The dark eyes flicked open and she caught him staring. He dropped his gaze and she gave a throaty laugh.

"Do I scare you that much *senor*?"

Bloody woman. She made him feel like a nervous schoolboy.

Jones fumbled in his pocket for his cigarettes. He pulled one from the case and struck a match. He turned to shield the flame from the breeze, cupping it in his hands. When the rough Irish voice sounded behind him, his mouth went dry and the cigarette fell from his lips.

"Turn around slowly, matey. Or I'll slit the whore's throat."

Jones did as instructed, to see Isabella held by the hair, her head wrenched back. She squirmed, straining away from the blade pressed to her neck. Her assailant gave a growl of warning as Jones moved forward.

"I'll gut her, I swear."

Jones forced himself to stand still. The man shuffled into the light spilling from the salon, pushing Isabella before him. Jones' breath caught in his throat at the apparition.

The skin of the hollow, sunken face and hairless head was so pale it seemed almost translucent, the ghoulish whiteness exaggerated in contrast with the rust-streaked metal plate covering half the skull. The man's right eye was wide – bloodshot and lidless within a circular socket of riveted iron. Beneath the hideous eye, the mouth opened out into a gaping hole, the cheek almost entirely missing, exposing teeth and gums in a cadaverous grin. Tendons and scarred skin stretched and shifted as the man spoke.

"You're the newspaperman? I've got a message for you..."

"You need to let her go. Right now."

"Or what? You'll write a nasty story about me?"

Jones brought his right arm up. With a flick of his wrist he activated the spring-loaded mechanism strapped to his forearm, flinging the derringer pistol from his sleeve and into the palm of his hand. He stared down the barrel of the snub-nosed weapon.

"No. I'll shoot off what's left of your face."

The lop-sided smile faded. "Nice wee toy you've got there matey." The Irishman pressed the knife against his captive's skin and Isabella pulled away from the metal's touch. "Don't make me kill her. T'would be a criminal waste of a fine doxy."

Jones' fingers flexed on the pistol grip. He wasn't sure he could take the shot without the man's reflex reaction cutting Isabella's throat.

"Let her go. We can put the weapons down and talk like gentlemen."

"Who says I'm a gentleman?"

"We can talk. Or you can die. Last chance."

The man's grotesque head tilted to the side as he considered Jones' proposition. "All right," he said. "But understand this, you touch me and Jack Rackham hunts you down like a dog. Not to mention what he'll do to your lady friend here. Clear?"

"Understood."

The man withdrew the knife and shoved Isabella forwards. Jones caught her in his arms and looked down, ready to offer comfort. Instead, he found himself restraining her as she turned, eyes blazing with fury. Spanish curses filled the air as she hurled abuse at the Irishman. A frown formed on the mobile half of the man's face at the stream of insults.

"Isabella..." snapped Jones, sensing a limit to his patience. "Enough."

The interruption seemed to bring the woman back to herself. The rage in her eyes remained, but the voice was cold and level when she spoke once more. "You and your kind are supposed to stay out of my place. Rackham gave me his word."

"I'm not inside now, am I missy? Besides, I'm here on business, not looking for any of your amusements." He waved her aside. "Run along now. The reporter and I need to have words. Like gentlemen."

Isabella spat a final curse and stormed from the balcony, slamming the door behind her hard enough to crack one of the glass panes.

"Fiesty one there..." The Irishman nodded after her. "Pretty though."

Jones was in no mood for banter. "Deliver your message and get the hell out of here before I change my mind."

"I get so much as a scratch, and Rackham torches this place and everyone in it."

"Ah yes, Jack Rackham – the infamous King of the Pirates."

"Some call him that. Some call him Calico Jack. Me? I call him Cap'n."

"And what do they call you?"

"Name's Rook. Ask your friend from Florida about me." He grinned – ghastly, skull-like. "There are stories."

"I'm sure there are. What does Rackham want with me?"

"What do you want with him? More's the question." Rook continued over Jones' attempt to speak. "Don't deny it now. You hired a boat to take you to Tortuga. Only you hired it from the wrong man."

So much for the fishing expedition. Jones shrugged, trying to hide his frustration. "I write stories. To sell papers. Pirate stories will sell. I wanted to see Tortuga."

"Exactly what I thought. A man getting too nosy is all, I says. Let me have a chat with him, I says." The mismatched eyes stared at Jones. "I'll encourage the nosy gentleman to be leaving Havana and heading on home before someone gets hurt."

"Message delivered."

"Delivered maybe." Rook raised his knife and tapped the point against his metal plating. "But is it understood?"

Jones' fists itched, but he mastered his anger. "Perfectly," he said through gritted teeth.

The hideous smile reappeared. "Good stuff matey. Because after noon tomorrow, if I sees you in Havana, or Cuba, or anywhere else in the Antilles, I'll kill you. Little toy guns or no." He paused, waiting until Jones gave a reluctant nod. "Now then, I'll be off. Old Rooky has work to do. Nasty work. Nothing a gentleman like you would want to be involved in."

Speech over, he placed his hands on the railing and vaulted off the balcony. Astonished, Jones saw the man land like a cat twenty feet below, spring straight to his feet and walk off with a jaunty stride, sauntering down the Malecon through the patches of gaslight.

Jones watched the Irishman disappear into the night then pushed open the door to the salon. The room was deserted except for Kowalski, crouched down behind the velvet drapes framing the balcony window.

"Been there long?" asked Jones.

"Long enough." The Floridian stood and tucked away his pistol. "Came downstairs when Isabella started her screeching. Sounded like you had things under control. Didn't want to interrupt."

"So you heard?"

"Most of it. Looks like our boat trip is scuppered. And it don't sound like a healthy idea for you to stay in Havana."

"I'll be damned if I let some messenger boy run me out of town."

"Rook's a bit more than the mail boy. He's Rackham's pet assassin, and he's good at his job. Enjoys it too."

"I have no idea where he appeared from. And the way he jumped off the balcony like some kind of bloody monkey? Not natural."

"Natural definitely ain't the word. Ways I heard it, he was born looking like that and got sold to the circus. Grew up a sideshow freak before graduating to acrobat. Fell in with Rackham's crew and developed a taste for killing. It was Jack paid to get his face all fixed up."

"Charitable of him..."

"It was worth it. Bought his loyalty. Rook does exactly what Rackham tells him to."

"Well he certainly seems to have my card marked."

Kowalski grimaced. "That he does. But at least we have until tomorrow to get you out of town."

*

Jones sat at the desk in his room, sipping at an indifferent cup of tea and flicking through the pages of the previous day's Miami newspaper. Isabella had them shipped across the straits for the benefit of the Mirador's English-speaking guests. It could have been a year out of date for all the attention Jones was paying its contents.

The hotel had returned to business as usual after the earlier disturbance, and sounds of laughter and music drifted up from the salon below. Jones considered heading outside for a smoke, but the thought of unfastening all the bolts put him off. Rook's sudden appearance and the agile fashion of his exit had made him feel quite uncomfortable. His first action on returning to his room had been to secure the window shutters.

The desk clock chimed midnight, reminding him he had planned to be fast asleep by now, resting before an early departure. Frustration filled him, mixing with the remains of the nervous energy stirred up by his confrontation with the Irishman. Drinking tea and reading bloody newspapers – he could have been doing that back in London. On a good night, he could have been doing it in the damned trenches, although the newspaper might have been considerably more than a day old.

What the hell was he doing here? On some ridiculous quest to track down a bunch of pirates – like something out of a child's storybook. He had raged at his inability to make a difference in the deadlock of France, wanting to do something, anything. And here he was again – hamstrung by events out of his control. He realised now his vague idea of exacting some kind of personal revenge for his brother's death had masked a deeper desire simply to be useful.

Jones pushed the teacup aside and reached for a tumbler. He grabbed one of the crystal bottles without looking to see what it contained and poured himself a large measure. He gulped a mouthful down. Gin – the bitter taste suited his mood perfectly.

Half an hour and half a bottle later, a soft knocking roused him. He thumped the glass down a little harder than he had intended, and moved unsteadily to the door. A flick of the wrist brought the derringer up into his grip, but as he made to turn the key he acknowledged any miscreant would be unlikely to knock. Better safe than sorry though.

Isabella stood in the corridor outside his room. She had changed out of the black dress from earlier into one of dark red silk, but once again the shoulders were bare and the neckline provocatively low. Jones made a conscious effort to keep his gaze fixed on her face.

"I asked after you earlier. The staff said you were indisposed."

"I needed a bath after that animal placed his hands on me." She looked over his shoulder into the room. "May I come in?"

"It's your hotel. I imagine you can go anywhere you like."

Isabella swept past him in a rustle of skirts and a faint trail of perfume. Jones closed the door and then reset the mechanism beneath his sleeve, concealing the small pistol once again.

"An interesting contraption *senor*. I am glad you were wearing it."

Jones nodded. "A gift from my Floridian friend. Proved itself useful."

The woman brushed at the front of her dress before looking up. "I want to apologise. For the unpleasantness earlier. And for you being forced to rescue me." She frowned. "It is not a position I am accustomed to. The, how do you say it, damsel in distress?"

"Of that I am certain. But please, the apology should be mine. Rook wouldn't have been anywhere near your establishment if not for me."

"Perhaps. How will you get to Tortuga now?"

Jones stared hard at her, eyes narrowed.

She gave a sly smile. "Oh please, *senor*. When I left you outside the salon, I ran straight upstairs to the next balcony. It was too good an opportunity to listen and perhaps unravel some of that mystery of yours."

Jones reached for his glass, lifting it in a toast. "Well played."

"So now I know what you are up to, but I don't know why. Perhaps it is time you enlightened me, no? You may be in need of more friends."

"And you're my friend?"

"I could be."

"That depends," said Jones. "I got the impression you were already familiar with our visitor..."

She waved a dismissive hand. "Everyone knows Rook."

"And Rackham? How well do you know him?"

Isabella's eyes flashed in anger. "That *pendejo*," she spat. "I know him. I know him from before he became so grand and mighty. I know him from when he was just another smuggler."

"And you have some arrangement with him?"

"My business involves many arrangements with many men. Expensive arrangements." She shrugged. "Culpepper, he takes his payment so I do not receive visits from the police. The customs men, they take payment so my whisky does not disappear from the quay. Rackham? I pay him so his filth will not darken the Mirador's door."

She poured herself a drink, taking more care over her choice than Jones had earlier. "Yes, I know Jack Rackham, but I am not one of his creatures. I would help you if I could." She turned back to him and the playful spark reappeared in her eyes. "Who knows? If you can get rid of Rackham, it could save me a lot of money..."

Jones thought for a moment. What the hell – she knew most of it already. She might even be able to help.

"It's a long story. Take a seat."

Settled, brandy in hand, she listened attentively as Jones spoke. He surprised himself, explaining more than he intended, going beyond the details of his mission, touching on his frustration at the futility of the war and his personal reasons for coming to the Caribbean. Her eyes filled with compassion as Jones talked of his brother, and then narrowed as the story drew to a close with his account of the conversation with Rook.

She stood as he finished speaking, crossing the room to stand before the large gilt-framed mirror. She pulled her long hair away from her shoulder and leaned her head to one side. Her reflected gaze met Jones'.

"Tell me, did he leave me with any bruises?"

Jones lifted his drink, holding her look over the rim of his glass. Placing the tumbler down on the desk, he moved to stand behind her. He ran his fingertip along the line of her shoulder. The drink made him feel clumsy, like he was pawing at her, but Isabella closed her eyes and leaned against him. He bowed his head and pressed his lips to her neck.

"No bruises," he said, lifting his eyes once more.

Isabella returned his reflected stare, pushing her body back against his. Her dark eyes shone and when she spoke her voice was low.

"*Senor* Jones, perhaps you could help me out of this dress?"

He turned her and kissed her, hands sliding around her waist as her own moved up to the buttons of his shirt. Her quick fingers made short work of the fastenings and he thrilled as her nails scratched down the skin of his chest. He felt giddy, filled with a heady mix of desire and gin.

She pulled out of the kiss and looked up at him. "And there I was, wondering how I might repay you for saving me earlier..."

Jones broke away, lightheaded, breathless. Unwelcome notions of chivalry bubbled up amidst his churning emotions, pushing more immediate passion aside. Repay? He didn't want repayment.

He reached up and held the woman's face between his hands, looking into her eyes for a long moment before he spoke.

"Another time Isabella."

She stepped back, confused. "Why?"

"You've just been held at knifepoint, and I'm a little drunk."

She stared at him, clearly unsure how to take the rejection.

"Believe me," he went on, "I will regret this decision in the morning. But right now, you'd best be going."

Isabella regarded him in silence before giving a crooked smile and stepping forward to plant a small kiss on his cheek.

"Your friend was right about you English gentlemen." She moved past him, pausing at the door. "Goodnight *Senor* Jones. Another time."

"I hope so."

"As do I." She pulled the door open and swept out of the room.

Jones slumped into his seat, shaking his head in disbelief at what he had just done. He reached for his drink, determined to tranquilise himself into sleep. Raising the tumbler to his lips, his eyes caught on the newspaper heaped on the desktop, a headline leaping out at him: *Great Ship On Verge Of Cable Completion*.

The gin returned to the desk untouched. Jones' mind began to churn.

*

The Englishman had already finished his breakfast when Kowalski joined him on the terrace. Kowalski waved the waiter over and ordered his usual Havana breakfast, *tostados* and Cuban-style coffee – strong, sweet and with a pinch of salt. Something Jones might have benefitted from instead of his tea. By the looks of him, he'd not had a lot of sleep.

Order placed, Kowalski regarded the bay beyond the sea wall. The lack of breeze left the water looking like a sheet of glass.

"Would have been a perfect day for that fishing trip," he said.

Jones glanced up at the cloudless blue sky. "It still could be. Just not the one we had planned."

"So you ain't following Rook's advice?"

"Oh, I'm leaving Havana. But return to London? Not bloody likely."

They fell silent as Kowalski's breakfast was served. He nodded his thanks to the waiter and sipped at his coffee, waiting until the man moved away before speaking.

"Why do I think I ain't going to like whatever you've come up with?"

Jones adopted a hurt expression. "Come now Captain, where's your sense of adventure?"

Kowalski waved in the direction of the sea. "Going that way. With my sense of self-preservation."

Jones pushed a newspaper across the tablecloth, tapping his finger on a column of type. As Kowalski read, the Englishman sipped at his tea.

Kowalski finished with the article. "Yesterday we couldn't hire a fishing boat, and now you're looking to commandeer one of the most famous ships afloat? You need to lay off the booze Major."

"A matter of a telegram or two." Jones waved a hand dismissively. "The Admiralty will arrange the details. The tricky part will be getting out to her whilst avoiding Rackham's eyes and ears."

"We start sniffing around the docks again, you've got to reckon Rook's going to hear about it."

The Englishman nodded. "Exactly so. But I'm hoping the solution to our problem will shortly be joining us for breakfast." He looked up over Kowalski's shoulder. "And here she comes now..."

Kowalski turned to see Isabella descending the steps from the hotel to the terrace. The two men stood as the woman joined them. She settled into her seat and nodded a good morning to Kowalski, her greeting less frosty than he had expected.

He had never understood the woman's antipathy towards him. As far as he could remember he'd done nothing in the Mirador to invoke her displeasure. Granted, that was no guarantee he was blameless. He'd had his fair share of evenings in her establishment where his recollection was less than complete – it was that kind of place.

He smiled back at her over the table, wondering if this represented some sort of thaw in relations. Maybe Jones had put in a good word.

"So *senor*..." said Isabella, turning her attention to Kowalski's companion. "It was a pleasant surprise to receive your breakfast invitation. Especially as our evening was cut short." She laid her hand on Jones' arm. "We must pick up where we left off sometime."

Kowalski thought Jones seemed uncomfortable. A little hot under the collar there, Major. Jones was a hell of a man in a fight, but when it came to women, or this woman at least, he was like a babe in the woods. Isabella smiled as Jones coloured. Like a she-wolf sizing up her prey.

"But such pleasantries can wait for now," she said. "What can I do for you this fine morning?"

*

They clambered down from the wagon's cargo bed, Jones reaching up to assist Isabella's descent.

Their escorts marched them down the muddy track serving as the village's main street. The buildings to either side were pocked with bullet holes and blackened with scorch marks. The place had come under heavy attack. And relatively recently, thought Jones, taking in a blood-spattered wall, the stain still fresh enough to attract a swarm of flies.

They saw no one as they made their way to the centre of the village, a small square before the steps of a whitewashed church. The guards motioned them towards the chapel, taking up positions behind the visitors, fingers as ready on the triggers of their carbines as they had been since meeting the wagon on the forest road an hour before.

Jones' suspicion that Isabella maintained contacts with the Cuban rebels had proved correct. Hardly surprising, the woman seemed to know everyone. She had agreed to set up a meeting and arranged for Jones and Kowalski to be spirited out of the Mirador – inside a laundry wagon of all things, hopefully foiling any watchers Rook might have put in place.

Now she smiled warmly up at the extravagantly-moustachioed man in khaki fatigues who emerged from the church's dark interior.

"General Estrada," she said, stepping up and kissing the soldier on each cheek. "You look well. Life on the run must agree with you."

The man blinked at her use of English, glancing at her companions before answering in the same tongue.

"The food is not as good as in Havana. But I survive." He looked her up and down. "Naturally, you look as fine as ever. Providing for the decadence of the Imperialists clearly agrees with you." He shifted his attention. "And these are the Englishmen you insisted I speak with?"

Jones stepped forward, hand outstretched. "Only one Englishman, I'm afraid. David Jones. Pleased to make your acquaintance..."

His voice tailed off as he saw the expression on the General's face change, the dark eyes hardening as they fixed over Jones' shoulder. The Cuban released Jones' hand, hawked noisily, and spat into the dirt. He turned on Isabella, unleashing a stream of Spanish invective, too fast and furious for Jones to catch even a word. Isabella responded in kind and the volume rose to match the passion in the voices.

Kowalski stepped up to Jones' side. "Sorry Major," he said, keeping his voice low as the argument raged back and forth. "Maybe better if you'd left me in Havana. He ain't too impressed with me tagging along."

Jones waited until the verbal combatants paused for breath. "*Senor...*" he said. "Listen to my proposal. It will be worth your while."

The man glared at Jones. "You will find we are not so easily bought and sold. You think we too are mercenaries?" He spat on the ground once more. "Come with me. Come and see why I have more pressing concerns than the earning of blood money."

With a venomous glance at Kowalski, the General stomped off towards the church. Isabella watched him go, hands on her hips.

"Pig-headed fool. He thinks his principles alone will feed his men and provide them with ammunition." She shook her head. "He'll come around eventually, but we may have to endure more of these performances."

"Let's get after him then," said Jones. He turned to Kowalski. "And you, best keep your mouth shut."

The air inside the church was cool in comparison with the baking heat outside. Their eyes adjusted to the dim interior and they became aware of the figures crammed into the pews. It appeared the entire population of the village was huddled inside the chapel.

Jones and Kowalski followed Isabella up the central aisle, taking in the blood-stained bandages and makeshift splints. Every one of the assembled men, women and children seemed to have suffered some form of injury. At the head of the chapel, before the dais, Jones counted twelve still forms laid out, shrouded in blankets. Half of the lumps beneath the cloth were smaller – child-sized. A kneeling friar in a black robe glanced up as they passed by then turned back to the corpses and his prayer.

The General crossed himself before the altar. "I spend my entire life telling the people religion is part of the machinery keeping them prisoner..." He indicated the bodies. "And yet, in response to this, I find myself praying for their souls."

"What happened here?" asked Jones.

"Men came. In the night. Bandits. They take what little these poor folk have, and kill any who resist. The Yankees? They do nothing."

"This has happened before?" asked Jones.

"*Si, si*. Every few weeks another village is raided." The General sighed, lowering himself to sit on the topmost step of the dais. "The Americans say Cuba is their Protectorate, and yet the only protection these people receive is the little I can provide. We spread men around the villages, hoping their presence will keep the raiders at bay." He grunted. "It does not work. Three of my soldiers lie beneath those blankets..."

A small girl in the front pew began to scream, repeating the same phrase over and over. Her mother shushed her, rocking her back and forth, smoothing her hair, comforting her until she eventually fell silent. The girl stared out from the shelter of her mother's arms.

Estrada shook his head. "She's been like that for hours. The same thing each time: *El diablo de hierro...*"

"The iron devil..." translated Isabella.

Jones' mind returned to the balcony: *Old Rooky has work to do.*

"General, perhaps we have more in common than we thought..."

*

Tortuga

Captain Turner stepped from the wheelhouse onto the starboard wing of the bridge. He felt the vibration beneath his feet die away as his ship's great paddles ceased their labours. The vessel began to slow, carried forward for the moment only by her considerable momentum. Turner pulled his pipe from his pocket and stuffed its bowl. He struck a match and held it to the tobacco, sending out sideways puffs of smoke. He scanned the southern horizon, teeth grinding on the pipe's stem in irritation.

"Any sign of our guests sir?" asked Jenson, joining him at the rail.

"Not yet." Turner checked his pocket watch. "But we're early."

"What do you think it's all about?"

"Damned if I know. But it's a bloody nuisance."

"We were well ahead of schedule. A few hours delay shouldn't cause us too much trouble."

Turner was unconvinced by his First Officer's optimism. The message thrust into his hand by the wireless operator an hour previously had been short and annoyingly opaque, even by the standards of the dolts staffing the company's offices – a set of co-ordinates, a rendezvous time, and instructions to set his vessel at the disposal of the men who would come aboard. It all smacked of a longer delay than Jenson's few hours.

The wireless message accomplished what supply problems, hurricanes, and the outbreak of a damned war had all singularly failed to do. For the first time in two years, the machinery running the near seven hundred foot length of his ship was still. No engineers tended the pistons and gears, no crewmen scurried around the five towering funnels and, worst of all to Turner's thinking, no thick black cable paid out over the stern in the vessel's wake.

The *SS Great Eastern*, the largest ship the world had ever seen, now sat idly in the Bermuda Strait waiting to take on passengers. Like some kind of pleasure cruiser.

"Look sir," said Jenson, pointing to starboard.

There, over the bow of their Royal Navy escort, a black speck could be seen against the sky's bright backdrop. Turner drew out his expanding telescope for a closer look. Sure enough – one of those whirlybird contraptions. He snapped the eyeglass closed. At least they were on time.

"Make sure that thing stays clear of the funnels and masts," he said. "I don't want it flapping around the deck and breaking something."

"Aye sir," replied Jenson, heading for the stairs.

Turner watched the ornithopter's approach with a frown. He'd flown in plenty of airships in his time, but no amount of encouragement would see him strapped into one of those things. He disliked the way the twin rotors above the cab thrashed at the air. It seemed a most aggressive means of achieving flight, a violent beating of gravity into only temporary and grudging submission.

The incoming aircraft swept in low, the rotors' downwash whipping spray from the surface of the water. The man at the controls left it to the last possible moment before pulling up in a steep climb to crest the forty foot wall of the *Great Eastern*'s riveted hull. The ornithopter slowed to a near hover as it passed over the ship's rail, its wheeled undercarriage six feet above the planks of the deck. Waved in by members of the crew, the aircraft inched forward and down between the aftmost smokestacks. The wheels hit the decking and the pilot eased back on the throttle. The rotors' manic spin dropped in tempo.

The door on the ornithopter's flank swung open and three figures hopped down, the leading pair each carrying a pack. The trio crouched low to avoid the spinning tips of the rotor blades and scuttled to where Jenson stood waiting. After exchanging handshakes, the group all turned to watch as the ornithopter's engine note rose and the rotors flailed at the air with renewed force.

The aircraft bounced once then pulled itself into the sky. The new arrivals waved to the departing pilot and Turner was irked to see his First Officer doing the same. He'd have words with the man regarding that overly-cheerful demeanour of his. Turner tapped the embers from his pipe and turned from the scene below, heading for the bridge.

If the engine room deep within the hull was the fiery heart of the *Great Eastern*, the wheelhouse was its calm, efficient brain. Crewmen patrolled the racks of gleaming brass gauges, jotting their readings down in leather-bound journals, monitoring the performance of the vessel's automated machinery. Turner ran a tight ship, based on a strict routine, and it was gratifying to see the men continuing their regular procedures despite the distraction of their unusual rendezvous.

He passed through the compartment, nodding to the crew and running his own critical eye over the dials. He paused to speak to the man standing watch by the chart table.

"Inform Lord Brunel our visitors have arrived."

"Aye sir." A crisp salute and the sailor made for the hatch.

Turner frowned at the chart and the markings on the glass pane holding it flat. He followed the line of the cable already laid, and its transition into dots illustrating the work still to be done. His irritation grew once again. What could be so important for the Admiralty to commandeer his vessel, keeping her from the task at hand?

He headed for the companionway. He would receive his new passengers in the ship's stateroom.

Maybe there he would get some answers.

*

Jones faltered for a moment during the round of introductions, unsure exactly how to describe Isabella. He eventually settled on introducing her as his "associate from Havana." Her eyes twinkled at this, but she resisted any temptation to embarrass him before their hosts, much to Jones' relief.

The woman had been determined to accompany Kowalski and himself out to the *Great Eastern*. Joining the expedition was her price for putting them in touch with the Cuban rebels and negotiating the deal to borrow an aircraft and pilot. She insisted she was coming along, unwilling to miss out on the twin opportunities of taking her first ornithopter flight and spending time aboard one of the most famous ships afloat.

She also appeared to relish the prospect of taking up a position, however briefly, as a clandestine agent of the British Empire. Now the newest, and perhaps most unlikely, of Her Majesty's special operatives sat on a sofa in the opulent surroundings of the *Great Eastern*'s stateroom, in a striking, if slightly scandalous, outfit of leather boots, riding breeches and a man's cream shirt, unbuttoned at the neck and complemented with a white silk scarf. Something she had "thrown together to suit the occasion", as she put it. It seemed an aeronautic excursion required a quite-specific style of clothing.

Far from being the distraction Jones had feared, Isabella was proving to be something of an asset. He had worried the officers aboard would be less than impressed with the commandeering of their vessel, but as De La Vega deployed her formidable social skills, it became clear their hosts were enchanted by her presence. The two men were practically falling over themselves to make their female guest comfortable. This warm welcome appeared to extend to her two companions.

As Captain Turner leaned forward to refresh Isabella's coffee, Kowalski caught Jones' eye and gave him a wink. Clearly the Floridian too had underestimated the usefulness of having the woman along. After fussing over the cups and saucers, Turner seemed satisfied Isabella had everything she required. He turned his gaze on Jones.

"Now Major, perhaps you can tell us what all this is about?"

"Yes, please enlighten us," said Brunel, the old man's frail appearance belied by the strong voice. He adjusted the control stick jutting from the arm of his wheelchair. The conveyance turned, bringing its occupant around to face Jones, a wisp of steam puffing upwards from the boiler behind the seat, mixing with the trail of smoke from the man's cigar. "The message from my offices contained little information."

"My apologies. The Admiralty kept details to a minimum, worried our wireless signal could be intercepted. And further apologies for this interruption to your great endeavour."

Turner harrumphed into his coffee, his frown confirming Jones' suspicions. Isabella notwithstanding, the *Great Eastern*'s captain was unhappy with their presence. Brunel however waved the apology aside.

"The world has made do with telegraph and wireless for long enough. It can wait a little for my optical cable. What can we do for you?"

Jones launched into his tale, outlining their need to get a look at Tortuga, and how the task had been complicated by the intervention of

Rackham's henchman. Brunel and Turner listened in silence until Jones finished speaking.

"I understand your predicament," said Turner. "But I don't see how we can be of assistance. The loan of our naval escort would seem to run the risk of antagonising the Americans."

"With the greatest respect to the *Iris*," said Jones. "She's getting a little long in the tooth. If she was fit for anything more than light duty, she'd be on the other side of the Atlantic."

"A single cruiser wouldn't do us any good anyhow," put in Kowalski. "Too big to get in unseen, and too small to cope with Rackham's fleet."

"So what exactly is it you need?" asked Turner. "This ship is hardly suited for any kind of clandestine approach."

Brunel plucked the cigar from the corner of his mouth and answered the captain's question before Jones could speak. "It's painfully clear what the Major wants. He's not after the *Great Eastern*." The eyes sparkled. "He wants to borrow the *Neptune*."

Jones smiled back at the man in the wheelchair. Even at eighty years of age it was obvious the precise, inquisitive mind of the great engineer remained as sharp as a tack.

"If you wouldn't mind..."

The old man's face lit up in boyish enthusiasm.

"Would you like to see it?"

*

Leaving the stateroom, they followed in the wake of Brunel's chair down the vessels companionways. An elevator took them down into the depths of the ship.

The indicator gauge clicked through the levels, settling on the lowest, and the brass-plated doors slid open onto an enormous space. The *Great Eastern*'s engine room was a vast cathedral to steam power, criss-crossed by piping and walkways, dominated by a series of piston heads connected to the massive crankshafts cutting across the chamber.

The pistons were still for the moment and crewmen clambered around the engines, taking the opportunity afforded by the temporary halt to make adjustments and apply a thick layer of grease to parts normally inaccessible. The atmosphere was filled with the smell of oil, warmed on still-hot metal. The shouts of the engine crew and the banging of tools echoed around the steel cavern, prompting Kowalski to imagine the fearsome din when the engines were running.

Isabella leaned down to speak to Brunel. "This ship of yours *senor*, it is most impressive."

"It's not really mine, my dear. I only designed her. She properly belongs to the blasted accountants who seem to run my affairs. And of course to Captain Turner here, who does a fine job of looking after her."

Turner puffed up at the engineer's praise. "His Lordship is too modest as ever. Thanks to his design, the *Great Eastern* practically sails herself. Much of her machinery is controlled by automated mechanisms. Stoking the boilers, trimming the ballast, laying the cable – all mechanical. We can run the whole shebang with a skeleton crew in comparison with other vessels." He gestured along the walkway towards a bulkhead door in the forward wall. "This way please..."

The party traversed the engine room, above the heads of the engineering crew and the gleaming machinery. Turner spun the wheel on the watertight door, swinging it open on oiled hinges. They passed through into a small compartment, square and featureless save for another heavy door, a twin to the entrance. The first door was sealed behind them before the next swung open accompanied by a hiss of air.

The next chamber was of lesser dimensions than the engine room, but was no less impressive. What immediately captured the eye was the pool of water in the floor. Surrounded by a low wall, the circular pool was a full fifty feet in diameter, its cloudy green waters lit from below. It took a moment before Kowalski realised the source of the pool's illumination was the sunlight beating down on the ocean beyond the hull and filtering round beneath the *Great Eastern*'s bulk.

Jones and Isabella stared at the water with pensive expressions which matched his own. Turner and Brunel shared a chuckle, clearly used to the effect the gaping hole in the bottom of the ship had on visitors.

"Don't worry," said Brunel. "The excursion pool is quite safe. All a matter of balancing the pressures."

Kowalski's attention was next drawn to the machine hanging above the impossible pool, suspended on thick iron chains with links as long as his arm. Whilst he had some experience with submersibles, he had never seen anything like this before.

The rear of the contraption was a chubby cylinder, perhaps twenty feet in length and fifteen across, a series of round portholes punctuating its riveted plates, and a pair of gleaming brass propellers protruding from below. The forward portion of the craft was a boxy section with six complicated leg mechanisms, three per side protruding out and down, each a mass of cogs and pistons, ending in a circular plate of thick metal.

A large dome of glass bulged outwards at the front – ten feet wide, crossed over with reinforcing straps of steel. The glass was surrounded by a circle of electric lamps, obviously designed to illuminate the dark depths into which the vehicle would descend. On either side of the bulbous viewport hung mechanical arms, similar in construction to the legs behind, but terminating in heavy pincer claw attachments.

Brunel gestured towards the craft. "There it is. The *Neptune*..."

"I'd read about it, of course," said Jones, "but the reality is much more impressive than the descriptions."

Kowalski leaned towards him and spoke in a low tone. "This is your plan? A steam-powered langoustine?"

Jones shrugged. "I figured if we couldn't sail to Tortuga, perhaps we could walk..."

*

The *Great Eastern* and her escort steamed south as the sun disappeared below the horizon. The two ships anchored over the horizon from Tortuga, beyond sight of any observers on the island's peaks.

Chains rattling, the *Neptune* hunkered down to the surface of the pool, the water now turned an inky, dangerous black. A gangplank was lowered and the crewmen filed over, descending into the craft's interior through a hatch in its metallic carapace. Jones and Kowalski followed, carrying their gear.

Jones nodded up to Turner and Isabella who observed from the gantry above. The gesture was returned with a salute from the *Great Eastern*'s captain and stony indifference from the woman.

Isabella had started with flirting and ended with a stream of Spanish cursing in her campaign to persuade Jones she should accompany them in the submersible. His flat refusal to even consider such an idea apparently confirmed him as the worst kind of chauvinist, clearly revoking his previous privileged status of "English gentleman."

Brunel wheeled up behind him. "You seem to have disappointed your lady friend Major," he said, noticing the direction of Jones' gaze.

"So be it. This isn't a pleasure cruise. Miss De La Vega needs to learn she can't always get what she wants."

The old man gave a curt laugh. "Not a lesson she will appreciate, unless I am very much mistaken."

Jones looked up once more at the feisty woman from Havana. She glared down at him, arms folded. "No," he sighed, "probably not."

With a deep-throated rumble, the submersible's engines sprang into life, the noise echoing off the walls of the compartment. Jones returned his attention to the man in the wheelchair.

"Thank you for coming to see us off. It wasn't necessary. You and Captain Turner have done more than enough."

"I'm not seeing you off," said Brunel, shifting his control stick and manoeuvring the chair off the ramp and onto the *Neptune*'s plating. He smiled around the stub of his cigar. "I'm your pilot."

With a loud clunk, a square section of the hull descended into the submersible, carrying the wheelchair and the engineer with it.

"One of a kind, ain't he?" said Kowalski.

The *Neptune*'s interior was a cramped collection of passageways dotted everywhere with valve wheels and pressure gauges, a jumble of machinery affixed to every available surface. The low ceilings were a twisted mass of piping, as were the bilge spaces visible through the metal grille of the floor. Jones and Kowalski ducked their heads and made their way forward through the narrow companionway, squeezing past crew members busy making minute adjustments to controls and checking the readings on hundreds of dials.

Only when they reached the control room was there headroom to stand up straight. They entered the chamber at the front of the craft just as Brunel's chair locked itself into place before the curved window. He waved his passengers forwards, the boyish grin once again animating his features as he gestured to the complex array of switches and levers running beneath the viewport.

"Best damned thing I ever built." He patted the small wheel of the *Neptune*'s helm. "I can't resist the slightest opportunity to take it out."

"What's it for? Other than your entertainment?" asked Kowalski.

"Surveying the bottom, checking the lie for the cable. We've used its charges to flatten a few seamounts, and we've repaired a couple of breaks too. Yes indeed, this little beastie has proved itself very useful."

Brunel flicked a switch. The vessel gave a lurch, dropping a foot or so before jerking to a halt. Both his passengers grabbed for handholds, prompting the engineer to release a bark of laughter.

"Don't worry. It's a smooth ride, all the way to the bottom."

"How deep?" asked Jones.

"Three thousand feet here. Should be interesting. We've never been below two and a half before."

"Great," breathed Kowalski.

"Fret not Captain," said Brunel. "I designed the *Neptune* to withstand the pressures of a five thousand foot dive."

"I'm mighty glad to hear it."

"Besides, if it can't cope, we won't know a damn thing about it. The water will crush us like an eggshell in less than a second."

Kowalski gave Jones one of his "What have you got me into?" looks, but Jones ignored him.

Their elderly pilot ran his fingers over the controls, adjusting valves here and there. He opened the cover on the speaking tube.

"All hands, all hands, the clock is set at ten hours."

"What clock?" asked Jones.

Brunel pointed to a large brass gauge mounted prominently above the other dials. Its face was surrounded by digits, like a regular clock face, although the vertical indicator needle pointed to a ten in the topmost position rather than the usual twelve.

"Our air supply." Brunel pulled a new cigar from his waistcoat pocket. "Twelve hours if I gave these up of course." He grimaced. "But some prices are simply not worth paying."

The engineer threw a lever. With a crunch, the chains disengaged and the *Neptune* smacked down hard into the surface of the pool. The submersible wallowed for a moment then began to sink, the water travelling swiftly upwards over the glass dome.

In seconds the light from the chamber inside the *Great Eastern* was gone, disappearing above them as the *Neptune* began its long silent fall towards the ocean floor.

*

Fifteen minutes had ticked from the air supply clock before a gentle bump announced their arrival on the bottom.

Brunel checked a gauge. "Here we are. Let's see what we can see."

He turned a dial on the control panel. The ring of electric lamps around the observation dome burst into life, throwing a harsh white light across the featureless sand. The sudden illumination startled a handful of fish, their silver shapes flitting away into the surrounding darkness.

In truth, Jones was a little disappointed by the view. He wasn't sure quite what he'd been expecting, but probably something a touch more dramatic. Kowalski leaned forward, peering out. He too, appeared nonplussed by the sights. He became more animated when a drop of water fell on his shoulder from a riveted joint in the hull above.

"Your Lordship..." he said, an edge of panic in his tone.

Brunel glanced round to see both his passengers staring in alarm at the damp patch on the Floridian's shirt.

"Condensation old chap. Nothing to worry about."

Jones and Kowalski shared a relieved glance and their pilot returned to his controls. Brunel checked the compass, pushed on the drive levers, and spun the *Neptune*'s wheel. The submersible strode forward.

The noise of machinery echoed up from the rear compartments, and Jones felt the engine vibration through the soles of his boots, but there was little of the jostling or lurching he had expected from being inside a walker.

"Smooth ride..." said Kowalski, clearly thinking the same.

"Six legs rather than four. That's the secret. Makes us faster too."

"That'll suit the Major here. Damned if he ain't always in a hurry."

Brunel turned to Jones. "Five hours or so and we'll reach Tortuga's northern shore. No trenches to slow us down in these parts. We can engage the screws and hop over a trench if we need to, but we're faster if we stay on our feet. And a damned sight more fuel efficient to boot. Besides, the *Neptune*'s an ungainly beast when it's forced to swim."

The conversation trailed off, the three men falling silent as the sinister shape of a shark drifted into view. Attracted by the lights, the grey form kept pace with them as they traversed the sand. At least a dozen feet in length, it slipped effortlessly through the water alongside the submersible. Twice it flicked across in front of them, jagged teeth jutting from its jaws at random angles, its black beady eye staring in at the men behind the glass.

"Ugly beggar," grunted Brunel. "But seeing things like this is one of the reasons I love the bloody *Neptune* so much."

After sizing up the submersible and apparently establishing it wasn't digestible, the predator turned away. With a flick of its sickle tail, it disappeared into the darkness beyond the reach of the lamps. Jones shuddered as the shark vanished. The brutal efficiency of its shape coupled with the fearsome mouth left no doubt as to its purpose – evolved, if Mister Darwin was to be believed, over hundreds of thousands of years into nature's perfect killer. He hoped to God his brother had drowned before those things had got to him.

"I've seen sharks before," he said. "But never up close. Not sure I cared for the experience."

"You sure don't want them any closer," said Kowalski. "Unless they're on the grill. Nothing beats a shark steak at a cookout."

Both Jones and Brunel stared at the Floridian.

"What?" he demanded.

Brunel voiced the shared sentiment of the two Englishmen. "You colonials really will eat absolutely anything, won't you?"

The hours slipped past as the *Neptune* bore them over the featureless seabed. Only as they approached the coast of Tortuga did the view from the dome change, the level bottom giving way to chunks of rock and tall formations of coral as the ocean floor angled upwards. Brunel slowed the pace of their advance, skirting the larger chunks of rock and taking more care with the *Neptune*'s footing as they left the smooth sand behind.

This was more like it, thought Jones. Or at least, more like the tropical depths of his imagination. Brightly-coloured fish darted between swaying fronds of seaweed, seeking refuge from the nocturnal predators of the reef. The night-time hunters themselves shied away from the lights of the *Neptune* as it strode through their domain – an octopus curling its tentacles into the shelter of the coral, a cruel-looking eel withdrawing into its dark hole. The observers spotted no more sharks, for which Jones gave thanks, mindful of the swim awaiting at journey's end.

With the depth gauge at fifty feet, Brunel flicked off all but one of the lamps, leaving them creeping onwards and upwards preceded by a faint patch of light.

"Don't want the Blackpool Illuminations rising from the sea, do we? Not likely to help a clandestine arrival."

"Indeed," replied Jones. He glanced up at the air supply clock above them. Four and a half hours had passed. "We've made good time."

"I promised to deliver you before dawn Major, and if there's one thing I can't abide it's a lack of punctuality. Height of rudeness."

"No complaints from us on that front," said Jones.

"Should hope not. It will still be nice and dark up top. We'll see you safely onto the beach and run the pumps to replenish the air flasks for our return to the ship."

Jones nodded. "And we'll take our little stroll and be back at high tide tomorrow morning."

"It would be just swell if you were here too, Your Lordship," chipped in Kowalski. "Elsewise we're swimming home."

Brunel's smile reflected back from the curved interior of the viewport, illuminated by the red ember of his cigar.

The *Neptune* climbed the slope until the silvery underside of the surface came into view, lit from above by the thin moon. Ghostly beams shone down from the undulating surface, a shifting dapple of light playing over the sand and rocks. Brunel extinguished the last of the lamps and the *Neptune* crept forward until the shimmering boundary between air and sea was only inches above the top of the dome.

The engineer's fingers danced along a row of switches, flicking them down, one after the other. He reached out and turned a valve wheel. With a gentle hiss, the *Neptune* settled, its machinery still for the first time since the long drop from the *Great Eastern*.

"Gentlemen, your destination awaits. The upper hatch should be clear of the water."

"Then we shall take our leave," said Jones. He and Kowalski shook the old man's outstretched hand and headed for the companionway.

"Three o'clock tomorrow morning," called Brunel after them.

"Don't be late."

*

They swam the thirty feet to the beach, pushing their floating packs before them, then crawled forward out of the gentle surf.

Jones lay flat on the sand, the chill night air setting him tingling as the lukewarm seawater ran from his skin. Behind him the waves hissed as they lapped against the shoreline. The only other sound was the chirping click of cicadas in the trees.

He peered left then right down the beach, discerning no movement. He whispered an all clear to Kowalski. They rose together, crossing the sand in a crouching run, dragging their gear into the cover of the palms edging the beach.

By the faint light of the pre-dawn sky they removed their equipment from the oilskin-wrapped packs and dressed. Each man pulled on a shirt, patterned in different shades of green and brown. The new French-made *camouflage* clothing was designed to break up the outline of a man, disguising him against a natural backdrop.

Like most Imperial officers, Jones had doubted the efficacy of the patterned material – it being somehow typical of the French that they would look to improve the practice of war through the application of fashion. However, having witnessed the effective invisibility of an entire squad of French scouts during a training exercise, Jones had quickly become enamoured of the cloth's value.

The pair finished their preparations by tucking their khaki trousers into the tops of their boots. "Stops any spiders sneaking up there," joked Kowalski. At least Jones hoped he was joking.

The oilskins that had kept the equipment dry during their swim were folded flat and stuffed into packs bulging with rations and gear. Each man carried a long curved blade, hanging in a sheath alongside their pistol holsters. In addition, Kowalski had a rifle wrapped in brown burlap, strapped upright to his rucksack.

Pulling his machete from his belt, Jones hacked down a large palm leaf and carried it to the waterline. He stared out over the waves, trying to discern the shape of the *Neptune*, but could see nothing. The submersible definitely beat any fishing boat when it came to a secret landing. He moved backwards up the beach, brushing the palm fronds across the sand, erasing any tell-tale signs of their arrival. Rejoining Kowalski, he opened his watch and checked the time by its luminous dots.

"Dawn won't be long," he said. "Let's get well clear of the beach before anyone's up and about."

The island was a strip of land running east-west, forty miles in length and a dozen in width. A spine of jagged peaks ran down Tortuga's centre, separating the jungles of the northern slopes from the barren scrub of the south. Whilst the northern shores were the more habitable, the southern edge of the island boasted the bay of Cayona, a sheltered deep-water anchorage lined with cliffs. This easily-defensible inlet had served as a pirate stronghold for near three hundred years.

Rumour was that under Rackham's leadership, Cayona's natural defences had been bolstered by some formidable man-made additions. Jones planned to find a spot on the ridge overlooking the bay for an initial look, then get down closer for a more detailed inspection.

"Got to reckon they've got men stationed on the topmost peaks," said Kowalski. "Let's make sure we don't go running into any of them."

"You're the man with the jungle experience. I'll follow your lead. Time to earn that exorbitant fee of yours Captain."

Jones could hear the smile in the Floridian's reply as both men shouldered their packs. "Heh. You stick close then. And don't go getting bit by anything too poisonous..."

*

Kowalski led them inland through the trees, sometimes skirting the tangled clumps of undergrowth, sometimes hacking a way through, but always heading south and always heading uphill.

The sun's disc climbed in the sky above and the gradient became more evident. Whilst the foliage grew less dense, the steepening incline and the rising temperature kept their progress slower and harder than Jones would have preferred.

Kowalski called a halt five hundred feet below the ridge's rocky crest. He pulled a canteen from his pack, frowning at the sky as he twisted the stopper loose. He took a drink and handed the bottle to Jones.

"I don't like the look of those clouds," he said. "When it rains in these parts, it don't mess around."

"Then the sooner we get up this bloody hill the better."

Jones swigged lukewarm water from the canteen before hoisting his pack once again, waving his hand in a futile attempt to dispel the cloud of flies buzzing around his head. Perhaps some rain would banish the insects. The bloody things appeared to have adopted him as a travelling buffet. He slapped at his neck, smearing another of his innumerable tormentors over skin already dotted with itching bites.

They trudged on through the thinning trees, the slope growing steeper still. Jones gasped for breath, his leg muscles burning with the effort. Crawling about in muddy trenches for months on end was clearly poor training for a mountain trek, especially in this clammy heat. To Jones' profound irritation, Kowalski seemed to be coping fine with the climb, and appeared oblivious to the flies.

They paused in the cover of a boulder, overshadowed by one of the last patches of greenery before the island's bare bones thrust themselves into the air. Kowalski scanned the ridge ahead with a pair of binoculars.

"There's some sort of shelter on the peak to our left," he said. "But it's set up to watch the sea rather than the slopes, and there are outcrops blocking their view along the ridge once we get up there."

"Still a fair stretch of open ground to cover from here."

Kowalski indicated the ominous bank of cloud rolling building up on the horizon. "Sit tight for half an hour. Reckon we're about to get all the cover we need."

They rested against the rock and ate some of their dry rations as the sun disappeared behind the advancing clouds. Within moments of the first fat raindrops falling it was hammering down. Water bounced off the rocks and poured from the tips of the palm fronds above. The initial trickles past their feet became a rush of mud as the rain built in intensity. Jones, already soaked through, leaned towards his companion.

"It's bloody tipping it down..."

"Almost as wet as those English summers of yours," said Kowalski. "Come on. Let's move."

Keeping low, they pushed on, shielded from the observers on the peak by the shifting sheets of rain. They struggled towards the ridge, slipping and sliding, on their knees as often as their feet, scrabbling for handholds as the face of the hill liquified under the relentless downpour.

Jones' feet went out from under him, casting him full length on the ground once again. He gave a wry smile as he hauled himself up for the umpteenth time. This was where his trench experience came in handy.

He knew all about mud.

*

The slope ended before a sheer wall of rock, rising fifty feet above their heads. The pair stood at the base of the cliff and eyed the obstacle.

Jones didn't like the look of the climb, not one bit. The rain might be concealing them from any observers above, but the water was streaming down the rockface, turning what would have been a treacherous enough clamber in fair weather into an almost impossible ascent.

Kowalski squinted through the downpour. "The ridge runs right across the island. Only gap for miles is where Rackham's got his boys."

"So we climb it here?"

"With a little help from Ramon Cuervo..."

Kowalski shrugged off his backpack and rummaged within. He withdrew the launcher – an ungainly tube, reinforced down its eighteen inch length with hoops of brass. The fat barrel was mounted on a wooden handgrip studded with dials. Kowalski began to fiddle with the settings and Jones hunkered over his own pack, setting to work on the projectile.

Twelve inches of gleaming steel, the harpoon flared at its tip into four viscous barbs. Behind the hooks, the shaft formed an eyelet. Jones pulled rope through the hole until he judged the harpoon sat at the line's midpoint, a hundred feet or so trailing to either side.

Fearsome needle threaded, he handed the harpoon across. Kowalski slotted it into place and primed the charge. He raised the launcher in both hands and took aim at the cliff top above.

The pair stood like statues beneath the hammering rain. Water poured down Kowalski's upturned face as his eyes flicked from one possible anchor point to the next. Jones' trigger finger itched at the wait.

"Whenever you're ready..." he said, unable to restrain his impatience.

Kowalski's brow furrowed, but he didn't divert his attention from the rocks above. "We only have one more of these spikes Major," he muttered. "Figure you don't really want me to miss."

The launcher barked and the harpoon blasted out in a billow of smoke, the loop of rope hauled into the air in its wake. A metallic crack echoed from above and Kowalski turned to Jones, eyebrow arched.

"Happy now?"

Jones stepped forward and gave the dangling ropes a sharp tug. "Seems solid enough. Here's hoping our chums along the way didn't hear anything over the rain."

Kowalski went first, rope tied around his chest. At the base of the cliff, Jones hauled at the other end of the line. His arm muscles burned with the effort and his hands were rubbed raw by the rough fibres of the soaking rope. He frowned up into the rain, convinced his companion could be making more of a contribution to the ascent.

When his own turn came he quickly forgave the Floridian. The rocks were sheer and slick with water, almost devoid of hand- or footholds. It was all he could do to fend himself from the wall as Kowalski hauled him up. Any attempt at actual climbing was lost amidst his efforts to prevent the bumps and scrapes turning into more serious blows. It was a relief when he finally hooked his arm over the protruding shaft of the harpoon and reached up for Kowalski's extended hand. He was pulled, soaked, filthy and aching, over the crest of the ridge.

Jones peered out over the scree and boulders of the slope, searching through the downpour for the outline of the pirate bay away to the south. The torrential rain concealed the details of the rocks twenty feet away, never mind any signs of the shoreline. So much for their elevated observation position.

He began to shiver, the wind against his sodden clothes chilling him now the effort of the climb was past. He regretted his lack of sou'wester and galoshes – not the first things he'd have on his list for a trip to a Caribbean island.

"We're going to need to get closer," said Kowalski, echoing Jones' own thoughts. "And find some shelter until this muck blows over."

Sitting as much as standing, they slid through the mud and stones of the upper slope down into the boulder field below. They picked their way carefully over the haphazard scatter of rocks, wary of the narrow gaps between the unstable stones – perfect for the twisting or breaking of an ankle. At the slope's base the clutter gave way to untidy scrubland dotted with stunted bushes and the occasional lump of rock. The barren scenery stretched away to the south as far as the rain allowed them to see.

They cast about for somewhere to wait out the storm. Neither man fancied moving closer to the pirate encampment without getting a better look at the lie of the land.

*

The tropical sun, now high in the sky, warmed the rocks as the rainclouds rolled clear. The whole island steamed as the fallen rain evaporated. To Kowalski, the wreaths of vapour rising up, coupled with the lack of vegetation, made this side of Tortuga look as if it had been newly-decimated by some volcanic eruption.

The two men left the shelter of the rock formation and headed south, confident the mists curling into the air would mask their approach from any but the most eagle-eyed of watchmen.

As the cliff tops came into view, they aimed for a spot where scrappy bushes appeared to overhang the edge, figuring it would provide a concealed position from which to survey the inlet below. They crept forward now, taking turns to move, pistols in hand, the barrel of each weapon fitted with a suppression cylinder, courtesy of Ramon Cuervo.

If they did run into any wandering patrols, Kowalski was determined to take care of things quickly, but more importantly, quietly. The thought of rousing the bloodthirsty population of the port and being chased across the island was enough to give him the chills, despite the thick humidity.

With a hundred feet to go, he waved Jones towards the shadow of a large boulder and they slipped their packs from their shoulders. They stashed the bags in a narrow crevice then crawled forward over the final stretch of broken ground. Jones burrowed in beneath the low branches.

Taking a final look around the mist-shrouded cliff top, Kowalski wriggled in after him. Thorns pricked at his face and arms as he pushed his way through. Baked, soaked, and now scratched to pieces in a damned briar patch – Tortuga was proving as welcoming as he had expected.

With a grunt, he pulled free of the clutching barbs and into the hollow beneath the boughs. Jones turned from his position at the crumbling lip of the cliff and waved Kowalski forward.

"Watch you don't knock anything loose."

Kowalski shuffled up alongside the Englishman and peered out over Jack Rackham's stronghold and the waters of Cayona.

Beneath them, the cliffs fell two hundred feet straight down, stretching out to enclose a circular bay perhaps a mile across at its widest point. The southern tips of the cliffs ended in tall spurs of rock facing one another above a narrow stretch of water offering passage out to sea. At the summits Kowalski could make out the squat shapes of blockhouses, the slits cut into their walls no doubt offering an expansive field of fire over the waterway below.

Alongside these bunkers, gun emplacements raised long thin barrels towards the sky. It looked like Rackham was well set to fend off any attack from the air as well as the ocean.

Opposite the entrance to the bay, the town sat piled untidily against the northern cliffs. It sprawled, a shambolic jumble of buildings, not one the twin of its neighbour.

Sheds with corrugated iron roofs rubbed up against brick warehouses, whilst tall chimneys leaned over adobe huts and Spanish-style houses. The burnt out shells of buildings stood open to the elements, while other gaps between the tiled roofs were draped with tarpaulins, providing makeshift shelter. Shutters hung askew from stained whitewashed walls and boards covered most of the leaded windows in the slouched wooden frontages along the wharf. Tortuga's three hundred years of undisciplined history could be read in the clash of decaying architecture on display.

A cobbled road traversed its way through the collection of dilapidated buildings. Back and forth it twisted, down the steep slope from clifftop to waterside, serving the triple purpose of thoroughfare, marketplace, and sewer. Down near the waterfront, the street was choked with figures, traders hawking their wares, stevedores laden with bales of cargo, and men rolling barrels between storehouses and the boats moored at the quay's rotting piles. A clapped-out airship hung over the activity on the wharf, tethered to a wooden tower, its sagging gasbag patched in twenty different shades of filthy canvas.

Tumbledown warehouses were dotted along the base of the cliffs to either side of the town, jetties and wooden docks jutting out into the bay. Off to the east, the smooth surface of the water was broken by the dark shapes of derelict boats, some floating, but most half-submerged, their hulls splintered and broken – a graveyard of ships providing a maritime echo for the ramshackle town.

"Well Major, there it is. Jack Rackham's metropolis."

"Delightful," said Jones, surveying the scene through his eyeglasses. "But I'm more interested in those ships..."

The bay itself was crowded with vessels of all shapes and sizes. Fishing boats and steam launches lay at anchor alongside larger rust-streaked tramp steamers. At least a hundred ships – a mixture of civilian cargo vessels, no doubt engaged in smuggling or other shady dealings, and the outright pirate vessels, plainly armed to the teeth. Amongst them, Kowalski spotted tiny craft fitted with boilers and stubby smokestacks. Little bigger than rowing boats, they seemed almost certain to capsize if they were ever to fire the cannons they sported.

Towering above the ragtag fleet, dominating the bay, was the imposing bulk of a warship – her rust-streaked hull four hundred feet long and fifty abeam. Her superstructure climbed in tiers from the patched planks of the main deck to a wide bridge flaring out ahead of three funnels. She had four sets of long guns down her deck, and every rail bore the mark of modification as a weapons mount. The ship fairly bristled with tacked-on armament of all kinds, from hand-cranked Gatling carbines, to swivel-mounted cannons.

Above it all, reaching up beyond the smokestacks, was a metal pylon, its criss-cross beams narrowing to a point thirty feet over the bridge. There, fixed at the tower's tip, sat a large brass sphere, its smooth surface gleaming in the sun. Thick cables emerged from its base, snaking down between the girders and in through a hole in the wheelhouse roof.

"What's that thing up top?" said Jones. "Looks electrical."

"Major, you need to keep up with advances in the world of science. That there is an Edison Ball."

Jones turned a baleful look on him. "In my defence, I've had limited opportunity to browse the latest periodicals."

"Heh. Fair enough. Only reason I know is 'cos Maria dragged me to a lecture on the thing last time I was in Boston. Edison himself no less. Can't say I was too impressed. Man's so dull I damn-near fell asleep."

In truth, the only thing preventing him dropping off had been the frequent blows from Maria's sharp elbows. She couldn't comprehend why he hadn't been enthralled, and he couldn't understand why anyone would be. The evening had ended in a fiery row and, eventually, an equally-fiery making-up. Kind of summed-up their relationship.

"Did you stay awake long enough to know what it does?"

"Not the details, God no." Kowalski shuddered. "But there was an awful lot of talk about electric fields and magnetism."

"What do a bunch of pirates want with a bloody magnet?" Jones rolled his eyes at the blank look Kowalski offered in response. "Perhaps I should have brought Maria along instead..."

Kowalski returned his gaze to the ship below. "Whatever that thing does, the boat's quite the flagship, despite the rust."

"Where the hell did she come from? Your Admiral's estimate of Rackham's strength didn't mention anything along those lines."

"We didn't know. Last time any of our boys sneaked a look at this place, Rackham had nothing like her floating around."

Jones frowned. "It certainly explains why he suddenly thinks he can go after British shipping with impunity."

Kowalski took a long look at the dreadnought. "Damn it Major. He might just be right. That thing down there is as big as anything the Free Fleet has afloat."

"Are you saying your chaps can't do the job?"

Kowalski regarded the collection of pirate vessels. If the entire Fleet rolled out they should be able to handle things down here. But it would get real messy, and the bill would be high – in blood as well as coin.

"We can do it," he said. "But whatever number you were thinking, there's likely an extra nought on the end of it."

"We'll discuss that later. In fact, I'd rather leave the grubby details of any contract to the penny-pinchers of Whitehall. It's the operational questions I'm concerned with..."

Jones' voice trailed off, both men distracted by engine noise. Below and off to their right, a launch came into sight between the pillars of rock at the bay's entrance. Jones lifted the binoculars and scanned the vessel as it steamed past their position, heading for the town. The Englishman stiffened, knuckles whitening as his fingers tightened on the binoculars.

"What is it?" asked Kowalski.

Jones handed over the glasses and gestured at the boat. "Rackham has visitors," he said. His voice was hard, matching the look in his eyes.

Kowalski peered down at the launch, running his magnified gaze along the gleaming white trim and spotless planks of the deck. The sun caught the polished brass portholes down her side whilst a cheerful red funnel puffed steam into the air above the honey-varnished wood of her wheelhouse. Nice boat, he thought – not your average pirate vessel.

Two figures stood at the stern. The first bore the unmistakeable features of Rook, sunlight bouncing off his metallic skull. Alongside him, hands on the rail, staring out at the surrounding ships, was the ample frame of Commodore Silas Culpepper of the United States Navy.

*

"I've stolen my fair share of things in my time Major – a train, even an airship once. But laundry? This is a first." Kowalski peered doubtfully at the threadbare garments they had liberated from the washing line.

"At least it's clean," replied Jones, removing his shirt and tugging a rough denim one on in its place. He sniffed at the cloth as he buttoned it up. "Well, cleanish."

The sight of Culpepper in the stern of the launch had changed the nature of the mission. A reconnaissance of Cayona was no longer enough. Jones needed to know what was going on, and he wasn't going to get any answers perched on the cliff top. They needed to take a stroll into town.

With the volume of shipping in the bay, and the amount of trade going on, they reckoned a couple of new faces would pass unremarked. Their *camouflage* shirts however, were quite another matter, and it had been a relief when they came across the drying line before penetrating too far into the jumble of narrow streets.

Unpegging a shirt or two certainly bested their original plan of clubbing someone over the head and stealing their garments – a risky undertaking at the best of times.

Knocking an adversary unconscious always left the thorny problem of them eventually coming round and raising the alarm. There was an easy solution for such a dilemma of course, but it seemed disproportionate to kill a man in cold blood simply because you wanted to borrow his outfit – unsporting somehow. Besides, as Kowalski had observed, the shirt from the fellow you had to thump on the skull invariably turned out to be too small, or came in a dreadfully unfashionable check. Looting the washing line, with its choice of size and style, had been like an appointment with a Savile Row tailor in comparison.

Now, clad in still-damp stolen garb, the pair stepped out of the shelter of the alleyway and onto the main street running down the hillside towards the waters of the bay.

At first there were few signs of life, and fewer still of any activity. A drunk slumbered in a doorway and a scrawny child scrambled past, chasing an equally thin and dirty dog. But as they moved into the lower town, the hustle and bustle grew – stalls lining the roadside, compressing the pedestrian traffic inward. Their downhill progress became a torturous dance, attention divided between negotiating their passage through the crowd, sidestepping the sewer channel running the centre of the street, and avoiding eye contact with the stallholders, beggars and doxies – all desperate for an opening to make their pitch for coin.

Most of the bartering was in English, but the pronunciation and accents ran the gamut from impeccable to near-incomprehensible. The variety of voices was reflected in the crowd's faces. It seemed every race and nation was represented – the mercantile low-life of the world, attracted by the promise of unfettered commerce and illicit opportunity.

Eventually the street met the square, and the press of people thinned. The stalls gave way to shops and taverns, their ancient wooden frames leaning drunkenly together, surrounding three sides of the wide cobbled space bordering the waterfront. Jones headed for the centre of the square, Kowalski doing his best nonchalant stroll alongside him. They stopped before a cart piled high with fruit and vegetables, taking turns to browse the wares whilst the other had a good look around.

"Busy place," said Kowalski, his voice low. "If Rackham's getting a cut of all this, he must be doing well for himself."

Jones lifted an apple and turned it over, examining it for bruises. "And he's keeping a close eye on things. Making sure he gets his share. Two men on the tavern roof. Another two by the wharf."

"You see the cannon? At least three of them, covering the jetties. Reckon you don't cause any trouble in Calico Jack's town. Not if you want to leave in one piece."

Jones tossed the apple to Kowalski and picked up another. He gestured over his shoulder with his thumb.

"And if they don't pop a round into your boat, other punishments appear to be on offer..."

At the square's edge stood a raised wooden platform, a scaffold looming above. A body hung from the crossbeam, face swollen and black above the noose digging into its neck.

Jones pulled out a coin and handed over payment for the fruit. "What did he do?" he asked the stallholder, indicating the dangling corpse.

The man shrugged. "Feller beat up a strumpet."

"One of Jack's favourites? That why he strung him up?"

"Don't reckon so. Doubt Jack gives a damn about the bint. Ways I heard it, feller thought he could thump her without paying for it." The stallholder turned away to deal with another customer.

"Delightful," muttered Jones as they moved off.

The pair paused in the shadow of the wooden tower acting as a mooring point for the airship tethered above. The rickety timber frame looked less than robust, unlikely to provide much security in the event of the wind getting up. But in fairness, the rickety structure was a good match for the airship's battered gondola and threadbare balloon. The decrepit craft made for quite a contrast with the luxurious dirigible in which Jones had soared across the Atlantic.

Another pylon of criss-crossed beams rose amongst the chimneys over the town, this one topped with a tall metal rod.

"Wireless tower," said Jones, indicating the structure. "Our pirate chums appear to enjoy all the modern conveniences."

Kowalski turned towards him, eyes wide. "Wireless..."

"What about it?"

"I know why Rackham has an Edison Ball..."

"Feel free to enlighten me."

"Edison kept droning on about reducing unwanted effects..."

"If you have a point to this story, now would be the time to reveal it."

"The magnetism – it blocks radio waves. And the bigger the ball, the bigger the effect."

They both turned to regard the dreadnought and the brass sphere catching the sunlight high above her decks. Knowledge of the ship's invisible power over the airwaves only served to increase the sense of menace she radiated. Jones imagined all those distress calls, tapped out by desperate wireless operators, gobbled up by magnetic disturbance, never to reach a friendly ear.

"Enough sightseeing," he said. "Time to find out what Rackham and Culpepper are up to."

"I know the best place for gossip in most ports. I imagine Cayona ain't any different."

They turned their attention to the largest of the taverns.

"A little early for whisky..." said Jones.

"Heh. Rum it is then."

Jones rubbed the apple on his sleeve and took a bite as they made their way across the square. He'd missed lunch, and rum on an empty stomach was never a good idea.

*

The pub's tables were as dirty as its floor, and the air was thick with the stench of cheap drink and stale sweat. The service matched the ambience, their only welcome a sullen stare from an ugly barman as he poured their drinks. The place was everything Jones had expected, a grim dive of a dockside tavern. Naturally, it was packed.

He and Kowalski stood pressed against the counter, nervous of their elbows lest they spill someone's drink and get embroiled in a fight. They lifted their rum, Jones wincing at the gutrot smell of the dark brown liquid. The taste was quite as awful as the aroma promised. He lowered his hand and tipped most of the drink out onto the floor. The stuff would likely burn a hole in the planks, but better the floor than his innards.

He kept his ears cocked for anything interesting, but the only snatches of conversation he could catch were slurred arguments over favourite ports, favourite pubs, even favourite knots. Sailors' drunken chatter was nothing if not predictable.

One robust discussion regarding favourite songs broke out into a competitive, simultaneous rendition of the verses in question. Within moments, the entire pub was engaged, either in tuneless support of one or other of the ditties, or in loud demands for the singers to cease their caterwauling.

Jones leaned forward. "This is hopeless. Let's get out of here."

He straightened and made to leave but found himself brought up short, Kowalski's grip tight on his arm.

"Don't go rushing off," said the Floridian, his eyes fixed over Jones' shoulder. "I just spotted someone we'll want to talk to..."

Jones in tow, Kowalski pushed through the crowd and over to one of the booths set around the walls. The seats held a solitary drinker, head bowed over a glass and bottle, both empty. Kowalski slipped onto the bench alongside the slumped figure and Jones took the seat opposite. The head came up, bleary eyes struggling to focus, then widening as the man's rum-soaked brain processed the identities of his new companions.

The mouth dropped open in shock, revealing a flash of gold.

"Hello Luis," said Kowalski. "You owe us two hundred dollars."

*

Jones tightened the rope around Luis' wrists and stuffed a wad of dirty rags into the Cuban's mouth, muffling his protests. Another strip of the same oil-stained cloth secured the gag in place. The Englishman straightened from the prone figure and Kowalski tucked his pistol away, no longer worried about their reluctant guide making a bid for freedom.

In the alley behind the tavern, Kowalski had forced Luis to his knees and pushed the fat brass barrel of the silenced pistol between the Cuban's gold teeth. Luis' eyes darted between the men standing over him, brimming with tears as Kowalski explained in lurid detail what would happen if he didn't help them get a closer look at Rackham's operations.

Luis caught movement behind them – a scullery maid from the tavern lugging a slop bucket out into the alleyway. Her appearance brought a flash of hope to the Cuban's eyes. The girl took a long look at the tableau before her, taking in the kneeling man and the gun. Without a word, she dropped her gaze, poured the pail's contents into the hard-packed earth and turned away. With what Kowalski had seen of Tortuga, he reckoned it wasn't the first such scene the girl had witnessed.

With the maid's silent departure, the last thin thread of Luis' courage snapped. He begged, agreeing to do whatever they wanted, the desperate words distorted, made almost incoherent by the gun between his teeth.

They made their way through Cayona's backstreets, Kowalski clutching Luis' arm, pistol shoved into the man's side. Away from the square and main street there were few people about, and those few who passed didn't pay the trio a blind bit of notice.

Luis' boat was twenty feet in length, with a raised wheelhouse towards the bow and an open deck astern surrounded by a low rail. Her timbers were patched everywhere with different kinds of wood and streaked with a variety of paint. A single rusted smokestack poked upwards from the centre of the decking, the dented metal held upright in a web of guy lines. She was quite the bucket, thought Kowalski.

He and Jones shared a look. The Englishman pointed to their captive. "He made it here from Havana. It must be reasonably watertight."

They slipped from the mooring and steamed into the bay. They picked their way through the crowded anchorage, course roughly parallel to the shore. Kowalski ensured Luis didn't take them too close to any of the larger pirate vessels. Ahead of them, glowing in the light of the evening sun, the cliffs reared up and around, forming an imposing backdrop beyond the moored flotilla and the shipwrecks.

At the town's edge, a brick-built warehouse stood apart from the others, a jetty protruding into the bay from the broad doors set into its frontage. Despite its proximity to the maritime graveyard, the building and its dock were in considerably better repair than the other structures along the crumbling waterfront. That, and the sleek lines of the pristine steam launch moored at the pier, suggested the building belonged to Rackham.

"That is the place," Luis confirmed, cutting the throttle.

The boat coasted to a halt on the calm water, drifting in close to one of the derelict hulks. The Cuban had flatly refused to go any closer in – his terror of Rackham and the consequences of treachery finally overwhelming his fear of Kowalski's pistol.

So now Luis lay trussed on his thin cot in the compartment below the wheelhouse and Jones and Kowalski waited for evening. Now they had a boat they wouldn't need to hike back overland for their rendezvous with Brunel. They had time to spare.

*

Beneath the high cliffs, darkness fell across the bay with a startling abruptness. Away to their left the lights of the town reflected in the water, but as the daytime bustle of the waterfront petered out, only isolated pools of flickering gaslight punctuated the gloom around Rackham's warehouse.

Their boat floated a hundred yards from the end of the wooden jetty. An easy swim, a creep along the pier, and then we shall see what we shall see, thought Jones. He tapped Kowalski on the shoulder – time to go.

The two men rose, ready to slip over the side, only to duck back into shadow as bright electric lamps crackled into life down the length of the pier, one after the other, harsh white light shattering the blackness. The warehouse doors rumbled open and a dozen men spilled onto the dock.

"What's all this about?" whispered Jones, peering from the cover of the rail towards the sudden burst of activity.

Kowalski tugged at his sleeve and nodded in the direction of the bay. There, moving towards them over the water was the dark outline of a trawler, running in without lights. Their ears caught the throb of its engine and the wake of its passage set their boat pitching to and fro. The noise died away as the new arrival approached the pier, low greetings called out and answered with tossed ropes. The vessel was hauled in against the wooden pilings and tied up alongside Culpepper's launch.

The fishing boat's crew began hauling sacks up from the hold, passing them in a chain from one man to the next, down the gangway and onto the jetty. The assembled dock workers took charge of the cargo, stacking it on wheeled carts.

Kowalski gave him another nudge. "We're not the only observers..."

Beyond the activity on the pier, standing in the wide doorway of the warehouse, were two figures. Even at a distance, Jones recognised Culpepper's rotund build.

"The other one. Rackham?"

"Yep. That's him."

Jones rummaged in his pack and pulled the binoculars free. He raised the glasses and adjusted the optics, bringing Jack Rackham into sharp focus. The pirate was a good six inches taller than Culpepper, and thinner, his sharp features cast into stark relief by the lights. Dark hair swept back from a high forehead, the brows casting deep pools of shadow on either side of a hook nose.

Too far away, thought Jones. He needed to be closer – needed to see the man's eyes. His hands tightened into fists at the thought of a more personal confrontation with his brother's murderer.

"Shame I left the rifle under that rock," said Kowalski. "Two bullets and I could have saved you and Buckingham a whole heap of cash."

"I'd give you Culpepper," said Jones. "But I'm old-fashioned enough to want Rackham to myself. Besides, I need to know what's going on, and dead men tell no tales, as I'm sure these characters would put it."

"So you still want to go take a look?"

"More than ever. I'm intrigued now. What sort of cargo is so important the King of the Pirates and the bloody overlord of Cuba feel the need to personally oversee its unloading?"

The Floridian eyed the stretch of water between the boat and the jetty, the glare from the electric lamps washing over the surface.

"A little bright out there, Major." He gestured to their right where the upturned boats and rusting shipwrecks cast patches of dark shadow. "We might want to take the long way around."

The swim took them a good twenty minutes, their pace slow and steady, strokes kept carefully beneath the surface to minimise any noise or tell-tale splashes that might catch the light. They hauled themselves up onto the rocks two hundred yards along the shore from the warehouse.

Out here, beyond the edge of town, they were sure nobody would see them clamber out of the water. All the same, they moved quickly, keeping low, finding a sheltered niche amongst the stones before pausing. Both men lifted the footwear which hung from tied laces over their shoulders, tipped out the water, and slipped their feet into damp boots.

Jones grimaced at the unpleasant sensation. "Wouldn't that be just the thing?" he whispered. "Spend a year crawling around in the mud, only to get trench foot out here."

"Heh. Tropical island life not living up to expectations?"

Kowalski slid an oilskin pack from where it had nestled in the small of his back. He unwrapped the silenced pistols and handed one across.

Jones hefted the weapon and regarded the dark bulk of the warehouse silhouetted against the lights of the pier.

"Shall we?"

*

Luis jerked out of his exhausted doze as something bumped and scraped down the side of the boat. The oily taste of the rag clogging his mouth made him gag for the hundredth time, but with an effort he resisted the urge to retch. With the balled up rag and the tight strip around his lower face, he knew throwing up would be the end of him.

He flexed his cramped limbs once more, wincing as the movement caused the ropes at his wrists and ankles to chafe. When his captors had left, he had squirmed against his restraints, earning himself nothing but raw patches of skin. Anger and fear burned through him as he blinked tears in the darkness. Bound and gagged – a prisoner on his own boat.

His vessel rocked as someone clambered aboard. Those gringo bastards were back. They would sail out of the bay and dump him overboard. Send down a trussed-up meal for the sharks. He was sure of it – it was what he would have done himself.

He heard footsteps in the wheelhouse above, and then voices. Strangers' voices, he realised with a sudden surge of hope.

"Nobody around..." said the first voice.

"Check below," answered another. "She shouldn't be out here. Locals know better than to moor in this part of the bay."

Luis wriggled around in the confines of his cot, straining to see as footsteps clattered down the wooden ladder. The door swung open and a figure stood in the companionway, lantern high, the light flooding into the tiny sleeping compartment. Luis blinked up at his saviour and tried to speak. The man ignored the muffled begging and called over his shoulder.

"There's a bloke down 'ere..."

More footsteps, and the shape of another figure behind the lantern.

"Well, well," said the new arrival. "If it ain't my old pal Luis."

The first man stepped aside and Rook squeezed past him into the cabin. The bloodshot eye stared down and Luis' pleas choked in his throat. He'd sooner have faced the sharks.

"Now matey, I'm going to give you a moment..." The Irishman brought his ruined face down to loom scant inches from Luis' own. "I want you to have a good hard think about the story you'll be telling old Rooky when I haul that there plug out of your mouth..."

*

Jack Rackham watched his men wheel the last of the sacks into the warehouse. He took a final draw on his cigarette and flicked the butt out over the jetty's rail. The ember glowed red as it flew its arc, before snuffing out abruptly in the dark water below. Rackham nodded to the guards and stepped over the threshold. The wooden doors grumbled shut behind him.

Crates and barrels rose up on either side in haphazard towers as he made his way through the warehouse, the contraband haul of a hundred raids and smuggling trips. Deep pools of cobweb-strung shadow filled the gaps between the stacks and the air was thick with the smell of damp and dust. Only at the building's centre was there any open space. Here, a single electrical lamp hung down on a long chain from the ceiling, casting a sickly illumination over the newly-arrived cargo and the portly figure engaged in its inspection.

Always the same, thought Rackham, Culpepper checking up on him again. Still, business was business. He fixed a smile in place. Time to play the jolly trader.

"Everything to your satisfaction Commodore?"

The American straightened. "Everything appears to be in order. The quantities are as agreed."

Rackham patted a hand on the topmost of the hessian bags. "All ready for refining. Bolivia's finest – as promised."

"As paid for," corrected Culpepper.

Rackham maintained his smile with an effort. "And the other matter? Mister Rook's work proved up to scratch?"

Culpepper glanced round at mention of the Irishman, seeking his distinctive features and displaying visible relief at their absence. Rook made people nervous. It was the reason Rackham kept him around. Nothing ensured your business partners remained honest like having a pet lunatic at your beck and call.

"Your man completed his task admirably," said Culpepper. "I received another delegation yesterday – villagers begging for protection. One more month and I shall give them what they ask. My soldiers will move into the villages and, as if by magic," a smirk formed beneath the moustache, "the bandit raids shall cease."

"Making you look quite the hero..."

"And Estrada quite the fool. His pathetic insurgency will have lost all credibility and support. Cuba will be pacified, and all without my men having fired a single shot."

"Although mine will have surely fired plenty on their behalf," said Rackham. It did no harm to remind the Commodore his hands were clean only because others' were stained crimson, right up to the wrists.

"A job for which you have been handsomely rewarded," snapped Culpepper, the whiskered cheeks flushing red. Not for the first time, Rackham thought how much he'd enjoy playing the American at cards – the man's podgy face was like an open book.

"And there you go again," he said. "Treating me like I'm the hired help, rather than a full-share partner in this here enterprise."

"You have your ship. And now you have your instructions. The cargo needs to be in New Orleans tomorrow evening."

"Deauchamp's boys are expecting it?"

"Yes," sniffed the American, mouth wrinkled in disapproval. "The negro will be awaiting delivery."

Rackham snorted. "I feel for your delicate sensibilities Commodore. Forced into associating with unsavoury characters like myself, and now, Heaven forbid, negroes?" He indicated the pile of sacks. "And all in the honourable endeavour of flooding your own country with cocaine."

Culpepper drew himself up, affronted, puffing out his chest until it almost matched the girth of his stomach. "My country? My country fell at Appomattox."

Rackham smiled. "You can't have been more than an itch in your daddy's britches when Lee surrendered..."

"My father died fighting the Yankees. The Stars and Stripes is nothing to me but a flag of convenience. Besides, we're hardly flooding the country, as you rather dramatically put it." He nodded towards the bags. "Somebody has to supply this filth to the degenerates who use it."

"And somebody has to make a pretty profit doing it..."

"For the moment." Culpepper's eyes narrowed. "But like the raids on the Cuban villages, all this is the means to an end. Suppression of the cocaine trade will be one of my first successes when I am ensconced within the White House."

*

At mention of the American seat of government, Jones and Kowalski shared a troubled look. From their concealed position amongst the crates, the infiltrators had eavesdropped on the conversation with an increasing sense of disquiet. In the minutes since Jones had put a silenced round through the padlock on the warehouse's rear door, their simple reconnaissance mission had spiralled downwards into a dark morass of murder, illicit substances, and political conspiracy.

Jones' mind churned, torn as to the course of action to pursue. Should he relay this new information to Buckingham, and let the top brass back home decide what to do? Or might he end things here and now?

Staring at his brother's murderer, Jones knew there was no choice at all. The old men sat in the comfortable offices of Whitehall might be put out at a lack of consultation, but Jones couldn't let an opportunity like this slip through his fingers. Then again, perhaps Buckingham and his cronies would be pleased? After all, a handful of bullets would prove a damn sight cheaper than hiring the whole Free Fleet.

He looked to Kowalski and tilted his head towards the pair in the centre of the warehouse. The usual playful glint in the Floridian's eyes was absent, replaced by a steely look, a match to Jones' own. The business of killing was at hand, and both men settled into a hard, ruthless professionalism.

"Well mateys, what do we have here?"

They whirled, hands reaching for weapons, but pulling up short when presented with the sight of Rook and his guns. The man squatted atop the crate at their rear, a pistol in each hand, the lower half of his face stretched into a skeleton grin.

"Mister Jones of the London Times, unless I am very much mistaken. And here I thought my old mate Luis had to be lying." He lifted his head and called out. "Jack, we've got visitors."

The conversation at the centre of the warehouse came to a sudden halt. Rook gestured towards the light with the wave of a pistol.

"Let's go see Cap'n Rackham, shall we?"

*

The infiltrators knelt on the rough planks of the warehouse floor, relieved of their weapons, hands lifted to the backs of their heads, an armed sailor covering them from behind. Rackham ignored the captives for the moment, seemingly more interested in rummaging through their equipment, piled on a barrel. It was Culpepper who spoke first.

"This is an unwelcome surprise. I had understood from Captain Rackham's associate that you would be leaving the Caribbean at the earliest opportunity. You appear determined to stick your nose in where it's not required."

"In truth, the threats only made me more interested," answered Jones. If Culpepper was still swallowing his cover as a reporter, Jones wasn't about to put him right.

"And now you've stumbled on a bigger story than you imagined. I assume you've been lurking back there for some time."

"Long enough," shrugged Jones.

"A pity."

"Don't want your sordid little scheme revealed to the world? Peddling cocaine – not the behaviour one expects from a military man."

It was Culpepper's turn to shrug. "Election campaigns are expensive."

"So you're going to buy the Presidency?"

"Not at all. I shall simply use the money to better inform the populace regarding my suitability for the post." The American gave a smile. "The masses do love a war hero."

The noise of the door scraping open brought a halt to the discussion. Luis stumbled into the warehouse's centre, pushed forward by Rook into the circle of light. Rackham turned from his perusal of the equipment to face the new arrival.

"Luis, my old friend," said the pirate, wagging a finger at the Cuban. "Seems you've been running a passenger service."

The sailor rubbed at his wrists and shot the captives a venomous glance. "These men *senor*, they kidnap Luis. They force him to –"

"Save your breath," said Rackham. "I don't care."

The pirate raised the weapon he'd pulled from the pile. Luis' face turned grey at the sight of the gaping muzzle. A hollow boom echoed around the warehouse and the Cuban staggered, clutching his stomach, coughing out ragged breaths. His fingers scrabbled at the steel bolt protruding from his guts. Rackham put the launcher down and reached for one of the silenced pistols, ignoring the harpooned sailor's moans.

He raised the gun, waving it before Luis' eyes, then adopting a theatrical duelling stance. He stood, arm straight, turned side-on, squinting along the barrel at the wounded man. Luis stared up, tears streaming down his face. The gun spat, the report little more than a muffled pop, the noise of the bullet's sickening smack almost as loud. Luis dropped like a stone, a neat red hole in his forehead.

Ignoring the fallen man, Rackham turned the pistol this way and that, admiring the shining brass of the suppression cylinder.

"Nice gun. And quite the arsenal for a journalist." He tossed the pistol aside and regarded the kneeling men. "I don't like the smell of this story of yours. Not for a moment." He waved a hand dismissively at Kowalski. "This one we know. A gun for hire –"

"Much like yourself..." said the Floridian.

Rackham paused, an eyebrow raised at the interruption. He peered down his sharp nose at Kowalski before lifting his gaze to Rook.

The Irishman's kick caught Kowalski in the back, pitching him forward, smashing his face into the floor. Immediately Rook was on him, knee between the shoulder blades, pulling his head up by a fistful of hair and pressing the muzzle of his gun to the captive's temple.

"Now matey, you don't want to be giving any cheek to the Cap'n..." He rapped the pistol hard against Kowalski's skull. "Behave yourself."

Rook stood and the Floridian pulled himself back to his knees. Rackham stepped forward, looming over Jones.

"As I was saying, before your friend's interjection, something don't smell right in this here tale. Not right at all. You've gone to quite some lengths for a newspaper story..."

Jones stared up. Silent. Defiant.

Rackham beckoned Rook forward and put an arm around his subordinate's shoulders. He reached up his other hand and beat a tattoo with his knuckles on the metal plating of the Irishman's head. "I'm thinking maybe I should let Mister Rook here indulge his passion for knifework. See if he can't winkle the truth out of you –"

"Ask him about his brother..." muttered Kowalski, prompting everyone to turn in his direction.

He lifted his head to meet Jones' accusatory gaze. "Don't look at me like that," he said. "Easier this way than trying to keep your secrets..."

Rackham's eyes gleamed as he took in this exchange. "Your mercenary friend is wise beyond his years. Secrets is it? What's all this about a brother?"

Jones knew Kowalski was right. Let Rackham and Culpepper think they had uncovered the truth, disguising the greater secret of his real identity and mission. All the same, nothing was feigned about the bitterness in his voice. "He was the skipper of the *Milford*."

Rackham grinned at this revelation, but Culpepper was mystified. "What is he talking about?"

"A merchant tub we took weeks past," answered the pirate. "Nice haul of weapons aboard. She made excellent practice for the gunners."

Jones could feel his anger burning in his face. Rackham saw it and gave a slow nod.

"That's more like it. That's a tale I can swallow." He turned to Culpepper. "I think we've found what really motivates our friend here..."

Looking down again, the pirate's eyes bored into Jones' own.

"Vengeance," said Rackham, relishing the word. "Now there's a cause worth dying for."

*

Kowalski splashed into the water off the bottom of the ladder, ripples spreading out over the oily surface, illuminated by the faint light from the shaft mouth twenty feet above.

The Pit – so Rackham had named it as he had given Rook his orders. The Irishman had summoned a couple of burly cronies to act as guards and the captives were marched through the alleyways to a courtyard off the town's central square. There, the pirates manhandled a heavy trapdoor up and back, revealing the gaping maw of an old well.

The footing was rough beneath the waist-high water as Kowalski stepped away from the brick wall towards the pool's centre. He watched Jones pick his way down the ladder, followed by one of their escorts. Beyond the descending figures, he made out Rook's distinctive features grinning down. The man's leer was given a demonic cast by the flickering orange flame of the lantern he held above the pit's circular opening.

Jones dropped from the lowest rung and into the water, joined moments later by their guard. The pirate grunted, shoving them towards the centre of the pool, apparently confident the prisoners would comply.

A fair assumption, granted Kowalski, seeing as Rook's companion at the top of the shaft was covering them with a formidable blunderbuss.

Pushed back to back, they waited in silence as their captor bent low, fumbling in the water at their feet. Kowalski felt cold metal clasp his ankle, then his foot was pulled roughly to the surface, almost tipping him over. The pirate attached a padlock to the shackle and released the leg, allowing Kowalski to regain his balance. Grunting once again, the man turned to perform the same procedure on Jones. Task complete, their taciturn jailer clambered up the ladder to rejoin his fellows above.

Kowalski crouched, feeling out the manacle, following the chain beneath the water to a metal ring fixed in the stone. He gave the anchor point an experimental tug, to no effect.

"Ahoy there..." called Rook, his voice reverberating down the shaft. "Accommodation to your satisfaction?"

"Just dandy thank you," shouted Kowalski, damned if he'd let the man's taunting get to him. Well, not so as the bastard would notice.

"You're a couple of characters, I'll grant you that," came the response. "But I predict there'll be a mite less banter when we come for you in the morning." The Irishman's laughter bounced off the walls. "You'll be looking forward to the noose by then. Likely arguing over who gets to die first."

The prisoners stood in the water, staring upwards as Rook turned away and the trapdoor was dropped into place. Its timbers smashed like thunder against the cobbles, sealing them in.

*

A thick, choking blackness closed around the two men at the bottom of the shaft. Deprived of sight, Jones found himself disoriented, staggering in the darkness, turning this way and that, desperate for a hint of light. When Kowalski spoke it was a relief to have something to focus on.

"Least they let us climb down. Surprised Rook didn't just toss us in."

"And risk upsetting whatever his master has planned? Not likely. Rook's a nasty piece of work, but I do believe even he's more than a little afraid of Rackham."

"Well if he ain't, he's even crazier than I thought."

"Shall we explore our lodgings?" suggested Jones.

The two men shuffled outwards as far as their restraints would allow. From there they reached out, leaning forward until fingertips brushed against the slimy brickwork of their watery prison. They ran their hands over every inch of wall within reach, finding nothing of note but the rusting steps of the ladder – a tantalising offer of escape, denied to them by their iron tethers. A similar fumbling search of the uneven stone beneath the water yielded the same result, nothing to help their predicament. Straightening up, Jones made an unpleasant discovery.

"The water is rising. Either that or my legs have shrunk." He lifted his fingers to his lips then spat. "Salt water. This bloody hole is connected to the sea."

"Gets better and better, don't it?" Kowalski's tired voice came out of the dark. "High tide was around three, when we'd arranged to meet Brunel. Don't suppose this is as deep as its going to get?"

Jones shrugged and shook his head, before realising his companion could see neither gesture in the Stygian darkness. "I've lost track of time somewhat since our chums relieved me of my watch, but it's probably only ten o'clock or so." He gave a bitter laugh. "That watch was my father's. Doubt I'll be seeing it again anytime soon."

"We get out of here? I'll buy you a new one. One of Ramon's finest."

"I'll hold you to that. However, I think we may have some swimming to do before then..."

The water level crept inexorably higher as time ground past. They stood for as long as they could, up on tiptoes, necks craned back, until they were forced to bow to the inevitable. They slipped their boots from their feet and began to tread water.

At first the motion was almost relaxing, Jones able to ignore the drag of the chain. Deprived of light, with arms and legs stirring the warm water in slow, hypnotic circles, his mind wandered. Memories of his earliest trips out on the Solent filled his head – he and Michael, stuffed into bulky cork lifejackets in the stern of a dinghy, listening earnestly as their father told them what to do if they were stupid enough to fall over the side.

"Don't fight the current. Don't fight the sea. You can't win. Save your energy for shouting." He and Michael had stared wide-eyed at each other, then back to their father. "Don't try and make for the boat," he'd said. "You'll only tire yourself out. Let the boat come for you."

No boat coming for you here old chap, he thought, a grumbling ache beginning in his muscles. Just as no boat had come for Michael.

The pain slowly grew in intensity, pushing memories from his head, dominating his thoughts. He and Kowalski shared the occasional grunt of acknowledgement as tired limbs bumped against one another, but mostly they were silent, intent on the simple, immediate task of staying afloat.

A stabbing agony of cramp seized Jones' leg and he cried out, clutching at his thigh before slipping beneath the surface, the shackle and his sodden clothing dragging him down. He panicked, gulping a mouthful of brine before he felt hands pulling him upwards. He was turned, held up from behind as he coughed and retched. Kowalski's legs flailed beneath them, struggling to keep both men above the water.

Jones stretched his leg out straight, desperate to get the knotted tendons working again. Eventually the vice-like grip of the cramp loosened and he was able to move once more.

"Thanks," he croaked into the blackness.

"Don't mention it," came the weary reply. "Reckon you'll be returning the favour before too long."

Kowalski's prediction proved accurate as the hours stretched out in a dark haze of aches and cramps, each man forced to help as the other floundered. Jones' entire world narrowed into a single purpose, keeping his leaden limbs in motion and his face out of the water.

The first time his foot scraped on rock the significance passed him by – the blow just another addition to his variety of pains. But at the second occurrence, his exhausted brain figured it out. He stopped the rotation of his legs and straightened them, the muscles screaming in protest. His toes discovered the bottom of the shaft and he stood, head clear of the water.

Kowalski's groan of relief sounded a moment later, indicating he too had found solid ground beneath his feet.

"Thank Christ," breathed the Floridian.

"Amen to that," answered Jones.

They stood in the darkness, leaning against one another, all energy spent, silent as the water ebbed away. Eventually able to sit, they slumped down, tortured leg muscles finally ceasing their trembling. Sitting quietly in the dark, aching in every joint, Jones fell into a fitful slumber.

The next thing he knew he was jerked into wakefulness, strong hands grabbing at him and lifting him up. The pirates had come for him.

*

The rough hemp scraped over Jones' face as Rook pulled the noose down. The pirate waved a hand and the line went taut, biting into Jones' neck, hoisting him up onto his toes.

Rook shoved him round, checking the knots binding his hands and feet before spinning him back to face the crowd of cutthroats gathered in the square. The Irishman pushed his face into Jones'.

"Don't you be running off now matey."

He grabbed a hessian bag and lifted it towards Jones' head. Rackham stopped him. "No hood. I want to see his face."

Rook shrugged and moved off, crossing the platform to stand at Rackham's shoulder. The pirate leader addressed the men below.

"Brethren of the Coast!" shouted Rackham. "I have a question to place before the assembly. A question of justice." He pointed at Jones. "This here visitor to our fine shores claims to be a reporter. For the London Times, no less. Now I know you all to be erudite and well-read gentlemen..." A ripple of laughter. "So you may be of a mind to let the pen-pusher go?"

A stony silence followed this remark and Rackham turned with a look of mock concern. "It's not looking too good here mate," he said in a stage whisper, drawing more laughter from the crowd.

Jones would have loved to cast back some witty retort, but the effort of balancing on tiptoe was beginning to tell. He tried to ignore the ache in his calves, his muscles reminding him of their efforts in the pit during the night. If Rackham was going to hang him, then he might at least cut out the bloody speeches and get on with it.

"On the other hand," called the pirate, continuing the charade, "perhaps you fine fellows are of a private disposition and object to gentlemen of the press prying into your affairs?"

A chorus of agreement sounded out. "That's right Jack, I hate showing up in the society pages," cried one wag.

"My sentiments exactly. I'd prefer the great unwashed didn't hear about all the fancy parties we're attending." Rackham's voice rose. "In fact, I don't want the English getting even a sniff of us. Not until we've picked off every last one of those juicy supply ships. Then, when we're good and ready, we'll kick them out of the Caribbean for good."

Shouting now above the cheers of his men, Rackham continued, gesturing out towards the rusting dreadnought dominating the bay. "And we've got the ship to do it. What say you lads? Shall we use her to give those English bastards a front page or two worth reading?"

The gathered pirates roared their agreement and Rackham's eyes shone. He waited for the cheers to die down and then raised his hand.

"But before we get started on that enjoyable task, let's be dealing with this here piece of flotsam." He adopted a solemn expression and lowered his voice, forcing the assembled crowd to lean forward, intent on his every word. "By the powers vested in me, as appointed Captain of these here Brethren, I do hereby sentence this man to be hanged by the neck..." he made a theatrical pause and gave Jones a wink "...until dead."

Once again the cheers rang out and Rackham revelled in the noise and approval, nodding his appreciation as he crossed the platform. The pirate prodded Jones in the chest, pushing him off balance, forcing him to make little hops on his bound feet to maintain his balance. Muscles complaining as the crowd hooted with cruel laughter, Jones decided he'd had quite enough of being the straight-man in Jack Rackham's cabaret.

"Get on with it," he said.

Rackham's smile turned feral. "Say hello to your brother..."

He raised his hand towards Rook, but the order didn't come. Instead, the pirate leader was ducking for cover along with his men as an explosion rocked the square, the air suddenly filled with noise and a hail of splinters.

Ears ringing, Jones hopped round, straining to see the source of the blast. The smouldering remains of a trawler floated beside the quay, its upper deck twisted and blackened, flames licking up from its exposed innards. A lazy ball of smoke rolled into the air above the wreckage as dazed men picked themselves up along the length of the waterfront.

The boat's hull shifted, shunted upwards as something struck it from below – something massive. The onlookers backed away from the quay as the water boiled, a dark shape rising beneath the turbulence. The nervousness in the crowd turned to naked terror as the mechanical beast tore through the floating debris and burst to the surface.

The *Neptune* surged forward, smashing jetties and boats into matchwood. The submersible reared up, clambering from the water, scraping its bulk over the edge of the harbour. The six legs straightened out and the *Neptune* towered twenty feet over the pirates who had resisted the urge to run. A moment of silence filled the square before the remaining buccaneers, as one, drew their pistols and carbines and opened fire at the invading contraption.

Bullets struck the *Neptune*'s carapace and ricocheted off in all directions, unable to penetrate the thick metal plating. The rebounding projectiles flew around the square, causing more damage to the pirates themselves than they did to the submersible. The *Neptune* strode over the cobbles, futile gunfire striking it from all sides. From his raised vantage point on the gallows, Jones watched as men attempted to rush beneath the mechanical creature, seeking some weaker point, only to be kicked aside or crushed by the *Neptune*'s heavy feet. He had to admit, the pirates were brave. Crazy, but brave.

In the first few moments as the *Neptune* rampaged ashore, the party on the platform stood motionless, mouths agape, transfixed by the unfolding chaos. Rackham was the first to recover, shoving Culpepper towards the stairs, shouting at Rook to get him to safety. The pirate captain moved to the railing. He yelled instructions and gestured to his men, who were by now too busy avoiding the metal beast in their midst to pay any attention to their leader.

The *Neptune* stomped around the square, sparks flying where its feet struck stone. The deadly pincers swung this way and that, sending the quickest of the buccaneers diving for cover, and the slower, less lucky men, flying through the air.

A cannon roared and the *Neptune* staggered, struck in the side by the shot. Jones twisted to see a smoke rising from the barrel of the weapon, manhandled round from its original position covering the bay. The submersible trembled and emitted an ear-splitting shriek as steam erupted from its damaged hull. The gun crew gave a ragged cheer as their metallic foe slumped to the ground, one of its legs crumpled beneath it.

The *Neptune* lay like a wounded animal, limbs twitching, dented plates oozing a trail of thick black oil. The gun blasted out once again and the round smashed into the submersible's rear section – the armour plates buckling, great gouts of steam spewing out. The pirates around the square regrouped, closing in on the helpless craft, weapons raised.

At Rackham's instruction, one squad of men concentrated their fire on the observation dome. Here the bullets had more effect than against the riveted hull. Fractures spider-webbed across the glass and Jones waited for the whole viewport to cave inward. But despite the cracks, despite the relentless hail of fire, somehow the dome held.

The submersible's frame jerked, the heavy feet scraping across the ground. Pistons straining amidst groans of protesting metal, the *Neptune* heaved upright, crabbing from side to side as it compensated for the damaged leg. With a crunch of gears engaging, a pincer-tipped arm scythed down and across, toppling the squad of gunmen like ninepins, leaving them broken in the wake of its passage.

The cannon fired once more, but its crew had miscalculated, failing to account for their target's movement. The shot flew beneath the *Neptune*'s belly, bouncing headlong over the cobbles. The men around the gun scrabbled to reload as the submersible recovered its balance and rumbled into motion once more. It turned, its cylindrical rear smashing through the corner of the tavern wall, scattering brick and timber.

The mechanical beast ripped through a pile of cargo, smashing crates and barrels aside. The massive claws opened with a sinister hiss and reached out, clamping around a cart. With no more effort than a child might toss away an unwanted toy, the submersible flung the cart across the square. The improvised projectile flew true, crashing down on the gun emplacement, boards and axles cracking apart, separated wheels bouncing away over the stones. The cannon and the limp bodies of its crew lay broken and still beneath the wreckage.

With the pirates scattered and injured men littering the flagstones, the *Neptune* paused in its headlong rampage. It limped round in a full circle, seeking more adversaries. Finding none, the injured monster fixed its attention on the gallows where Rackham stood, transfixed by the carnage unleashed upon his men. As the submersible approached, the pirate shook free of his paralysis and made to flee. Turning from the scene he came face-to-face with Jones, still teetering on tiptoe. Rackham leaned in close, eyes filled with rage.

"This won't stop me," he spat. "And it won't save you."

He pulled the trapdoor lever. With a horrifying lurch, Jones dropped.

The fall was only inches, but it seemed to last forever before his descent was cruelly arrested by the noose. The drop wasn't so far as to break his neck, but the rude halt was more than enough to knock the breath from his lungs at the very moment the rope dug in, making the expelled air impossible to replace.

Dangling, bound hand and foot, Jones squirmed, the hemp at his throat a crushing iron trap. His chest heaved, muscles in spasm as he tried to breathe. He was vaguely aware of the *Neptune*'s bulk as it lumbered closer, but his vision contracted into a narrow tunnel and his ears filled with the frantic pounding of his pulse. He spun at the end of the rope, limp, his existence reduced to a slow, grey dizziness.

The last shreds of his consciousness slipped away. The world swung first one way and then the other and then he was weightless, falling, floating, down into darkness.

*

Kowalski stood in the knee-high water, staring up at the tantalising circle of daylight, trying to work out what the hell was going on up above.

The noise of the blast had echoed down the shaft, bringing him to his feet. His ears caught the unmistakeable crack of gunfire, mingled with crashes and thumps, and the cries of men.

He hollered up the shaft. "Hey!"

A head appeared over the rim of the hole. The pirate who had hauled Jones away earlier scowled down at him. "What?"

"You having a little trouble up there?"

"Shut your trap," came the reply.

Another booming impact rang out, this one causing a noticeable tremor through the stones. The guard disappeared from Kowalski's narrow field of vision. A gunshot sounded, followed by a loud mechanical crunch and the smash of metal on stone.

Without warning the shaft was full of tumbling bricks and lengths of splintered timber. Kowalski crouched for cover, hands over his head. A hail of gravel and rock spattered down into the water, chunks of masonry sending up huge splashes. The roar of the descending wreckage filled the air, echoing around the narrow space. A lump of brickwork smashed into Kowalski's shoulder and he hunkered down under the avalanche of debris and noise, convinced he was about to be buried alive.

When the thunderous downfall subsided, he gingerly unfolded himself, sloughing off his crust of fragmented stone. A thick cloud of dust clogged the air, and Kowalski coughed, peering at the pile of rubble and jumble of timbers. It seemed someone had picked up an entire street's worth of houses and dropped them down the hole. Looking up, he spotted a thick spar wedged across the width of the shaft directly above him. Lord bless that piece of wood, he thought. It had clearly acted as a shield, deflecting the largest lumps of tumbling stone.

And at least now he wasn't alone. There, inches above the water, sticking out from the chaos of bricks and broken beams, protruded a hand. Kowalski sloshed forward and tugged at the appendage. The arm flopped out from the debris, dislodging a tumble of gravel and revealing the face of his pirate guard, lifeless eyes staring out from the rubble.

Kowalski started to dig.

*

The throb of the engine worked its way into Jones' awareness, a rhythmic match for the pounding ache in his temples. The particular tone of the machinery noise seemed familiar. He cracked open an eye and took in the curvature of the riveted plates above him. The *Neptune* – somehow he was inside the *Neptune*. And somehow he was still alive.

He crawled to the bulkhead and pulled himself into a seated position, groaning as he lifted his head, his vision swimming with the effort. Stabilising himself against the wall, he raised a hand to the tender skin of his throat, grimacing as he swallowed.

"*Senor* Jones, whatever is that terrible smell?"

Isabella peered down from the compartment's doorway. Jones gave a weak smile and indicated his filthy clothing.

"That would be me," he croaked. "I'm afraid my overnight lodgings were not quite the Mirador."

Her eyes travelled over his bruised and battered frame. She crouched and leant in, planting a kiss on his cheek.

"When I saw you on the gallows, I was sure we were too late."

"I'm a little stretched. But I'll survive. Here, help me up..."

With Isabella's assistance, Jones clambered to his feet. He swayed and his vision blurred once more, but he steadied himself and stared down at the woman. "What are you doing here?"

She batted her eyelashes and adopted a doe-eyed look. "I convinced your Lord Brunel to take me on an excursion. Somehow he found it impossible to refuse." She grinned, the girlish expression vanishing. "I think he is rather fond of me..."

Isabella remained at his side, supporting him as they made their way forward through the companionway. The *Neptune* had been in the wars, that much was clear. Dirty water sloshed beneath the metal grilles and sharp bursts of spray erupted from cracked bulkheads, misting the air. The crew scurried around, lugging spanners or repair plates, grim purpose etched in their faces.

The control room itself was awash, the deck inches deep. The great round dome was cracked and starred, trails of liquid seeping down its curve. Brunel turned from the watery gloom beyond the fractured glass and nodded to his passengers.

"Good to see you up. I rather worried we had misjudged our timing."

"Tight timing or no, I appreciate the intervention." Jones gestured to the viewport. "Your vessel seems to have paid a high price for the effort."

"We had to scarper when that bloody warship opened up." The engineer grimaced. "I wouldn't trust us below twenty feet, but the pumps are coping for the moment."

"Good to hear. Now, forgive me, we have little time. How far to the *Great Eastern*? I have important information for London. We can't afford for Rackham to overtake us."

"All the stops are open, we're at full speed. Well, as fast as we can go in this state." The old man's frown gave way to a sly smile. "But I risked a deeper dive before our departure, improvising a little something to slow our friends down. Shame I used the charges back at your execution, otherwise I could have put that warship on the bottom of the bay."

Jones shook his head. "The dreadnought is the least of our concerns, if you can believe it. This affair has become more complicated than we thought. And much more serious to boot."

He looked around the bridge.

"I need to speak to Kowalski. Where is he?"

*

The streets around the square were in ruins, making Cayona look even more dilapidated, something Kowalski would have thought impossible. Buildings were missing walls and sections of roof, the displaced bricks and tiles scattered across the cobbles. Flames licked up amongst the damaged structures and everywhere there were wounded men. Some limped through the rubble, seeking their fellows, others sat with blood-soaked rags pressed to their wounds.

Kowalski overheard enough conversation to work out Brunel's submersible had made quite the nuisance of itself, tearing up buildings as it smashed its way through the streets. Wide-eyed accounts of the *Neptune*'s rampage were accompanied by dark glances cast towards the dreadnought out in the bay. It seemed her gunners' ill-advised attempts to drive off the mechanical monster had done nothing but add to the devastation. Poor Jack would have his hands full keeping the townsfolk happy after this little episode.

Liberating the padlock keys from the dead pirate had filled Kowalski with a burst of energy and enthusiasm. But hauling his leaden limbs up the ladder and out of the shaft had drained the reservoir. His legs and arms ached after his night of treading water and his face was scratched and bruised from the rubble shower he had endured.

Of Jones he could see no sign. He hoped this meant good news and the Englishman was still alive. He figured it would take more than a gang of disorganised thugs to cause that one any real problems.

Regardless of Jones' fate, Kowalski had to get out of Cayona. It was only a matter of time before somebody realised their prisoner was missing. The pirates of Tortuga had taken a bloody nose this morning – he didn't much fancy them taking out their frustration on him.

He pulled a piece of flapping curtain from the window of a wrecked house. He wrapped a strip around his forehead, tugging it down over one eye, practically covering half his face. He fashioned a sling from the remaining material and tucked his arm inside. He was was banking on the fake bandages and his dishevelled appearance to ensure he fitted in with the other men moving about, but all the same he kept his head down as he hobbled through the streets.

He limped along the waterfront, heading for the docks at the edge of town. His night of captivity had been deeply unpleasant, and that kind of treatment always brought out the worst in him. Before he sought a way off Tortuga he was of a mind to see if he couldn't add to Jack's woes.

*

Rackham watched as the squad of sailors gathered at the dreadnought's stern hauled in the line. The man clutching its end was hoisted up the ship's flank, spitting seawater onto the deck as he clambered over the side. He pulled goggles from his face, bare chest heaving as he recovered from the dive. Rackham drummed his fingers on the railing, waiting for the report.

"A length of anchor chain fouling the screw," panted the diver. "Explains why the *Gertrude*'s over there..." He gestured towards the cliffs.

The crewmen turned as one. Across the bay a steamer rubbed against the rocks with the ebb and flow of the waves, wearing more holes into her patched and rusted hull.

"How long?" demanded Rackham.

A shrug. "I don't know. Yards of the bloody stuff I suppose."

Rackham's temper surged. He lashed out, swiping the diver with a vicious backhand. "Idiot," he snapped. "How long to get it cleared?"

The diver rubbed at his jaw, eyes downcast. "We'll have to cut it. Two hours? Maybe three?"

Rackham's fists tightened. He turned on the *Revenge*'s chief engineer. "I want us moving in an hour. Understood?"

The engineer hesitated, caught between agreeing to the timing or making his Captain unhappy. Best make the consequences of failure clear, thought Rackham.

"Mister Rook!" he called.

The Irishman materialised at his shoulder. "Aye Cap'n?"

"Do everything you can to assist and ah, encourage, these gentlemen in their efforts to free the screw."

Rook tilted his head. A wicked grin crept across his ravaged features. The crewmen shared nervous looks.

"Why sir, it'll be my pleasure."

Evil little bastard, thought Rackham. He'll be hoping for a damned delay so he can enjoy making an example of someone. Rook's particular skills were often useful, but the man's predilection for cruelty could sometimes prove counterproductive. Best ensure this particular task was a genuine team effort.

"One hour Mister Rook," said Rackham. "Or it's your head too."

The ghastly smile faded. "Aye sir," muttered the Irishman.

Rackham turned away and headed forward. He flexed his knuckles, hand still tingling where it had struck the hapless diver. The sudden release of violence had felt good.

More of that might be in order if things didn't start going his way.

*

Kowalski approached the warehouse only to have his path blocked by the burly seaman standing watch. The sailor regarded him from beneath a heavy brow, taking in the filthy clothes and bandages.

"What do you want?" he grunted.

Kowalski jerked a thumb towards the town. "Jack wants every able-bodied man. He's mustering a crew to go after that steel lobster."

The man pondered this, then swung his head from side to side. "Got to stay here. Jack said so."

"And now he says otherwise. I'm taking your place." Kowalski indicated his bandaged arm. "I ain't no use to them with this..."

The sailor rubbed his unshaven chin with tattooed knuckles. "S'pose not," he said eventually.

He pulled a pistol from his belt and Kowalski's stomach lurched, but the weapon was turned and offered grip-first to him. "Here. You've to shoot any feller who tries to talk his way past."

"Will do," nodded Kowalski gravely.

The sailor padded off towards the town.

Thank the Lord for the less-than-bright, thought Kowalski. How would the rest of us get by without them? He slipped through the narrow gap in the doors and into the warehouse.

He pulled the fake bandages off and threw them aside as he made his way between the stacks of crates. The illicit cargo was still where it had been the previous evening, piled up at the warehouse's centre. Kowalski eyed the fat hessian sacks with distaste. Some of his fellow mercenaries swore by the stuff – the airmen in particular. But he'd never seen the attraction. Black coffee and strong tobacco worked fine for him, he'd never felt the need to resort to the Bolivian Marching Powder.

Atop a barrel alongside the sacks was the equipment from his and Jones' packs. Kowalski rummaged through the climbing gear and rations before his hand closed around the hard metallic sphere of one of Ramon Cuervo's explosive charges. Perfect.

With the sharp point of a climbing piton he sawed at the sackcloth of one of the lower bags. When the hole was big enough, he turned the dial on the clockwork timer and set the orb quietly ticking. He shoved the charge into the bag, pushing it as far as he could into the chalky beige paste. Regardless of what else happened, this particular batch of Bolivia's finest wouldn't be making Culpepper a single cent.

Kowalski stepped out of the warehouse's gloom, emerging blinking into the light. The sun bounced from the waters of the bay, forcing him to squint as he ran his eyes over the boats moored along the harbour.

Whilst the warehouse guard clearly hadn't been the sharpest tool in the box, even he'd eventually work out he'd been duped. Wouldn't be long before the man came lumbering back along the waterfront, buddies in tow. Kowalski needed to be well on his way before then.

His eye fixed on the sleek lines of Culpepper's launch, tied up on the wharf. Her two crewmen stood idly, smoking cigarettes and leaning on the stern rail. Kowalski tucked the pistol into the back of his belt and made his way down the wooden jetty towards the launch. If he was going to borrow a boat, he might as well leave town in style.

The flat crump of an explosion rolled out from the building behind him and the sailors' heads whipped round seeking the source of the noise. Their eyes flitted between the man on the jetty and the trails of smoke curling out of the warehouse door. Neither man seemed overly alarmed, likely inured to such blasts following the excitement of the morning's events. The sailors appeared unarmed too, which was a relief. Less likely there would be any foolish heroics.

Kowalski pasted a broad smile onto his face.

"How you doing boys? Any chance of a smoke?"

*

Rackham made his way up the ladders towards the *Revenge*'s bridge, anger pounding behind his eyes with every step. He had rushed out to his ship, determined to pursue the mechanical menace out to sea, only to be baulked when the dreadnought refused to move. The enforced delay added to the rage bubbling in his veins, but denied the release of action and pursuit, he was forced to think. Even if the *Revenge* was temporarily incapacitated, he refused to sit idly by whilst his tormentors got clean away. He kicked open the bridge door and snapped instructions to the sailor sitting before the wireless.

"Get the airship aloft. That thing that attacked us must have come from a ship. A nearby one. I want it found."

The crewman lifted the flared trumpet of the mouthpiece and began to speak, relaying the orders to shore.

Rackham stood, fists clenched, surveying his fleet. It rankled sending a damned balloon out, but needs must. On principle, he harboured a deep resentment towards flying machines and their pilots, holding them responsible for the gradual shift of trade from the ocean into the air. He could smell the end of piracy in the change.

But for the moment, the clumsy dirigible offered a better chance of finding his enemy than all the vessels at his disposal.

All those ships. All those guns. More firepower than even Teach or Morgan could have dreamed of, and yet that bloody machine had waltzed in and out of the bay with barely a scratch. The only shots the *Revenge* had fired had missed the submersible completely, doing nothing but more damage to his town.

The whole thing had been a shambles. Made him look like a fool, unable to hang onto a couple of prisoners. There would be questions amongst the Brethren – whispered at first, but they'd grow louder if the attackers weren't caught, and quickly. Frustration banged around inside his skull once again.

"Not your finest hour," said Culpepper's voice behind him. "Your incompetence has risked exposing our activities."

Rackham whirled on the American, pushing close, his face inches from the other man's. "Don't try to blame this on me," he snarled.

Culpepper's podgy countenance darkened, but Rackham ploughed on, unwilling to let the pompous American speak. "You told me he was a journalist," he roared. "You think a bloody newspaperman has access to machinery like that?" The Commodore reared back from the tirade and Rackham pressed forward, pointed finger raised in the other man's face. "And you, you damned fool. Couldn't keep your fat mouth shut. Had to go blabbing off about your ridiculous scheme."

The American's nostrils flared and he found his voice. "The only thing ridiculous here is you and your ragtag bunch of cut-throats."

Cut-throats is it? Rackham's mind filled with the image of Culpepper's blood spewing from a ragged slit in his fleshy neck, down over the ever-so-smart uniform. God but that would be a satisfying sight.

A costly one though. The Commodore was still worth more to him alive than he was dead, despite any short-term satisfaction gutting him might provide. Rackham hauled his temper into check, packing it away for future use. He fixed the American with a flinty gaze.

"And yet this ragtag bunch are all that stands between you and a noose. Assuming, that is, you want us to go and catch the bastards for you, rather than doing it for yourself?"

Culpepper stared at him, face flushed with anger but unable to deny the point. "Distasteful as it may be," he said eventually, "it appears I still have need of your services."

Damn right you do, you arrogant arsehole, thought Rackham.

The American turned from their exchange and waved a sailor over, his casual command of the pirate crew, without so much as a by-your-leave, set Rackham's blood pounding once more.

"Call my launch. Have them come alongside." Culpepper returned his attention to Rackham. "I will be in Havana. Inform me when the situation is resolved." The eyes in the fat face narrowed. "Don't let me down."

Rackham stared out at the wreckage of his town, the broken buildings and curls of smoke stinging at his pride.

"I'm not doing it for you," he said.

*

Windward Passage

The excursion pool became a cauldron of churning water as the dark shape of the *Neptune* rose through the gap in the hull. The submersible blew the last of her ballast and broke the surface, water streaming from her riveted plating. Turner looked down from the gantry, taking in the bent metalwork and the starburst cracks across the glass. Brunel's pride and joy appeared to have taken something of a beating.

The submersible's hatch cracked open and Jones' head emerged.

"Thank God you're back," Turner called. "We feared the worst."

The army man gave him a tired nod in return, reaching down to offer a hand to the De La Vega woman. Turner frowned, reminded of the argument before the *Neptune's* departure. Dead-set against letting a female passenger aboard the submersible, Turner had been unable to reason with Brunel. The woman from Havana appeared to have the old man twisted around her little finger.

With a hiss of hydraulic pressure the engineer himself rose from the craft's innards. "The worst very nearly occurred," said Brunel. "The Major here was late for his rendezvous. We found him just in time."

"Where is Captain Kowalski?" asked Turner, becoming aware of the downcast faces opposite.

Jones raised weary eyes. "He won't be joining us. We left him behind." The voice was dejected, edged with bitterness.

Brunel stared up from his chair. "Not through choice, Major. How many more times do I need to repeat myself? We practically tore the town apart looking for him."

Jones straightened his shoulders, mastering himself. When he spoke, his voice held a note of contrition. "My apologies. You couldn't have done any more. Not once Rackham began to bombard his own town."

Mollified, Brunel nodded and reached for the control stick on his wheelchair. Turner watched the engineer lead the party over the gangplank, amazed as ever at the old man's stamina. Despite the extended stay at the controls of the submersible, the engineer appeared his usual spritely, cantankerous, brilliant self. He seemed in considerably better shape, in fact, than the man trailing behind.

Jones looked exhausted, and from the sounds of it, had enjoyed the dubious hospitality of the Tortugan pirates. Turner itched to hear the tale, but more pressing matters awaited.

"Excuse me. I must return to the bridge and get a message to the *Iris*. Commander Warburton has been insisting we head to a friendly harbour and report you as missing."

Brunel's mechanised chair headed for the pressure door. "I believe we could all do with some fresh air. Much as I love the old *Neptune*, it is rather like being packed inside a tin can."

They trooped through the engine room to the elevator. Turner pushed the selector lever to the topmost position. The conveyance gave a shudder and started upward.

"Warburton will be relieved. He's become rather frustrated – both with the lack of news, and our inability to discuss matters properly."

Brunel looked up, a quizzical frown in place.

"It's been like the old days," explained Turner. "Reduced to sending messages by shutter lantern. Bloody wireless is playing up. Can't get through to anyone."

*

With a jerk the elevator came to a halt and the doors slid open, the passengers emerging into the wheelhouse. Sunlight flooded in, sparkling off the gentle waves. Bloody weather, thought Jones. Better a storm. Or fog, or mist – anything to help them slip away. On a glorious afternoon like this, the bulk of the *Great Eastern* would be visible for miles.

The deck officer stepped forward and snapped off a salute. "Welcome back Your Lordship."

"Thank you Mister Jenson," answered Brunel. "Now get on the lantern and tell our Navy chums we're back –"

"And tell them we need to get moving. Now."

All heads turned in Jones' direction.

"There's nothing wrong with your wireless," he said. "This is Rackham's doing." He went on, ignoring Turner's incredulous look. "There's a dreadnought on its way Captain. We need to get out of here as fast as we bloody well can –"

The conversation came to an abrupt halt as the unmistakeable sound of an explosion rattled the bridge windows. Heads snapped round to see a huge plume of spray raining back down onto the sea's surface a hundred yards in front of their Royal Navy escort.

"What on earth?" blurted Jenson.

"Range-finding shot," said Jones. They had already run out of time.

As he spoke, another fountain of water erupted, closer to the *Iris* this time, followed a moment later by the noise of the blast. Jones winced. Their escort's guns couldn't match the range of those on Rackham's warship. When the pirate gunners got their eye in, the cruiser would be pounded into the sea before she could return a single shot.

"There's your dreadnought..." said Turner, pointing south and handing over a spyglass. "By the size of her bow wave, she's making twenty knots."

"Faster than us I presume?" asked Jones, raising the telescope.

"We'll do fourteen. Maybe fifteen at a pinch. With our paddles we're much more manoeuvrable, despite the difference in size, but a screw-driven warship will have this old girl for speed every time."

Jones watched through the lens as a bright muzzle flash erupted from the dreadnought. Long seconds later the shell struck home, the shot finding its mark this time. Black smoke burst from the cruiser and, moments later, the mournful sound of an alarm klaxon echoed across the stretch of water between the ships.

All activity on the bridge came to a halt, the crewmen frozen, appalled at the scene. The men of the *Great Eastern* had clearly spent their war years very far from the bloodstained waters of the North Sea. A second impact rocked the *Iris*, and then a third. More smoke darkened the air, and the orange glint of flames could be seen.

It was Isabella who broke the silence. "We must do something..."

The woman's voice seemed to break the spell transfixing Turner. He tore himself from the window and bellowed into a tube, his voice echoing out from speakers throughout the vessel. "All hands! All hands! Launch the starboard boats."

As the crew burst into activity, preparing to mount their rescue effort, Jones regarded the stricken ship across the water. She had already adopted a noticeable list, her deck leaning away from them, the rust-streaked plating of her lower hull lifting into view.

"Captain, our time is short..."

Turner spun, his face like thunder. "If you're propoding we abandon those sailors, you're not the man I thought you were Major."

"You misunderstand. I'd never suggest such a thing. But we need to think about our own vessel."

Brunel bristled. "This ship can take a lot more punishment than our unfortunate escort."

"I don't believe sinking us is in Rackham's plan. He hasn't taken a potshot at us yet which rather suggests he's seeking a new addition for his fleet. Rackham is a showman – he won't be able to resist a temptation like the *Great Eastern*."

"This ship? In the hands of pirates? Over my dead body."

Jones stared down at the old man in the wheelchair. "Your Lordship, I fear that's exactly what Calico Jack has in mind."

"What do you suggest?"

Jones regarded the speck on the southern horizon and then turned his attention to the more immediate scene as the *Great Eastern*'s boats headed for the stricken cruiser. The *Iris* was now keeled over almost ninety degrees, the remaining crew leaping into the water and swimming for the approaching lifeboats. It would be a matter of minutes before the water found the hungry openings of her twin funnels. From there it would be sucked down into her belly, condemning her to the deep.

"We can't outrun the dreadnought, but we might at least draw her away from the boats." He gestured to the rescue flotilla. "We'll never get them back aboard in time, and I dread to think what Rackham will do to them. I doubt he's in the mood to take on passengers."

Turner contemplated the view and nodded. "Go on..." he said.

"If he wants the *Great Eastern*, let's at least make him work for it."

Brunel turned his wheelchair away from the windows. "I'd sooner see this vessel on the bottom than part of a pirate fleet."

"I'll see it done," said Turner, steel in his voice.

Jones regarded the sailor. "No you won't Captain. I commandeered your vessel. No need for you to go down with it." He held up a hand to silence Turner's protestations. "I'll be leading Rackham on this merry chase. Get your crew into the remaining boats." Turner's frown deepened but Jones continued. "I admire your sense of duty. But the Admiralty placed you at my disposal, and I've just given you an order."

Brunel's chair trundled forward between the two men. The engineer stared up at the *Great Eastern's* master. "By playing the Admiralty card, I do believe the Major is holding trumps. It's time to look to your crew's safety. The ship belongs to Major Jones now."

Turner gave a reluctant nod. "Very well," he said. "Mister Jenson, signal the men to abandon ship. All hands to the boats."

Emergency klaxons began to sound throughout the vessel, and the crewmen in the wheelhouse made for the companionway. Turner and Brunel conferred briefly before the old man spoke to Isabella.

"My dear, I would be happier if you would accompany myself and Captain Turner in the *Neptune*. It may be bashed and bruised, but it will still provide a more comfortable ride than an open rowboat."

Isabella ignored Brunel, stepping close to Jones, scowling up at him.

"For this you throw your life away? You men are all the same. Always looking for a cause worth dying for..."

Once again Jones found himself at a loss for words to respond. Looking down into Isabella's black gaze he knew he could never make her understand. He made do with a shrug.

The gesture infuriated the Cuban woman. She swung her hand, catching Jones across the cheek with a sharp slap that echoed around the wheelhouse. His face stung from the contact and he couldn't help but flinch as the arm was raised again. But this time Isabella's hand anchored around his neck and pulled his face down, her lips locking onto his own.

Before he realised what was happening the woman broke away, heading for the door. At the threshold she turned, dark eyes blazing.

"Perhaps *senor*, there are some causes worth living for, no?"

With that, she left.

Jones felt the colour rise in his face. The flush of embarrassment would at least mask the tingling redness from where she had slapped him. Speechless he looked to the remaining occupants of the wheelhouse. Turner stood open-mouthed in astonishment, whilst Brunel chuckled at Jones' discomfort.

"I suggest you make it out of this adventure alive Major," he said. "Because Miss De La Vega will surely kill you if you don't."

*

"Gunners say she's in range Cap'n," shouted the young sailor standing by the rank of speaking tubes.

Rackham frowned. "She's been in range for some time now Billy. Inform the gunners that when I require their advice, I will ask for it."

The sailor blanched at Rackham's tone, flicking up a cover and muttering into the opening. Rackham shook his head and turned to Rook.

"All those idiots want to do is fire their bloody guns."

The Irishman looked up from his chair. "Shouldn't give them such big toys to play with. What do you expect?"

"I expect them to do as they're told."

Rook scratched at the plating on his head, picking flakes of rust from the metal and dropping them onto the deck. "The boys don't understand what you want with that ship. Can't say I blame them overmuch. Not rightly sure I understands it myself."

Rackham bent and spoke into the man's ear, his voice low and hard.

"You don't need to understand Rooky-boy. You're just like the others. All you need to do is what you're told." He placed a hand on the Irishman's shoulder, stopping him from rising. "Easy now. No need to get uppity. Always remember, these men won't follow you. They hate you a lot more than they hate me."

And I've been very careful to keep it that way, thought Rackham as Rook glowered up at him. Using the Irishman as an instrument of discipline meant the Brethren universally loathed his lieutenant. Much more so than the Captain who ordered the punishments in the first place.

A strong second-in-command was necessary – but no point letting them get too popular, or developing ideas above their station.

"You're a good lad Rook. You've a talent for dirty work. But don't ever be thinking it makes you Captain material."

Rook stared at him, the living portion of his face twisted in sullen anger. After a moment, he muttered an "Aye sir," and looked away, acknowledging his place in the proper order of things.

"Good boy," said Rackham. He rapped his fist on the man's iron skull. "Now make yourself useful. Go and kill some Englishmen for me..."

Whoever remained on the *Great Eastern* must have thought Rackham was stupid – banking on him being so intent on chasing after his prey he would ignore the lifeboats she had left in her wake. They would enjoy no such luck.

Rackham made his way out onto the wing of the bridge. Down on the main deck his sailors were untying the ropes securing the squat shape of the gunboat. Shallow of draught and mighty fast, the gunboat had proven herself on many a smuggling expedition. Now she was hoisted aloft by lines at her stern and bow, the derricks swinging round, taking her out over the side rail. The crew clambered aboard and the winch turned, lowering her until the keel hung scant feet from the water thundering down the dreadnought's flank.

Rook arrived on the deck below. He clambered onto the rail, balancing for a moment before launching himself outwards. He flew out and down, arresting his fall on the rope supporting the gunboat's stern. Hanging there, the Irishman looked up to the bridge, sunlight glistening off his metallic plating. He waved a hand in a salute and Rackham nodded in return. Rook wrapped a leg around the line and slid down in a controlled descent, hopping away from the rope and onto the deck.

With Rackham's lieutenant aboard, the cables were released and the gunboat splashed down into the waves. The prow dug in to the surging spray and for a moment she seemed sure to founder, but her screw bit at the water and she levelled her trim. The small vessel turned away to port.

Rackham eyed the defenceless flotilla in the distance – the lifeboats clustered around the cruiser's upturned hull. Another load of English sailors to feed the sharks.

He returned his attention to the *Great Eastern*. Bursts of spray shot up on either side where the ship's massive paddles thrashed at the water. By God but they were driving her hard. Whoever stood at the helm of the enormous merchant ship was pushing her to her limits. And for nothing. The continued flight was futile – the *Revenge* visibly closed the gap with every passing moment.

The thrill of the chase gripped him again, his blood afire as it had been when the airship's captain had first radioed him with news of the massive ship lying offshore. He gripped the rail and gave a fierce smile.

Not long now, and she would be his – the prize jewel in England's maritime crown, very nearly in his grasp.

*

Alarm bells clamoured for attention and warning lamps winked urgently above the gauges, every needle quivering in the red. Jones couldn't have said what information the dials were designed to impart in the first place, so he did the only thing he could and ignored them all.

The telegraph levers for each paddle wheel were pushed forward to the stops and the *Great Eastern* thundered across the water, requiring a tight grasp on the helm to keep her heading fixed. Exactly what her heading was remained a mystery. The compass needle spun crazily in its housing, useless within the magnetic disturbance created by Rackham's ship. All Jones was sure of was every passing second drew them further away from the helpless lifeboats and the *Iris*.

The deck shook beneath Jones' feet as the engines pounded away – boiler pressures and paddle speeds no doubt far in excess of what Brunel had envisaged. Thus far the vessel was holding together, despite the shaking, a testament to the engineer's skill.

Jones looked aft through the rear windows. There, barely a quarter mile behind, closing on the starboard quarter, was the sinister shape of the dreadnought, black clouds belching from her trio of smokestacks. The warship cut through the water, her fearsome speed putting the lie to her decrepit appearance as she closed in on her quarry.

Time was running out. The dreadnought would catch the *Great Eastern* in minutes. Jones knew he could do no more. The ship was lost – what remained was to decide the manner of the grand vessel's passing.

*

Jenson stood in the stern of the lifeboat, supervising as the last of the survivors was hauled spluttering from the water.

The white hulls of the open boats floated low, laden with men rescued from the cruiser. The *Iris* herself had slipped beneath the surface moments before, a patch of oily water dotted with bobbing debris the only remaining evidence of her existence.

The sound of an engine brought his head up and he spotted a squat vessel closing on the pack of milling lifeboats. The new arrival coasted to a halt, bobbing in the swell fifty yards from the nearest craft. A figure stood in her bows behind a formidable-looking machine gun, his misshapen face cracking into an awful smile as he reached for the crank handle.

Bullets flew from the revolving muzzle in a terrible mechanised fusillade. Jenson gawped as fountains of water sprang up, marching over the surface, the procession of splashes dragging his gaze along with its progress. The hail of lead reached one of the boats and the impacts tossed chunks of wood and men into the air. The helpless crewmen packed into the lifeboat jerked in a gruesome dance, tugged this way and that as the bullets flew in.

Only a handful of the sailors survived this first barrage unscathed, leaping into the water on the opposite side – the possibility of drowning or sharks proving less immediate than the threat of the gunman.

The harsh chatter of the gun fell silent and cries and moans from the men on the decimated boat drifted over the water, carried on a breeze stinking of cordite and blood. It took Jenson a moment to comprehend the next sound he registered, so alien was it to the scene. Shrill laughter was ringing out from the man in the gunboat's bow.

Recovering from their shock, the sailors in the lifeboats scrabbled for their oars, desperate to put distance between themselves and the madman. But the flotilla was packed too tight, and the men were too disorganised. The swinging oars clattered against one another or made only ineffective swipes at the water.

Jenson's boat had moved no more than half a dozen yards before the fearsome machine gun was hauled round in their direction.

*

The *Revenge* ploughed through the water, her course parallel with the larger vessel. They had caught up with the *Great Eastern* easily and now Rackham chafed, irritated by the stubbornness exhibited in his quarry's continued flight.

"Billy," he called. "Tell the boys to shove a couple of rounds past her wheelhouse. Past it mind – not through it. I'll have their hides if they so much as scratch her."

The sailor relayed the instructions through the speaking tube and Rackham stepped out of the wheelhouse. He looked down to the main deck, watching the heavy turrets grind round, the long guns rising to the required elevation.

The muzzle flashes were brighter than the sun, leaving after images behind his eyelids when he blinked. His ears rang as the wave of noise rolled out, rattling the windows behind him. The shells moved too fast for the eye to follow, but the shriek as they tore through the air gave an indication of their course.

A second after the guns sounded, two mountainous splashes erupted in the water beyond the merchant ship. The crew lined up along the dreadnought's rail gave a ragged cheer.

The huge vessel steamed on, paddles working as hard as ever. Rackham's irritation bubbled up into naked anger, becoming a physical thing trapped inside his head, seeking release. Seems they'd have to put some scratches in his quarry after all – maybe some holes too.

He waved down to the sailors manning the variety of weapons mounted on the port rails.

"Right lads," he yelled over the wind. "I've had enough. Put in the windows on her bridge. Everything but the big guns."

The crew turned to their weapons, eager to have their fun. At the bark of "Fire!" fuses were lit, crank handles turned, and triggers were pulled along the length of the ship's rail.

Rackham thrilled to the sound of a hundred carbines and swivel cannon unleashing hell against the enormous craft that had the temerity to defy his will.

*

The distant rumble of gunfire startled Jenson, breaking his rapt fascination with the gaping muzzle pointing his way.

"Get over the side!" he shouted, pushing at the nearest men.

A futile gesture, but he was damned if he'd simply stand there and let them all be shot. He looked back across the water, a sick knot forming in his stomach as the gunner fixed him with his uneven stare.

Suddenly, the sea beneath the gunboat boiled upwards, and she lurched, tipping over at a sharp angle, pirates tumbling over the rails and into the turbulent waters below. In a fountain of spray, the *Neptune* surged to the surface, smashing the gunboat aside, staving in its keel.

The submersible reared over the floundering vessel, mechanical arms raised, pincer claws spread wide. The arms hung there for an awful moment before plummeting down, flattening the wheelhouse. The remaining crew fell from the buckled deck — all bar the figure who managed to stay balanced in the bow, hanging on to the gun mounting.

As the boat pitched and tossed, the pirate hauled his weapon round towards the submersible. The barrels spun, the gun's report accompanied by high-pitched ricochets as bullets bounced from the *Neptune*'s plating. A metal limb swept up from the water once more, pistons extending. It snapped out with terrible speed, grasping both man and machine gun in the claw's steel grip.

Clamped around the chest, mashed together with the wreckage of the gun, the pirate howled as he was lifted into the air, his unnatural features stretched into a hideous scream. Higher and higher rose the arm, accompanied by the rising pitch of the trapped man's screeching.

Finally, at the apex of the submersible's reach, fifteen feet above the water, the blades of the claw snicked horribly together. Separated sections of man and machinery tumbled into the sea.

Stumbling to the lifeboat's stern, flooded with a mixture of horror and relief, Jenson dropped to his knees and threw up over the side.

*

The roar of the small arms broadside from the dreadnought carried to Jones even over the thunderous vibration caused by the *Great Eastern's* exertions. A few scattered impacts cracked the panes of the starboard windows and then, in an avalanche of noise and glass and splinters, the gunners on the ship opposite found their mark.

Jones threw himself to the deck. He scrabbled into the shelter of a control console as the windows exploded inward, showering him with glass. He hunkered down out of the storm, the air filled with the angry buzz of bullets, as if a swarm of wasps had been released into the wheelhouse.

Rounds smacked into the banks of dials, shattering gauges and clipping pipework. Sharp squeals of steam added to the bedlam, jets of billowing vapour clouding the air. Jones smelled smoke and spotted the hungry orange flicker of flame bloom to the rear of the compartment. A spark must have found the stacks of charts.

Something a hell of a lot bigger than a bullet blasted through the wooden panelling inches from his head, sending shrapnel whistling past. A hot streak of pain lanced down his cheek. He touched trembling fingers to his face. The tips came away crimson. Too close, too bloody close by half.

The incoming barrage seemed to fade in intensity, or perhaps Jones had simply got used to it. Either way, he had to see what was going on. He crawled across the deck, trying to avoid the worst shards of metal and glass with limited success. He raised himself to his knees by the helm, making the most of the insubstantial cover offered by the brass column and the wheel. His raised line of sight revealed the view through the shattered windows.

The dreadnought was closing the gap, the stretch of water between the two vessels down to a hundred yards. Keeping as low as he could, Jones lifted Turner's eyeglass and pulled it open, raising it to bring the pirate ship into sharp focus.

Rackham's vessel swarmed with sailors, although most appeared to have abandoned their guns, explaining the reduced amount of lead flying in Jones' direction. Instead the men opposite were now engaged in preparing coils of rope, vicious-looking hooks dangling from the lines.

They were getting ready to board the *Great Eastern*, that much was clear. The dreadnought would pull alongside, matching speed with the merchant ship, and the grappling hooks would fly. Of course, Jones could veer away, putting off the inevitable, perhaps even sending some pirates tumbling into the waves, but Rackham had men to spare, and wouldn't give a fig how many of them died. He'd bring the dreadnought in again, keeping at it until the boarders finally made it aboard.

Or more likely, he'd lose patience and settle for putting a couple of rounds from the big guns into the wheelhouse, ending the chase for good.

Jones snapped the telescope shut and ran his gaze around the ruined bridge as isolated bursts of gunfire continued to whistle overhead. The bulkhead walls were riddled with holes, the glass panes from the windows now redistributed in razor fragments over every surface. Steam jetted from a hundred burst pipes, mixing with the acrid smoke billowing up from the fire amongst the charts. The flames had taken proper hold now, licking up the wooden panelling of the rear wall.

Who was he kidding? The chase was at an end already. He hauled himself to his feet, ignoring the ricochets. He stared across at the dreadnought, a thin smile forming on his lips.

"Plenty of guns on that ship of yours Jack," he said to himself, gripping the helm with one hand and reaching out for the telegraph levers with the other. "But how's her turning circle?"

Bracing himself, he spun the wheel to the right and threw the starboard paddle control to 'Full Astern'.

*

A brutal crunch of machinery rang out from the *Great Eastern*'s innards. The mechanical clamour echoed across the water, causing the pirate crew to turn as one from their boarding preparations. The vast ship groaned and visibly shuddered, her deck pitching to starboard as the near side paddle abruptly changed direction.

Water blasted upward where the wheel gouged at the sea. From his elevated position on the bridge, Rackham saw first one, then another of the blades wrench free from their mountings and skip away across the surface before sinking. The great ship pitched further, heeled over hard as the paddle bit in. Machinery and material slid down her inclined planking, smashing into the starboard rail, barrels and crates bouncing up and over, tumbling into the waves.

Howling in metallic protest, the seven hundred feet of the *Great Eastern* surged round – impossibly fast, impossibly huge. Rackham stood open-mouthed, frozen in place as the bows of the merchant ship swung into the path of the dreadnought.

Awful comprehension of the sudden danger blossomed in Rackham's mind. He threw himself at the wheelhouse door, bursting in and screaming at the transfixed helmsman.

"Hard-a-starboard!"

The sailor snapped from his trance, spinning the wheel, trying to turn the *Revenge*. The wall of steel was now perpendicular across their course and only fifty yards ahead. The dreadnought's bow began to move, but too slowly, too late. The *Revenge* thundered on, straight for the riveted plates of the vessel blocking their way.

Rackham gripped the rail beneath the windows, staring forward, unable to look away. A helpless rage burned within him as the gap between the ships disappeared.

*

The force of the impact threw Jones from the helm and across the wheelhouse. He smacked down hard on the deck, sliding sideways before coming to an abrupt and painful halt against the bulkhead. Something cracked in his side and he released a roar of agony.

In tears of pain he rolled over and gingerly pressed a hand to his torso. At least one rib, he thought, sucking in shallow breaths through gritted teeth. Bloody sore, but it won't kill you. Stop whining. Worry about it later. He pulled himself up, shuffling forward to see how much of a mess he'd made. The carnage that presented itself was well worth a broken bone or two – he had never seen anything like it.

A quarter of the way down the *Great Eastern*'s starboard side, beyond the still-churning paddle, the ship was rent by a massive fracture – the plates of the hull buckled and torn, the deck planking splintered upwards and out. From up on the bridge, Jones could see down into the gaping wound. There, plunged into the heart of the great vessel like an axe head, was the foremost twenty feet of the dreadnought.

Although rusted and patched, the warship's armour plating had sliced through the thinner hull of the merchant vessel like a hot knife through butter. Now the two ships ground against one another, the dreadnought's screw continuing to flail at the water, driving her deeper into the side of her quarry, whilst the *Great Eastern*'s thrashing paddles impaled her sideways on the sharp prow.

The tall smokestack nearest the impact point leaned drunkenly and toppled, adding to the cacophony of screeching metalwork. The entire vessel shuddered and the fracture widened, a new section of planking splintering up as the dreadnought lurched, penetrating further.

Jones became aware of a figure on the warship's bridge, gesticulating wildly at a crew only just picking themselves up from where the collision had tossed them. Jones smiled through the pain from his ribs. Not quite what you'd planned, eh Jack?

Someone on the dreadnought finally thought to throw her engines into reverse, attempting to withdraw her bow. The noise of tortured metal from the fracture grew in intensity as the warship tried to pull free, but the tangle of steel held fast.

Jones reached for a lever on the panel before him – the only control beyond steering and throttle he had asked Turner to explain. He threw the lever and felt a low tremor grumble its way up from below.

Deep in the bowels of the ship, vents had opened, releasing the air in the pressurised compartments, allowing the ocean to flood in through the excursion pool. The *Great Eastern* was going to the bottom, and she would be taking Rackham's pride and joy with her.

The fire crackled up, smoke finally overcoming steam in the two-way contest to fill the wheelhouse. Struggling to breathe, Jones lurched out onto the wing, his injured ribs complaining as he coughed the vapours from his lungs. He wheezed his way down the ladder towards the main deck, clutching the rail with one hand and his aching side with the other.

He turned toward the stern and the welcome sight of the ship's final lifeboat. He limped aft, up the noticeable incline of the planks, reaching the lifeboat's davits and grasping hold of the rope ladder. Before taking on the climb, he paused to look back along the side of the ship.

The *Great Eastern* had taken on a sharp slant, down at the bow as water poured into her interior. This in turn had dragged the front section of the dreadnought downwards, hoisting the screw at her stern clear of the water. The brass blades of the warship's propeller now churned air rather than the ocean, powerless to drag the trapped vessel free.

Jones watched as the dreadnought's crew began lowering boats over the side, abandoning any attempts to save their ship, concentrating instead on saving their own skins. The figure on the bridge opposite bellowed at his men – Jones heard him from across the water, the exact words unclear, but the tone in which they were delivered all too plain.

The King of the Pirates was less than impressed with the misfortune dealt his beloved vessel. Rackham's helpless rage confirmed Jones' suspicion – without the warship, the pirate was nothing. The task he'd been handed by Buckingham was complete.

He contemplated the waiting lifeboat, but then his gaze drifted back to Rackham. Black emotion rose, clouding out thoughts of escape. The job might be done, but his brother was still dead. And that bastard over there was still alive.

He turned from the lifeboat and staggered forward, heading for where the two ships ground against one another, locked together in a deadly embrace.

*

Billy shouted across the wheelhouse, the words lost amidst the noise of the dreadnought's suffering.

Rackham lifted his head. "What?"

"Time to go Cap'n." The sailor gestured towards the door. "We've stripped all the guns we can, but she's going down."

Rackham's temper surged up inside him. He hurled the glass from his hand. The improvised missile flew across the compartment and smashed against the bulkhead.

"Think I need you to tell me she's sinking?" he roared. "Get out of here. Wait for me at the boat."

Rackham raised the rum bottle and took a swig, sucking air over his teeth as the raw spirit burned its way down his throat. Billy continued to hover in the doorway, shifting from one foot to the other, casting nervous glances through the forward windows. Rackham hauled out his pistol and brandished it at the sailor.

"Get going," he snarled. "Afore I put a bullet in you..."

Billy fled. Rackham gave a snort of disgust and tossed the pistol over his shoulder. He pulled himself up from the chair, stumbling as he compensated for the angle of the deck. He stared out through the windows, down the length of the dreadnought to her bow, now scant feet above the roiling water.

The forward portion of the *Great Eastern* too was nearly submerged, the two vessels drowning together, dragging each other in, sucking all his plans down with them. The debacle at the hanging had been bad enough, but losing the *Revenge* would spell the end. The Brethren would never follow a man who had lost the biggest ship ever to fly the colours.

Quietly, behind his back, there would be a ballot. The newly-elected Captain would put a round between Jack's eyes, or cut his throat, and that would be that.

Such dreams he'd had. Such schemes. All for naught. He lifted the bottle again, spilling rum down his chin as the ship lurched. The waves lapped up the deck as the dreadnought slipped further into the sea. Looking away from his tortured ship, Rackham scowled towards the *Great Eastern*'s superstructure, where flames poured up from the bridge windows. He hoisted the bottle in a toast. Hope you're happy, he thought, whoever the hell you were.

Rackham tore himself from the view and stumbled for the door, clutching the rum to his chest. Time to find out if Billy and the lads had held on for their gallant leader, or if he was going down with his ship. Filled with bitterness and drink, he found he didn't care either way.

A figure darkened the doorway. Good lad Billy, thought Rackham, come to collect your Captain.

But the voice was not that of the young sailor.

"Going somewhere Jack?"

*

Jones entered the wheelhouse, keeping his pistol fixed on the pirate.

"You?" choked Rackham, staggering back, eyes wide.

"Not sure what you're celebrating," said Jones, nodding to the bottle. "Climbing up here, I noticed your lads all heading south as fast as their oars could carry them. Seems you've been left behind."

Rackham adopted a sour expression, swaying on his feet.

Jones looked around the bridge. "Nice boat. Shame she's sinking."

His eyes caught on a familiar piece of equipment. There, sitting above the ship's wireless, was a wooden box, its front panel a mass of dials, a tangle of electrical cables sprouting from its rear. A hard knot of anger formed in his chest.

"Coded messages, eh?" he said. "How long have you been working for the Germans?"

"I don't work for nobody..." spat the pirate. He took a swig from the bottle, spilling as much as he swallowed. "Partners, more like."

"Their spies told you which ships to attack. Targeting the cargo they didn't want to reach France."

Rackham sneered. "Made it all the sweeter – knowing I was helping kill more of you bastards."

Jones adjusted his aim. "And knowing that makes this even sweeter for me..."

"Ah, to hell with you," said Rackham. He spread his arms wide and stepped forward, bringing his chest to within inches of the pistol's muzzle.

"Do it," he said, voice flat and cold.

Like shooting a rabid dog, thought Jones – a kindness to everyone.

The deck pitched beneath their feet and both men stumbled. Jones' aim faltered and Rackham seized his chance.

The pirate swung his hand and the rum bottle shattered against Jones' skull. Glass ripped his skin and stinging liquid splashed in his eyes, sending him rearing back, his free hand flying to his face. Before he could recover, Rackham was on him, fingers scrabbling at the gun.

Already off-balance, and reeling from the blow to his head, Jones fell back. The pirate crashed down on top, driving Jones' breath out of him and sending a flare of agony up from his damaged ribs. Caught in a blaze of pain, unable to summon any strength, the pistol was wrenched from his grasp and sent tumbling away over the deck.

Rackham pressed down, rum-tinged breath hot in Jones' face. His fingers closed around Jones' throat. Jones clawed at Rackham's hands and got hold of a single finger. He hauled it outwards and the bone gave way with a sharp crack. The pirate howled, rolling clear, and a fierce satisfaction overcame the pain from Jones' side. You already tried to strangle me once Jack, he thought, sucking in great gulps of air.

Rackham rose unsteadily and lurched for the door, abandoning the fight, clutching his injured hand and cursing. Jones reached for the rail and pulled himself to his feet. Bent almost double over his aching ribs, blind in one eye through a combination of dripping blood and cheap rum, he glowered after the retreating pirate.

"No you bloody don't."

He threw himself at Rackham, smashing into his back. They burst through the doorway, careening across the wing. Locked together, they crashed into the rail and tipped over the edge.

The lower deck came rushing up and everything went black.

*

Jones was shaken into befuddled consciousness as hands gripped his shirt and hauled him up.

His returning awareness was accompanied by a flood of pain. The broken ribs he could endure, almost accustomed to their grumbles, but entirely new hurts now clamoured for attention from across his body. He almost blacked out again as he put weight on his left foot, streaks of agony shooting up from his ankle. But unconscious twice in one day was quite enough. He concentrated, swaying, but managing to stay upright.

"Easy there Major..."

Jones cracked an eye open, wincing as the sunlight sent spots swirling across his vision. He mustered his scattered wits and Kowalski's face swam into focus.

"You're alive..."

"Heh. A sight more than you by the looks of it." The Floridian regarded the bridge above them. "Still, you're in better shape than I expected after your tumble. Reckoned I was coming aboard to sweep up the pieces and take 'em back to Isabella for a keepsake."

Jones ignored the jibe, mention of the fall sparking recollection of his struggle in the wheelhouse.

"Where's Rackham?"

"You must have hit your head harder than I thought. Where's Rackham? Damned if you ain't been sleeping on him..." He gestured and Jones hobbled round to look.

Calico Jack Rackham, King of the Tortuga Pirates, lay on the sloping deck, head askew, blank eyes staring up into the cloudless sky.

"Broke your fall..." said Kowalski. "And his neck."

Their contemplation of the dead man was interrupted by a surge of water as the dreadnought shuddered, slipping further into the sea. The wave's backwash sucked at Rackham's corpse, dragging it down the deck.

Fully half the warship's length was beneath the surface. Disturbed by air escaping from the wreckage, water now boiled above the tangled steel of the collision point where Jones had clambered between the vessels.

The *Great Eastern* herself was settling low, bows submerged, her paddles finally motionless. Like the dreadnought, her stern was pushed upwards as she sank at the bow, raising the blazing superstructure of her wheelhouse like some sacrificial offering. The flames roared up, belching thick black smoke into the air.

Kowalski followed Jones' gaze. "Never have found you without the smoke. My little boat couldn't keep up when Rackham tore off after you."

Jones turned from the stricken merchant ship. "Little boat?"

Kowalski waved towards the side rail. "Right this way Major. Although you may have to swim some. I didn't dare tie her up to any of this mess."

Jones flexed his ankle, sucking his teeth at the stabbing pain. "I fear I'll be floating more than swimming. I may require a tow."

Kowalski stepped close, offering his support. Together they shuffled towards the side, Jones practically carried by his companion.

"Typical top brass," muttered Kowalski. "Always leaving the lower ranks to do the heavy lifting."

At the rail, Jones turned for a last look at the chaos he'd created.

Rackham's body was floating now. It sloshed about amongst the debris – one more piece of flotsam as the waves devoured the ship.

*

Kowalski dragged the Englishman out of the water, hauling him over the launch's stern rail. The pair slumped to the deck, a stain of seawater spreading out from their sodden clothes, darkening the planks.

Jones was pale and drawn, clearly struggling with his various injuries. Kowalski winced in sympathy. Whilst he felt pretty beaten-up himself, the Englishman was in a whole other class of hurt – dog-tired and broken.

Kowalski clambered to his feet. "The Commodore's bound to have some liquor stashed somewhere. You look like you could use a drink."

"I could at that." Jones looked round at the launch. "I thought I recognised her. Nice boat."

"Seemed a criminal waste to leave her tied up in Cayona," said Kowalski, shouting over his shoulder from the wheelhouse. "And her crew proved none too keen to die repelling boarders." He pulled a whisky bottle from a storage locker, waving it in triumph as he returned.

Jones eyed the label. "Proper Scotch," he grunted. "Bloody luxury." He pulled the cork from the neck with his teeth and spat it over the side. He hoisted the bottle and took a deep swallow. "God, but that's better."

Jones handed the bottle up and Kowalski swigged from it himself. The spirit burned his throat, the warming tingle spreading down and out through his core. He looked at the label.

"Have to find out where Culpepper gets his booze," he said. "This stuff is pretty good."

"Talking of the Commodore, how did our would-be President feel about losing his pretty little boat?"

Kowalski moved to the steps leading up to the wheelhouse. He couldn't help but smile as he reached for the locker door beside the stairs.

"Why don't you ask him?"

He turned the handle and the man stuffed inside the locker popped outwards, his hog-tied frame thumping to the deck. Piggy eyes glared above a gag that reduced the man's anger to a series of muffled grunts.

Jones goggled at the sudden appearance of the American. He stared at the captive open-mouthed before recovering himself and looking up to Kowalski, face full of questions.

"Heh. Wireless started squawking as I was fixing to leave. Our friend here wanted collecting from Rackham's ship. Figured I'd oblige." Kowalski nudged the trussed man with his foot. "He didn't pay a blind bit of notice as to who might be at the wheel. Too busy getting his fat behind down the ladder. Damn near pooped his britches when I said hello."

The expression on the American's face had been beautiful – a memory Kowalski would treasure to the end of his days. "Since then, he's been packed away in his compartment there. I reckoned you might want to discuss some things with him. Assuming you were still alive and all."

Jones pulled himself up, clutching the rail as he hobbled over to the steps. He lowered himself onto the bottom rung and stretched his injured leg out before him.

"You reckoned correctly. Untie him."

Kowalski handed his pistol over and Jones covered the captive whilst Kowalski loosened the ropes. Culpepper manoeuvred his bulk into a sitting position against the stern rail and pulled the gag from his mouth.

He worked his jaw, jowls wobbling, pink tongue flicking out to moisten cracked lips. The eyes darted from Jones to Kowalski and then back again.

"Perhaps..." he said. "Ah, perhaps we can come to an arrangement?"

Jones said nothing and Culpepper flinched from his silent regard, fixing his gaze on Kowalski instead.

"Name your price Captain..."

"Ain't that easy. Us mercenary types, we can be mighty choosy about our employers."

Jones spoke, iron in his voice. "You're a disgrace Commodore. A stain on the honour of your country and your service." His face twisted. "You disgust me."

Culpepper swallowed. "The degenerates will find their supply, whoever delivers it. All I was doing —"

"This isn't about your drug-running," interrupted Jones. "And it's not about your deal with Rackham..." He paused, eyes downcast, staring at the deck for an age before lifting his gaze, focused once more. "It's not even about my brother."

The pistol came up, the weapon rock-steady in Jones' grip. "This is about the villagers you've been terrorising for months. The people you were supposed to protect."

Culpepper's lip curled beneath his whiskers. "And for those peasants you'll appoint yourself judge and jury?"

The gun roared in Jones' hand.

The American clutched his leg and howled. Jones struggled to his feet, staring down at the injured man. Culpepper quailed before the look, his screams fading into strangled sobs. Blood seeped up between his fingers from the ruined meat of his thigh.

"I'll cheerfully stand judge and jury over the likes of you," said Jones. "But I draw the line at executioner. Instead, I'm going to give you the same chance your pirate friends gave all those British sailors." He turned a stone cold gaze to Kowalski. "Throw him over the side."

Culpepper's keening returned at full pitch. "No!" he screeched. "The blood... the sharks..."

Jones turned his back on the injured American, plucked the whisky bottle from Kowalski's grip and shuffled up the steps into the wheelhouse.

Kowalski grabbed Culpepper's lapels. The man sobbed, pleading, podgy fingers pawing at him. Kowalski hauled him upright and stared into the flushed, sweating face.

"You picked a fight with the wrong man there Commodore..."

He gave the American a shove.

Culpepper's mouth gaped wide as he toppled backwards over the rail. He struck the water with an almighty splash. He disappeared beneath the waves before struggling upwards, arms flailing.

The boat's engine rumbled into life, prompting renewed howls from the man in the water. Incoherent calls rang out interrupted by frequent dips under the surface. The launch steamed away from the floundering American and the ships sinking behind him.

Culpepper's desperate pleas echoed inside Kowalski's head long after they had faded from his hearing.

*

Havana

Jones shaded his eyes to follow the course of a fat airship as it passed across the bay, heading for the docks.

He raised his teacup and took a sip, pleased at the lack of trembling clatter as he returned the cup to its saucer – a definite improvement from the previous day. However, the motion did prompt grumbles from the ribs beneath the tight bandages and, not to be outdone, the dull throb from his ankle flared up. He ignored both complaints and closed his eyes, soaking up the morning sun.

The peace was interrupted by Kowalski, bursting through the doors and out onto the balcony. "Have you seen the papers?"

Jones nodded, tapping a finger on the stack of folded publications beside his breakfast tray. *Navy Hero Lost Defending English Ship From Pirates* proclaimed the headline on the topmost page.

The periodicals beneath all recounted similar stories, and had done for days – ever since the news had made it to the American mainland. The only aspect of the tale to vie with Culpepper's passing for top billing had been the arrival in Havana's harbour of the wounded *Neptune*, Brunel at the helm, towing a flotilla of lifeboats laden with survivors.

"Unbelievable," said Kowalski. "Next thing they'll be trying to canonise the bastard."

"The authorities know the truth. Let Culpepper enjoy his posthumous glory." Jones adjusted the cushion beneath his raised foot. "How are the negotiations proceeding?"

Kowalski snorted. "A damned talking shop is all they are. Nobody willing to quit yapping long enough to hear what the other side is saying."

"Better than the alternative..."

The American administration, embarrassed by the revelations of Culpepper's activities had reluctantly entered into discussions with Estrada and his insurgents. The Floridians were moderating the talks and Kowalski had been pressed into service monitoring security.

"Nearly forgot. I picked something up for you..."

Kowalski fished a small wooden box from his pocket and deposited it on the table, nodding to Jones to open it.

Inside, nestled on a bed of dark blue velvet, shone the brushed metallic casing of a pocket watch. Jones lifted it out, sliding the catch to reveal a mechanical marvel – an intricate mechanism of cogs, springs and levers gleaming beneath the glass of the watch's open face.

"Ramon assured me it was a good one," said Kowalski.

"I don't know what to say…"

Kowalski got to his feet. "Then don't say anything." He waved a hand towards Jones' ankle. "Buy me a drink when you're up and about."

Jones returned the Floridian's smile. "I might even buy you two."

"Heh. I'll see you around Major."

Kowalski departed, leaving Jones running his fingers over the smooth matte surface of the watch. His reverie was broken by Isabella's arrival. She bent over him and pressed her lips to his own, her black curls tumbling across his face. She pulled away and beamed down at him.

"And how is my patient this morning?"

"Better. And better still if more of that treatment is forthcoming."

Her eyes sparkled. "Perhaps. But we must be careful. You are an invalid after all." She settled herself in her seat, slipping her fingers beneath the silk at the top of her dress to withdraw an envelope. "More correspondence from the telegraph office. You are a popular man."

The past three days had seen an endless procession of visitors traipsing through the Mirador to speak with Jones. Most – like the Americans or the British Consul – to discuss the political ramifications of the events on Tortuga. Others – like Brunel and Turner – more interested in the progress of Jones' recuperation. The whole period had been punctuated with regular telegraph messages from London – a mixture of congratulations for a job well done, or admonishment for the cost to the Treasury of scuttling the *Great Eastern*.

Isabella handed the envelope across. The paper was still warm from contact with her skin. Jones tore the flap and removed the card.

Return at earliest opportunity. Still a war on. – B

He stared down at the printed words.

"What is it?" asked Isabella.

Jones lifted his gaze to the woman across the table, regarding her for as long as he had stared at the telegram. She gave an uncertain smile under his scrutiny, her fingers twisting at a strand of hair.

He folded the message card over on itself and tore it into two neat halves. He stacked the pieces and tore them through again before depositing the resulting scraps amidst the remains of his breakfast.

Leaning back in his chair, Jones clicked open the pocket watch and peered at the mechanism. The tiny gears spun as the second hand ticked its way round the dial.

"Nothing," he said, returning his attention to Isabella. "Nothing that can't wait a while."

***

Titan's Fire

Rod Gillies

The Mediterranean

The cough rattled round the compartment, echoing over the engines' rumble and snapping Jones awake. He watched O'Neill tug a handkerchief from his uniform pocket, the movement hampered by the attaché case handcuffed to his wrist. The man huddled over the crumpled cloth and quaked through the coughing fit. The spasms subsided and O'Neill frowned at the contents of the handkerchief. He tucked the offending article away and raised his gaze, bloodshot eyes sunk into grey skin.

"Always hated flying," he croaked. "Thin air up here don't you know."

And cold too, thought Jones, the men's breath hanging in the air between them. He pulled out his watch and checked the time.

"Not long now sir."

O'Neill made a lopsided attempt at a smile. "I suppose not."

Jones hauled himself up from his seat. He stomped life back into legs numb from the long hours of inactivity since their dawn departure.

"I'm off to see Wilberforce."

A new bout of coughing swamped O'Neill's attempt at a reply. Jones made for the bulkhead door leaving the Brigadier hunched over his handkerchief once again.

The sunlight blazing in through the cockpit windows offered a dazzling contrast to the enclosed aft compartment. The row of metal-framed seats before the windows held a single occupant, his gaze fixed forward, gloved hands on the controls. Jones clapped his hand down on Wilberforce's shoulder in greeting and peered out. The Mediterranean sunshine was a poor match for the cabin temperature, its brightness bouncing back from the clouds for as far as the eye could see. The airship felt tiny against the vast white expanse.

"Pretty, isn't it?" said Wilberforce round the stem of his pipe, his expression hidden behind an extravagant moustache and a pair of goggles, the lenses tinted black against the glare. The bowl of his pipe bobbed up and down as he spoke. "Don't be fooled. Nothing but big bags of rain. And generally stuffed with bloody great mountains." He gave a sniff and nodded towards the window. "Clouds – not to be trusted."

"Unless your map-reading is even worse than your flying, there's nothing down there but waves."

"And the small matter of an Ottoman fleet."

"That too," smiled Jones.

Wilberforce tapped a finger on the compass housing and ran his gaze across the multitude of dials and gauges.

"I normally pay someone for all this nonsense. However, from what I recall of my navigation classes, I believe we're approaching our rendezvous. You'd best fetch our passenger."

"And you'd best put that thing out and open a window." Jones pointed at the pipe. "He's hung on this long. I don't want him hacking up a lung because of your cherry leaf."

"Philistine..." said Wilberforce. "It's applewood." All the same, the pilot pushed open a glass panel and knocked the contents of the pipe's bowl out into the whistling slipstream.

"You can smoke to your heart's content when we're finished."

"It'll go nicely with those drinks you'll be buying." The airman nodded to himself. "Yes, pale ale I think. None of that pilsner muck you've developed a taste for."

"It's cold and wet. What more do you need?"

"Still unrepentant?" Wilberforce craned round in his seat, grin just visible beneath the fringe of his moustache. "I'm beginning to suspect you genuinely enjoy the damned stuff."

It had become a standing joke between the two men, a bone of genial contention as they passed the time in Gibraltar, awaiting the perfect combination of weather forecast and intelligence report.

"We may be at war with the Germans," said Jones as he made for the door. "But we can at least acknowledge they brew a decent pint."

He pulled the hatch closed behind him, the pressure seal cutting off Wilberforce's accusations of treason. Jones checked his watch once more – time to get this ridiculous parlour game started.

*

The gunner spotted the airship first, bringing it to the pilot's attention with a kick in the back and a wave to starboard. Shouting over the roaring wind would have been futile. Besides, up here, near the limits of altitude for an open cockpit, it was better to save your breath.

The pilot twisted round and nodded to the man perched above him in the tiered cockpit, raising his gloved hand, thumb aloft. He turned his attention to the distant dot and pulled on the joystick. The controls vibrated in his grip, cables thrumming the length of the fuselage as the flaps on the wings shifted. The biplane swung round, settling on an intercept course. He reached for the throttle and tugged the stop out to its fullest extent, the growling pitch of the engine rising in response. The prop clawed at the air with increased vigour and he was pushed back into the canvas webbing of his chair. The engine's accelerated rhythm echoed in his pulse as they closed on the target.

The dirigible grew larger, the gondola now distinct beneath the grey bulk of the gas envelope, engine pylons protruding to either side of the airship's red, white and blue tail markings. The pilot pushed forward and brought the biplane down before swinging her into a tight s-shaped turn. He'd make the final approach from the airship's rear quarter, offering the best field of fire to his gunner.

The remaining distance disappeared in moments, chewed away to nothing by the propeller blades, the airship suddenly massive before them. He throttled back, almost to a stall, and the biplane and its clumsy prey hung together, frozen in the sky, scant yards apart.

The chatter of the machine carbine cut through the wind and the engine's roar. The biplane's frame shuddered as the gun spat a torrent of lead up towards the helpless target. Then they were past, ripping through the shadows beneath the balloon and out into the sunlight once more.

The pilot pulled them up into a steep climb and hauled the stick to the side, working at the pedals with his feet. The aircraft seemed to stand on her tail for an age, then her nose tipped to port and she dropped. The view filled with the wide white blanket of cloud, the airship fat and stark against the backdrop. The slipstream howled over the wings as they dropped, arrowing down towards their quarry.

Thick oily smoke spewed from the dirigible's portside engine pod. The skin of her gasbag, previously smooth and taut, was now puckered and wrinkled, noticeably sagging towards the tail. Even as the biplane closed the gap, the stricken craft was losing altitude, dipping towards the clouds. The pilot craned round in his seat and waved the gunner off. No need to inflict further damage, the airship was going down.

The biplane settled into a turn, a hawk circling above its wounded prey. Below, the dirigible ploughed a furrow into the clouds, deeper and deeper, until it disappeared from view, swallowed up by the vapours.

*

"Nothing to worry about chaps," shouted Wilberforce. "The buggers left us one engine…"

Jones stared across the cockpit at the pilot. The man was clearly some kind of bloody lunatic. Goggles discarded, features set in a manic smile, Wilberforce cackled with the gondola's every lurch.

The console before the three men was festooned with winking lamps, the needles on each dial quivering firmly in the red. One gauge in particular demanded Jones' attention, his eyes returning to it over and over. Ignorant of the purpose of the majority of the instruments, he understood only too well the importance of the altimeter, and the significance of its rapidly unwinding dial. Beyond the windows, clouds rushed past in a dark blur, the airship's headlong descent squeezing water droplets out of the grey fog, sending them streaming up and across the glass in wavering silver streaks.

O'Neill leaned across and gave Jones' arm a weak punch.

"A proper pea-souper out there, eh Major?"

Good God, thought Jones. Am I the only one not enjoying this? The Brigadier settled back in his chair, crossing his hands over the attaché case in his lap – a picture of calm. Like a damned businessman on an omnibus, heading off for work in the City.

Daylight banished the gloom as the airship dropped free of the clouds' embrace. The return of visibility immediately reduced Jones' sense of helplessness. At least now he could see where they were going.

Ahead, the sun's rays broke through the grey ceiling of clouds, dappling the ocean. Distracted by the sparkle of light, it took a moment before Jones recognised the dangerous shapes of the warships below.

A cluster of ironclad frigates, eight in all, trailed wakes of foam across the water, plumes of smoke billowing from their multiple funnels. At the heart of the flotilla a larger vessel loomed, double the length of her companions, her superstructure climbing in tiers to tower above the others – the *Sultan Osman*, flagship of the Ottoman navy.

Even at a distance the dreadnought was an impressive sight – a marvel of British engineering, Jones thought with a wry smile. The largest warship afloat, fresh off the Belfast slipways, she had been delivered to the eager Turks only six months before the outbreak of war. Perhaps memory of the nuisance the vessel was now making of herself in enemy hands would give the Admiralty pause before they approved future shipbuilding contracts.

Wilberforce hauled at the stick and the airship's nose lifted, slowing their rate of descent, even if only a little. He eyed the closest of the ships.

"Five pounds says I can put her down on the deck."

"We're certainly close enough," said O'Neill, voice crackling with phlegm. "My compliments on your navigation."

The airman was abruptly sombre, all levity banished. "Thank you sir."

O'Neill crumpled in his seat, wracked by a bout of coughing. When the spasm passed, the man pulled his head erect, blinking moisture away to stare at his companions.

"When you're ready Major."

"You're sure about this?"

"Of course I'm bloody sure." O'Neill frowned. "Just get on with it."

Jones pulled his pistol from its holster. The Brigadier eyed the muzzle of the gun and gave a crooked smile. He closed his eyes, a mercy for which Jones offered up a guilty prayer of thanks.

"It's been an honour sir."

Jones pulled the trigger.

*

"Let me be sure I understand this correctly..." Jones had said around his cigarette as he raised a flaming match to its tip, privately amazed his fingers were not trembling. "I've to be shot down by our own side, and then deliver a dead man to the Turks?"

"You've to deliver the briefcase. The Brigadier is window dressing."

"I've served with the man. You're asking me to commit murder."

Buckingham's eyes softened, not a phenomenon Jones had witnessed often. "Hardly murder. Bertie O'Neill is rather unwell."

Doesn't matter, thought Jones. He sucked hard on the filter pinched between his fingers. As with the majority of the orders Buckingham dished out, the head of Special Operations failed to comprehend these things were, almost without exception, easier said than done.

"With all due respect, you won't be the one doing the dirty work."

"I was under the impression dirty work was your speciality."

"And thinking up crackpot schemes appears to be yours."

Buckingham's moustache twitched, the closest the old man ever came to a smile. "Touché. But I'm afraid in this instance you would be mistaken."

"So this little gem is Hanson's idea?" Jones ground his cigarette into the ashtray atop the Duke's broad mahogany desk. "Where is he? It's not the same without him lurking at your elbow."

"He's otherwise engaged. On a trip to the Americas if you must know. Overseeing a job we've given to your old chum Kowalski."

Kowalski would be delighted, thought Jones. The Floridian mercenary liked nothing better than a client hanging around like a bad smell, second-guessing his every move.

"But my deputy has nothing to do with this either," said Buckingham, returning to the matter at hand. "The whole affair is O'Neill's idea. His last hurrah, if you will. Didn't really feel I could refuse."

The Duke leaned forward, his sharp gaze burning across the table.

"I would imagine you feel much the same."

Jones avoided the stare, reluctant to admit to the growing tingle of excitement at the prospect of a proper mission. Truth was, he was bored. He'd not seen any decent action since returning from Havana. The light duties were a punishment, he suspected, repayment for his extended absence following his last assignment – his "Caribbean holiday", as the Duke insisted on referring to it.

"Well?" pressed Buckingham.

Jones took a breath. "I'll do it."

"Excellent. Knew I could count on you…"

"Don't be too smug." Jones' mind was already churning over the operation's logistics. "I have some changes to your precious plan."

"Really?" The Duke regarded him with an arched eyebrow. "You genuinely think you're better at all this than everyone else, don't you?"

"So do you. Otherwise I wouldn't be here."

Buckingham frowned at the rejoinder, but didn't disagree. "Very well. If I must indulge you. What elements do you think could be improved?"

"Grab a pen," said Jones. "I have a list…"

*

The airship limped through the sky, low now – no more than five hundred feet above the water and perhaps a mile from the nearest vessel. Jones kept his eyes on the ironclad, avoiding the slumped form in the seat beside him. He could make out a flurry of activity on the ship's nearside deck, tiny figures scuttling around – Ottoman sailors, no doubt preparing a welcoming party for their unexpected aerial visitor. Wilberforce interrupted his observation.

"Need to put this old girl in the drink beside the first ship we come to. If I don't put her down soon I'll lose any say as to how she goes in."

"That settles it then." Jones stood. "Watch yourself…"

He raised his pistol and stitched three rounds across the windows. Glass splintered, crystal fragments scattering across the cockpit.

"You meant that," glowered Wilberforce, brushing at himself.

Jones gestured at the windows, now spidered with cracks. "Stops Johnny Turk seeing you sitting there. And we need some damage up here…" He looked at O'Neill's body. "As an explanation."

Wilberforce followed his gaze. "Bet the old bugger's enjoying this. Wherever he is."

The airman was probably right – O'Neill had always had a black edge to his sense of humour.

Jones contemplated the neat circular entry wound in the Brigadier's forehead and the thin trail of blood which leaked from it. He tried to avoid the spray of gore spattering the cockpit wall behind, but once glimpsed it drew the eye regardless of any contrary desire. The aircraft shuddered, shaking Jones back into the moment. He packed away his guilt – it would have to wait. He made for the door, leaving the dead soldier behind him.

"I'll prepare our last charade," he called back to Wilberforce. "You get ready to ditch her."

Bullet holes riddled the aft compartment fuselage, wind whistling in through the aircraft's wounds. Jones eyed the multiple punctures. If he got out of this in one piece, he'd seek out the biplane's gunner and buy him a pint. The man had put his shots exactly where he'd been instructed. Just as well – a couple of degrees out and the fusillade would have ripped through the thin walls of the cockpit and shredded its occupants.

The airship creaked and groaned around him as he moved up the incline of the deck to the floor hatch. He spun the wheel and hauled, swinging the door up and back, allowing the angry slipstream easy access to the compartment. The opening revealed the tops of the waves scudding past beneath them.

He opened a storage locker and manhandled its contents out into the cabin. The mannequin had been requisitioned from an unimpressed Gibraltarian tailor, the dummy press-ganged into service as the final member of the airship's crew. Wilberforce, delighted with their new recruit, had promptly christened him Charlie. Now, clad in ill-fitting uniform and parachute harness, it was time for their wooden comrade-in-arms to play his part.

Jones clipped a line into the ring affixed to the deck and turned the figure onto its back. He rummaged in the oilskin pouch stitched to the parachute harness and withdrew a small metallic sphere. He twisted the dial set into its surface, activating the clockwork timer. Five minutes ought to do it. He tucked the device back in place and stood, hefting the mannequin over the hatchway.

"*Bon voyage* Charlie."

The wooden figure slipped through the opening, the line spinning out, its anchor clip rattling. The rope jerked once, and then hung loose, task complete. Jones crouched and peered back through the hatch. There, drifting towards the water, was the pale canopy of an open parachute.

The expanse of silk and the dangling figure beneath couldn't help but be spotted by the telescopes undoubtedly trained on the descending airship at this very moment: a pilot abandoning his doomed aircraft – a pilot that would never be found. The small explosive charge would release the parachute, and the lead weights sown into the uniform would consign the mannequin to the depths. Only the canopy would be left, floating on the surface, a soggy marker for Charlie's watery grave.

Jones got to his feet and kicked the floor hatch closed. Now comes the tricky part, he thought. He and Wilberforce had to avoid a similar fate.

*

The two men floated together, weightless beneath the water, thirty feet beneath the silhouette of the ditched airship. Jones peered through the streaked glass of his mask, gaze following a stream of bubbles up through the water to the undulating surface. The expelled gas rose in a glittering cascade, dissipating into the rainbow shimmer formed by the oil and kerosene leaking from the wreck above.

He checked the luminescent dial on his depth gauge. He unclipped a weight from his harness and let it drop away into the abyss, compensating for his reduced buoyancy as he drained the air from the flask strapped to his chest. He pulled at Wilberforce's wrist and mimed a tugging action, instructing his companion to do the same. The airman swung round in the water, struggling to retain his orientation, arms and legs flailing, overcompensating first one way and then the other.

Jones regarded this aquatic performance until his patience evaporated. He snatched a weight from Wilberforce's straps, sending it to the distant bottom. He grabbed hold of his companion's harness and gave a single scissor kick, taking them up a few feet. He released his grip with his left hand, but kept a tight grasp of the ungainly pilot with his right.

Wilberforce continued to float upwards, Jones' anchoring serving to spin him round until once again he was facing downward. The airman scowled through his mask, curses round his rubber mouthpiece releasing a burst of bubbles. The pilot appeared much less comfortable beneath the waves than amongst the clouds. Served him right, thought Jones. Should have spent more time practising with the diving equipment, and a little less time in Gibraltar's pubs.

They had ditched the airship a scant quarter mile from the Ottoman fleet. Jones had to acknowledge Wilberforce had fully earned his beer money – smacking the aircraft into the swell hard enough to simulate a real crash, but gently enough not to crush the gondola and the men within. A furtive look through the broken windows had revealed a ship's launch, already in the water and heading their way. Jones was relieved – it would have been just the thing to have gone to all this trouble only to have the airship sink before Johnny Turk roused himself to put a boat out.

Material from the punctured gasbag had torn free of its buckled frame, settling over the wallowing gondola like a shroud. Jones and Wilberforce tossed their boots through the side hatch, pulled on the clumsy breathing apparatus, and then clambered out, following their footwear into the water. The cylindrical flasks strapped to their chests contained enough compressed air for an hour-long underwater sojourn. Whilst the air tasted foul, tinged with nasty hints of rubber and metal, it was infinitely preferable to a lung-full of seawater.

They had watched the hull of the launch glide overhead, or at least Jones had. Wilberforce was more concerned with his position in the water, continually paddling this way and that like a wayward turtle, spending much of his time upended, facing down into the indigo depths.

Sailors splashed over the side of the boat above and swam for the gondola, ignorant of the submerged observers. Minutes dragged past, and then the launch nudged in closer, its hull rocking as something heavy was transferred from the wreckage. Brigadier O'Neill was on his way, embarking on his final mission. The boat pulled away, oar strokes digging churning furrows of foam across the surface. The divers were left alone once more, suspended in the half light of the sea.

Jones regarded the ghostly glow of the depth gauge once again, then flipped it over to examine the timepiece attached to the reverse. Forty-four minutes elapsed. Shouldn't be long now, he thought. He hoped. His gaze returned to the play of sunlight on the waves above.

Wilberforce stopped floundering. An urgent grip dug into Jones' arm and the pilot gestured downward, eyes wide behind his mask. Jones turned his attention to the deep.

Below them a patch of blackness formed, darker than the midnight blue of the surrounding water. Indistinct at first, more shadow than physical presence, a long shape materialised out of the depths. It grew – some lurking denizen of the ocean, rising up to claim them.

*

The dull clang of the inner airlock echoed up the companionway and around the *Nautica*'s control room. Anderson winced at the noise and his bridge crew exchanged frowns in the dim light before returning their attention to the banks of dials. Nobody knew if the Germans had shared the new-fangled hydrophones with their Ottoman allies, but not one of the crewmen aboard was about to risk a racket to find out.

Nautica would have made a fine Trappist monastery over the past fortnight as she stalked the Turkish fleet. Conversations were kept short and conducted in whispers, the men practically tiptoeing across the deck, wary of any unnecessary noise. The submersible had surfaced only at night to hoist the wireless mast and send coded reports, the radio operator's fingers lent extra speed by the desire, held in common with his crewmates, to return to the safety of the depths as quickly as possible.

Anderson was proud of his lads for maintaining their discipline and nerve over such an extended hunt. He only wished he could reward them by putting a torpedo into that bloody great dreadnought. But orders were orders. The Admiralty appeared to have other plans for the *Sultan Osman*.

The submersible's two new passengers were escorted into the control room. Water seeped from their sodden clothing, pooling around their stockinged feet. Dixon, the *Nautica*'s chief engineer, stood behind the new arrivals, regarding the spreading puddle with a black look.

Anderson was surprised the man hadn't already summoned a work detail. Seawater inside the boat – he imagined the very sight of it was giving Dixon palpitations.

"It's alright Chief," said Anderson. "I doubt it will sink us." He thrust his hand towards the first of his visitors.

"Welcome back on board Major Jones. Good to see you again."

"The feeling is most assuredly mutual Captain." Jones offered a weary smile as he returned the handshake. "You're making a habit of plucking me from the waves."

"My pleasure," said Anderson. "Although I'm disappointed you don't appear to have any young ladies in tow on this occasion..."

"Sadly no." Jones turned to introduce his companion. "Captain Anderson, meet Wing Commander Wilberforce of the Aeronautic Corps."

"A flyer? We'll try not to hold that against him." The two shook hands. "First time aboard a submersible?"

Wilberforce peered round at the control consoles, eyes travelling up to the glass dome and the watery gloom beyond.

"Do these things always smell like goats? Or is that just the sailors?"

Dixon bristled behind the airman, but Anderson returned Wilberforce's smile. "The latter unfortunately. But we'll likely get some time up top to freshen the air on our way back to Gibraltar."

"We're not heading for the Rock," put in Jones. He reached inside his shirt and withdrew a leaf of waxed paper. "Sorry Captain, new orders."

Wilberforce's shoulders slumped. "Where are we off to now?"

The dejected look coupled with the damp drooping moustache lent the airman the aspect of a half-drowned St Bernard. Alongside him, Dixon looked similarly unimpressed as Jones' words. The two men exchanged a long-suffering look, the natural antipathy of sailor and flyer subsumed, at least temporarily, by a shared disgruntlement.

Anderson turned his attention to the typewritten text. He scanned the terse instructions as Jones pulled the other two men towards the map table in the control room's centre.

"The documents O'Neill is carrying should have the *Osman* and her chums bustling off for Gibraltar to prevent the arrival of half the Royal Navy. Always assuming they can decode the papers of course – they're in cipher, but not a very good one." He indicated the expanse of the chart. "Johnny Turk has been keen to keep the Med a private boating pond up until now. He's unlikely to let our ships waltz in unopposed."

"All a fiction I presume?" said Wilberforce.

"Not at all. The fleet left the Solent last week."

"So why make a bloody appointment?" growled Dixon. "Sounds like the perfect way to waste some sailors' lives."

"Cold arithmetic," said Jones. "The risk to ships and men has been deemed less than the value of keeping Ottoman eyes fixed firmly on the Western Med for the next few weeks."

Dixon frowned. "And whilst the Turks are distracted?"

Anderson finished his reading and answered for Jones. "We can finally get the fleet that's been bottled up in Egypt out to sea." He turned to the Duty Officer. "Set course for Alexandria. Best possible speed."

"Aye sir." The man bent to his assignment, plotting out the new heading, greaseproof pencil marks over the glass panel atop the chart.

"What's in Alexandria?" asked Wilberforce, eyeing the map.

"Ships," said Jones. "And troops. Thousands of them – Australians and New Zealanders mostly, itching to get back into the fight since they scared the Turks away from Suez. They've been cooped up by that fleet for months, of no use to man nor beast." He smiled at the airman. "They've got airships too, but not many pilots. They'll be delighted when you put in an appearance."

Wilberforce's shoulders straightened at this, a twinkle in his eye at the thought of getting back in the air. Dixon however, retained his furrowed brow.

"Where will this expeditionary force be headed?" asked the engineer.

"We're not messing about," replied Jones. "We're after the Turk's grandest prize – Constantinople itself."

"Bloody hell," said Wilberforce and Dixon in concert.

"That's why Buckingham took O'Neill up on his offer. The stakes are too high to turn down any advantage." Jones paused, a flicker of guilt playing across his face. "However unsavoury the means of obtaining it."

Anderson leaned over the map. He pointed to its Eastern edge, where a narrow stretch of water ran between the Mediterranean and the inland sea lying before the Ottoman capital.

"The Dardanelles are too well defended for ships to force a passage through to the Marmara. The first objective is to establish a beach-head and capture the gun forts."

He looked back to the printed paper, checking the unfamiliar place name. He tapped a finger on the chart, indicating a long peninsula.

"Gallipoli..." he said.

"You'll be going ashore at Gallipoli."

*

Extracted from 'A History of the Ancient Sects and Societies of the East'...

Only the windblown sands and bare rock of Arabia and Persia could have offered an appropriate stage for the dismal deeds of the infamous Old Man of the Mountain.

One Hassan, a missionary of the School of Cairo, and possessed of a fierce and determined character, did distinguish himself and acquire much influence in that great city. This influence however, coupled with his haughty demeanour, excited the envy of others and Hassan found himself exiled. Forced to flee the land of his birth he passed through trials of storm and fire, enhancing further his reputation, rather than diminishing it, which had surely been his enemies' intent. By dint of his strength of character, he gathered a great host of followers, and seizing a fortress in the hills, there established his Rule.

In that inaccessible nest he composed theological works, and gave himself up to frequent religious exercises. But also he killed with calculation to gain fame and power, to inspire fear and devotion in equal measure. And this need not surprise us, for theological studies are no bar to ferocity, and a mystical nature is often found united with a vicious fury.

Always this Hassan sought new ways whereby he might increase his dominion, and so gathered about himself a great many scholars and alchemists, who through his patronage began to unravel the many Mysteries of the world. Counted chief amongst these men of learning was one Al-Kalil, whose desire for knowledge was as unfettered by gentleness and love as Hassan's own hunger for power...

Boston, Massachusetts

"God damn it Tank. You're about as stealthy as a locomotive. Could you make any more noise?"

"Your problem. Not. Mine," said the big man, words punctuated by a low mechanical wheeze. "Your idea. To bring. Me along."

Fair point, acknowledged Kowalski. The bruiser hulking beside him in the attic was only there at his invitation and Kowalski was glad of the company, despite the racket. He needed a man he could trust, a man who could handle himself if things turned sour. Tank O'Connell was that man – notwithstanding the iron lung which had earned him his moniker.

Kowalski returned his attention to the task at hand, scraping at the brickwork. Whilst the groans emerging from O'Connell's torso sounded loud enough in proximity, Kowalski figured it wasn't any worse than the scratch of the knife and the patter of mortar tumbling to the planks. Besides, they could have had an entire marching band up here and the clamour would be lost amidst the muffled din emanating from the packed tavern below: the Black Dog – roughest pub in Charlestown, itself the roughest neighbourhood in the whole of Boston.

Even their brief reconnaissance the previous night had seen two fights spill out from the tavern. The first of these altercations ended in a stabbing, the victim either unconscious or dead, dragged away by his fellows whilst the victor and his cronies went back into the bar.

The later fracas had been less deadly, but considerably noisier – two formidable doxies scrapping like cats over the attentions of a well-to-do gent in a top hat. The shrieking and scratching was eventually brought to a halt by a wobbly intervention from the man. After a brief discussion, he staggered into the night, a floozy hanging off each arm.

"Mistake," wheezed O'Connell as he and Kowalski watched the scene unfold from the rooftop opposite. "He'll get out. Of his. Britches. Then robbed blind."

Kowalski figured he'd only be getting what he deserved. Seeking cheap thrills in Charlestown was a foolish vice, one liable to get its adherents killed. The uptown swell would have stuck out like a sore thumb amongst the Dog's clientele, men and women who could sniff out a purse at a thousand yards. And there would be no strolling beat cop happening by ready to lend a hand, that was for sure. Boston's finest kept well away from these streets, especially after dark.

The evening's observation had given Kowalski first-hand knowledge of the tavern's surroundings, well worth the delay of putting the plan into action, even if it left them precious little time to get everything into place. Hanson had grumbled at the waste of a day, but then Hanson was never happy, and it wasn't like the Englishman was doing any of the actual work.

"Dim the light," said Kowalski. "I think I'm through."

Tank twisted the dial on the side of the boxy metal lamp, reducing its glare to a dull orange glow. Kowalski tucked his knife into its sheath, making a mental note to polish the scratches from its tip. His father would have been appalled at this latest mistreatment of a fine blade. The right tool for the right job – Kowalski senior's favourite refrain, and a good excuse for the old carpenter to have amassed an extensive collection of gleaming ironmongery. The six-inch hunting knife with its wicked serrated edge was most definitely the wrong tool, but as Kowalski's fingers worked the loose brick free, he figured it had done the job all the same.

More bricks followed until the expanse of wall beneath the roof contained a jagged hole, three bricks across and five rows high. The extracted brickwork was piled carefully to either side, the weight distributed evenly across the joists. Whilst the storehouse beneath them was empty, neither man wanted to risk the noise of collapsing masonry.

Kowalski contemplated the opening. "Give me the lamp," he said.

O'Connell handed over the lantern and Kowalski aimed the bulbous lens forward, pushing the blackness away from the hole, banishing it to the deeper recesses of the building next door. The light revealed a crawl space, the rafters sloping down on either side to form a tight triangular tunnel above a floor of joists and cracked plaster. Spiders scuttled away, seeking refuge in the twilight. Further back, at the edge of the illumination, a pair of eyes reflected the lamplight. They blinked once and disappeared, a faint scrabbling marking their retreat.

"Rats," said O'Connell in a grave tone. "Don't like 'em."

Don't particularly like them myself, thought Kowalski. And small dark spaces even less. But it ain't like I've got a choice. Nobody had ever described Kowalski as small, but there wasn't a chance of Tank's bulky frame squeezing into the space beyond the bricks. What the hell – you had to play the hands you were dealt. Kowalski waved his companion aside and moved towards the hole.

He twisted his shoulders and reached through to place the lantern on a joist, its light spilling across the floor. He pushed himself in, scraping his chest, then stomach across the brickwork. He gripped the rough wooden beams and pulled, hauling his upper half further into the attic and dragging his legs after. Each creak and scrape made him cringe, but the muted revelry from below remained unchanged as he inched forward. He wriggled round, lifting the lamp to reveal O'Connell's features peering in.

"Pass me the cable."

Tank thrust an arm through the gap, a bundle of cable clutched in his meaty fist. Kowalski took the rubber-coated wire and shuffled forward into the attic space.

The lamp illuminated the way ahead for six feet or so, the triangular tunnel cast in shades of hellish orange. But behind this patch of light, the darkness and the sloping walls closed in around Kowalski. He wriggled on, ignoring the splinters digging into his palms, spitting dust and cobwebs from his mouth, his shoulders scraping against the rafters to either side.

A clammy sweat materialised on his forehead, a magnet for the dust stirred up by his awkward passage. Time stretched out and bile began to burn in his throat. He stopped, all forward momentum leeched away by the confines of the tunnel. His pulse thundered in his ears as the wood and slates above squashed down. The suffocating weight of the dark itself settled around him.

He closed his eyes and blew out the breath he'd been holding. He gobbled down a lungful of air and then pushed it out in turn. He forced himself into a series of deep breaths, one after the other – in through the nose, out through the mouth, ignoring the smell of must and dust and rat droppings. He concentrated on the simple act of breathing, its continuation providing evidence the rafters were not collapsing in on him – rational proof he was not about to choke his last in the airless dark. Calmer, if still far from comfortable, he forced his eyes open and scrambled forward.

After an eternity of crawling he met a wall of bricks blocking the left half of the passage and proceeding upward between the rafters. He cast a look down the dark recess to the right, relieved he wouldn't have to negotiate this narrower space. Twisted on his side, he reached for his knife and went to work on the mortar binding the bricks together.

*

Nearly an hour had ground past since he had shuffled out of the attic but Kowalski was still relishing the airiness of the warehouse's upper storey. His gaze followed the line of cable across the wooden planks and up to the hole in the wall above. He pictured the dictograph's receiver dangling at the end of the wire. The damned thing had better work after all this trouble.

He turned his attention to the contraption on the floor. He had expected to have to make multiple trips, hauling the dry cell batteries up to the warehouse's top floor. O'Connell had other ideas, grabbing a container in each hand and lugging them effortlessly up the creaking stairs. He'd left one for Kowalski, who'd made more of a meal of the ascent, clutching the handle bolted to the metal cylinder in both hands and cursing his way through the entire climb.

Coils of wire looped from the wing nut contacts, linking one battery to the next and then on to the box – a cube of polished wood, eight inches to a side, its front occupied by a grille of wire over a round opening. A small lamp glowed on its top, indicating the unit was receiving power.

If Hanson's information was correct, the rooms above the Dog served as a meeting place for Boston's most vocal supporters of Irish revolution. These friends of St Patrick had come into money, a substantial amount it seemed, and had dedicated the funds to the cause. Dockhand gossip had crates stuffed with contraband guns recently arrived in the city, the cargo ultimately destined for the Emerald Isle. Needless to say, Hanson was eager to hear details of any such shipment.

The second lamp atop the dictograph emitted a faint flicker, accompanied by thin scratchy sounds emanating from the speaker grille. Down the wire, carried on electrical impulse, the dictograph relayed noises from next door – banging doors, shuffling feet, chairs scraping on floorboards. Distorted and muffled by the passage through the cable, yet still comprehensible, a voice called a meeting to order.

A room above an infamous Irish pub – Kowalski figured the Republicans might have chosen someplace a little less obvious. Still, they likely reckoned no Englishman would dare set foot in this, the darkest green corner of the darkest green city in the United States.

And they'd be right, he thought, that's why the British had hired him.

*

Hanson looked up from the transcript, brow furrowed over the rims of his spectacles. "I hope you didn't engage some pretty secretary to type this up on my account."

"Heh. Don't fret none," said Kowalski. He raised his index fingers and waggled them in turn. "I can drive one of those typewriter contraptions all by myself, even if the going is a mite slow. Nobody knows about our little adventure 'cepting you, me and O'Connell."

Hanson's frown deepened. "I would rather you had consulted me before subcontracting on our agreement."

"You hire me to do the job. You ain't paying enough to mandate how it needs doing. Besides, no cause to worry. I trust O'Connell with my life."

"You've trusted him with something considerably more important."

"A fact which ain't altered by you complaining about it. You want to keep bitching about what can't be changed, or do you want to talk about the guns?"

Kowalski lifted his cup to mask a smile at the Englishman's irritation. The hotel's coffee was good, the quality a match for the opulent suite. He ran his gaze around the room, taking in the wood-panelled walls, the heavy velvet curtains, the polished expanse of the walnut desk between the two men. He was impressed. He would be sure to stay here next time he was in town. Maria would love it, although she'd surely make a show of tutting at the expense.

"The guns then…" said Hanson, returning his attention to the transcript. "It appears your fellow Americans have acquired quite the arsenal for their chums in the Old Country."

"Ain't my fellows – I'm Floridian. But yes, they've managed to get themselves a whole heap of munitions. Decent merchandise at that. All packed and ready to go."

"On this airship, the *Maverick*?"

"Leaving for Dublin in two days."

Hanson leaned back in his chair. "If I seriously believed they'd head straight for Dublin it would be more convenient all round – we'd simply seize the cargo at the docks. But doubtless they'll unload in some remote spot well before they reach the city."

"Why not go to the authorities here? Like as not they'd take a dim view of gun-running. Especially if they ain't getting a cut of the deal."

"We're on the verge of convincing the Americans to join the war effort. We can't upset the applecart by making this business public. It's not the time for debate of the Irish question, either here or at home."

"Figure life would be simpler if you folks just left Ireland well alone."

"Personally, I wouldn't argue with your assessment." Hanson removed his spectacles and massaged the bridge of his nose. "But Irish emancipation isn't top of anyone's agenda at the moment. The last thing we need is an armed insurrection in our own back garden."

Kowalski gestured towards the transcript. "Seems that's exactly what this Von Gossler character is hoping for. Sounds to me like he put up the money for the guns."

"Doubtless. Von Gossler is known to us – a distant cousin of the Kaiser himself no less."

"Don't that make him British royalty?"

"Very droll. As it happens, his father was an honorary Colonel in the Queen's Guards. Needless to say he wasn't invited to take up his commission upon the outbreak of hostilities."

"But daddy's boy ain't a soldier?"

"Drummed out of military school apparently, much to pater's irritation. He's been in the United States for a year, a trade attaché at the embassy." Hanson snorted. "Bloody Germans. Their cover stories are as unimaginative as their plans." He paused, eyes flicking down once more, roving across the page. "All the same, supporting the Fenians this brazenly is rather a blunt instrument, even for them."

"Blunt and heavy can work just fine," said Kowalski. The British sometimes needed reminding that not all schemes should be judged on their elegance and complexity. When it came to strategy and plans, Kowalski was an advocate of big and stupid — such schemes were seldom pretty, but in his experience they usually worked.

Hanson nodded in unhappy agreement. The Englishman had run out of options, both of them knew it. Kowalski stayed silent, waiting for the other man to suggest the obvious course of action.

He had discussed the eventuality with the Admiral even before departing Florida. If it came to it, he was authorised to negotiate a new contract between the Free Fleet and the British to deal with the weapons.

The Admiral had stipulated only two restrictions: first, the Fleet's involvement must remain secret — nobody wanted to upset Florida's larger neighbour by blatantly operating inside her borders. And second, whilst the guns themselves were fair game, there were to be no American casualties. Kowalski had agreed to the first requirement, something he had fully expected. But he had committed only to "try his best" on the second — a response the Admiral had clearly expected in turn.

Eventually Hanson spoke. "Are you familiar with the events of 1776 when the Bostonians tipped tonnes of British cargo into the harbour?"

Kowalski nodded. The history of the Revolution was still taught in school, even if Florida was no longer part of the Union.

The Englishman gave a thin smile. "I wonder if now might be a good time to return the favour?"

*

The electric lamps strung along the dock front crackled, their light reflecting in the black waters of the Charles. In the circles of illumination beneath the lamps the bustle of commerce continued, the night's chill no obstacle to the pursuit of the dollar. Stevedores lugged crates and barrels between warehouses and paddle steamers, whilst more cargo rose on wooden platforms, hauled up the freight elevators to the airships tethered above. The underside of the gasbags caught the light from below, the bunched aircraft resembling a fixed bank of low cloud somehow defying the cold wind blowing in from the sea.

Kowalski and O'Connell strode down the cobbled quay, hopping out of the paths of men laden with produce – trays of fish packed in ice, wooden crates of clinking bottles, and a hundred other kinds of trade goods. Kowalski leaned towards his companion as they walked.

"I thought it would be quieter at night."

"This is quieter," said O'Connell. "But still. Cargo to unload. Plenty of men. Work nights. Get away from. A nagging wife." He smiled. "Done it myself. A few times."

"Thought you'd retired? Pension not enough?"

"Fleet looks after me. But cash. Goes to the lady. Elsewise I'd spend it. On whiskey." He shrugged his broad shoulders. "Truth is. I get bored."

Figures, thought Kowalski. His companion had enjoyed an eventful career with the Fleet. An aerial dragoon like himself, O'Connell had dropped out of the sky into Cuba, Bolivia, and a dozen other tropical conflicts. Kowalski had served with him for years, had been alongside him when he'd taken three bullets in the chest, and had helped drag him clear of the jungle. The iron lung which saved Tank's life had also ended his time with the Fleet. He'd stayed as long as he could, but the moisture and heat played havoc with his new insides. Forced to flee Florida's humidity, he'd headed north to colder climes and a quieter life. But once a mercenary, always a mercenary – the big man had jumped at the chance for a little adventure when Kowalski came knocking.

O'Connell stopped. "That's her."

Kowalski eyed the aircraft looming above the last of the elevator towers. She hung in the air, a hundred and fifty feet of rigid frame dirigible – big enough when she'd floated free of the construction yards two decades previously, but a dwarf by the standards of the modern giants. Despite her obvious age, the *Maverick* looked to be in decent repair, her gas envelope neatly patched, bashes and dents in the gondola's frame concealed beneath a reasonably fresh coat of paint.

To all appearances she was an honest ship, her crew earning their crust picking up small freight contracts here and there, combining them into full holds to ferry across the Atlantic.

Only Kowalski's knowledge of her current illicit cargo prompted him to look any closer. The shutters welded to her lamps so the beams could be shielded, the extra floor hatch in addition to the regular loading doors, the dark grey paintwork and canvas, chosen to blend into the backdrop of an overcast sky – these details combined to form a different picture, one where the *Maverick* was at least occasionally engaged in the transport of contraband goods.

"You're sure the guns are aboard?"

"Pretty sure," said Tank. "Two big crates. Went up earlier."

"And just one man still around?"

O'Connell nodded. "Short straw. Rest of the crew. Gone to the pub."

The two men looked to the high deck of the freight tower. A lone figure shuffled back and forth, transferring the remaining packages and crates from the elevator platform to the waiting airship. Kowalski ran his eyes down over the tower itself, gaze fixing on the steep stairs winding their way around the wooden structure.

"Time for a climb then."

*

They crouched in the shadows behind a stack of crates, Kowalski's heart pounding from the exertion of the climb. His ragged breath stood in sharp contrast to the even mechanical wheeze emerging from the man beside him. O'Connell looked as if the ascent hadn't bothered him a jot. Maybe there was something to be said for steel innards after all.

The view from the tower's upper deck was impressive. A line of airships stretched away down the dock, each pulling at their ropes, tugged by the wind. A hundred feet below, the white glare of the waterfront contrasted with the city across the river.

As far as the eye could see, Boston spread out, a dark jumble of rooftops and chimneys, silhouetted against the orange gaslight spilling up from the narrow streets. In the distance, the domed tower of Faneuil Hall stood stark against the uplit cloud.

Kowalski turned from the vista to observe the platform's only other occupant, now perched on a crate at the tower's far edge, taking a break from his labours, puffing on a tightly-rolled cigarette. Damned fool – he surely wouldn't be smoking if his boss was around. In Kowalski's experience, airship captains tended to take a dim view of naked flames.

"You think you can take care of our friend?" he said. "Quietly mind, and less than lethally."

O'Connell pulled a billy club from his coat – six inches of leather, filled with sand. The weapon looked tiny in the big man's fist. "Depends how thick. His head is."

"Heh. I ain't kidding Tank. Admiral's orders."

"Not working. For the. Old man. No more."

"Then do it for me. Or try to, at least."

O'Connell rolled his eyes then slipped away amongst the crates and barrels, crouched low, moving with exaggerated care on the balls of his feet. His steps were quieter than his breathing, itself quickly swallowed up by the wind and the creaks from the *Maverick*'s tethers. O'Connell had always been a stealthy one – a ghost when he needed to be, sent in ahead of the rest of the squad to deal with sentries or lookouts. It was uncanny, the way the brute, normally a lumbering ox, could disappear into the shadows when the occasion demanded. Kowalski had always been glad Tank was on his side rather than part of any opposition.

He raised his head above the boxes and attempted to follow O'Connell's progress, occasionally catching a glimpse of movement, but only because he knew roughly where to look.

The crewman finished his smoke, flicking the remnants of his cigarette over the platform's edge towards the water. He turned back to his task and bent to lift his next load. Tank closed the gap, rearing up behind his unsuspecting prey. A massive fist swung and the leather sap caught the unfortunate soul behind the ear. The crewman keeled over.

O'Connell dragged the unconscious form into the shadows as Kowalski left his cover and crossed the platform. Tank straightened, his grin visible in the darkness.

"Been. A while. Enjoyed that."

"Figure he didn't. Good to see you ain't lost your touch." Kowalski nodded towards the waiting airship. "Let's go and break something."

They made their way up the gangplank into the *Maverick*'s hold. The compartment was long and narrow, stuffed with barrels, bolts of cloth, boxes and packages, all stacked around the curved walls, lashed to the ribs of the gondola's frame with cargo netting. Two larger crates sat apart from the others, alongside the floor hatch – the guns, ready for a drop off in some secluded part of the Irish countryside. And perfectly placed for an unscheduled drop off right now, thought Kowalski, imagining the dark water waiting a hundred feet directly below the hatch.

"Come on," he said. "We've got cargo to unload…"

Before either man could move, a voice sounded behind them.

"Raise your hands," came the command. "Turn around slowly."

Kowalski's heart sank. He lifted his hands and shuffled around. O'Connell did the same.

A thin man stood in the forward hatchway, a heavy revolver in his grip. He looked no more than twenty, black hair close-cropped at the back and sides, flopping forwards at the front, the colour a match for the wispy attempt at a moustache dusting his top lip. Above the stiff collar of his jacket the man's Adam's apple bobbed up and down as he swallowed. The pistol wobbled from Kowalski to O'Connell and then back again.

With his free hand the gunman beckoned to another figure lurking within the cockpit. "Disarm them." The voice held a hint of an accent, and more than a hint of a sneer.

The second man stepped through the hatch – a deckhand, clad in rough denim overalls and cloth cap. He patted down the two interlopers, relieving them of their pistols. He lifted a gun in each hand and offered the captives a smirk, his teeth chipped and dirty. Kowalski smiled straight back. The man's cursory search had failed to uncover the knife sheath strapped at the small of his back. That was something, thought Kowalski. But it wasn't much – pistol beat knife every time in his experience.

"Go and see to your crewmate," said the gunman. "Then fetch your captain from his tavern."

The deckhand hesitated, eyeing the two captives. The gunman took umbrage at not being obeyed immediately.

"Be quick about it," he snapped. "Or I'll shoot you first."

The crewman curled his lip. "Aye, you probably would at that," he said in a surly Irish brogue. He turned away and left the trio in the hold.

"Gossler I presume," said Kowalski.

"Von Gossler if you don't mind. And you are?"

"Nobody important. You know how it is, all this cargo lying around. Thought there might be some going spare. Clearly we picked the wrong ship." Kowalski offered his best winning smile. "We'll be on our way." He shifted sideways towards the gangplank.

"Common thieves? I think not. How would you know my name?"

Kowalski cursed himself for a fool and decided to remain silent – less chance of making things worse. Von Gossler gave a thin smile and nodded towards O'Connell.

"Might I suggest a less memorable specimen for undertaking reconnaissance? One could hardly miss this brute hanging around all day."

As the German regarded Tank, Kowalski took the opportunity to edge further towards the hatchway. The movement brought Von Gossler's attention and the weapon swinging back round.

"Don't test me. I will not hesitate to shoot."

Maybe, thought Kowalski. But his sideways shuffle had reduced the German's ability to cover both men. O'Connell saw it too and took a small step to his right, widening the gap further. The move brought a rush of colour to the gunman's cheeks.

"I'm warning you..." The pistol barrel swung back and forth with increased vigour, the movement following the German's darting eyes. "You must listen to me..."

"Whoa there friend," said Kowalski. "No need to get all riled."

The young man turned again, the gun back on Kowalski. "I informed the captain about our observer..." The pitch of his voice rose. "He did not listen either. Ignorant peasant. More concerned with whiskey than –"

O'Connell interrupted Von Gossler's rant, pouncing forward, huge hands extended, reaching for the revolver. The German lurched round, eyes wide, staggering back from Tank's looming menace. The gun fired and the weapon's roar echoed through the compartment. The bullet thumped into O'Connell and threw him backwards. His heavy frame smashed headlong to the deck.

"I warned him," shouted Von Gossler as the reverberations of the shot faded away. His entire body shook as he waved the gun at the fallen man. "He did not listen." The wild stare turned on Kowalski and the muzzle of the pistol came up again.

"Easy there," said Kowalski, backing away.

Von Gossler closed the gap, the revolver trembling in his grip. "He should have listened..."

The sap struck the German across the back of the head with a dull thud. His eyes rolled up into his skull and he crumpled to the deck, the pistol tumbling from numb fingers to clatter on the planks. Kowalski blew out the breath he'd been holding and looked up at O'Connell.

"Thanks."

"No problem," wheezed Tank, the loud gurgles emanating from his chest giving the lie to his reply. The big man stood over the fallen German, sap dangling from one hand, the other held to his torso, index finger plugged to the knuckle in the bullet hole beneath his shirt.

"Going to. Need. Patching up."

"Can it wait?"

"Long. As you. Don't need. Any help."

"You keep watch then."

Kowalski moved towards the crates and the floor hatch. The wooden boxes were long and broad and no doubt heavy – he hoped he'd be able to move them without assistance. But taking a closer look at the hatchway, he saw his original plan would require revision regardless of the heft of the crates. The doors were secured with a heavy padlock.

Behind him the rumble of machinery split the night. He whirled round to see Tank gesturing towards the freight elevator. The centre platform shook, the heavy gears at each corner rotating, teeth meshing with their counterparts on the supporting pillars as they carried the elevator down into the tower's frame. God damn it, thought Kowalski – no time to look for any keys now. The *Maverick*'s captain and her crew would be on their way up soon, likely unimpressed at being dragged from their drinks.

He lifted the fallen pistol and took aim at the padlock. The revolver bucked in his hand, its roar followed immediately by the harsh ping of a ricochet and Tank's breathless swearing as the bullet flew past the big man's ear. Kowalski turned from the undamaged lock to meet his companion's irate stare.

"Sorry."

The situation required a new strategy, something bigger, something dumber – Kowalski's speciality. He tossed the pistol aside and fumbled in his jacket pocket. He pulled out a box of matches and struck one. The match flared up and he stuffed it into the box's open drawer. The resulting conflagration singed his fingers and he cursed, tossing the blazing package towards a bundle of rolled cloth.

The flames licked at the material and caught hold. Hungry fire scurried along the lengths of twine and rope securing the cargo. In moments, the whole pile was ablaze. Satisfied, Kowalski made for the gangplank. He grabbed O'Connell's arm.

"Come on."

Tank shook him off and limped back towards the slumped form of Von Gossler. "Can't. Leave him. Just a kid."

"A kid who shot you."

O'Connell ignored the jibe. He reached down with his free hand and gripped Von Gossler's lapels, hoisting him upwards. Kowalski shook his head but moved to help all the same.

"Civilian life's made you soft."

He grabbed the man's ankles and together they lugged the German down the gangplank, dumping him at the tower's edge.

Kowalski manoeuvred through the crates and peered over the shaft's rim. The platform was beginning its journey back up, doubtless laden with grumpy Irishmen. Returning his attention to the *Maverick*, he pulled his knife from its sheath and made for the forward mooring. Acutely aware of the rumbles from the lifting gear behind him, he hacked at the rope, dragging the serrated blade across the tough fibres. His arm was aching by the time the line parted with a twang, whipping away into the darkness.

He bounded across the platform for the second mooring point, this one nearer the stairs where O'Connell waited, hunched over, hand pressed to his chest. He watched as Kowalski bent to the line.

"Just. Leave. It."

"Get out of here Tank," answered Kowalski, jaw tight, forcing himself not to shout. He couldn't leave the airship tethered there. The crew might be able to extinguish the flames and he doubted the fire had done much damage to the cargo as yet.

O'Connell lurched out of sight down the steps and Kowalski set to it. The anchor line positively sang under the pressure as the craft strained to be free, the breeze pushing the airship's nose out and away from the tower. The knife was barely a third of the way through when the cable surrendered to the strain, a whiplash crack echoing across the platform. He made for the stairs, the *Maverick* bobbing away from the tower in his wake, fire blossoming inside her.

Kowalski was half a flight down when the elevator platform rumbled past, and a full flight down, turning the corner, when angry cries rang out as the crew discovered their aircraft adrift. He had caught up with Tank, almost at ground level, when the airship erupted in crimson fire.

The explosion ruptured the dark sky. An infernal illumination rippled across the docks and the buildings on the opposite bank, painting the scenery with shifting patterns of orange light and shadow. Tongues of fire spewed out, flames rolling across the face of the tower, scorching the timbers and bringing howls from the men trapped on the upper deck.

The airship's frame hung in the centre of the fireball for a moment before gravity rudely reasserted its dominion. The burning mass plummeted from the sky, flames hissing in the cold waters of the Charles.

*

"Why didn't you tell me you were in town?" demanded Maria, hands on hips, pleasure and irritation battling for control of her features.

Kowalski stepped into the office and back-heeled the door shut behind him. He slipped his arms around her and pulled her close. He pressed his lips to hers until the stiff pose melted and she returned his embrace. Eventually she pushed him away.

"Don't think you're forgiven," she said, struggling to maintain a disapproving tone.

"Pleasure to see you too."

He looked around the room, taking in the piles of papers, the shelves groaning beneath their burden of books, a blackboard scrawled with indecipherable equations. The office was a near twin to the room in which he had first set eyes on her, deep within an underground laboratory.

"Busy?"

She brushed hair from her face. "Of course I'm busy." She waved at the expanse of paperwork. "I have work to do. Not like your other women, sitting idly by waiting for you to come a-calling."

"Heh. There are no other women. Well, none that count."

She scowled up at him, but the slap he half-expected failed to materialise. He decided to push his luck. "Not too busy for dinner? The Lenox – my treat. And I have a suite reserved..."

"How very forward. I like that in a man – refreshingly modern." She raised an inquisitive eyebrow. "The Lenox? What are we celebrating?"

"A job well done."

"One you can tell me about?"

"Nope." Kowalski turned for the door. "But I guarantee there'll be plenty of other stories. Tank does love a tall tale."

"Tank?"

"A friend," said Kowalski over his shoulder. "He's joining us."

"In which case I shall make an effort," she called after him. "I would scarcely bother on just your account."

Kowalski smiled as he walked away. Maria could turn up in a length of sackcloth and he'd still think she looked good.

*

Sure enough, she did indeed look damned fine. The ivory dress emphasised her curves and provided a handsome contrast to her tumble of black hair. She turned heads as they entered the restaurant and

Kowalski was filled with the peculiar mixture of smugness and bewilderment he always experienced when she was on his arm in public. What was Maria doing with him? Beautiful and smart – a damn sight smarter than he was, that was for sure – she had to have other admirers.

Maybe one day he'd have to make an honest woman of her, he thought, not for the first time. But deep within he already knew that particular resolution would founder in the face of their next argument. They seemed able to go three days or so in each other's company before something would spark an explosion.

For the moment though, the inevitable conflagration lay safely in the future and he was determined to enjoy the evening.

O'Connell stood as Kowalski escorted Maria to the table. The big man towered over her petite form, his burly frame stuffed into a new three piece suit – one of the proceeds, Kowalski guessed, of their recent payoff from Hanson.

The debriefing had gone well. "Nicely done, if a tad extravagant," Hanson had said, tapping his finger on the lurid newspaper report regarding the immolation of the *Maverick*. An unfortunate accident apparently, being blamed on a drunken crewman.

Kowalski had taken the cheque and headed for the First Boston Bank, wiring the funds to the Fleet's headquarters in Tampa. He made a withdrawal too – Tank's agreed fee, plus a sizeable bonus on top to meet the costs of the welding job O'Connell's innards required. Seemed Tank had visited both blacksmith and tailor.

"Maria Eisenstein, Tank O'Connell..."

O'Connell took Maria's hand in his paw and bent to give it a kiss.

"A pleasure," she said. "John has been telling me all about you."

She leaned in and rapped his chest with her knuckles. She gave a smile at the clang which emanated from beneath the waistcoat.

"My apologies, I couldn't resist."

Tank gave out a deep-throated rattle, his version of a chuckle.

"Pleasure. To meet you too. The lady who. Tamed this. Reprobate."

"Tamed?" Maria turned a caustic look towards Kowalski. "This one?"

"You have. No idea."

"No Mister O'Connell, I don't." Maria moved round the table to take a seat. "But I insist you tell me everything I ought to know regarding the scandalous past of this beau of mine."

Kowalski made a show of helpless surrender and took his chair. "Heh. Just don't go believing even half of what he tells you..."

His gaze was drawn to the street beyond the window. The few people braving the wind bustled along, collars up, hats pulled down against the elements. All but one – a lone figure across the street, clad in a top hat and long coat, stood motionless in a shadowy patch between the gas lamps.

The figure lifted a hand, doffing his hat to reveal a head completely wrapped in bandages. His features were hidden beneath the folds, but the black holes where his eyes would be seemed fixed upon the trio of diners.

Kowalski felt a cold knot form in his stomach. He stood, his chair clattering back, the noise drawing frowns from other tables and bringing his own companions' small-talk to an abrupt halt.

"What's wrong?" said Maria.

He looked down at her. "I'm not sure."

He turned back to the window but the bandaged man was gone. Kowalski stepped up to the glass and peered in both directions down the street. No sign of their observer – if that's even what the figure had been. He lowered himself back into his chair, shaking his head. Maria and O'Connell stared at him across the table.

"Ignore me. It's nothing."

Too much damned sneaking around recently, he thought. This underhand stuff was getting to him. He preferred a stand-up fight to all this skulduggery. He beckoned the waiter over – what he needed was a drink, a large one.

The window caved in with an almighty crack, shards of glass spraying across the dining room. A hard black sphere bounced once on the white linen and rolled to a stop in the centre of the table.

The trio froze, staring at the grenade, the only sound the tinkling of falling glass. Time ground to a near standstill, everything moving as if mired in treacle.

Maria turned towards Kowalski, her mouth opening in the beginnings of a scream. He rose, reaching for her – slow, too slow.

He saw Tank stretch out his hands, the man's meaty fingers scrabbling across the tablecloth, closing around the black ball, pulling it towards himself.

And then the world turned red.

*

Extracted from 'A History of the Ancient Sects and Societies of the East'...

The scholar Al-Kalil, by virtue of his great intelligence did advance himself to become foremost amongst the lieutenants of Hassan. Primary amongst the services he provided the Master was the creation of an army of devoted followers, known as The Faithful. These souls – if such description is suited, there being some doubt they possessed such an essential element – despising fatigue, dangers and torture, immune to pain and ignorant of fear, would joyfully surrender their lives whenever it pleased the Lord of the Mountain, who might require them to protect himself or carry out his mandates of death.

One Persian Caliph, passing close by the territory of Hassan, and hearing wondrous and fearful tales of the sect, requested an invitation to the fortress. Hassan eagerly assented, suffering – as all tyrants will – an urge to validate his majesty with the respect of other rulers. On making the round of the towers, two of the Faithful, at a sign from the Master, stabbed themselves to the heart, and fell at the feet of the terrified Caliph, whilst Hassan coolly said, "Say but the word, and at a sign from me, you shall see them all thus on the ground."

How such devotion was secured was a secret Al-Kalil kept tightly unto himself. The scholar's mania for secrecy extended even unto his Master, and whilst Hassan revelled in the use of this cadre of devout adherents, and saw his power and fame grow in direct proportion to their employment, greatly he desired to comprehend the method of their creation...

Washington, District of Columbia

Von Gossler opened the window and leaned out, his bandaged fingers fumbling with the handle. At the second attempt the door swung free, smacking back against the side of the carriage. He stepped from the train and joined the flow of passengers traipsing up the platform.

The fans suspended from the high curve of the station's ceiling stirred the clouds of steam leaking from the engine at the train's head. He passed through the vapours, the heat radiating from the locomotive's boiler causing beads of sweat to dampen the strips of cloth binding his face. The moisture reactivated the itch which plagued his skin beneath the covering, but he resisted the urge to scratch, a painful lesson learned from previous lapses in control.

His wrapped face and hands drew curious glances from his fellow passengers but Von Gossler ignored them. He joined the line and concentrated his attention on the knot of people waiting beyond the barriers. He had telegraphed ahead, arranging to be met from the train.

The queue for the inspection of tickets was a microcosm of America – all walks of life represented, the different strata of society jumbled together without thought for hierarchy or precedence. How very democratic, he thought, eyeing the mixture with distaste. The line served as a fine illustration of everything wrong with the nation – men of quality forced to wait, intermingled with the lower orders. What, pray, was the point of having first class carriages, if this vulgar melee awaited travellers upon disembarking?

He finally reached the barrier and brandished his ticket. The inspector waved him on and he passed through the gate. He was immediately intercepted – a face he recognised from the embassy.

The man touched his fingers to the brim of his hat and gave a curt nod. "Allow me," he said, holding out his hand. Von Gossler was only too happy to pass over his valise. He flexed his fingers as he was led from the station. Carrying the case along the platform had set the cracked skin stinging beneath the bandages.

His guide led him to an automobile, a Benz, its black and silver bodywork polished to a brilliant shine – near twenty feet of gleaming mechanical muscle. The vehicle drew admiring glances from passing pedestrians. This dazzling example of German engineering had been shipped across the Atlantic to impress the American politicians. A simple task – most of them were representatives from backwoods territories, still traversing the streets of Washington by horse, thinking trolley cars and locomotives the height of modern technology.

The driver's seat was positioned behind the long slope of the bonnet, the passenger compartment further back, its windows tinted – protection against both sun's glare and casual observation. Von Gossler's guide tucked the valise away into the vehicle's luggage compartment, then opened the rear door and waved him towards the shady interior.

The leather seats within already held another occupant. Von Gossler arranged himself, settling into the deep cushioning under the stern gaze of Johann Heinrich von Bernstorff, the Ambassador himself. This was unexpected. Von Gossler licked his lips beneath the bandages.

"Your Excellency. There was no need to come and meet me..."

"On the contrary, I deemed it essential."

Von Bernstorff leaned forward and rapped on the glass pane separating the two men from the driver. The Benz's engine purred into life and they pulled away from the station.

"How are your injuries?"

"The burns are healing." Von Gossler swallowed, determined to keep any tremor from his tone. "Although I am told there will be scarring."

The diplomat's eyes flicked down, taking in the cloth-wrapped hands before returning to meet Von Gossler's gaze. "Good. It will serve as a reminder of the perils of exceeding one's abilities."

Von Gossler's blood thumped in his ears. How dare this functionary speak to him in such a fashion? "Bernstorff. You forget yourself –"

"No. It is you who have forgotten yourself – setting up this Irish affair without authority."

"At least I took action," snarled Von Gossler. "If I left matters to you, we would still be talking. All you do is talk."

"Idiot. All I appear to do is talk. An important distinction – one you seem incapable of grasping."

"I dealt with the Floridians —"

"Once again you are mistaken. If anyone dealt with the Free Fleet, it was I. Can you comprehend just how much money it took to prevent a mercenary vendetta?" The diplomat shook his head. "Your thirst for revenge has compounded your original foolishness."

The ambassador looked away, staring out through the smoked glass as the buildings of Washington rolled by. Burning with a bitter mix of anger and shame, Von Gossler did the same. The view brought him to an uncomfortable realisation – they were not heading for the embassy.

"Where are we going?"

"You are leaving the Americas. I have convinced your father you can better serve Germany somewhere very far from here..."

Von Gossler began to tremble, a cold sweat seeping from every pore. His guts clenched at the thought of his father's steely gaze poring over a telegram from the ambassador. Von Bernstorff let him stew in his fear, then patted his bandaged hand, a humourless smile in place.

"Don't worry. You are not bound for the Front. Germany needs soldiers, not foolish boys."

Von Gossler hated himself for the flood of relief which coursed through his veins. "Where am I being sent?"

The ambassador ignored the question. He reached into his waistcoat and withdrew a slip of paper. He unfolded it and regarded its contents.

"You had a tutor? Falke?"

"Yes..." said Von Gossler, bewildered by this turn in the conversation. "Years ago..."

"Wilhelm has indulged a fancy and financed one of Falke's projects." Von Bernstorff waved a dismissive hand. "Something scientific I believe, and no doubt doomed to expensive failure."

"What of it?"

"I have recommended you as an assistant."

"I'm no scientist..."

"No." The thin smile appeared again. "But then you were hardly much of a trade attaché."

"I warn you Bernstorff, you can't speak to me like this."

The ambassador observed the tantrum with disdain. "We won't have to put up with each other for much longer." He pointed forward through the windscreen.

In front of the Benz, the road descended towards Washington's aerodrome terminal – an open field surrounded by hangars, the meadow playing host to a diverse collection of aircraft. Single-seater biplanes rubbed wingtips with ornithopters, and balloons and airships of all sizes bobbed at their tethers.

Looming over everything, dominating the view was the unmistakeable bulk of a Zeppelin. Normally this giant of the skies would have filled Von Gossler with nationalistic pride, but now the sight of it only added to his gnawing uncertainty.

"The British persist on prowling the North Atlantic with an admirable thoroughness," said Von Bernstorff. "You will travel south, then make the crossing from Buenos Aires."

"And my final destination?"

The diplomat stared at Von Gossler, his eyes cold and grey.

"As I said before, somewhere very far from here."

*

Gallipoli Peninsula

"That's a round pound you owe me now Sarge."

Macgregor glowered down at the coins, the pennies barely perceptible in the gathering twilight. Two tails – a losing throw. Another one. His run of poor luck was approaching legendary status. The boys were beginning to whisper about it. Bloody stupid game.

He wasn't supposed to allow the men to gamble, never mind participate himself – strictly against rules and regs. But what else was there to do when they weren't fighting Abdul or digging graves? Macgregor figured the odd game of Two-Up wasn't going to kill anybody. Although Private Bell's smug satisfaction might well result in someone getting a good kicking. Macgregor shifted his dark look from the coins to the foxhole's other occupant.

"No need to be quite so cheerful about it Bluey."

"Sorry Sarge," said Bell. His grin suggested he was anything but.

"How about we write it off against some of your debt from Wozzer?" Bell's smile faltered as Macgregor continued. "Don't think you've worked off your obligation just yet."

Depending on who was spinning the yarn, the "Battle of the Wazir" had been either a dark stain on the Corps' honour or a bloody good laugh. Outraged at the prices charged in the Cairo brothels, a bunch of drunken lads had kicked off – the disturbance spreading until a full two thousand of the Diggers were embroiled. Macgregor and his squad were swept up in the chaos and it took a few hard words, and a couple of harder knocks, for him to keep the rowdiest of his boys from joining in. He'd led them all clear of the red light district, sticking to back streets, extricating them just before the Red Caps arrived. The military policemen restored order in their usual robust fashion – wading in, batons swinging.

The morning after, sobered-up and beholding the unfortunate souls on punishment duty, Bluey and the others had acknowledged the debt they owed their gruff sergeant.

Pleased at Bell's discomfort, Macgregor reached for the pennies once again. Might as well have another throw. Better to work his bad luck out on the coins – maybe use it all up before the next run-in with Abdul. He placed the pennies on the kip and made to flick the wooden paddle. But before he could send the coins skyward, Bell's hand shot out and grasped his forearm.

"You hear that?"

Macgregor hadn't heard a thing, but that meant little. A decade of blasting for opal back in Lightning Ridge had left him near deaf years before he'd enlisted. But Bell? The boy could hear a bloody pin drop, and had the eyes to match. There wasn't a better scout in the Corps – exactly why Macgregor had brought him out here within spitting distance of the Turkish lines.

Bell scrambled up the front bank of the crater, inching forward until his eyes crested the rim. Macgregor let the coins and paddle drop to the mud. He hefted his rifle and moved to join his comrade. Side by side they lay, pressed into the damp earth, peering out into the gloom.

A torn and shattered landscape lay beyond the foxhole. Pocked with craters and dotted with gnarled and stunted trees, the scene was rendered in shades of grey by the moonlight leaking between the clouds. Beyond the scrub, the escarpment's bulk reared up, a blacker patch against the sky.

Macgregor stared hard into every shadow. His imagination conjured up flickers of movement, sinister shapes creeping forward, but the half-seen figures would resolve themselves into branches, or rocks, or mounds of earth – into anything but an advancing Turk.

"Nothing," he whispered.

"I heard something..."

Macgregor slumped against the side of the crater and stared up into the sky. Stars twinkled for a moment, before disappearing again, swallowed by the drifting cloud. No great loss. The night sky made him uncomfortable. They were so far from home even the constellations were strangers. Was it any surprise they were all getting twitchy?

"Just one of the bloody Abduls visiting the little boys' room."

Bell maintained his silent vigil.

"Come on Bluey – no need to be so jumpy."

His companion gave a sigh and turned round. He leaned back alongside Macgregor. "Sarge... Can I ask you something?"

"Ask away mate. Can't promise a sensible answer mind. Us sergeants don't hear much more than the rest of you Diggers."

"Is it true? About the Tommies at Suvla? The Sandringham lot?"

"What's the story doing the rounds?"

Bell was silent for a moment, then the words spilled out of him in a rush. "I heard they marched into the mist and vanished. Forty men – gone. No injured. No bodies. Just gone. Like something... took 'em."

Macgregor had heard the story too, and more embellished versions of the tale besides. Truth was, nobody knew what had happened to the Sandringham Company – it was as if the ground had opened up and swallowed them whole. But he would be buggered if he'd let his squad scare one another witless with ghost stories.

"There's nothing out there but Abdul. Worry about him, not some damned bunyip. The Tommies are dead. Or captured. Or having high bloody tea with the Sultan himself." He punched Bell in the shoulder. "I don't know which, but I do know they weren't eaten by any monsters."

The feral growl which followed this pronouncement froze the two men in place – eyes wide, staring at one another. The hair on the back of Macgregor's neck stood on end and a chill tremor skittered its way through his bones. Bell was the first to react, fumbling for his rifle.

Something flew over Macgregor's head, smacking into the Private, knocking him down into the puddle in the bottom of the foxhole. Bell flailed on the ground, pinned in the mud by an emaciated figure. An initial yelp of surprise transformed into a high-pitched screech as his assailant bore down. The attacker was shirtless, pale skin criss-crossed with welts and scars, bone and muscle standing out stark on the scrawny torso.

Macgregor raised his gun and fired. The bullet struck true, he was sure of it – he would have sworn he heard the wet smack of the impact. But the half-dressed figure didn't even flinch, staying hunched over atop the struggling soldier. Bell's screams trailed off into a rasping gurgle as Macgregor fumbled with the bolt of his rifle. The click-clack of its action brought the attacker's head swinging round towards him. Macgregor's stomach lurched as he took in the sight.

The creature, for it could surely be no man, had a face wrecked by open sores, frayed into sagging strips of flesh, the eyes sunken, hidden deep within the hollow shadows of their sockets. The lips, tattered and torn, drew back from teeth stained black with Bell's blood. The thing hissed, its muscles bunching across its shoulders. Macgregor hauled his rifle up and yanked at the trigger as the thing leapt.

The beast crashed into him, sending him stumbling back against the crater wall. It scrabbled at him, its teeth snapping down into his upraised arm. Macgregor let out a roar and thumped his free fist into the creature's face. With a crunch of gristle, its nose crumpled, smeared sideways across its cheek, but the jaws maintained their vice-like grip even as Macgregor threw in another punch. The creature shook its head back and forth, gnawing at Macgregor's arm, worrying at the bite, oblivious to the desperate blows raining in.

Through a flood of pain and fear, Macgregor abandoned his strikes and scrabbled for the bayonet at his belt. Filthy skeletal fingers closed around his throat as he tugged the long blade free. Gasping for breath, he plunged the knife deep into the thing's side.

The claws tightened, digging into his neck as he stabbed again, and again. He felt a hot rush of agony as the skin of his throat ruptured. He coughed gouts of blood, the sprayed fluid mixing with the gore pumping from the creature's wounds. A part of his mind, somehow divorced from his ravaged body, kept focused on the knife in his hand – thrust, to the hilt, pull it back, thrust again. Nothing else mattered.

The beast's grip loosened, the jaws falling slack, the head lolling away. But the knife too fell still, tumbling from Macgregor's frozen fingers. Locked together in the bottom of the foxhole, bathed in each other's blood, the combatants lay still.

*

"Major Jones, I've heard a lot about you..."

The stranger stood stooped in the dugout entrance, his shock of ginger hair brushing the low lintel. The hair topped a wiry frame clad in a tweed three-piece suit. The man removed his spectacles and wiped at them with a handkerchief.

"From all the stories, I'd assumed you'd be taller."

Jones swigged a final mouthful of tea. He put the chipped enamel mug beside the remains of his breakfast and pushed himself to his feet.

"Any taller and I couldn't stand up in here."

"Doctor Gordon Sullivan," The man stepped forward with a smile, hand outstretched. "I'm here to see your specimen."

Jones returned the handshake. "That was quick."

"Three days on the most uncomfortable airship it has ever been my misfortune to board. But after your telegram, what did you expect?"

"There's been many a message to London in the last few weeks. None of them garnered such an immediate response." Jones glanced down at his visitor's medical bag. "Not much ammunition in there I'd imagine. I don't suppose you've another battalion or two along with you by any chance?"

"Sadly no. Soldiering's not really my line of work."

"What is?"

"Your mysterious telegram for starters. Buckingham thought it sounded right up our street." Sullivan's green eyes sparkled. "I'm with Porton Down."

"And my message was enough to drag you from your bubbling cauldrons?"

"Most definitely." The doctor pulled his handkerchief out again and dabbed at his brow. "Perhaps I could see the specimen now?"

Jones led the way. He ducked beneath the wooden frame of the entrance and stepped out into the trenchworks. He surveyed the camp – a drab clutter of canvas shelters and makeshift hovels cut into earthern walls. A muddy path was tramped into the trench bottom, winding its way past a campfire where a tin pan balanced precariously above the flames on a makeshift tripod of scrap metal. The pot was surrounded by a bedraggled collection of soldiers. They looked up as the two men emerged, nodding to Jones before turning back to the sorry stew of corned beef and water which constituted today's rations. And yesterday's. And every day for a month now.

The blazing sun sparkled off the sea away to the left, bringing an ill-fitting Mediterranean cheer to the scene. The waves lapped around the metal carcass of a stranded walker, a casualty of the initial assault on the beach. Off to the right, perhaps two miles distant, two of its more fortunate fellows could be seen, standing proud above the battlefield, their mortars trained on the Turkish lines. The great machines looked impressive, yet had proved all but useless on the uneven rocky terrain, unable to breach the defences atop the escarpment.

It had all started so well – the airships pounding the Turks as men poured ashore and established the beach-head. But three days in, the storm had taken half the dirigibles, snatching them from their moorings, along with all chance of a swift victory. Freed from constant bombardment, the Turks had held on long enough for reinforcements to arrive and the Imperial advance stumbled to a halt.

This narrow strip of land between the cliffs and the sea was the sum total of ground gained over three months of hard campaigning. A few miles of Ottoman soil – damned poor return for the blood spilled thus far. The original plan had seen them marching into the Turkish capital four weeks after stepping off the boats.

"I need to source some more appropriate attire," said Sullivan, his tall frame wilting in the heat. He gestured down at his tweeds. "Savile Row's finest. But more suited to London than Constantinople."

"We're still a long way from Constantinople Doctor," said Jones. "A long way indeed."

*

The cave was the coldest place they had to act as a morgue.

Other bodies had been buried in common graves during breaks in the fighting, the dead afforded as much dignity as time would allow. Not this corpse however – more ceremony, and more luxurious accommodation, awaited this particular casualty of war. A tarpaulin had been rigged over the cave's entrance. The shade, coupled with the seeping groundwater, served to keep the niche in the rocks relatively cool. If not for the stench, the cave would have made a pleasant refuge from the heat.

Jones lifted the lantern and hung it from the hook wedged into the rock overhead. The light spilled across the narrow cave and its gruesome contents. Sullivan's eyes were wide, darting behind his glasses, flicking from one part of the cadaver to the next, sucking in the details.

"Worth the trip?" asked Jones.

"Most assuredly," said Sullivan, his attention fixed on the body. "Four days dead you say? And yet look at the decay..." He stepped forward. "You don't mind if I...?"

"He's all yours. We're sick of the sight of him. And the smell."

Sullivan placed his bag on the table. He removed his jacket and hung it over the cave's lone chair before turning back to the case and thumbing the catch. He withdrew a pair of gloves made of some thin rubber, the material stretching almost translucent over his knuckles as he wriggled long fingers inside. Hands covered, brandishing a pair of gleaming metal tongs, he bent over the corpse.

Jones pulled out his cigarette case. He contemplated the solitary smoke it contained. Tobacco was in short supply, along with everything else. The irony wasn't lost on him – here he was, standing in the Ottoman Empire itself, yet the Turkish blend he could have picked up from any of London's better tobacconists proved stubbornly unavailable.

Sullivan shifted the body and putrid air assailed Jones' nostrils with renewed intensity. That settled it – now was definitely as good a time as any. He plucked the lonely cigarette from its resting place and struck a match. He held it to the tip and inhaled deeply, savouring the light-headed rush brought on by the smoke. One thing to be said in favour of enforced abstinence, it certainly made an infrequent indulgence all the more pleasurable, regardless of the setting. He breathed out a lungful of thin blue vapour and watched Sullivan work his way over the corpse.

The doctor's attention roved across the cadaver, manipulating the tongs with delicate precision as he poked and prodded at the emaciated form. Strips of grey skin were peeled away from wounds, the black and rotten flesh beneath sniffed at and explored.

The examination was accompanied by exclamations of excitement quite at odds with the reaction the corpse had provoked in Kendrick, the regiment's own surgeon.

"Good God," said Sullivan, his movements coming to an abrupt halt, gangly frame hunched over the end of the table.

Jones smiled to himself. Now that was exactly the same expression Kendrick had employed. He took a final draw from between pinched fingers, relishing the last of the tobacco's smoke. He flicked the cigarette butt away into the mud.

"You found the bolt then?" he said.

Sullivan had twisted the corpse's neck, the awful face turned away to reveal the back of its head. Near the base of the skull the matted hair was shorn down to a patch of stubble. At its centre, a hexagonal metal bolt protruded from skin streaked with rust and dried blood.

"Don't suppose that thingamabob is keeping the bugger's head attached do you?" Sullivan didn't wait for an answer, instead going to his bag once more and rummaging within.

He turned back, armed with bulky pair of pliers and a broad smile. Too broad by half thought Jones, discomfited by the obvious glee the man was taking in the ghoulish proceedings.

"Hold him still would you Major? It's time for a little engineering."

Sullivan tossed over another pair of gloves. Jones pulled the rubber over his fingers, mouth gone dry in anticipation of the grisly task. He made his way around the table and, bracing himself, reached out, clamping his hands around the corpse's head. He felt the skin shift beneath his grip, its mooring to the bones beneath grown rotten and weak. Between his hands the milky grey eyes glared out above the ghastly snarl of the mouth, the chipped yellow teeth standing proud from withered gums – like tombstones. Jones swallowed and looked away.

"This is the most unpleasant thing I've done this morning."

The doctor shifted his grip on the pliers and placed his other hand across the back of the corpse's neck. "Try being on this end..."

Sullivan gave a sharp tug and the bolt slid free with a stomach-churning squelch. The man from Porton Down held his prize aloft between the pincers – a metallic spike, three inches long, streaked with blood and flecks of fibrous tissue. Its tip was hollow, and protruding from within, flaring out to glint orange in the lamplight, was a crown of splayed copper wire. Jones eyed the grisly artefact with distaste.

"I assume there's little chance that ended up in there by accident?"

"No chance at all."

"You know more about what's happening here than you're letting on Doctor." Jones pulled off his gloves and tossed them away into the recesses of the cave. "I don't appreciate being kept in the dark."

Sullivan held the bolt close and gave it a sniff. His nose wrinkled in disapproval. "I had my theories. Supposition I believe can now be advanced from informed conjecture to fact."

"Facts you'll be sharing any time soon?"

"Patience Major," said Sullivan. He produced his handkerchief and wiped the bolt clean of gore before slipping it into his waistcoat pocket. "It's rather a long story, and one I don't care to recount more than once. I need you to arrange a meeting with Sir William."

"Birdie's a busy man."

"Come now. A chap with your reputation? And Buckingham's patronage? If you can't get us in to see Birdwood, nobody can."

Jones turned his back on the doctor and made for the cave mouth. He pulled the tarpaulin aside and stepped out into the fresh air. Sullivan followed him out into the daylight.

"I'll get you in to see Sir William," said Jones. He gestured back towards the cavern. "Your examination seemed thorough enough, but whilst trying to prove your pet theory I predict you missed the most important detail..."

"Really?" Sullivan's lips compressed into a thin line, his brow furrowed. "Do enlighten me."

"That thing in there is wearing the remnants of a British uniform," said Jones. "The poor bastard used to be one of ours."

*

The projector's lamp gave out a low fizzing crackle, its light focused onto the pull-down screen. It provided the only illumination within General Sir William Birdwood's command bunker, the beam swirling with smoke from the old soldier's pipe.

With a click and a flicker, an image appeared on the screen, a sepia-tinted group portrait – a collection of austere-looking figures in dark coats and top hats. In the centre of the gathering, determined stare burning outward, upturned moustache familiar from a thousand newspaper photographs, stood Wilhelm of Prussia, the Kaiser himself.

Sullivan loped out from behind the projector.

"I'm sure you recognise our friend Willy. The cheery looking chaps around him are the committee of the Leopoldina, Germany's equivalent to the Royal Society." He reached up and tapped a finger on the screen, indicating a hawk-faced woman, the only female present. She stood at the edge of the photograph, the severe cut of her dress a match for her face, her hair scraped back beneath a black hat. She looked like she was fresh from attending a funeral.

"This formidable lady is Karla Falke – professor, chemist, and all-round dabbler in the darker corners of science."

Sullivan turned from the projected image and faced Jones and Sir William, the only members of his audience. He blinked in the mottled spotlight of the projector and waved a hand.

"Next slide if you please Major."

Jones pressed the lever protruding from the projector. With a clunk, a new image appeared.

"Good grief," muttered Sir William. He plucked his pipe from his mouth and waved its stem towards the screen. "It's like something from the damned circus, a bloody carnival trick."

The photograph had been taken in a laboratory, tiled walls and shelves stacked with specimen jars forming a backdrop to the central scene. There was Falke – clad in a white smock, no hat this time, but hair still pulled tightly back, enhancing the sharpness of her features. She reminded Jones of the vultures he'd seen in Africa, their heads bereft of feathers to make for more efficient scavenging from carcasses.

The woman stood alongside a second figure – a young man staring directly into the camera. The youth had close-cropped blonde hair and his shirtless torso was muscular in build. He looks like a soldier, thought Jones. But what demanded the eye's attention, and made the man's calm expression remarkable, was the series of metal skewers punched through the meat of his arm.

All down the left limb, from shoulder to bicep and on into the corded muscles of the forearm, sharp metal rods penetrated the skin, pushing up bulges of flesh before emerging once more. Seemingly oblivious to the thin trails of blood dribbling from the punctures, the soldier stood impassive, blank eyes fixed on a distant point.

"This is no trick," said Sullivan. "Falke has been experimenting for years, exploring pain and the body's capacity to ignore it. Mesmerism, chemistry, surgery – she's tried everything." The medical man stared up at the screen. "Naturally we've tried to replicate some of her work, but with little success. We've been limited to using rats and mice –"

"You sound disappointed," said Sir William.

Sullivan met Birdwood's frown. "We must understand the weapons of our enemy if we are to counter them."

Jones spoke up. "You think that thing in the cave is some military experiment gone wrong?"

"No Major. I'm not sure it went wrong at all." Sullivan returned his attention to the screen. "Last we heard, Falke was claiming she'd made a breakthrough. She was begging for more funds to continue her research."

"Did she get them?" asked Jones.

"We don't know. Our man in the Leopoldina can't seem to find out. But we do know Falke hasn't been in Germany for some time." Sullivan pulled the bolt from his waistcoat pocket and held it up. "This little contraption suggests to me the professor is enjoying a Turkish holiday."

Sir William took the bolt from Sullivan's outstretched hand. He peered at the length of metal and its crowning halo of copper wire.

"This was in the creature's head?"

Sullivan nodded. "At the base of the skull. The wires would be tangled up in exactly the portions of the brain Falke gets excited about. A few jolts of electrical energy up there and who knows what might result?" He continued, becoming more animated, his words coming faster. "Many of the specimen's wounds are old, showing signs of corruption and decay from long before the time of death. Classic symptoms of untreated infection – almost like leprosy." He waved his hand at the image on the screen, at the skewers in the young soldier's arm. "That's what pain is for, you see? It's a warning system to make us look after ourselves. Without it, we might miss a cut or a scrape that would otherwise become infected. It's a useful thing is pain."

The doctor paused, eyes distant, peering at a vision of the future.

"But it's also a tyrant. We exist in fear of its touch. Imagine if we could live beyond its reach..."

Jones and Birdwood shared an uncomfortable look at this sermon.

"Come now gentlemen," said Sullivan. "Soldiers who feel no pain? Men without fear? Surely any officer would long for such bravery amongst the men he commanded?"

Sir William puffed out a cloud of smoke. "Doctor, you are sadly mistaken – a common misapprehension amongst those who have not pursued a military career. Bravery is not the absence of fear. Far from it." He brandished his pipe at the man from Porton Down, fingers wrapped around the bowl, punctuating his words with little stabs of the stem. "Bravery is being afraid, but overcoming your fear to act in spite of it."

And Birdy should know, thought Jones. He was famous amongst the Diggers for his "dawn patrols" – the morning tours he took of the forward positions, well within range of the Turkish guns. His frequent presence on the front lines, even in the thick of battle, had earned him the respect of the Australian and New Zealander troops he commanded – men who normally harboured an abiding distrust of authority. Birdwood could have easily overseen his command from a comfortable cabin aboard the *Elizabeth*, moored offshore. But no – he ran the show from amid the trenches, and the mud, and the stacked bodies of the dead.

Jones' thoughts returned to the decaying corpse in the cave. "And what use is a man without fear if he's rotting to pieces as some kind of feral beast? Whoever and whatever he was before, that thing we found is anything but a soldier."

Sullivan's shoulders slumped, crestfallen at the comments. "Well, yes, clearly Falke's process has some unfortunate side effects..."

Good God, thought Jones – there's an understatement.

"But research always proceeds uncertainly," said Sullivan. "Progress occurs in fits and starts. Imagine if Falke can perfect her methods?"

Jones' mind pictured another situation, more immediately unsettling. He recalled the report of the scene in the foxhole – a pair of soldiers torn asunder, seemingly by the creature's bare hands and teeth.

"Even if she doesn't, imagine if the Germans or the Turks were to release a horde of the bloody things at us."

Sir William's grave look offered a mirror for Jones' own concern. He returned his attention to the man standing before the projection screen. "Well Doctor, what do we do about all this?"

Sullivan straightened his lanky frame, brightening at the opportunity to make his suggestions. "We need to find out where Falke is working. We have intelligence chappies looking into it from the London end, but perhaps your reconnaissance boys can join the hunt? Maybe question any Turkish prisoners too? See if they have any ghost stories to tell?"

Birdwood nodded. "Very well, consider it done. What else?"

Sullivan's eyes slid towards Jones. "The Major here tells me there have been more sightings since you recovered the original specimen."

"I doubt even a tenth of the reports are true," said Sir William. "The lads are so spooked they're seeing things."

"Vampires and werewolves," put in Jones. "Straight from the pages of the penny dreadfuls..."

"But however they're being described, chances are there's more of them out there?"

The soldiers shared an unhappy look. In an effort to preserve what little morale remained, officers throughout the Corps had been instructed to squash flat any rumours making the rounds. But suppression didn't necessarily make the stories untrue. Sullivan smiled at their silence, his eager gaze darting back and forth between the men seated before him.

"I'd very much like to take a look at a live example..." he said.

Jones knew where this was headed. A grim chill solidified in the pit of his stomach. Sullivan stared at him, gaze magnified through his glasses, quite as intent as that of the German scientist on the screen behind.

"Perhaps you might catch one for me?"

*

Anderson peered into the periscope's eyepiece, hands cupped round the mounting, shutting out even the faint red glow of the control room lights. Slowly his eyes grew accustomed to the dark and the solid black circle reflected down through the optics resolved itself into a shifting collection of greys.

One of the half-glimpsed shadows seemed more regular in form than the others and Anderson centred the periscope's view upon it. He turned the dial to bring a magnified image into focus. He blinked, quarry lost in the changed perspective, and then he had her again – the straight edge of a funnel, a faint white glimmer hinting at a bow wave. He pulled back from the eyepiece, his gaze flicking down to the brass compass housing.

"Target bearing twenty-two degrees."

A second later the deck officer's reply came back. "Same heading sir. She hasn't altered course."

The Turks were placing too much faith in the dark, thought Anderson. It wouldn't help them. On a cloudless night like this, with a pale sliver of moon glinting off the waves, the *Nautica* and its crew had proved themselves adept at hunting down the Ottoman ships.

"Range?"

"Eleven hundred yards sir. Assuming she hasn't changed speed."

Not likely. Darkness or no, the supply vessel's skipper would have her fires stoked to bursting, coaxing every ounce of speed from her engines.

After the *Nautica*'s exploits the previous evening, the Turks would now know the submersible was back in the Marmara. Their merchant captains would be running scared, even as the gunboats took up the hunt.

Anderson and his crew had run riot on their last visit to the near-landlocked body of water which lay between the Mediterranean and the Black Sea. After negotiating the fierce currents of the Dardanelles, slipping past the lone submarine net and a smattering of mines, the remainder of the cruise had been relatively plain sailing. The *Nautica* was unstoppable, sinking ship after ship, running rings around the Turks.

They had returned to the fleet moored off Gallipoli as heroes. Anderson and his officers were hosted for drinks by Commander Keyes aboard the *Queen Elizabeth*, Birdwood himself appearing, ferried out from shore to thank them in person. When Anderson was caught up in the hunt, eyes pressed to the periscope, it was easy to forget his mission was only a small part of a wider theatre of operations. It sharpened his mind somewhat when the commander of the land offensive informed him the

Nautica's lonely efforts were the only thing stopping the Turks pounding the Tommies and Diggers back into the sea. Thanks to the supply ships now littering the bottom of the Marmara, the Ottoman gunners were running just as short of ordnance as the invasion force.

The conversation left Anderson motivated and burdened in equal measure, restless to get back into the fray. But engine troubles kept the submersible floundering alongside the supply tender for nigh on a month and by the time Dixon had the *Nautica* seaworthy once more, the Turks had strengthened their defences. The layout of the new anti-submersible features suggested the Ottomans had sought advice from their German allies – a wise strategy. After all, nobody had more experience than the Hun in underwater warfare, and in defence against it.

The run up the Dardanelles this time had been an altogether cagier affair. They had skirted the new clusters of mines and probed at the heavy netting now strung across the narrow passage every few miles. A full night and day had passed whilst they worked their way slowly eastwards through the Straits – every man aboard grateful when they could finally surface and replenish the submersible's gamey atmosphere with the clean, warm air of the Turkish evening.

Since then, they had roamed the Marmara, seeking prey. The previous night, they had sent two supply ships to a watery grave. But a pair of torpedoes had ploughed harmlessly past a third target, much to Anderson's irritation. After the stressful journey through the Straits, and the looming prospect of the return trip, he was determined to make the voyage worthwhile. They couldn't afford any more misses – *Nautica's* supply of ammunition was not inexhaustible.

Anderson swivelled the periscope and placed the crosshairs on the dim outline of the target vessel's bow. He turned further and moved the sight half the ship's length ahead of her. He flicked his eyes down to the compass once more.

"Helm, three degrees port."

"Three degrees aye," came the immediate response.

The bridge crew waited in silence – one second, two, then three – before the helmsman spoke again, confirming the course change.

Anderson ducked his eye to the periscope once more. There, closer now, the Turkish vessel thundered into the starboard edge of his view.

"Fire!" he called.

The deck officer relayed the order into the speaking tube and the *Nautica*'s frame shuddered as the torpedoes leapt from the submersible in a surge of compressed air. Anderson remained glued to the eyepiece, counting under his breath. The count ran on. And on. Past the mark he had in his head. Damn it – more wasted shots.

But then a flash of white erupted in the view, sprays of foam bursting into the air at the ship's bow. A fountain of water caught the moonlight, silver droplets cascading back down like molten metal. A moment later a second blast surged up, 'midships this time.

The detonations rumbled through the water, the submersible's hull vibrating as the concussion waves rolled past. Anderson watched long enough to confirm the kill, waiting until the target's outline adopted a noticeable list. He raised his gaze and ran it around the control room, nodding to each of the bridge crew in turn.

"Fine work gentlemen."

He pressed his foot on the pedal in the deck and stepped back as the periscope descended, its oiled tubes contracting in a smooth hiss of hydraulics. He rolled his neck, easing out tensed muscles before turning his attention to the chart table.

"No rest for the wicked," he said. "Find something else to shoot."

*

Von Gossler woke with a start, fists clenched around twisted folds of sheet. His hair clung to his forehead, the skin slick with clammy perspiration, his pillow damp with moisture. He blinked in the darkness, blind in the shuttered room but glad to be awake – better to stare sightlessly into the void than return to his nightmares. The dreams were getting worse – more vivid, more frequent – filling his nights with visions of fire and remembered pain. His wounds had healed, the agony reduced to a dull itch in his skin, but his scars remained, some visible, some not.

A muted sound caught the edge of his hearing, the barely-audible echoes of an anguished howl bouncing from stone to stone around the crumbling fortress. One of Falke's pets, giving voice to its torment. At least one of the damned things was always screeching – morning, noon or night. When they all joined in dreadful chorus, the caterwauling could have wakened the dead. Why the scientist didn't remove their damned tongues was a mystery.

He rolled onto his side and reached for the bedside cabinet, his fingers finding its edge and searching across the surface. His hand closed around the glass and he raised it to his mouth. A thin dribble of water met his lips, worse than nothing at all, the dampness on his tongue serving only to make him more aware of his parched throat. He smacked the glass back down and cursed the lack of a bell-pull with which to summon his manservant. He stretched out further, fumbling in the dark for the lamp's cable, following its twisted length to the switch box.

The lamp fizzled into life behind its shade, the glass bulb's filament casting a yellow glow across the room. He tossed the sheet aside and sat up, slipping his feet into a pair of pointed slippers. Ridiculous things, like something from the Arabian Nights – the footwear of some debauched potentate. But still better than the cold flagstones of the floor. The walls of the castle offered a blessedly cool refuge during the day, but after sunset the temperature plummeted, a bone-numbing chill creeping out from the ancient stone.

He shuffled over to the washstand where the water jug waited beside the porcelain basin. He lifted the jug and filled his glass, gulping it down before pouring another. The water was lukewarm, and like everything in this Godforsaken country, it carried the taint of dust and remnants of the spices the Turks insisted on adding to every dish. He longed for some pure Alpine spring water, fresh from the mountains, or even better, an overflowing stein of beer. He replaced the jug, starting back as he caught sight of himself in the oval mirror hanging above the cabinet. He resisted the pull of his reflection for a moment, then found himself leaning forward. His eyes roved across the mirror's surface in morbid fascination, transfixed once again by his own ruined features.

The left side of Von Gossler's face was a mass of wrinkled scar tissue, shockingly pink in juxtaposition with the whiteness of the right. Puckered folds of new skin surrounded an eye puffy and red, whilst the fringe of his hair sprouted in uneven patches. He made to smooth down the wayward locks and received a jolt of surprise all over again at the raw flesh of his fingers. From the monkey's paw of his hand the burn continued up under the sleeve of his nightshirt, the skin a foul half-cured leather.

To think, at college he had enjoyed a reputation as something of a dandy – a follower of the latest fashions and a breaker of hearts. He had joked with his fellow students, swigging beer from deep steins, discussing which of the girls might be pretty enough, and of good enough breeding, to make him a wife. He glowered at his reflection, wrinkled face twisting. A single tear rolled down the pale unblemished cheek beneath his healthy eye. He scrubbed the moisture away, loathing his weakness.

He dragged himself from the mirror and pulled open the dresser, reaching for his clothes. A return to sleep was a remote prospect, and besides, slumber offered no comfort.

Dressed, and with a heavy greatcoat pulled close for warmth, Von Gossler made his way down the spiral stairs. He held his candle out at arm's length, glad of the light but uncomfortable with the naked flame. He passed a landing, a silent corridor leading off, empty rooms beyond the doorways studding the walls. The fortress keep was near-deserted, the small garrison force content to spend their time in the gatehouse and patrolling the walls, well away from Falke and her activities. Aside from Von Gossler and the scientist, the building played home only to a handful of laboratory assistants and the experimental subjects themselves.

Another howl rolled around the tower. A second voice took up the dreadful refrain and Von Gossler's descent was completed to the accompaniment of a mournful duet. He reached the base of the stairs and stepped out into the main hall, scaring the wits from the Turkish soldier who stood guard. The man whirled at his sudden appearance, rifle raised.

"Idiot," muttered Von Gossler, pushing past.

The Turk let out a great gulp of breath and offered a tobacco-stained smile and a shrug by way of apology. The smile disappeared as the wailing started up once again. The soldier's eyes grew wide, swivelling in their sockets to scour the shadows, of which there were plenty.

Von Gossler found he could hardly condemn the man for his nervousness – his own heart pounded faster as he crossed the expanse of the hall, thankful for his small circle of light, a protective aura against the cold darkness. The only other illumination in the great room was provided by a handful of isolated torches, flickering in their wall sconces, their light serving only to animate the edges of the dark, sinister movement haunting the corners of his vision.

He steeled himself to ignore the shifting shadows and strode the length of the room. He tried to keep his gaze from both the surrounding darkness and the tongues of fire licking up from the torches, much larger than the flame of his candle. But averted eyes could not stop the smell of smoke reaching his nose, bringing back half-remembered flashes of his nightmares. The crackling sound of fire, amplified by his imagination, mingled with the unearthly screeches emanating from the archway.

He ducked his head to step through the low opening. Another stone spiral led down, this one a part of the original fortress, older still than the masonry of the upper levels – the slabs pitted and uneven, worn and weathered from centuries of feet. He made his way round and down, nervous of his footing, right hand holding the candle, the fingertips of his left brushing the wall, new skin tingling at the rough rub of the stone.

After four revolutions the stairs came to an end, levelling out into a narrow passageway. His breath clouded in the cold air and he tugged the lapels of his greatcoat tight around his chest. With every forward step, the moans and groans grew in volume, the punctuating screams now loud enough to set his teeth on edge with each occurrence.

He stopped before a heavy wooden door, its timbers bound with straps of rusted metal. He raised his fist and banged on the timbers. At the first blow, an eerie silence fell beyond the portal.

He waited, alone in the gloom, counting off the seconds, resisting the urge to swing his candle round to check his rear. Finally, a clatter and scrape of ironmongery rang through the tunnel as bolts were thrown and keys turned. With a shriek of antique hinges, the door swung open, light flooding out. Von Gossler squinted, recognising the outline of his former tutor silhouetted against the brightness.

"Ah, Viktor. Come in." Falke stepped back and waved him inside.

He extinguished the candle and stepped through the portal. The woman pushed the door closed behind him, slapping the bolts back into place. She rummaged in one of the pockets dotting her dirty apron and withdrew a watch on a chain. She rubbed smears from the glass and peered at the timepiece before turning a penetrating gaze on her visitor.

"It's late. Or early. Whichever you prefer."

"I couldn't sleep."

The eyes narrowed. "More nightmares?"

Von Gossler felt the colour in his cheeks. He ignored the question and moved past the scientist, out of the low passage and into the high vaulted space of the laboratory proper. Ancient masonry soared up in columns, the supports branching out into arches, their spans criss-crossing the roof, creating a curved patchwork of stone. He ran his eyes across the ceiling, cringing at the thought of the bulky fortress squatting above.

A row of cages took up an entire wall. The crossed wire fencing of the gates offered half-glimpsed outlines of the shapes within. An unsettling silence emanated from the enclosures, disturbed only by an occasional hiss of breath or a faint scrape of movement. Eyes glittered in the dark to the rear of the cages, their quiet observation an almost physical sensation against Von Gossler's skin. He shuddered and turned away.

The other walls of the chamber were lined with bookshelves and equipment – electrical generators, a refrigeration cabinet, distilling apparatus, smelting ovens, and a dozen other devices whose purpose eluded him. This elaborate array of machinery surrounded an open space dotted with workbenches. The nearest of these was home to a collection of specimen jars, each containing an unappetising portion of pickled flesh.

Organs of all sorts bobbed alongside severed limbs, the process of decay frozen at various stages. Most of the grisly trophies were unrecognisable, flabby remnants of pale meat, floating in formaldehyde or slumped at the bottom of their jars, little more than sludge. Von Gossler found these mysterious articles much easier to contemplate than the more immediately identifiable remains.

Falke tapped the side of a jar, gnarled grey tissue suspended within.

"My latest exhibit..." She nodded towards the chamber's centre. "A moment earlier and you could have assisted in its removal."

The dissecting table held a corpse, clammy and pale, laid out on the stained timbers, its arms by its sides. The crown of the skull had been removed and the space within gaped towards Von Gossler, illuminated in merciless detail by the white glare of an angled lamp. His stomach lurched at the sight of the empty cavity.

"You are too gentle a soul Viktor," said Falke. "You will need to stiffen those nerves of yours if you are to become more engaged in the practical aspects of our studies."

"I am no butcher. Nor am I interested in becoming one."

"Ah yes. You believe you are only here to report back to your masters in Berlin..." She gave a thin smile in response to his jolt of suprise. "I know all about your little telegrams. Your attempts at espionage have been painfully transparent."

He swallowed. "It's not spying. But High Command feel –"

She silenced him. "Having them peer over my shoulder is a minor inconvenience. They understand even less than you do."

She made her way across the laboratory to the cages. Her approach created a ripple of nervous movement within the shadowy enclosures.

"Our work is important enough to put up with Berlin's curiosity."

She lifted a metal box and brandished it with a thin smile. In a theatrical gesture, she extended a finger and flicked the switch affixed to the unit's top. The box gave out a click and a high-pitched buzz began to hover at the edge of Von Gossler's hearing – low, insistent, more felt than heard, like the irritating drone of a nocturnal insect.

There was a moment of calm, punctured only by the barely-audible whine, and then a riot of screeches and howls erupted from within the cages. Falke turned towards Von Gossler, arms spread wide. She raised her voice to carry over the din.

"After all, this is where we create the future."

*

Lying on the hard-packed earth, Jones regarded the entrance to the ravine. Walls of sandstone rose up on either side of the dry stream bed. The canyon was narrow, maybe six feet across, and wound its way back into the escarpment, a shadowy gouge in the rocks.

"You're sure it's in there?" he said to the soldier lying alongside him.

"It dragged Billy off..." The New Zealander looked at Jones, then away. "I followed it this far. But I couldn't go in after it. I just couldn't."

"For God's sake Simpson, there's nothing more you could have done. Like as not your Billy was already dead."

"Too bloody right he was dead. It ripped his damned head off."

The three-man patrol had been jumped on the edge of No Man's Land – the unfortunate Billy hauled away by the creature after a brief and one-sided melee. His surviving companions had followed the beast to the crevice before the youngest had returned to camp to raise the alarm. Jones regarded the man at his side. The sergeant might not have entered the ravine, but he'd stayed out here alone for over an hour, awaiting the arrival of reinforcements, in full knowledge of the horror lurking nearby.

"There's no way out at the other end?"

"Box canyon. Cliffs all round. Been up there a few times on patrol." Simpson offered a half smile. "Good place to stop for a smoke." He shook his head. "It's still in there, unless it can climb like a bloody monkey."

I wouldn't put it past it, thought Jones. Who knew what the blasted creatures were capable of? Still, it was the first confirmed report they'd had for a week. Hopefully the beast wasn't going anywhere, just seeking a little privacy for its lunch. Jones hated himself for the thought, and what it meant for the luckless Digger providing the meal.

He wriggled his way back from the crest, crouching low until he could stand without being visible from the other side of the ridge. He scrambled down the hill and joined the half-dozen men who stood clustered at its base. He felt Sullivan's eager gaze on him the whole way down. The doctor was practically hopping from foot to foot in nervous excitement.

"Well?"

"It's in there," said Jones. "We think."

"Capital. About time one of the beasties put in an appearance."

"This isn't a church outing Doctor. This beastie of yours has already killed a man."

Sullivan glanced round at the men, blanching at the range of stony expressions directed his way. "Well, yes," he said, blinking behind his spectacles. "Regrettable. Obviously."

Uncomfortable under the soldiers' cold regard, Sullivan crouched and wrestled with the buckle of his rucksack. Jones eyed the pink scalp beneath the thinning crown of ginger hair as the doctor rummaged in the bag. Whilst the medical man had swapped his tweeds for more appropriate attire, he hadn't yet appropriated one of the distinctive bush hats the Diggers all wore. More fool him.

Jones tipped his own hat back and rubbed a grimy fist thought the sweat on his brow. He hoped they could get this damned circus over and done with before the sun climbed much higher – not even the Australians liked being out in the searing heat of midday.

Sullivan straightened and offered Jones a cloth-wrapped bundle. Jones removed the covering, and lifted the weapon. He had seen air pistols before, but never one like this. The gun was stubby, the barrel short and wide, its grey steel bound with thin hoops of brass from gaping mouth to wooden grip. A metal flask protruded from the weapon's top, a reservoir for the compressed air which would send its projectiles on their journey. The line of the gun continued back from the grip over Jones' wrist in a feeder tube of wire runners.

A polished wooden box was produced from the rucksack next. Sullivan fished out a small key on a chain from beneath his shirt and turned it in the lock. As the curious soldiers leaned in, he flicked back the lid with a flourish, displaying the box's contents like a music hall illusionist at the climax of his best trick. Nestled within the velvet-lined contours of the box were six glass spheres, each the size of a golf ball, green liquid sloshing within.

"What are those?" asked one of the Diggers.

"Magic bullets," said Sullivan. He lifted one of the spheres from its resting place and held it up to the light. The liquid nearly filled the ball, flashing emerald where it caught the sun's rays, only a small bubble of air trapped beneath the crown.

"Opium, curare and valerian. Dissolved in the strongest gin we could find – Plymouth, obviously." He smiled at the soldiers staring up at the green orb. "I daresay if we had enough tonic we could organise quite a party with this little liqueur."

"Will it work?" asked Jones.

Sullivan tucked the glass sphere back into the box. "The contents of just one of these would see all your comrades here as drunk as lords. Against an individual? I think we can guarantee unconsciousness, and a fairly appalling hangover."

"I'd not be so sure about these boys," said Jones, drawing grins from the Diggers. "They can handle their drink. How quickly does it work?"

"Depends on the size of the beastie..." Sullivan turned to the soldier at his side, Simpson's fellow survivor from the ill-fated patrol. "How large was the creature that attacked you?"

"It was a scrawny thing. Short too. Shorter than me." The man swallowed. "Bloody strong though. Not natural."

The doctor returned his attention to Jones. "One shot ought to do it."

"Would two prove fatal?"

"I'd rather we didn't take the risk."

"I'm sure you would. But seeing as I'm taking all the risks anyway, I may put two rounds into the thing, just to be sure."

Sullivan offered Jones a sour look. "Those tranquiliser globes aren't cheap you know."

Jones took the box and began slotting the glass spheres into the pistol's feeder rack.

"I'll do my best to capture your prize in one piece," he said. "But if something goes awry, I'm afraid my primary concern is unlikely to be Porton Down's finances."

*

It was all quite different from his last proper hunt – a sociable affair on the banks of Loch Tay, two years before the outbreak of war. He'd bagged a brace of birds, and won a sizeable wager too, if he remembered rightly. However, no tartan rug and wicker picnic hamper waited at the end of this excursion, and Jones reckoned his current quarry was a touch more dangerous than a flustered grouse.

He inched forward, back pressed to the dusty sandstone, stepping carefully, testing the ground with each movement. He eased pebbles aside with the toe of his boot, seeking solid ground before he risked any shift in weight. He approached the bend in the ravine – an almost ninety-degree corner, obscuring his view of the way ahead. He advanced towards it as he had the previous blind spot in the gorge's twisting course – sideways on, hard against the rock, pistol raised to cover the bend and anything which might emerge around it.

The burning indigestion in his throat was worse this time than the last, the odds of an unpleasant encounter increasing with each step he took. Thoughts of the ravine's occupant grew more lurid, memories of the terrible corpse back in camp exaggerated by fevered imagination.

He reached the sharp edge of the outcrop which marked the bend. He leaned his head against the stone and took a series of deep breaths, eyes fixed on the thin strip of blue sky visible between the cliffs above. He willed his heart to stop thumping and slid forward the final inches. He grimaced at the scrape of his shirt on the stone, hideously loud to his ears.

Beyond the kink in its course, the canyon continued for ten feet or so before opening out into a round sinkhole, perhaps thirty feet across, the ochre banding of the sandstone cliffs rising up all around. A thin trickle of water spattered down the far wall, a pathetic remnant of the once-mighty torrent which had carved out the ravine. A shallow pool, little more than a puddle, washed the base of the rocks.

At the water's edge the man-thing squatted, huddled over a grisly mound of tattered clothing and torn meat. The creature was painfully-thin, its skin mottled with bruises and scabs, stretched taut over skeleton and tendons. As Jones peered from his vantage point, the beast reached out a wiry limb and dug fingers into the body before it. The claw twisted, a fistful of flesh wrenched out then gulped down to the accompaniment of chewing noises and wet grunts. Jones swallowed hard and raised the air pistol, wishing it were a proper weapon, with proper ammunition.

He drew a bead on the half-naked creature, but before he could pull the trigger, the thing dropped to all fours, meat forgotten, its head tipped back, sniffing at the air. A tumble of loose stones rattled down from above the pool. The beast's head snapped towards the noise, its gaze dragging Jones' own attention upward – just in time to see the shape above launch itself out from the cliffs.

The figure plummeted into the edge of the pool, dirty water erupting at the impact. It rose from the mud, unfolding its powerful frame. Jones gawped at the new arrival. It was huge, its shoulders, arms and chest bulging with muscles beneath the threadbare remnants of a vest. The damned thing was like some circus strongman gone wrong.

Water ran in streams down the exaggerated torso as the giant lurched from the pool. It raised its head and fixed a feral gaze on the canyon's other occupant and its meal. It spread its arms wide and roared, clearly intent on assuming possession of the food.

Jones was amazed the smaller creature didn't turn tail and flee at the monster's approach. Sullivan was right, this Falke woman had to be doing something to their sense of self-preservation. The scrawny beast's lack of concern for its safety was evident in the way it charged straight at its challenger, determined to defend its lunch – fingers twisted into claws, mouth agape in a frenzied howl.

The assault of flailing arms and snapping teeth was met with indifference by the hulking giant. It ignored the flurry of blows and scratches, thrusting out a massive arm, hand catching in a vice-like grip around its assailant's neck. With a grunt, it flexed corded muscles and hoisted its assailant into the air. The giant stood frozen for a moment, opponent raised aloft, oblivious to the talons scrabbling at its arm. Then it squeezed, and with a sickening squelch the smaller beast went slack, limbs dangling loose.

The brute cocked its head to one side, lips pulled back over yellowed teeth in a grin of victory. It pulled the corpse close and hissed its triumph into the dead thing's face before tossing it into the dust alongside the remnants of the unfortunate Billy. The monster squatted and surveyed its feast, broad chest rising and falling in a series of ragged breaths.

The entire encounter had taken a handful of seconds – a menace which had overwhelmed a three-man patrol disposed of as little more than a minor irritation. The barrel of the air pistol wobbled as Jones raised the weapon once more. He slowed his breathing and focused on stilling the tremors. He took aim, recalling Sullivan's faith in the effectiveness of even a single round of the tranquiliser.

He yanked the trigger six times, emptying the magazine at the giant.

*

Jones ran, his heart fit to burst, pounding in his throat, the thunder of his pulse almost as loud as the growling hate which filled the canyon behind him. The sounds of pursuit bounced from the rock, filling his mind with the thought of claws grasping his shoulder, or snatching a fistful of hair, or closing around an ankle. He ached to look back, desperate for reassurance he was further ahead of the beast than he thought – but he didn't dare slow down, even for a moment.

He threw himself around the bend in the ravine. Halfway out. How could it only be halfway? His lungs burned and his thighs felt like lead, but he pushed himself harder, arms pumping, head down.

His foot turned on a loose rock and he was suddenly flying. He flung out his arms to break the headlong fall and the rocks tore at his palms as he smacked down. The impact drove the breath from his body and he scrabbled forward, trying to get his feet under him once more. He glanced back over his shoulder as he rose and was flooded with a peculiar cocktail of emotion – relief the beast was not right on top of him, mixed with a renewed rush of horror at its continued pursuit.

The brute crashed around the twist in the gorge, smacking from one wall to the other in its drunken rage. Sullivan's potion was having an effect all right, but was not yet creating the intended stupor, rather a berserker fury. Jones had a flash of memory, ludicrously inappropriate. A Portsmouth pub – The Registry if he remembered rightly – an ogre of a deckhand, drunk as a lord, a half-dozen sailors required to restrain him.

The creature lifted a baleful gaze, eyes struggling to focus before fixing on its prey. It came on, arms outstretched, face twisted in animal fury, spittle flying from gaping jaws as it gave voice to its anger. Jones turned away and tried to shut out everything but the run.

He burst from the crevice into the bright sunlight. He reeled, dazzled by the glare, and then threw himself flat at the harsh crack of gunfire which erupted from the bottom of the hill. He rolled down the slope in a flurry of dust and ricochets, wincing as bullets and splintered rock buzzed around him.

Panicked cries of "Hold your fire!" rang out from below and the barrage came to a merciful end. He regained his feet and the incline bore him forward and down, a chaotic pell-mell descent, as much falling as running. He risked a look to his rear and spotted the monster staggering from the canyon mouth. But then his foot twisted on the uneven ground and he went down once more. He thumped to the ground, forehead smashing against the rock.

Everything became muffled and muted and slow. He tumbled, limbs tangled and leaden. He rolled onto his back, squinting up into the sun. The light stabbed down, exacerbating the splitting pain behind his eyes. He shook his head, trying to clear the fog filling up his skull. His blurred vision caught movement and he turned, and there it was – the beast lurching towards him, only yards away.

He scuttled backwards, ignoring the scrape of his hands on the stones, unable to drag his attention from the brute. It careered forward, movement erratic, limbs and senses clearly dulled, but on it came all the same. It closed in, rearing up, fists raised like massive clubs. And then it tripped on the loose scree and smacked to the ground. Its momentum carried it past in a shower of rock before it ground to a stop in the dust.

Jones skidded to his own halt with only a little more grace. He lay, propped up on his elbows, gaze fixed on the prone figure of the giant. He pulled in one lungful of air after another, frankly astonished to have made it out of the gorge in one piece. He tore his eyes from his fallen pursuer as Simpson heaved into view, breathless from the charge up the hill.

"Sorry sir. About the shooting," The New Zealander looked mortified. "The lads got twitchy, what with the roaring and screaming and all."

Jones accepted the sergeant's outstretched hand and hauled himself to his feet, becoming slowly aware of the aches and pains from across his body. He wiped a hand across his forehead, the sweat setting his grazed palms stinging. He prodded at the egg-shaped lump already swelling at his hairline – bloody sore, but he'd had worse. Besides, a handful of bruises was infinitely better than the alternative.

"At least the nerves affected their aim…"

Simpson gave a lop-sided smile. "I'll have words with them about that sir. Arrange a bit more rifle practice."

Sullivan appeared, face red and shining in sweaty excitement, eyes fixed up the slope. He barely even glanced at Jones.

"Well done," he called as he passed. "A magnificent specimen."

"You're welcome," muttered Jones after the lanky figure.

The man from Porton Down reached the prostrate form and crouched down, fascinated by the fallen giant, oblivious to all else.

"You've made the Doc's day there Major," said Simpson. "He looks delighted with his new pet."

"He'd better be. I'll be buggered if I'm getting him another one."

*

"He's a big lad, isn't he?" said Birdwood.

The observers stood at the rim of the pit and stared down at the hulking figure. The giant crouched against the wall, casting the occasional sullen glance up through the criss-crossed wiring which capped his accommodations. This was all a far cry from when the beast had first woken – its fury at finding itself caged had seemed boundless. It had thrown itself at the walls of its circular prison, clambering up the rocks to attack the wires above. The skin of its fingers wore down to bloody tatters as it scrabbled at the stones and the bolts of the cage. Only a goat carcass tossed from above had distracted it from its efforts, and only the narcotics in the meat had prevented their immediate resumption once the food was consumed.

The creature was now quiet – blessedly so. Whilst a circle of canvas screens shielded the pit from curious eyes, the roaring had echoed across the camp. Little chance of the monster's capture remaining a secret now, despite the members of the hunting party being sworn to silence.

"He wasn't to begin with…" said Sullivan.

Jones and Sir William turned with matching looks of enquiry.

"Big," said Sullivan. "He wasn't like that to begin with. Falke has been busy – the clever old witch."

"Explain," ordered Birdwood.

Sullivan removed his spectacles, using a corner of his shirt to polish the lenses between finger and thumb. He blinked as he spoke to the two soldiers – a tall, sunburned, ginger owl.

"I had little time with the specimen before we had to put it in its hole. Didn't fancy it waking up whilst I was poking at it." He slipped his glasses back on. "But even a cursory examination revealed some interesting differences to the other examples. The, ah, deceased ones."

He beckoned them forward, pointing at the figure below. "Look at the muscles across its shoulders for a start. Not natural. They've been attached somehow – stitched on or something."

Jones and Sir William peered over the pit's rim. Sullivan was right. The beast's physique was bulging with layered strips of tendon and sinew – the enhanced musculature pushed up in ridges beneath the skin.

"Looks like he's draped in streaky bacon," said Sir William.

"I very much doubt it's pork," said Sullivan. "In fact, I would be surprised if those added extras weren't of a decidedly human origin."

Jones looked back to the doctor. "So now Falke is cobbling men together from spare parts..."

"Not quite. But she's using muscular tissue from donors to enhance strength far beyond natural limits." His eyes took an unhealthy gleam. "Absolutely fascinating. I wonder how she's stopping the grafted muscle being rejected. And how on earth is she connecting everything together? There's no point having extra power if the brain can't control it." He gave a grin. "That would be like providing you gentlemen with a shiny new howitzer and yet neglecting to build a trigger mechanism."

Jones shook his head. "I'm more concerned about those donors you so casually mention. This isn't a damned scientific puzzle – men are dying for these experiments. And those that survive..." He gestured downward, words escaping him for a moment. "They're less than men at the end of it all, no matter how much stronger they may be."

He turned from the pit, sick to his stomach with the thought that the creature below had been a soldier – perhaps a husband, or a father.

"This has to be stopped," he said.

Sullivan grabbed at Jones' arm.

"No. This has to be understood." The man's green eyes shone with excitement. "Don't you see it? Falke has accomplished things modern medicine has only dreamed of. Who knows where this might lead?"

The two men stared at one another. It was Sir William who broke the silence. "That's exactly what I'm afraid of..."

Sullivan released his grip and turned towards the General. Sir William pulled his pipe from his pocket and stuffed tobacco into its bowl.

"Major, you're right. That thing down there is an abomination, an offence to God's creation." Sullivan bristled at Jones' side, but Birdwood continued before he could speak. "And yet, the Doctor too is correct. As he said, we need to understand the methods of our enemy if we are to properly counter them."

Jones could cheerfully have knocked the teeth out of the condescending smile which Sullivan turned in his direction – probably would have too if he hadn't been stood before his commanding officer. He made do with a stare which saw the scientist's smirk replaced with a gratifyingly nervy series of blinks.

"Don't worry Major," said Sir William. "We'll shut down Falke's operation, but in the process I want us to gather every last scrap of intelligence we can get on what she's been up to."

"So we can create monsters of our own?"

Birdwood regarded Jones over the flickering match he held to his pipe. He sucked at the stem, holding Jones' gaze, expelling sideways puffs of smoke until the tobacco smouldered to his satisfaction. He shook the match out and flicked it away into the dust.

"That decision will be made considerably higher up the tree than you or I, my boy. But I shouldn't worry – I'm not sure ravenous beasties are really our sort of thing."

Our sort of thing isn't what it used to be, thought Jones. Poisonous gas, the aerial bombardment of cities, putting torpedoes into passenger ships – none of these had been anyone's sort of thing at the outbreak of war. Now both sides routinely acted in ways which would have been deemed despicable only a few years previously.

But then, what was the alternative? Fight with a hand tied behind one's back as the enemy sought the advantage? And hadn't he himself engaged in his fair share of dubious activity, not least the recent fun and games over the Med? Maybe Birdie was right — such questions would have to be settled well above his pay grade.

"The whole argument is academic," said Jones, shrugging off his discomfort. "We've no idea where Falke is."

"That's where you're mistaken. I received some interesting information on that front whilst you were out hunting."

Birdwood turned and called to his aide. "Bring in our visitor." He looked back to Jones. "An old friend of yours I believe…"

The flap in the canvas screen was pulled aside and a tall, broad-shouldered man stepped through. He straightened to reveal a handsome, square-jawed profile, and a dark gaze which took in the enclosure and the creature within the pit.

Jones recovered from his shock, feeling his facial expression transform from stunned surprise into a smile. He found his voice.

"What the bloody hell are you doing here?"

Kowalski looked up, eyes hard, the habitual grin which Jones remembered nowhere to be seen.

"Major," he nodded in acknowledgement. "I can tell you where your scientist is hiding out. But we need to get one thing clear…" He pointed towards the hole and its occupant. "I ain't here for your monster hunt. I just want Von Gossler."

"Who?" asked Jones, flummoxed as much by Kowalski's attitude as his words.

"Von Gossler – the man I've followed halfway round the world…"

Kowalski's tone, cold before, was now steely-hard.

"The man who killed Maria."

*

Extracted from 'A History of the Ancient Sects and Societies of the East'...

In the fullness of time Hassan's desire to apprehend the knowledge of Al-Kalil came to dominate his thoughts, depriving him of peace and satisfaction. This despite the growing reach of the Order's influence, the expansion of which had previously provided his sole desire and ambition.

He insinuated his own spies amongst the scholar's assistants but received their reports with increasing frustration. Al-Kalil's methods remained secure, his secrets recorded only in cipher within a great book.

This tome, this chronicle of Mysteries unlocked, stayed always at his side, chained to the wrists of a slave, the only man who ever witnessed the scholar put pen to paper. This unfortunate's tongue was cut to a stub and the drums of his ears punctured, reducing his nature to that of the mute beast of burden. This rendered him incapable of recounting Al-Kalil's alchemical secrets, even were he to fall under the vilest of tortures.

Great was Hassan's frustration. Was he not The Master, the Lord of the Mountain, unto whom tributes flowed like water? Did this lowly scholar – this individual whom history would scarce have noticed even as a scribe had Hassan not raised him up – dare to keep from his benefactor the details and procedures of the artifice practised in his name?

Such were Hassan's private thoughts and so cunning as the fox he laid a trap for Al-Kalil. Although advanced in years and growing frail in body, the Master remained sound of mind and in full possession of his skills with all manner of poisonous preparations and potions. He prepared a sumptuous feast for Al-Kalil, claiming to honour him the most illustrious of his Lieutenants, but filling the food with ingredients to dull the mind and make it pliable and open to suggestion. By dint of this ruse Hassan would discover the key to the scholar's cypher – or so the Master's plan would have transpired had Al-Kalil, as wily as Hassan himself, not divined the feast's entire purpose at tasting the very first morsel of the tainted food.

Rising from his place at the Lord of Mountain's side the scholar named him traitor and addressing the assembly declared "By betraying me he has betrayed our Order. Call him Master no more." He raised up his staff – a curious device of his own crafting – and used its power to take the very will of Hassan's guards under his own command.

At Al-Kalil's bidding these men, whom ever before had proved stout and loyal, removed the Master from the table and dragged him to the terracing on the walls. Mindless and without mercy in their obedience to Al-Kalil's instruction, they ignored Hassan's pleas and flung him from that high place unto his death on the rocks.

Thus passed the infamous Hassan, the Old Man of the Mountain, at the hands of his own followers. And in this dreadful fashion so ascended Al-Kalil to Mastery of that Order which the native of Cairo had founded so many years before...

Gallipoli Peninsula

"...and then on to London where I talked old Buckingham into getting me out here." Kowalski peered down into the stained depths of his cup.

"That was awful," he said. "Got any more?"

Jones pushed the bottle towards him. "My apologies, the bar selection is somewhat limited."

Kowalski poured himself a healthy measure. He waved the remaining inch of liquid at Jones. The Englishman shook his head.

Suit yourself, thought Kowalski. He topped up his mug and took a mouthful. The smoky burn tortured his sinuses and scorched his throat.

"Jesus," he growled.

The booze tasted rotten, but it took the edge off the ache in his arm. He rubbed at his shoulder. The muscles throbbed, still slowly knitting themselves back together. The docs had prised some hefty chunks of shrapnel out of him in the hospital – fragments of metal from Tank's iron lung, fragments of bone whose origins he didn't want to think about.

"Now what?" asked Jones. "You'll find this Von Gossler character?"

"Already found him."

"He's at this castle? This Boo-hannay?"

"Burhanli," corrected Kowalski. "He's there."

"How do you know?"

Kowalski gave a tight smile as he hoisted his drink, his thoughts flicking back to Washington.

"I had a reliable source..."

*

His only regret over the whole affair was not being able to keep the automobile. The Benz had been magnificent. Say what you like about the Krauts, they made some beautiful machinery. Hardly surprising the driver was so reluctant to give up the keys. Looking back, Kowalski knew he'd underestimated the German. The man was a bodyguard as well as a driver – he'd have been selected for his ability to handle himself at least as much as handling the Benz.

The pistol's appearance hadn't helped, that was for sure. Tiny snub-nosed thing – it looked like a damned toy. Besides, Kowalski himself probably didn't present the most credible threat – limping, left arm in a sling, face scraped and bruised. Like as not, the embassy man had figured him for little more than a hobo. Small wonder the driver had fancied his odds and made a leap for the gun.

The weapon worked better than it looked. With a crack like a champagne cork, the shot took the man in the neck and a second later he was down, eyes rolled up into his skull, a thin dribble of saliva running from the corner of his mouth to the cobbles beneath his head.

Kowalski tucked the pistol away and checked the street. The leafy boulevard remained deserted. The faint gunshot had done nothing to disturb the American capital's slumber. The house behind him was the only one in the street where light still shone behind the curtains.

He crouched, fumbling with his good hand at the fallen driver's neck, checking for pulse and breath. Both were present, if slow. His fingers found the dart and he pulled it free, careful to avoid its sharp tip.

The letter which accompanied the pistol's delivery had gone into laborious detail regarding the poison's origin. Ramon Cuervo, the Free Fleet's armourer, was nothing if not thorough, assuming everyone shared his passion for detail. Kowalski had got as far as the first paragraph – something about Amazonian frogs – before his eyes glazed over.

He slipped the dart back into the leather pouch and regarded the slumped form of the German. He'd be sure to inform the diminutive Cuban gunsmith both poison and pistol had performed admirably in this, their first, and most definitely unauthorised, field test.

He patted down the driver's pockets and withdrew the keys. He grabbed the unconscious man by his lapels and dragged him to the vehicle's rear. In the shadows behind the bulky automobile, he stripped the man of his coat and hat, then bundled him awkwardly into the luggage compartment. It was a tight fit – unconscious Germans generally occupying more space than the typical gentleman's trunk – but he finally got the unfortunate cargo stowed and the hatch squashed shut.

Breathing heavily, Kowalski leaned back against the Benz, cursing the sling and the injured shoulder it supported. He had always made for a poor invalid, invariably too quick to be up and about. This time he'd been even worse, forcing himself from his bed against the advice of the doctors and the Admiral's express orders. He couldn't just lie there, staring at the ceiling, mind returning over and again to the bombing and its aftermath. He had places to go, people to kill. He owed it to Tank, and to Maria.

Clad in purloined coat and hat, he waited in the driver's seat for an hour before the door of the house opened. A portly gentleman emerged and made his way down the steps, pausing at the bottom for a tip of his hat to the woman who stood framed in the doorway. Her nightdress was of a respectable enough length, but the gaslight behind shone through the flimsy material, making for an impressive silhouette. The lady knew her business, thought Kowalski. Like that showman feller Barnum put it, "always leave them wanting more."

The door closed, consigning the vision to memory, and the man continued towards the automobile, a noticeable spring in his step. He hesitated as he reached the Benz, clearly expecting his driver to emerge and open the door for him. When such service failed to materialise, he pulled at the handle himself, clambering into the rear compartment, mood soured, a scowl reflected in Kowalski's rear-view mirror.

Settled in the plush upholstery, the man reached forward and rapped with his cane on the glass partition, barking something in German. Kowalski assumed his passenger was enquiring if he was awake. He turned in his seat and slid open the panel.

"Howdy," he said, his English prompting Von Bernstorff to gawp at him like a stranded fish. "Hope you enjoyed your evening."

The gun popped and the ambassador's eyes went wide. A second later he was unconscious.

*

The German came round slowly. Kowalski let him become aware of the ropes binding his hands and ankles before he showed him the pistol – a real one this time, rather than the dart gun, its purpose intimidation over incapacitation.

"We took a little drive out of town," he said. "Nobody round these parts to hear a shot. Or any screaming."

Von Bernstorff's eyes flicked from the revolver, to Kowalski, to the windows. Finding no help beyond the tinted glass, he composed himself.

"I must warn you..." he said, his English bearing only the faintest trace of an accent. "I have no money upon my person."

"If I was after money, I'd have interrupted your night before you visited your lady friend. All I'm after is your help."

The German nodded to the weapon. "A rather dramatic fashion in which to seek assistance."

"I've always reckoned you get further with a gun and a smile than with a smile alone."

"Quite." Von Bernstorff leaned back, trying to make himself comfortable despite his bonds, more relaxed as it became apparent he wasn't about to be shot, at least not immediately. "You have me at something of a disadvantage. You are aware of my identity, yet I remain ignorant of your own..."

"Name's Kowalski. Figure you've heard of me."

"The Floridian Captain? I, ah, understood that matter had been settled to everyone's satisfaction."

Kowalski squeezed the pistol's grip, struggling to keep his voice low and even. "Your blood money might have kept the Fleet off your back. But this? This is personal. Call it a freelance operation."

"And I assume your desire is not for further compensation?"

"You assume correctly."

Von Bernstorff regarded Kowalski with an expectant gaze, refusing to acknowledge the gun. "So what can I do for you Captain?"

A born diplomat, thought Kowalski – always ready to negotiate.

"Way I hear it, you and Von Gossler were not on the best of terms..."

"My relationship with a junior functionary is none of your concern."

"Junior functionary? I don't think so. It must have stuck in the throat, being forced to keep an eye on daddy's little boy."

"Perhaps." A thin smile. "And now you wish to know his location."

"Are you going to tell me?"

"No."

"Pity," said Kowalski. He pulled back the pistol's hammer and raised the muzzle so the German could no longer pretend to ignore the weapon. Von Bernstorff did his best to look bored, but Kowalski detected a flicker of apprehension.

"Death before dishonour? Please, spare me the dramatics." Kowalski stared at the man in the back seat. "Whatever you've sent Von Gossler to do, I figure it can't be that big a deal, elsewise you wouldn't have trusted it to a clown like him."

The ambassador remained silent. Kowalski tried a different tack.

"Besides, better a private indiscretion than the rather public disgrace of being found dead outside a brothel. No matter how fancy the joint might be." Kowalski jerked a thumb over his shoulder. "Ain't that far back into town. Your body'll still be warm when they find you…"

The German's air of confidence visibly eroded as Kowalski spoke. That was the trouble with the aristocracy, thought Kowalski – caught up in a web of honour and obligation, as much trapped as empowered by their names and inheritance. Little wonder Europe was in such a mess. A whole damned continent run by a handful of squabbling inbreds – entire countries duking it out in a glorified family feud.

"What's it to be Your Excellency? One small piece of information, or your good name dragged through the mud?" He waggled the gun. "Not to mention you ending up, you know, dead."

Von Bernstorff met Kowalski's gaze, his authority evaporated, his expression almost pleading. "I require your assurance as a gentleman you will never reveal the source of the information."

Jesus, thought Kowalski. Where did they dig up these old fossils?

"If I were a gentleman, you'd have my word. But I ain't." He shrugged in the face of Von Bernstorff's discomfort.

"Either way, you're going to tell me what I want to know or I'll kill you and ruin your precious reputation. You can have my assurance as a gentleman on that front…"

*

The screech echoed through the submersible's passageways and compartments. It reverberated from the riveted plating of the hull and set Anderson's hair standing on end, like fingernails down a blackboard. Every man aboard tracked the rub of the cable down the *Nautica*'s flank towards the propellers churning at her stern.

The entire crew held their breath. If the steel cable tangled in the screws that would be it – either the mine would blow them to Kingdom Come, or they would be forced to surface and the Turkish shore batteries would deliver them to the same end.

Anderson closed his eyes and offered up a silent prayer. On land, he was agnostic at best – what little faith he'd possessed had evaporated with the passing of his wife. But beneath the waves it was another matter entirely. He was yet to meet a submariner who didn't become a devout believer the instant the ocean washed over the upper ports.

The sheer variety of faith was impressive, running well beyond mundane Anglican tradition to encompass all manner of superstitious rituals and good luck totems. Even Dixon, hard-nosed practical man that he was, favoured a tatty rabbit's foot, rolling it between finger and thumb in times of stress. The charm would be in Dixon's hand right now as the engineer stood in the aft compartment, doubtless growling at his men, to all appearances unmoved by the noise, yet internally willing the cable to pass unsnagged.

The scraping ceased, plunging the *Nautica* back into blessed silence. Lucky boat, thought Anderson. His jaw muscles relaxed, releasing teeth he hadn't realised he'd been grinding. Lucky, lucky boat. He opened his eyes to see the sweaty, smiling faces of his bridge crew turned in his direction. He took a breath, thankful he could, despite the taint in the air of men cooped-up with their fear.

"Well done lads," he said into the quiet. "That should be the last of them for a while."

He turned his attention to the chart table as the Duty Officer marked their position. The *Nautica* had already negotiated its way through a half-dozen minefields and skirted the nets. Nearly there.

By any measure, their second voyage to the Marmara had proved as successful as their first. A trail of Ottoman shipwrecks scattered the seafloor in their wake. They had led the Turkish gunboats a merry dance, always one step ahead of their pursuers, dragging them from coast to coast. But ammunition and fuel supplies were not bottomless and Anderson was forced to call time on their adventure – making for the Dardanelles rather sooner than he would have liked.

He had dreaded the return passage down the narrow stretch of water. The currents were bad enough, not to mention the added dangers of net and mine. Three times the *Nautica* had picked its way along this course – a fourth attempt was pushing their luck, if not stretching it to breaking point. But it wasn't as if they had a choice. The tender floating off Suvla represented the only safe haven for hundreds of miles, and the sole way to reach her was down the throat of the Dardanelles once more.

The added requirement for speed complicated matters all over again. He would rather have made the attempt at night, giving them at least a chance of remaining undetected if forced to surface. But orders were orders, and so the screws turned faster than Anderson would have liked and the merciless glare of the sun waited for them to make a mistake.

He pulled the scribbled note from his pocket and deciphered the scrawled handwriting once again, much as the radio operator had decrypted the coded bursts of the wireless transmission in the first place.

The instructions had come through as they were preparing to submerge, having just sent notification of their intent to return to the fleet. The wireless operator had burst into the control room, thrusting the transcription into Anderson's hand.

Congratulations on a successful cruise. Your presence required urgently. Make all possible haste.

Anderson tucked the message away and regarded the chart. Three miles of blessedly clear passage before the shaded rectangle which marked the final Turkish minefield. One last obstacle before they reached the relative safety of the Mediterranean.

"All ahead full," he said. "Let's get this over and done with."

*

Von Gossler watched the automobile follow the twisting road, working its way back and forth across the face of the hill. The vehicle skirted the potholes and crept round the tight corners, nervous of the yawning drop waiting beyond the road's tattered edge. He remembered his own arrival at Burhanli months before – the vertiginous view from the windows, the chill realisation his life was in the hands of his driver.

A twist in the road took the vehicle behind a dusty outcrop of rock, momentarily shielding it from the observers on the wall.

"What do they want?" he asked his companion.

Falke squinted into the sunlight. Von Gossler wondered how long it was since the old woman had felt its warm touch. "The occasional update on our progress is the price of Ottoman hospitality."

"You call this hospitality?"

"I call it remote. And secure. All the comforts I require. Besides, they have been of greater assistance in our labours than you realise."

"The Turks?" Von Gossler snorted. "Herdsmen – scrabbling in the dust. They build nothing of their own. Even their battleships are British." He gestured with contempt at the automobile as it puttered back into view. "That thing down there is Italian, unless I am mistaken."

Falke's look was sharp. "The Sultans kept the flames of science and reason burning through five hundred years of European ignorance and superstition." She raised a bony finger and prodded Von Gossler in the chest. "Our visitor belongs to a rich scholarly tradition. I will not see him insulted. Have some respect."

The scientist turned and made for the stairs. Von Gossler offered a silent curse at her back. He hoped she took a tumble and snapped her scrawny neck. Respect for the Turks? What of the lack of respect the woman offered him?

He shifted his attention back to the landscape beyond the walls. The dry, cracked hills rolled off to the horizon to the west while the cliffs fell in a near vertical drop into the waters of the Straits to the east. God but he hated this place – the dust, the heat, the crushing inactivity. Nothing to do but observe Falke's increasingly revolting experiments, jotting down her mumbles. She seemed convinced her thoughts were worth preserving for posterity, a chronicle of her glorious scientific achievements. If so, Von

Gossler was destined to be remembered as nothing more than the woman's lowly assistant – a passive note-taker on the margins of history.

He closed his eyes, enjoying the feel of the breeze against his scarred skin. Despite the heat, the air made for a welcome change from the carrion atmosphere of the laboratory. At least this visit would spare him an afternoon of duty at the woman's side. With a final look out over the walls he headed for the stairs. Below, the automobile negotiated the last of the hairpin turns and began to pull itself up the track towards the gate.

*

The garrison captain stepped smartly forward and pulled the door open, snapping off a salute. The soldiers lined up in the courtyard stamped to attention. Von Gossler was unable to resist a smile. He couldn't recall the men better turned out. Boots freshly blackened, buckles gleaming, and clean shaven – they looked almost like a real army.

Their visitor emerged from the automobile, old bones clearly stiff from the uncomfortable journey. He was short and stocky of frame, clad in a dark three-piece suit of decidedly Western and expensive-looking cut. The dark red fez atop his head was the only exotic element to his clothing. His face was deeply lined, the tanned leather of the skin contrasting with the whiteness of his hair and beard. Sharp eyes peered out from beneath heavy lids, sweeping across the assembled men, the black stones of the fortress, and the blue sky above the walls.

The man offered a nod to the still-saluting captain then turned away, ignoring the soldiers' polished finery. He made his way across the courtyard, attention fixed on the waiting Germans.

Falke stepped forward. The Turk took her hand and bent over it, lips brushing her parchment skin. He straightened and Falke babbled something in Turkish, presumably a welcome. Von Gossler's stomach churned – his first Ottoman dignitary, and here he was, unable to even grunt a hello.

"And to you," replied the visitor, filling Von Gossler with relief at the excellent German. "It has been too long my dear."

"Minister, allow me to introduce Viktor Von Gossler, my admirable assistant, and a distant cousin of our own Wilhelm no less..."

Not that distant, thought Von Gossler, lip curling as he offered a bow.

Falke continued with the introductions. "Viktor, this is Kaan Pasha, Minister for Education and Industry, trusted advisor to the Caliph, and a very great friend of Germany."

The two men shook hands and regarded one another. Von Gossler tried to remain unflustered as the old Turk's gaze roamed across his burned features. His stoicism under such obvious scrutiny drew a nod from the Minister.

"As you can see," put in Falke. "Viktor has suffered somewhat in service to his country..."

Von Gossler stood a little straighter at the woman's comment. They had never discussed the circumstances in which he had acquired his scars. In truth, he was ashamed to raise the matter, assuming she had been provided with Von Bernstorff's version of events. The scientist's words brought another nod from Pasha, setting the tassel on his fez swinging.

"So many young men have already given so much. Not twenty miles away, yet more are staining the hills with blood to keep the invaders from our lands." The Turk scowled. "That is why I am here. First, to view your demonstration. I am keen to see what use you have made of the artefact." He turned an intent gaze on Falke. "I have heard positive reports of your most recent experiments."

The scientist blinked at this. Von Gossler realised Pasha was making it clear he had informants within the castle.

"And then we shall discuss putting your work to practical use. Now, let us waste no more time. Show me the laboratory."

*

"Well well, you have been busy..."

Pasha Khan's leathery features split into a smile as he took in the expanse of the underground chamber. He turned to Von Gossler.

"When I first brought your mentor here, it was just a damp cellar."

Perhaps the old Turk's eyesight was failing him. In Von Gossler's opinion the description remained apt, despite Falke's recent efforts. The scientist had seen fit to have the various cadavers removed, making the laboratory more presentable for Pasha's visit. Even the planks of the dissection tables had been scrubbed – although no amount of effort would get the more stubborn stains out of the wood.

The cages along the far wall were empty – their usual occupants getting a rare glimpse of the sun, gathered in the courtyard above for the afternoon's demonstration. The laboratory's atmosphere was considerably fresher for their absence. The Minister would likely be less enamoured of the space if he were to spend hours locked down here, breathing in the reek, documenting the woman's butchery.

Pasha's eyes flicked to the bookshelves in the corner. Falke followed his stare. "You wish to check on your precious volume?"

"Of course," said the Turk. "You have no idea the favours it cost me to have it brought here."

Falke shuffled away between the workbenches, beckoning them to follow. She swept a dustsheet from a reading desk to reveal an ancient leather-bound book, the tattered parchment pages stacked six inches deep. She laid her hand on the blotched red vellum of its binding.

"It is safe. And it is used. Better than mouldering in your archives, gathering dust whilst your librarians stared stupidly at the cypher."

Pasha turned a half-smile on Von Gossler. "She's insufferable when she's right. Nobody could make head nor tail of it until she came along."

"What does it contain?" asked Von Gossler. The book was something new to him. He'd seen Falke at the desk of course, her fingers tracing lines of text, but the scientist had never hinted at the old book's importance.

"Ancient knowledge," said the Turk. "The key to everything that has been accomplished here..."

"Not quite everything," snapped Falke.

"My apologies." Pasha's eyes twinkled. "I do not intend to belittle your achievements."

"And yet you do." The scientist's tone was acidic. Von Gossler found he was enjoying seeing Falke have her nose tweaked out of joint.

The woman spun on her heel. She hauled another sheet aside to reveal an alcove in the wall. "Your ancient knowledge provided clues. But I have taken the next step…"

The two men regarded the glistening machinery which stood beneath the arch. Pistons and gears connected polished steel rods and iron struts into a criss-crossed sculpture – man-shaped but massive. Hydraulic tendons coated in heavy rubber coiled around the skeletal frame, like some species of giant leech adapted to survive on a diet of rust and oil.

"My my," said Pasha. "What do we have here?"

"The future," replied Falke, the gleam in her eyes a match for the metalwork behind her. "All it awaits is a suitable subject."

The Turk gave a rueful shake of his head. "You haven't changed Karla. Obsessed with what is next – never ready to say the work is complete."

"It never is."

"And yet we cannot simply research forever." Pasha indicated the contraption behind the scientist. "Your future will have to wait. It is time to put your current brood to use."

"It is still too early…" stammered Falke. "They are not ready."

"They are ready enough. I am informed the British are about to receive a rather distinguished visitor. I plan to arrange for some guests amongst the welcoming committee…"

*

The soldiers stood massed on the beach to either side of the jetty, cheering the incoming boat at the top of their lungs.

Mechanical walkers towered in the midst of the crowd, men clambering up their steel legs, eager for a better view. A band, hastily cobbled together for the occasion, struck up a tune and eventually tumbled together into a rhythm of sorts. Five thousand Diggers broke into song and the words of "Waltzing Matilda" echoed around the bay. Even the New Zealanders joined in, habitual competitiveness with their Australian cousins forgotten in the moment. With one voice, the Diggers welcomed Field Marshal Kitchener ashore.

Jones, Kowalski and Sullivan forsook the melee on the sand, choosing to observe the scene from the crest of one of the low hills which surrounded the camp. They watched General Birdwood step to the fore amongst the officers on the jetty and offer a parade-ground salute as the commander of the Empire's military forces crossed the gangplank.

A fusillade of cannon shot thundered from the rank of walkers and the soldiers' cheers doubled in volume as the smoke from the explosive acknowledgement rolled across the beach. Above it all, high in the sky, silhouetted against the orange of the sunset, a pair of dirigibles floated. The tenor blast of their foghorns rang out, adding to the din. Jones wondered if Wilberforce was at the helm of either, and if so, what the pilot thought of the airships' somewhat ornamental role in proceedings.

"Grand to see the men's spirits raised, eh?" said Sullivan.

"Perhaps," said Jones. "Would they cheer quite as loud if they knew Kitchener had insisted the Dardanelles could be secured with half the troops requested?" He watched the man below accept the Diggers' raucous welcome with a series of nods and waves. "If he'd listened to advice, this expedition of ours would be in Constantinople by now."

"I wouldn't know about that." Sullivan frowned. "As I said at our first meeting, military matters aren't really my line of work."

Kowalski indicated the jetty. "Sounds like they ain't in his neither."

That was a little harsh, thought Jones, feeling a peculiar obligation to defend the great Imperial hero. "Maybe I'm being unfair," he said. "The man's bright enough, and he's a soldier through-and-through. You can see how much the lads think of him. But he appears incapable of seeing beyond France. I suspect he's always viewed the Dardanelles as something of a sideshow to the main event."

"Which is exactly how it plays out if you ain't going to allocate the men," said Kowalski. "Back in London, Buckingham suggested old Kitchener didn't go all-in because that Churchill feller had been so involved in the planning..."

Sullivan turned from the scene below. "Are you seriously suggesting personal politics would interfere in the running of the war?"

"Heh. Figure you've got a whole heap of book learning Doc, but if you're even asking that question, you maybe ain't so smart after all."

Sullivan declined to respond. He stomped away down the hill.

"Come on," said Jones, giving Kowalski a nudge. "Let's grab something to eat and then we'll see Anderson get what's coming to him."

*

Von Gossler stood at the bend in the stairway and marvelled at the cave's extent, wondering how he could have remained unaware of its existence until now. Hundreds of feet across and almost as high, the space echoed to the sound of footsteps. The noise bounced back and forth from columns of calcified stone before being swallowed by the darkness beyond the torches' reach.

The ancient stairway spilled down the chamber's wall, dropping away from the clustered stalactites of the ceiling in a series of narrow flights chipped out from the living rock. Slow, patient droplets of water slipped from the tips of the hanging stones above, gleaming gold in the torchlight as they dropped to the pool, their impact sending great round ripples across its black surface.

Beneath Von Gossler's feet the stairs continued their serpentine descent, twisting round and back on themselves until they reached a broad flat area surrounded by water. At this natural quay a battered launch was moored, a Red Ensign hanging limp at her stern. The putter of her engine drifted up from below, a curl of smoke from her stubby smokestack adding a kerosene taint to the air.

"Look..." said Falke, drawing Von Gossler's attention to a crevice on the far side of the chamber. A faint play of orange light tinted the water before the crack – remnants of the sunset leaking in from outside. "There is a passage out to the Straits."

Von Gossler stared at her. Did the woman think he was some kind of complete imbecile? Of course there was a damned passage. How else had the boat got there?

Kaan Pasha shuffled down the stairs at the head of a line of Turkish soldiers. The squad of commandos, freshly arrived by truck from the capital, was everything the Burhanli garrison was not – disciplined, quiet and radiating an air of dangerous capability. The Minister joined the two

Germans on the ledge, surveying the cave as the rest of the men filed past. Von Gossler shied away from the flaming torches his companions held aloft. He himself had refused the offer of a light, preferring to risk his footing than hold one of the hissing, spitting brands. In truth, he'd have preferred not to come down here at all, but he couldn't bring himself to show weakness in the face of Falke and Pasha. If those elderly fools would brave the depths of the cavern, then so must he.

Pasha pointed towards the boat. "My spies acquired her straight off the jetty at Suvla – her and a pile of uniforms." A sly smile. "Together they should serve admirably as a disguise."

Only now did Von Gossler realise the half-dozen Turks were all clad in British khaki rather than their regular fatigues.

"Captain Kemal," called Pasha, beckoning over the last of the soldiers. "Listen closely to the professor here. Mark her words well."

Falke produced a small box, its metal faces giving off a dull gleam beneath the torchlight. The Turkish soldier leaned close, examining the device as the scientist spoke.

"The switch sends the radio pulse to awaken the subjects from their stupor. It has a range of perhaps a hundred yards, definitely no further." Falke raised her hand, stabbing at the air with a long finger. "I would suggest you do not use it if you are within arm's reach of any of the subjects. Doing so would almost certainly prove unfortunate."

The Turkish captain gave a solemn nod. Falke handed over the device and the man made off down the stairs, heading for his comrades on the quay and the waiting launch.

"Ah," said Pasha, hoisting his torch. "Our unsuspecting heroes..."

An awful procession descended the steps – eight of Falke's man-beasts, shackled at the neck and wrists, heavy iron links tethering each to its fellows. Eyes glazed, they lurched in somnambulant parade, a single overseer leading the way.

"Incredible," breathed Pasha. The Turk appeared fascinated by the creatures, indeed had spoken of nothing else since the afternoon's demonstration. "Look how docile they are..."

"Only until awoken," said Falke, a note of maternal pride in her voice.

The things shambled closer, bringing with them a hideous stench – part animal, part chemical, part decaying meat. Von Gossler gagged and raised a hand to his face in a futile attempt to filter out the rancid odour. At least as terrible as the smell was the sight of the different creatures, each more twisted and deformed than the last.

One had no fingers below the first knuckle, the digits replaced with long metal knives, the blades screwed into rotting stumps of bone. Another's mouth gaped open, jaws unable to close around the unnatural teeth transplanted within – a big cat's perhaps, or some baboon's.

Yet another caught Von Gossler's attention for the swollen venom sacs pulsing in its neck. The sight repelled and fascinated him in equal measure – he was unable to tear his gaze from the throbbing lumps at the creature's throat. He thought he'd seen every aspect of Falke's work in his role as the scientist's assistant – this horrific vision proved otherwise.

All the creatures bore the scabs and weeping sores typical of Falke's creations, and most slouched along under the added burden of grafted muscle, their arms and torsos bulging with enhanced strength. Von Gossler offered silent thanks for the restraints they wore, and for whatever dark science had been employed to harness their rage.

The last of the beasts reached the turn, slouching past the ledge where the observers stood. Its head lifted, nose wrinkling, and it turned a glassy stare towards Pasha.

"It sees the fire," said the Turk, waving the torch back and forth. The creature's head swung ponderously from side to side following the flame.

"Don't…" said Von Gossler, appalled at the proximity of the thing, its looming bulk, the gag-inducing odour rolling from it.

"Viktor my boy," said Falke. "There is nothing to be afraid of…"

The chain at the creature's neck went taught, tugged forward by the procession ahead. The beast, hauled off-balance, stumbled forward into the Turk. Pasha staggered, his arms flailing, clutching at Falke for support with one hand, the other swinging the burning torch towards Von Gossler.

The flames surged up, filling his vision and flooding his mind. He batted his hands at the torch. The sharp shock of the heat awoke terror within him, overwhelming his senses with remembered pain.

He reeled back from the fire, and suddenly there was nothing beneath his heels but air. The horrified faces of his companions flew up and away. He floated, caught in a strange calm as the wind rushed past, its touch cool on his skin.

He smashed into unforgiving stone in an explosion of snaps and cracks and agony. His body shrieked its disapproval at this treatment and then he was gone – awareness fading into welcome, silent darkness.

*

For most conspicuous bravery, in command of Her Majesty's Submersible Nautica whilst operating in the Sea of Marmara, Captain Michael Frederick Anderson is awarded the highest military honour the Empire may bestow, the Victoria Cross.

In the face of great danger he succeeded in destroying one large Turkish gunboat, two troop transports, two ammunition ships, and three store-ships, in addition to driving a further store-ship ashore. All this alongside forcing a submersible passage through the Straits, a task many had believed impossible.

In recognition of their bravery, the Nautica's officers are awarded the Distinguished Service Cross, and her regular crewmen the Distinguished Service Medal.

The aide finished reading from the citation, folded the sheet of paper, and stepped back. Kitchener stepped up onto the low stage and regarded the soldiers gathered before him in the command bunker. The Field Marshal's solemn expression, familiar from a thousand recruitment posters, cracked into a broad smile as he beckoned Anderson forward.

The submariner looked petrified. From what Jones could see, peering over the shoulders of the more senior men, he reckoned the poor chap would cheerfully have faced the Dardanelles a thousand times over rather than this mortifying ordeal.

The two men shook hands, the Field Marshal leaning close and exchanging a few quiet words with the sailor. He lifted the cruciform medallion from the table at his side and pinned it to Anderson's chest.

The decoration in place, Kitchener took a step back and offered the submariner a salute. At that the assembled men broke into loud applause.

Anderson turned towards the gathering, flushing crimson above the collar of his dress uniform as he reluctantly accepted their acclaim. Like the Captain, every man present was dressed in his finest – Generals, Admirals, Commodores and Colonels, all scrubbed up and well-polished to show their appreciation for the sailor.

Even Wilberforce had made an effort, the sole representative of the Aeronautic Corps clad in his dress whites, moustache tips freshly waxed, trying but failing not to look impressed with the honour bestowed upon the man from the rival service.

Clapping along with the rest, Jones reckoned the applause was well-deserved, and only to be expected. Despite Anderson's modesty and obvious embarrassment, the *Nautica*'s accomplishments had been one of the few bright sparks in this otherwise dismal campaign.

The boat and her crew were approaching legendary status, both here amongst the Diggers, and with the public back home, helped along by the enthusiastic exaggeration of the press. From what Jones had heard, Anderson would be lucky if he didn't receive a second citation for his more recent excursion. Although by the look of it, a repeat of this experience might be the end of the poor man.

General Birdwood raised his hands for quiet.

"Gentlemen, thank you for joining us in this pleasant duty, but now the Field Marshal and I need to talk." Sir William smiled. "In the Mess you will find tea. And cake – fresh from the counter at Selfridges, courtesy of the Field Marshal."

The assembled officers began to file out the door, wrapped in a low hum of conversation. Kowalski leaned in close to Jones.

"Shiny medals and some afternoon tea – that really all it takes to gee up the troops?"

Jones decided to take the question as a joke, although with the Floridian's current mood, it was impossible to be sure.

"Most definitely," he answered, keeping his tone light. "You know the English. We'll do just about anything for a decent cup of tea."

"And risk your lives for a worthless piece of tin," replied Kowalski, nodding towards Anderson with something approaching a sneer.

"Keep your voice down for God's sake. You know as well as anyone how much he deserves this."

Kowalski was unimpressed. "Your boys are more in want of ammunition than cake. Or medals."

Jones turned away, determined not to say something he might regret. They shuffled forwards in uncomfortable silence, eventually reaching the head of the line where Anderson was engaged in an endless round of handshakes.

Jones offered the sailor his hand in turn. He regarded the new medal affixed to the man's uniform. Regardless of what Kowalski might say, the decoration did make a difference – an acknowledgement of the risks the submariners faced every time they ducked beneath the waves.

"I've known a few men who've earned one of those," said Jones. "You're the only one who's stayed alive to collect it. I genuinely couldn't imagine a more worthy recipient. Congratulations old chap."

Anderson squirmed. Jones let him. He meant every word. Eventually he decided to put him out of his misery.

"Just don't expect us to start saluting as you go strolling past."

The sailor's face cracked into a smile for the first time since the beginning of the ceremony.

"Those Army salutes aren't worth as much as the Navy ones, you should know that by now..."

Sir William called out, interrupting the exchange. "Major Jones, perhaps you and your associates could join me?"

Anderson nodded towards Birdwood and Kitchener. The two men conversed in low tones before the wall map, fingers stabbing at different locations across the chart.

"Watch out," said the sailor. "Those two look like they're cooking up a task for you."

"Unfortunately, I may have contributed to the recipe..."

"You army chaps never learn – always suggesting new ways to get yourselves killed." Anderson made for the door. "I'd best go and face my own battle. Good luck with whatever it is you're mixed up in."

Jones watched him go. He wasn't sure which of them had it worse – himself, or Anderson with his Mess full of senior commanders all intent on further congratulation. At least the sailor would be getting a slice of cake.

General Birdwood turned from his conversation and beckoned the waiting trio towards the chart. He introduced them to Kitchener.

"Field Marshal, these are the men I've been telling you about. Let me explain the operation we've been planning..."

*

Birdwood summarised, marking each point on the map with a tap of his finger. "So the push out from Suvla focuses Turkish attention here in the north, allowing the ANZAC forces to break through. The mayhem will allow Major Jones' detachment to strike out for Burhanli. At a stroke, we sever the supply lines to the defences at Helles, as well as getting our hands on this Falke woman's research." Birdwood eyed his commander. "It's our best chance to finally make something of this campaign."

Kitchener regarded the tangle of lines and arrows illustrating the proposed operation. Jones winced to see it marked up like this – too many objectives, too many simultaneous manoeuvres. The plan looked like the work of desperate men.

"The strike for Burhanli will be exposed until reinforcements arrive," said the Field Marshal. "What if they're cut off rather than the Turks?"

"It's a risk sir," said Birdwood. "But we can pull the men out by sea if we have to, and at least we'd have the German research."

"But little else to show for your efforts." Kitchener frowned. "These scientific secrets could prove an expensive acquisition. The feint to the north alone could cost a thousand men."

"It's worth the price," blurted Sullivan, prompting the soldiers to turn in his direction.

"Sorry to interrupt..." He blinked furiously behind his spectacles. "But this information could prove as valuable in the long-term as Constantinople itself."

"Forgive the good Doctor," said Birdwood. "He may be overstating the case somewhat, but equally, he may not be wholly incorrect." He paused. "You'll understand when you've seen the creature for yourself."

Kitchener turned his penetrating gaze on Jones. "Major, you'll be leading the assault on the fortress. What do you think?"

"It's a sound plan sir. We should be able to accomplish the task."

"Yet you don't appear overly enthusiastic."

Of course I bloody don't, thought Jones. What man with any sense would be keen to lay siege to a Turkish castle? The last Englishmen to attempt that trick had been the damned Crusaders, and look how well that had turned out. He took a deep breath.

"It's less the plan I have reservations about sir, more the requirement for it in the first place."

"Major Jones and I don't see eye-to-eye on this matter Field Marshal," said Birdwood, eyes narrowed. "Although I had assumed the question was settled."

Jones cringed. Reopening this particular can of worms likely hadn't been the wisest move – especially in front of Kitchener of all people.

"Sorry sir," he said, unsure himself which of the senior men he was addressing the apology to. His discomfort twisted within him, turning to anger. "But I'll be damned if I agree with the Doctor here..." The look Sullivan shot him was poisonous. "Risking all these lives to get hold of some obscene science – it's not right."

Birdwood made to speak – to bellow more likely, judging by his face's crimson shade. But Kitchener raised a hand, his expression intent.

"You have an alternative?"

Jones could feel Sullivan's stare burning into him. Alongside the doctor, Kowalski offered a matching sullen glare. Seems I've managed to upset everyone, thought Jones. Might as well finish the job properly.

"The Turks' aerial defences are a joke," he said. "If we'd had more airships this whole affair might have been over weeks ago."

"You're not the first to have lectured me on the supply situation Major." Kitchener's tone was icy.

Jones hurried on. "A couple of dirigibles loaded up with bombs would reduce this fortress to rubble, solving the problem once and for all."

"Yet depriving Porton Down of its prize," said Kitchener.

Jones decided to keep his thoughts on that particular matter to himself. "We should concentrate on beating the Turks sir. Let the Aeronautic Corps deal with this Falke woman and her creations."

He stopped speaking, the die cast. Whatever happened now, at least he'd made his views clear.

Sir William leaned forward, hands on the back of a chair, knuckles white around the wood as he glared at Jones. "Thank you Major," he said, his tone quite at odds with the civil nature of the words. "If you're quite finished, the Field Marshal and I require some time alone."

Jones offered a salute and turned for the door. Sullivan and Kowalski followed behind. The weight of their dual stares was heavy between Jones' shoulder blades.

*

Sullivan ignored Jones when they emerged from the bunker. The doctor stormed straight past him and off into the warren of trenches, his lanky figure swallowed up by the gloom. Kowalski, on the other hand, had no intention of letting Jones off so lightly.

"What the hell was that about?"

"It's the right thing to do." Jones had stood up to Birdwood and Kitchener, he wasn't about to back down from the Floridian.

"And so you'll ignore all our planning and assume you know best? You God-damned arrogant son of a bitch."

"What is the matter with you?" shot back Jones. "I thought you wanted Von Gossler dead?"

"I don't just want him dead. I want my hands at his throat. I want to look into his face. I want to hear him beg." Kowalski's voice dropped to a dangerous growl. "Then I'll see him dead – not before. And not by some other feller's hand."

"It won't bring her back..."

"You think I don't know?" Kowalski glared at him. "Don't you dare tell me it ain't worth it. You've always had your purpose – well now I got mine. Maybe it ain't as high and mighty as Queen and Country, but it's all

I've got." Kowalski shrugged, the venom gone from his tone, replaced with weary resignation. "Ah, what the hell would you know about it? You left Isabella in Cuba."

Jones watched him stomp off into the darkness. He debated with himself if he should go after him, but settled on letting the man go. The mood they were both in might see more than words being exchanged.

Besides, what would he say? That only shame at duty undone had dragged him from Isabella's side and back to war? That he kept every letter she sent and regretted his choice every day?

No. He'd be damned if he'd justify himself to the mercenary, especially when the man was in such foul temper. Bugger it — what he needed was a drink. More than one in fact. Time to find some of that bloody awful Turkish paintstripper.

He'd taken barely a half-dozen steps along the trench before screams and the harsh clatter of gunfire ripped through the night.

*

Chaos swept through the camp around the command bunker, bellowed orders and panicked shouts competing with animal roars and the mechanical crack of carbines. The noise of fighting surrounded Jones, mayhem echoing out from every point of the compass.

He unclipped the flap on his holster and withdrew his pistol, all the time whipping his head first one way and then the other, peering into the darkness at either end of the trench. His dilemma on which way to proceed was resolved as the battle came to him.

A soldier limped out of the shadows, face streaked with mud, his eyes wide and white.

"Run!" he shouted. "It's coming —"

The cry was cut off — the man snatched backwards into the dark. A shriek rang out, tailing off, swallowed up in an awful scrabble of wet snapping noises.

Jones backed away, revolver raised in the direction of the unseen struggle. A hand clamped down on his shoulder and he nearly jumped out of his skin. He swung round, heart in his throat, his pistol coming to a halt aimed between Kowalski's eyes. The Floridian held up his palm.

"Easy Major. Save your ammunition for whatever's back there..."

A shadow appeared in the doorway behind them and the two men whirled in unison, bringing their guns to bear. Jones managed to avoid putting a round through General Birdwood's face. Christ-be-damned, he thought, would people please stop sneaking up on me?

"What the bloody hell is going on out there?" demanded Sir William.

"Stay inside," shouted Kowalski, shoving Birdwood back into the bunker, ignoring the old soldier's outraged splutters.

Jones' attention was drawn back to the trench, captured by the monstrous vision which lumbered out of the gloom. The thing moved forwards on its hands and feet in an awkward loping motion, head low, snout swinging back and forth. It lifted its face, glittering menace lurking in the depths of shadowy eye-sockets. Its jaws dark with filth and blood, it snarled, lips sliding back over gums bristling with yellow teeth.

The creature reared up and spread its arms wide, hissing and spitting at the two men who blocked its path down the trench.

"The head..." muttered Jones. "Aim for its head."

The beast leapt, throwing itself forward in an apelike bound. Jones' finger tightened on the trigger and the pistol barked in his hand. Kowalski fired beside him, the pair shoulder to shoulder, shooting over and again. In the glare of the muzzle flashes, the creature's approach became a flickering nightmare of monochrome images.

Bullets spattered into the man-thing's chest and shoulders, knocking chunks of pale flesh flying. Still it came on, rocked by each impact, but oblivious to the damage. Finally a round struck true, snapping the beast's head up and back. It tumbled forward, limbs caught beneath it, bringing it sliding to a tangled halt in the mud.

Jones lowered his gun and breathed once more. Kowalski took a step forward and nudged the fallen creature with his foot. The thing gave out a rasping grunt and squirmed round, its jaws opening and closing, attempting even in its death throes to attach itself to Kowalski's boot. The Floridian brought up his pistol and fired a single shot into the beast's face. Its limbs twitched once and it lay still.

The two men regarded the grotesque corpse.

"Maybe I'll join this monster hunt of yours after all," said Kowalski. He cocked his head at the continuing bedlam reverberating around the camp. "Sounds like you could do with the help –"

His eyes went wide, gaze fixed over Jones' shoulder. Jones turned, trying to raise his pistol at the looming shape. But the gun was batted aside and claw-like fingers caught his arms and hauled him off-balance.

He flailed, caught in an iron embrace as the fetid stink of his attacker's breath rolled over him. He caught a vision of red eyes in a pale face and a mouth stretched wide, and then it was upon him.

Pain lanced up from his neck as the beast's teeth sliced through his shirt, gouging furrows into the meat of his shoulder.

*

Kowalski took aim, drawing a bead on the creature's head as it gnawed at its captive. Stay still, his mind screamed at Jones. The last thing he wanted to do was put a bullet through the struggling Englishman. He banished the ironic thought that he would cheerfully have done so only minutes before. He pulled the trigger.

The pistol did nothing but emit a loud click. Kowalski blinked stupidly at the weapon for a moment then cursed. He sprang forward, wielding the empty revolver like a cudgel. His strike would have brought a baseball crowd back home to their feet. The roundhouse swing battered the beast full in the face. The blow rang its way up the gun barrel, setting his fist stinging from the impact.

The creature staggered back, releasing Jones from its grip. It wobbled off a few paces, shaking its head. Jones clapped a hand to his collarbone and stumbled. Kowalski hauled him upright.

"Thanks," grunted the Englishmen.

We're not out of this yet, thought Kowalski as the beast straightened up, glowering at the pair, bloodshot eyes filled with animal hunger. It took a step towards them.

"Shoot it," he snapped. "I'm out of bullets."

"No gun," said Jones. "Dropped it."

Well that's just swell thought Kowalski. He raised his empty pistol, preparing to meet the creature's charge.

The ear-splitting clatter of the carbines almost scared him witless. He threw himself into the mud and dragged Jones down beside him as the fusillade burst over their heads. The torrent of lead picked up the beast and threw it back against the trench wall where it danced, plucked this way and that by the unforgiving hail of bullets.

Kowalski and Jones hunkered down, arms folded over their heads until the explosive reports came to a stuttering halt. The creature slumped motionless to the ground, its frame riddled with punctures – an almost unrecognisable mess of mangled flesh.

The prone men raised their heads, craning round to see Birdwood and Kitchener stationed in the bunker doorway. Each of the old soldiers brandished a machine-carbine, cordite drifting up from the multiple barrels as they spun slowly to a halt.

Sir William stared down, teeth clamped on the stem of his pipe. He offered them a nod before turning to Kitchener. "Good shooting sir."

The Field Marshal lifted his weapon to hold it vertically, admiring the gleaming brass mechanism. He reached out and patted a hand on the carbine's barrels, pulling his fingers away at the metal's heat.

"Always wanted to try one of these things," he said, a grin appearing beneath the moustache. "Bloody marvellous."

Birdwood turned his attention to the men lying at his feet.

"Come along you two. No time for lounging around. We appear to have an infestation which needs clearing out…"

*

Dawn revealed the extent of the havoc wreaked upon the camp. A full hundred men were dead, the fallen arranged in silent rows, shrouded in blankets. Alongside the victims lay the bodies of their unnatural attackers, a collection of twisted rotting figures. The sight of them haunted Jones' mind long after he'd turned away.

From their vantage point on the hill above the camp, Birdwood's senior officers watched plumes of smoke curl up into the morning sky from the smouldering remains of their stores. A felled walker offered mute testament to the Turkish saboteurs' effectiveness, its buckled limbs lying askew, its mortars smashed loose from their mountings and scattered around its metal corpse.

Confused reports had come in throughout the night, eventually coalescing into a coherent picture. The Turks had used the mayhem created by the monstrous creatures to infiltrate the defences and work their way across the encampment, targeting supplies and ammunition stores. The explosive results of their efforts had provided spectacular if sporadic illumination for the fighting in the trenches as hunting parties sought out the inhuman foe.

The infiltrators had even managed to destroy one of the last remaining airships. The burnt and broken curves of its crumpled frame littered the stretch of beach which served as an airfield. Jones spotted Wilberforce, standing disconsolate at the edge of the hilltop gathering, hands in pockets, glowering in the direction of the smoking wreckage. The Aeronautic Corps on the peninsula was now reduced to a grand total of one serviceable aircraft. All-in-all the night had been a disaster for the campaign – the Diggers' morale would sink lower than ever after this.

"Damned impressive operation," said General Birdwood. He looked at Jones. "Almost something you and Buckingham might have cooked up."

Although I hope we'd have stopped short of employing those obscenities as a diversion, thought Jones. He decided to leave that particular argument closed for the moment, making do with a nod instead. The motion caused him to wince and lift a hand to the wad of blood-stained cloth stuffed beneath the collar of his shirt.

Birdwood frowned and nodded towards the bandage. "Be sure you see Kendrick. Get that wound seen to."

One of the Brigadiers piped up – not one whose opinion Jones valued overmuch. The man was a bloody fool, the worst sort of upper-class rugger bugger, convinced the entire war was an extension of the fun to be had on Eton's playing fields.

"We're just lucky the Turks didn't use this as a prelude for a serious attack. Old Abdul must be stretched mighty thin not to have grasped an opportunity like this."

Kitchener turned from his contemplation of the scene and offered a sharp look at the man who had spoken. "The primary lesson to take from last night is not one regarding the weakness of the Turks."

The man coloured and decided to keep any further observations to himself. Kitchener shifted his gaze to Birdwood.

"You knew my opinion before I arrived General. Nothing I have witnessed over the last two days has altered it."

Sir William slumped, like a boxer finally defeated after a long and tiring fight. The Field Marshal turned from the General to address the assembled men, raising his voice to grab their attention.

"I have decided to call an end to this venture in the East." He ran his stern gaze across the gathered officers. "You and your men have fought bravely and well, but the campaign for the Dardanelles is lost. Return to your troops and begin preparations for withdrawal."

The announcement brought a hubbub of conversation amongst the officers on the hilltop. Jones took in the variety of reactions – some men looked angry, some ashamed, but more still appeared relieved, glad the whole sorry affair was at an end. Jones himself couldn't be sure how he felt about it – his aching muscles and the insistent throb from his wound dominated all else for the moment.

Kitchener beckoned Jones and Sir William closer. Birdwood appeared to have recovered his poise – now the order had been given, the old campaigner stood ready to carry out his duty.

"As for our other concern..." said Kitchener. "I would see an end to this unholy science." He nodded at Jones and then looked at Sir William, his stare as hard as flint.

"Send in the airship General. Pound this Burhanli into the dust."

*

Jones found his way to the medical tent. He ducked his head beneath the flap and stepped into the welcome shade. He'd seen the place worse, stuffed with wounded and dying men in the terrible aftermath of one failed offensive after another. It was quieter this time, in both numbers of casualties and the cries of the injured, but the nature of the wounds on display somehow made it different. Numb to the regular perils of war, Jones found these injuries unnerving – instead of the usual bullet or shrapnel wounds, today the soldiers nursed bites and scratches and wicked claw marks.

He spotted Sullivan, his sleeves rolled up, bent over a stretcher, bandaging a wounded man's arm. Jones caught his eye, and offered him a nod, glad the man from Porton Down had mucked in to help. Sullivan frowned and turned his back – it seemed Jones was still in the bad books.

Just wait until word of Kitchener's decisions circulated – the doctor's mood was unlikely to improve. Never mind Kowalski's. Jones hadn't seen the Floridian for hours, not since the search parties had flushed out the last of the creatures. He didn't relish his next encounter with the man.

Kendrick straightened up from a patient and noticed his newest arrival. The surgeon waved Jones towards a canvas chair. He sank into it – the first time he'd sat down since the previous evening. He leaned back and offered a wry smile to the medical man. The doctor looked exhausted, likely as much in need of a seat as Jones.

"Busy night?"

"Busier than some," said Kendrick. He shrugged. "Calmer than others we've had." He pointed to Jones' makeshift dressing. "How long have you been walking about like that?"

"A while. It stings a bit, but I'll survive."

"I'll be the judge of that."

Kendrick crouched. He pulled Jones' shirt aside and peeled the crude bandage from the wound. Jones gritted his teeth as the blood-soaked cloth was tugged free, reopening the lacerations.

"Good Lord," said the surgeon, eyeing the multiple gouges. "How did you collect this badge of honour?"

"Ran into a beastie. It thought I might make a tasty morsel..."

Kendrick jerked back, his tone suddenly sharp. "It bit you?"

"Yes..."

Almost before Jones had finished his answer, the man was up on his feet. Kendrick practically ran across the tent. He grabbed at Sullivan's arm, hauling him close and speaking to him in a low voice. Sullivan's eyes flicked to Jones, the initial scowl turning to concern at the surgeon's words. Whatever was going on, Jones didn't like the look of it at all. A clammy sweat broke out across his forehead as Kendrick returned, Sullivan in tow. Jones took in the pair's serious expressions.

"You two need to work on your bedside manner…"

The doctors said nothing, Kendrick standing back whilst his colleague bent to examine Jones' wound. Sullivan prised the gouges open, peering into their depths. This was quite bad enough, but when he pinched the entire wounded area between his fingers and squeezed, Jones almost shot out of the chair.

"Bloody hell! Is that entirely necessary?"

Sullivan ignored him, leaning in close to sniff at the fresh fluid leaking from the bite. He frowned, then turned to Kendrick.

"Get my bag."

The surgeon grabbed the case from the trestle table and handed it over. Sullivan delved within and pulled out a leather wallet and a vial of amber liquid.

"What's that?" demanded Jones, increasingly unimpressed with both his treatment and the lack of commentary.

Sullivan flicked open the wallet and withdrew a syringe.

"You've been poisoned Major. Whatever bit you was venomous."

Jones' skin crawled at the thought. He imagined his blood, pumping round his body, carrying a black taint to every organ. He swallowed a mouthful of saliva, mastering a compulsion to throw up.

Sullivan extracted a syringe-full of liquid from the vial, tapping it with his finger to work the air bubbles out of the mixture.

"We've had three other men infected," he said, lifting Jones' arm. "They were more badly mauled and ended up with a good deal more poison inside them." He met Jones' gaze and answered the unspoken question. "Two of them are already dead. The third isn't far behind."

Jones didn't feel the pinprick. He watched, dazed, as Sullivan pushed down on the plunger and the syringe's golden contents disappeared into the veins of his forearm. The needle pulled free and Sullivan pressed his thumb over the tiny red dot of the puncture.

"That should help."

Jones felt a flood of relief. "You had me worried there."

The medical men shared a look and Jones' stomach lurched once more. "What?"

"If only I had a laboratory..." said Sullivan, his voice tight with frustration. "I could rustle up an antidote, set you right as rain in a jiffy."

Jones stared at him, not wanting to hear the words, but needing to know all the same.

"The serum I've given you will slow the effects," continued the doctor. "But I can't stop it."

He removed his glasses and blinked down, clearly searching for words. The ones he settled on sent a chill lancing into Jones' heart.

"I'm sorry Major, but you'll be dead in a day. Maybe two."

*

"The lads did a bit of scrounging," said Simpson, sheepish, shifting from foot to foot. "They, ah, came up with these sir. For you."

The soldier produced a small package and placed it on the table. Jones leaned forward and lifted a corner of the wrapping to reveal a box of cigarettes. Turkish, and a decent blend too – not his usual, but by God they would do. The smokes were the best news he'd had all day.

"Pass on my thanks. I know how hard these things are to come by."

"Least we could do sir." The New Zealander looked down, meeting Jones' eye for the first time since he'd entered the dugout. "And if there's anything else you need, you let me know."

"Thank you." Jones raised the cigarettes. "But now I have everything I could possibly want."

Simpson eyed the table, the enamel mug, and the bottle of Turkish brandy – a quarter-drunk already. "Reckon you do sir."

Jones returned the man's smile. "That will be all Sergeant."

The soldier straightened his spine, dirty boots clumping together as he came to attention. He saluted, his stare fixed over Jones' head.

"It's been a bloody honour sir."

Jones pushed himself up from his seat and returned the man's salute.

"No," he said, a catch in his voice. "The honour is mine. And pass that on to the lads as well."

Simpson turned on his heel and ducked under the lintel, heading back out into the afternoon sun. Jones returned to his chair and opened the cigarette box. He pulled one of the slender tubes from within and rolled it between finger and thumb, letting his anticipation build. He struck a match, holding the flame to the cigarette's tip, sucking in a hungry mouthful, relishing the moment.

He leaned back and lifted his feet to rest on the table's corner, his weight settling into the chair's creaking canvas. He sent a stream of blue smoke billowing up towards the ceiling. More followed until a cloud hung beneath the uneven rafters and the cigarette was burned down to a stub, the heat at its tip threatening his fingers. His aunt had always berated him for smoking – a filthy habit, she'd maintained, one which would hasten him to an early grave. He plucked another cigarette from the pack, lighting it from the smouldering embers of the first.

He regarded the bottle on the table, wishing it were Scotch. His eye was drawn to the scattered leaves of paper beneath the bottle and mug – a half-written letter to his aunt and uncle, and then more sheets, intimidating in their blankness, reminding him of the note to Isabella he had yet to attempt. What could he say? Should he even try? Would a letter from him be any better than some telegram from Buckingham? Jones sneered at his weakness. Of course it bloody would. He just couldn't bring himself to reach for the pen – more scared of the search for words than of what the coming hours would bring.

A knock interrupted his thoughts. Sullivan stood in the doorway, wafting a hand before him in an attempt to dispel the fug of smoke.

"Good Lord," he coughed, eyes watering behind his spectacles. "Are you trying to scare off visitors?"

"Not by design," said Jones. "Although if that's the effect..."

Sullivan stepped fully inside, followed by Kowalski. The Floridian took a look round the dugout, gaze drifting across the mess on the table before fixing on Jones. He gave a shake of his head.

"Figured you'd coop yourself up somewhere dark and miserable, seeking refuge in bad booze and cheap tobacco."

Jones brandished his cigarette.

"Actually, I suspect these were rather expensive."

"Melancholy don't suit you Major." Kowalski jerked a thumb over his shoulder in the direction of the door. "On your feet. Time to get moving."

Jones' boots stayed on the table. "I don't believe I have anywhere I need to be."

"I disagree. Ways I figure it, we got ourselves a common purpose for the first time since I got here."

"I don't follow."

"You, me, and the Doc."

"What about us?"

"Doc says you're a goner without an antidote – something he can't cook up without a laboratory to play with…"

"I'm well aware of the situation," said Jones. He reached for the bottle. "I was planning on forgetting all about it. Please don't remind me."

Kowalski plucked the drink from Jones' hand and shifted the bottle out of easy reach. "Maybe you need reminding there's a perfectly good laboratory a few miles that way." He gestured, in entirely the wrong direction as it happened, but Jones caught the gist of his meaning.

"Burhanli?" He gave a snort. "The castle will be rubble by dawn."

Sullivan joined the exchange. "So we need to get a move on."

"We?"

"I want Falke's research. Captain Kowalski here wants his reckoning with Von Gossler." The doctor offered a thin smile. "Your own interests appear self-evident."

Jones couldn't believe what he was hearing. Either the brandy was stronger than he thought or everyone had gone insane. "So we just waltz through the Turkish lines and knock on the door?"

"Of course not," said Kowalski. "We're going to hitch a ride…"

He ducked out of the doorway, returning a moment later with a third man in tow.

"I understand you're in need of transport," said Anderson. "Perhaps I can drop you off on my way up the Straits?"

Jones eyed the submariner, nervous of the glimmer of hope the man's words had ignited. "You're heading back to the Marmara?"

"One more cruise," came the reply. "Birdwood wants the Turkish gunboats kept busy during the evacuation. The *Nautica* leaves in an hour.

I believe we have room for three passengers. Steerage obviously – I'm afraid our first class cabins are fully booked."

The trio waited, their inquisitive stares a matching set.

"What's it going to be Major?" said Kowalski. "You going to sit and get drunk on some frankly God-awful booze, or you going to come get yourself killed with us?"

Jones tugged out his watch and thumbed the catch. The casing clicked open to reveal a cutaway face, the mechanism ticking and whirring beneath. He contemplated the rotating gears and the sweep of the hands, each passing moment marked off with a tiny click.

He swung his feet down from the table and pushed his weary bones out of the chair.

"What are we waiting for?" he said. "I haven't got all day."

*

Extracted from 'A History of the Ancient Sects and Societies of the East'...

Under the stewardship of Al-Kalil the Order grew in power and infamy. Its very name struck fear in the hearts of Princes – Mohammedan and Christian alike. By the ruthless employment of the Faithful, and the judicious spreading of dreadful rumour regarding their capability, so this new Master sought to elevate himself above all other Rulers.

Much wealth he gathered to his stronghold, and all was spent in pursuit of the Great Mysteries of the World. A vast laboratory was constructed to the Master's design, with forges and crucibles for the purifying of base materials, and mirrors and lenses arranged into grand telescopes. In this place the Master would sequester himself for days on end, foregoing all sustenance and sleep, lost in his search for Knowledge.

These labours, perhaps to be judged a worthy pursuit by the standards of our own time, proved Al-Kalil's undoing. Those more junior adherents of the Order, not yet initiated into the Higher Degrees, thought little of their Master's endeavours. Instead they remained desirous of the more material rewards which Hassan, less-learned perhaps than Al-Kalil, but a wiser judge of his fellow man, had bestowed upon them in recognition of their fealty.

In the absence of these fruits of loyalty, more than one of these disillusioned adherents sent messages to the Seljuk Princes – they who had suffered most at the hands of the Order and did greatly desire its destruction. And so the Seljuks came to the fastness and laid it siege by both land and sea, and despite the sacrifice of a thousand of the Faithful, the stronghold fell by betrayal, the Turks entering in and sacking it.

Last to fall was the central tower where the Master sought refuge, sending man after man to perish defending the stair until none remained but the mute slave burdened with Al-Kalil's great book. The Turks' victory plain, the Master took this unfortunate servant and threw him down, breaking him upon the spears of the host below. Then cursing the Seljuks, Al-Kalil himself leapt from that pinnacle and in this fashion passed the second and final Master of the Order, and that terrible organisation, bereft of both leadership and home, never again troubled the world.

Burhanli

Darkness. And then light – searing, painful light. Then darkness once again, a blessed return to peace.

A voice – muffled, indistinct through fog, calling. He tried to ignore it, unwilling to hear the words which summoned him, but the voice grew louder, clearer, more insistent.

"Open your eyes again," it said.

He clung to the darkness and willed the fog to swallow him up once more. But the vapours receded, leaving him exposed, unable to hide.

"I know you can hear me," said the voice, stern now, unforgiving. "Open your eyes."

Perhaps if he complied with the instructions they would leave him alone, stop shouting at him. His father had always said that was all he wanted, for him to do as he was told. If he opened his eyes, even just for a moment, maybe they would leave him be. He cracked an eyelid open, and then the other, scraping them back over gritty eyeballs, granting the stabbing light access to the inside of his skull.

A blur – the shape slowly resolving itself into a face. It leaned in close, a hawk's stare boring down into his own bleary gaze.

"Good," said the face. "Good boy."

See – just give them what they want. Now he could go back to sleep. His eyelids drooped.

"Ah ah..." said the woman, wagging a long thin finger. Falke, came the thought, her name is Falke.

The face vanished for a moment. It reappeared accompanied by a hand clutching a syringe.

Sight of the needle disturbed him, but he couldn't tell why. The woman fumbled with something beyond his vision and then a warm glow began to tingle outward from behind his eyes, jangling, itching through the jumbled pathways of his consciousness. The last vestiges of the black fog evaporated and his mind broke free of the dark.

He lay flat, gazing up at a stone ceiling. His name was Viktor Von Gossler. He was in a castle in Turkey. And something was very wrong.

"What..." he croaked, his voice a broken whisper.

"You had an accident," said Falke, hovering over him. "Don't you remember?"

Von Gossler made to shake his head but could not move. He swivelled his eyes in their dry sockets, glimpsing the edges of some sort of iron collar and headpiece. The metal held him immobile, pinned in place. He rotated his gaze back to the scientist.

"Don't worry my boy. It's for your own good." She offered him a joyless smile, the skin of her face stretched into a rictus grin. "We don't want you suffering any more damage, do we?"

"I don't..." Von Gossler tried to swallow, his tongue a foreign thing, swollen and clumsy in his mouth. "I can't... feel anything."

"I would be astonished if you did."

Falke raised a scalpel, its blade streaked with crimson.

"I severed your nerves some time ago."

*

Wherever they stood, the three passengers found themselves in the way – either blocking the passage or preventing access to storage lockers and maintenance hatches. The *Nautica*'s crewmen were nothing if not polite as they squeezed past their guests, but Jones detected a difference in the atmosphere from his previous voyages aboard the submersible. The sailors were tense, coiled tight – their heads swivelling round at the slightest noise. The repeated trips through the Straits were taking their toll, fraying the nerves of every man aboard.

"Spare cogs round here, ain't we?" said Kowalski as they were ushered away from yet another cluster of valves.

Sullivan stepped aside and cracked his skull off a girder. Jones winced at the sound. Half a head taller than anyone else aboard – you would think the doctor would have learned to duck by now.

"Don't think I'm built for this submersible lark," said Sullivan.

"You're certainly not built for the uniform." Jones pointed to Sullivan's trousers, hems flapping a good three inches short of his ankles.

They had snuck aboard the *Nautica* disguised as crew, clad in khaki trousers and navy-blue rollneck sweaters. Jones deemed the subterfuge necessary and Anderson agreed. Whilst Kowalski and Sullivan were technically outside Birdwood's jurisdiction, the submersible was not, and nor, despite his current medical status, was Jones.

Nobody knew what the General might make of their self-appointed mission, but better to seek forgiveness than permission was Jones' motto.

"Half mast," said Sullivan, glancing down with a wry smile.

"Not on my account I hope."

The doctor's smile evaporated. His eyes flicked away, avoiding Jones' own. Typical civilian, thought Jones, uncomfortable with gallows humour.

"Come on," he said. "Let's find out where we are."

He led the way forward through the narrow companionway. They ducked through a pressure door and straightened up under the control room's glass ceiling. Anderson turned from the chart.

"How are you enjoying your cruise?"

"Not much of a view," said Kowalski, indicating the heavy darkness above the dome.

"The sun set an hour ago," said Anderson. "No moon yet. Shame really. We're not so deep the moonlight wouldn't have reached us. It can be quite beautiful you know."

"A warrior and a poet..." put in Jones.

Whatever retort the submariner intended to throw Jones' way was placed in abeyance as the Duty Officer straightened from the map table.

"Sir, we're coming up on the first minefield."

"Very good," said Anderson. He raised his voice to carry across the control room. "All ahead slow. Make our depth forty feet. Let's see if we can't sneak over the top. We spent too long trying to find a deeper route the last time."

Instructions delivered, he returned his attention to his passengers.

"Two miles through the mines and we'll drop you gentlemen off." He gave Jones a look. "Poetry aside, the lack of a moon should be perfect for your evening swim."

"Swim?" Sullivan looked aghast at this statement. "I thought we would be going ashore by boat?"

"Sadly no," replied Anderson. "You're going to have to get wet."

"Don't worry Doc," put in Kowalski. "Ain't like those pants of yours can shrink any smaller..."

*

"God damn it!" cursed Anderson. "We were almost clear."

The *Nautica* floated dead in the water, hanging in the blackness, the hum of her engines silenced by the cable which fouled her screw.

At the first screech of contact the helmsman had employed a deft touch, swinging the submersible round, clear of the mine's anchor line. It was a skilful manoeuvre, the achievement undermined only when the *Nautica*'s new path took her full-on into another cable. The line scraped down the hull in a metallic cacophony and tangled itself in the propellers.

"Sorry sir," said the sailor at the wheel.

"Good Lord man," said Anderson. "It's not your bloody fault."

The crewman turned back to his station, relief at his commander's words plain. Jones was impressed – he'd served with many an officer who'd have ranted and raved at the turn of events, desperate to find someone to blame. Such displays were clearly not Anderson's style.

The submersible's captain hunched over the chart table, examining their position from beneath a furrowed brow. Dixon clambered through the hatchway. The engineer nodded to Jones, his expression grave, then moved to Anderson's side.

"Any good news Chief?"

"By the feel of it, she's fouled good and proper. We run her at all and we'll reel the mine in like a fish on a hook."

"We could dive, see if the movement shakes it loose," said Anderson. His tone revealed what he thought of his own suggestion.

"Aye, we could. But like-as-not the bloody thing's got a pressure switch and the change in depth will set it off."

The two sailors traded black looks.

"I'll get the boys to go for a swim," said Dixon in a heavy voice. He made for the door.

Anderson moved to the periscope column, activating the footplate. The eyepiece mount slid up into place with a quiet hiss. He nodded to a crewman who flicked a switch. The lamps in the control room changed colour, the chamber illuminated in a malevolent red.

"A tad ghoulish, no?" said Sullivan.

"Maybe," said Anderson. "But it's good for the old night vision..."

He grasped the periscope's handles and bent to the eyepiece. He crabbed his way round the column in two slow revolutions. Double circuit complete, he pulled his head back and glanced over his shoulder to Jones.

"Care for a look-see?"

Jones made for the periscope and took hold of the grips. He hunkered over and pressed his face against the rubber cowl around the lens. The view of the world above was a black disc, a distant cluster of pinprick lights the only details to be discerned. The tiny pearls of illumination were stitched across the centre of the reflected view, winking on and off in a random pattern. It took Jones long seconds before he realised the lamps were ashore, the flashing caused by the rise and fall of intervening waves on the surface. Anderson was keeping the periscope low in the water, an understandable precaution given the Turks were likely on the lookout for any signs of the submersible's return.

"Cannakale," came the voice at Jones' shoulder. "The narrowest point in the Straits. Home to a half-dozen gunboats. I'd prefer we were further off, but at least we're not right outside the damned harbour."

There was a push on the right-hand grip and Jones turned with the motion, the view from above swinging round. A low shape slid into sight, darker than the backdrop of the sky – the northern shore.

"Keep going," said Anderson. "There, that should be it."

The land rose up in the periscope sights. A hill loomed over the undulating water, its summit crowned with a square-edged shape, too regular to be natural. A single light shone out from the walls, a gleaming beacon in comparison with the faint stars.

Jones straightened up from the eyepiece, blinking at the control room's hellish illumination.

"Burhanli?"

Anderson nodded and sent the periscope sliding down into its housing.

"So what now Captain?" asked Sullivan.

"We wait." Anderson's gaze drifted in the direction of the stern. "And we pray the divers can cut us free."

*

With the bulkhead hatches sealed, the atmosphere in the control room grew stuffy, the tension climbing along with the clammy heat as the minutes ground past. The bridge crew sat silent at their consoles, eyes directed up and aft, as if their blind attention might somehow assist the divers. Jones imagined it was the same throughout the vessel, the compartments locked up tight, sailors in each section stuck with little to occupy them but worry. The long quiet stretched out.

The wait made the sudden detonation all the more shocking.

The deck bucked beneath Jones' feet. He was tossed into the air and across the chamber, the control room filled with clumsy, tumbling men. He struck his head against the hull and slumped to the deck, stunned. The explosion's roar rumbled through the *Nautica*'s frame, the vibration threatening to rattle teeth loose from gums and setting hull rivets popping, flying across the chamber like bullets.

The awful clamour and shaking tailed off, replaced with an altogether more sinister backdrop of creaks and groans – the tortured noises of injured metalwork. A thin jet of water sprayed across Jones' face, sharp and cold, rousing him from his daze. He eyed the leak with a sick feeling in his stomach – unnerved by the enthusiasm with which the sea forced its way in through this tiny buckle in the hull. He spotted a dozen more sprays just like it, water hissing into the compartment from multiple points, misting the air. The vapours swirled in the crimson lighting, eruptions of white cracking through the red where fountains of sparks burst from shorted-out switch boxes. The control room was a waterlogged vision of hell itself.

Jones scrambled to his feet as the submersible's crew regained their order. Men staggered into action around him – turning valves, cranking at pumps and shouting incomprehensible jargon at one another.

Jones, Kowalski and Sullivan huddled together, nursing their knocks. They regarded the frenzy of activity – once again reduced to staying out of the way, more aware than ever of their status as useless ballast. Anderson barrelled past, bellowing orders. His gaze swept across the consoles and he snapped out instructions based on the gauges, or shook his head in frustration before moving to the next station.

After a few frantic minutes, the situation appeared to stabilise, the levels of activity and the volume of the shouts ebbing away. The crew took the opportunity for a moment's rest, and Jones took the opportunity to grab Anderson by the arm.

"What's happening?"

The submersible captain stared at him, momentarily confused. He blinked as he appeared to remember about his three passengers.

"We've taken a thump, but we're not sinking." He frowned at the inch of water slopping about the deck. "Well, not yet anyway." He pointed a finger upwards. "Just be glad the dome didn't give way."

Jones glanced up at the glass panels and the heavy darkness beyond. He offered a silent prayer of thanks for the diligence of the shipyard workers who had bolted the submersible together in the first place. Any further discussion was put on hold as the pressure door swung open, admitting Dixon and another inch of water. Anderson turned immediately to his engineer.

"What's the damage Chief?"

"Engine room's gone. Flooded to the top." Dixon offered a sour expression and wiped a grimy hand through the water and grease coating his face. "We've had to seal the aft companionway too. Filling fast and no way to stop it."

All activity around the control room came to an abrupt halt at his words. The engineer dropped his gaze, unable to meet the looks of his fellow crew.

Anderson's face was ashen. "Casualties?"

"Seven," said Dixon into the silence. "And the divers, obviously."

"Good God…"

Dixon returned to the matter at hand, as brusque as ever.

"Steering's gone. Engines too. Ballast tanks are stable though – that's something. And we still have the air pumps. We're not sailing anywhere Captain, but we can go up…" he cast his eyes at the waterlogged deck beneath his feet, "…or down."

"Let's avoid the latter for as long as possible," said Anderson.

"Aye sir." The engineer headed off to oversee the crew's efforts at staving off the inevitable.

Anderson leaned on the chart table, head lowered. He stayed like that for a long moment before lifting his gaze towards his passengers.

"Not where I'd planned to drop you, but we've been deprived of any choice in the matter." His tone grew firmer, his course of action apparently decided. "Your swim will be a little further than envisaged, and will have to begin in more dramatic fashion than I had intended."

Sullivan frowned. "What do you mean?"

"The Turks are bound to be on their way – they can't have failed to hear the mine. We'll have to put you out before we surface – let you get clear, then we'll pop up and grab their attention." Anderson pointed a finger aft. "The airlock's lost, along with the engine room. And we can't use the regular hatches or you'll flood the rest of the boat."

He paused, seemingly unable to resist a smile despite the situation, the red lights lending his grin a decidedly diabolical cast.

"I'm afraid there's only one way off the *Nautica*…"

*

"Ain't a chance in hell you're cooping me up in there."

Kowalski eyed the hatch and the dark round hole of the torpedo tube. Alongside him Sullivan looked equally appalled at the prospect of clambering inside. Jones' expression was as calm as ever, but even he seemed a little pale. Although granted, thought Kowalski, the man's pallor might have more to do with him being poisoned and all, rather than their proposed exit from the submersible.

Anderson slapped a hand on the top of the tube and a hollow boom emanated from its gaping mouth.

"It'll be a bit of a squeeze, but you won't be in there for long." He cast a look at Sullivan, the medical man's lanky frame hunched over, head tilted sideways beneath the curve of the hull. "Well, perhaps more of a squash for the Doctor."

"It's not as if we have a choice," said Jones, nodding towards the deck and the water washing across it. He crouched and pulled the knots from his laces, slipping off his boots. Kowalski did the same, wincing at the chill as his stockinged feet splashed into the water. He pushed his boots down into his pack and folded the oilskin-wrap around the bag.

"Pack first?" he asked.

Anderson nodded. "The extra buoyancy will help pull you to the surface." He turned to where Dixon waited, laden with gear. "Chief?"

The engineer splashed over and handed each man a bundle. Kowalski unfolded the stiff material to reveal round glass lenses fixed into a canvas hood. He regarded the contraption, his apprehension multiplied by its makeshift appearance.

"It goes over your head," said Dixon. "Then you pull the drawstring around your neck. The canvas is waterproof, but the seal isn't. Some water will get in but, don't worry, the pressure will keep you mostly dry."

Kowalski didn't like the sound of "mostly" – figured it wasn't far from "mostly dry" to "mostly drowned". He flipped the hood over and examined the stubby metal flask attached to its reverse – a grand total of four inches long and one across.

The engineer spotted his grimace. "Plenty of air to see you to the surface. You'll be moving at a fair old lick..." He offered a smile. "Like a cork from a bottle."

Great, thought Kowalski. Just great.

"They're adapted from gasmasks," said Anderson. "Designed to get trapped crews off the boat in shallow waters. Not as fancy as proper apparatus, but perfectly serviceable nonetheless."

Kowalski's attention shifted from the canvas headgear, drawn once more to the yawning mouth of the torpedo tube. He shuddered at the idea of putting himself in there, the very thought of it setting his toes curling in his sodden socks. He leaned in close to Jones.

"Ain't sure I can do this," he said, voice low, ashamed at the words.

The Englishman stared at him, eyebrow raised. "So what's it to be? Are you going to sit here twiddling your thumbs, or are you coming with us to get yourself killed?"

Kowalski smiled. "Figure I deserved that…"

Jones clapped him on the shoulder. "Let's just get out of here and get on with the job."

"I'd appreciate it if you would," said Anderson. "There's a limit to how long our pumps will run. The quicker you're about your business, the quicker we can be on the surface."

"I'll go first then," said Kowalski, steeling himself. "Sooner it's started, sooner it's done."

The tube was as dark and cramped and airless as Kowalski had feared. He lay, arms hunched before him, fingers tight around the binding of his pack, his shoulders pressed hard against the smooth metal to either side. The stifling closeness wasn't helped by the canvas hood, its fastening tight around his throat. The hood's glass lenses fogged as his breath quickened into tight shallow draughts.

"You all right in there?" came a muffled voice.

He banged the heel of his palm twice on the base of the tube, the signal intended to convey a message – no I'm not alright, you're about to drown me in here, and I wish you'd just get on with it. At least some of his meaning must have been transmitted for the last traces of light vanished as the hatch at his feet swung closed.

The tube was secured, the clang of bolts rattling through the metal and setting his ears ringing. He wriggled a hand up to the back of his neck and scrabbled for the valve on the air flask. He fumbled at it, fingers straining as it refused to budge. His building panic transformed itself into embarrassed relief as he realised he was turning it the wrong way.

He twisted the valve open, delighted at the hiss of air and the cool draught which whispered at his ears. His relief was short-lived, replaced by creeping fear, rising over him in direct proportion to the level of the cold seawater now pouring into the tube. He kept his head raised, pushed against the curve of his metallic prison, skin prickling as water insinuated itself between the canvas and his throat. He gulped air, trying not to vomit as the suffocating press of the water settled around him.

And then, in a deafening growl of pressure, he was away. Buffeted by bubbles in a surge of current, Kowalski was flushed out of the *Nautica* and into the dark.

*

Kowalski bobbed on the surface, hood removed, revelling in the wide open sky and the gentle breeze. He hung onto his pack and floated in the water, staring up at the scattered stars.

Ten feet away one of his companions burst up in a riot of bubbles. Kowalski waited until the figure had pulled its head free from its hood and finished coughing and spluttering.

"Sullivan," he hissed. "Over here…"

The doctor turned this way and that in the water, seeking the source of the voice. Kowalski's eyes had adjusted to the starlight, but newly surfaced and without his spectacles, the other man would be blind.

"Where are you?" called Sullivan, far too loud for Kowalski's liking. Noise could carry for miles over water, especially on a still night. He could already hear the distant rumble of engines, probably half the Turkish navy, no doubt heading their way.

"Keep your damn voice down," he said, injecting as much command as he could muster into a whisper. He struck out for the floundering medical man, swimming one-handed, pushing his pack before him.

The two men bumped together in the water, Sullivan's relief at the rendezvous plainly apparent. He squinted at Kowalski and spoke, his tone blessedly reduced in volume.

"Which way is the beach?"

"This way…" came Jones' voice out of the dark.

Kowalski smiled to himself – trust Jones to have surfaced with considerably less fuss and racket than his compatriot. He grabbed Sullivan's pack and tugged both bag and hapless doctor towards Jones and the waiting shore.

The trio made steady progress against the light surface current, their approach to land marked by the black shape of the hill, looming ever higher as they swam in. All the same, Kowalski was taken by surprise when his feet brushed against the bottom. A couple more strokes and then all three of them were upright, wading in through the shallows.

They scrambled from the water onto the thin strip of pebbles which marked the boundary between the sea and the rocks. They found shelter amongst the rocks and the trio began to strip off their wet clothes.

"It's bloody freezing," said Jones. Kowalski could hear the man's teeth chattering as they hauled fresh garb from their packs. "Thought it was supposed to be warm in this part of the world?"

The breeze whispered across Kowalski's damp skin — refreshing maybe, but hardly freezing. Sullivan too picked up on the comment.

"It's not that cold Major. Are you feeling quite alright?"

Jones tugged his sweater on and looked towards the medical man, his eyes deep in shadow.

"Your patient's not dead yet," he said. He tilted his head back to examine the rocky hillside. "All the same, I'd prefer if we didn't hang about. I hear there's a hospital full of nurses up there…"

It was a weak joke and Kowalski could tell Jones knew it, but he admired the Englishman for making the attempt. They all had their reasons for being here, but even Kowalski, with his restless itch to get hold of Von Gossler, had to acknowledge the particular urgency of Jones' situation. The three men pulled on their boots in awkward silence.

Dry and dressed, they turned their backs on the water. Jones pointed out a goat track, the tramped-down line of earth barely visible in the gloom. The path wound its way back and forth across the face of the incline, climbing up and out of sight. They picked their way over the tumbled stones at the base of the hill and made for the track.

Behind them, the drone of engines echoed through the night and beams of light stabbed into the dark. The Turkish gunboats had arrived, prowling the Straits for whatever had detonated the mine.

*

Anderson raised his hands as the searchlight swept over the stricken submersible. "Big smiles lads," he called, squinting into the glare. "Don't give them any excuses to take a pot-shot at us."

The crewmen around him dutifully hoisted their hands, but smiles remained conspicuously absent. To a man, the *Nautica*'s crew frowned in the direction of the approaching gunboat. What sort of reception would they get from their captors? Anderson couldn't imagine the submersible and her sailors were the toast of Constantinople at the moment.

The Ottoman vessel swung abeam, foam churning at her stern as she came to a halt in the water twenty feet off the *Nautica*'s flank. The swell sent out by the manoeuvre set the crippled submersible rocking. Anderson adjusted his footing, compensating for the motion as well as the steadily increasing list of the deck. A second lamp snapped on and the twin beams of light transfixed the clustered crewmen.

Anderson felt a rush of relief as a voice rang out. Words were infinitely preferable to the carbine fire he'd been half-expecting.

"You take rope," came the shout, heavy with accent, but the English a damned sight better than Anderson's Turkish.

A line flew, tossed from the darkness between the searchlights. Its knotted end thumped onto the deck as its length splashed into the water between the two craft. A second rope followed.

"Pull her in boys," said Anderson.

Sailors hauled on the lines. The gap between the vessels inched closed until the Turkish boat bumped alongside the *Nautica* – half her length but rising high above her. Grim-faced sailors lined the rails, guns aimed at the men on the submersible's deck.

"You climb," came the voice from above. A cargo net was flung out, clattering against the gunboat's hull.

"Up you go lads," said Anderson. "Help the injured."

He watched the first of his men reach for the net then turned away, searching for Dixon. The Chief appeared in the hatchway, clambering up from below. The engineer stood, his features set in a harsh frown under the glare of the spotlights. He caught Anderson's eye and offered him a stiff nod before shuffling forward to join the queue to ascend.

Anderson was the last to leave the deck, hanging back until the hindmost of the crew had begun their climb. Alone atop the submersible, he regarded the length of her, from the glass dome of the bridge, back to the jagged tear in her plates which ruined the lines of her stern.

"Goodbye old girl."

He made for the net and hauled himself up the side of the gunboat, leaving the *Nautica* silent and lifeless in his wake. He scrambled over the rail and was immediately grabbed by a Turkish sailor and shoved through the press of his men.

Pushed out into an open space on the deck, he stumbled to a halt before two figures – officers judging by their uniforms. He pulled himself erect and saluted his captors, thinking it wise to at least attempt a show of good manners. The gesture brought sneers from the pair.

The Turkish officers babbled to one another, the conversation punctuated by much gesticulation and a number of meaningful glances in Anderson's direction. The speech was incomprehensible but their excitement was obvious. Finally, one of the men turned to Anderson and spoke in English.

"Captain says I welcome you aboard." A sly grin formed on his face. "And I thank you..."

"For what?"

"Sultan offers great reward to men who stop British pirates." He gestured towards the stricken *Nautica*, his smile growing wider. He rubbed his finger and thumb together. "Reward even greater when we tow in captured boat..."

Right on cue a sharp thump emanated from within the submersible's hull. Every man on the gunboat whipped their heads towards the noise. The captain and his interpreter shouldered their way through the crowd, joining the sailors, Ottoman and British alike, peering over the railing. Alongside the Turkish vessel, the *Nautica* rocked in the water, smoke curling from her hatch to swirl in the searchlight beams.

"Sorry to deprive you of your prize," said Anderson to their backs, injecting more cheer than he felt into his tone. "But we can't just let you waltz off with our ship."

The *Nautica*'s stern settled lower in the water, half her length now submerged, the movement accompanied by a deep metallic rumble. Dixon's explosive charges had done their job. Just like the man, thought Anderson – meticulous to the last, even when scuttling his beloved boat.

One of the *Nautica*'s crew began to sing, a lusty but tuneless rendition of 'Rule Britannia'. Before the end of the first line, the entire contingent of British sailors had taken up the refrain, bellowing out a salute to their ship's passing, much to the astonishment of their captors. Of dubious musicianship but admirable volume, the singing carried out over the water, a faint echo rattling back from the rocky cliffs.

"*... and Britons never, never, never, shall be slaves.*"

As if recognising her crew's farewell, the *Nautica*'s blunt bow rose up in acknowledgement. With an angry roar, a plume of water spouted from her hatch. The spray glowed in the lights, spattering back to the hull in gobbets of brilliant white. And then, her steel frame protesting her demise, air whistling from her torn hull, she slipped down and back.

The midnight black waters of the Dardanelles closed over the *Nautica*. Fragments of wood bobbed in the centre of an oily rainbow of leaked fuel, the only evidence the submersible had ever existed.

Turning away from the swirl of debris, the Turkish captain gave a bark of command. The English crew were herded away from the rail, rifle jabs bringing a rough halt to the impromptu choral recital. The men huddled together, quiet under the eyes of their guards.

After an agitated exchange, the gunboat's master stomped off towards his bridge, leaving his interpreter to address Anderson.

"Captain says you are brave, but stupid. You would have been forced to explain undersea boat. Unpleasant yes, but you stay alive." The man shrugged. "No boat? No reason to take you to Constantinople."

"Excellent news. He can drop us off wherever he likes."

The Turk blinked, Anderson's attempt at a joke lost in translation.

"We have orders regarding prisoners..." The man waved to one of the guards and uttered an unintelligible command.

Good grief, through Anderson – *they're actually going to gun us down.* He swallowed a sick mouthful of fear and braced himself, determined to meet his Maker with some measure of dignity and the minimum of fuss.

No bullets flew. The guard lowered his weapon and moved off, returning a moment later with a length of rope. However, any sense of relief died stillborn for Anderson. The interpreter's next words chilled his blood more effectively than any death sentence.

"We take you to castle," he said. "The German madwoman can have you now…"

*

The moon put in an appearance, making their final approach to the fortress slower than Jones would have liked, the trio forced to pick their way from shadow to shadow. At least there was plenty of cover – the broken landscape surrounding the castle was scattered with boulders and weathered outcrops of rock. The walls reared above them as they moved in, the crumbling masonry jagged and black against the stars. The last stretch was steep, and made all the more tiring by the need for constant vigilance. A single ill-placed step would have sent the loose scree skittering down the slope, alerting the guards.

They had watched from a distance, establishing the rough pattern of the Turkish patrols. The guards spent most of their time towards the front of the castle, meeting above the gate at regular intervals. They stood together, idling for a minute's conversation on each occasion, doubtless engaged in the universal pastime of soldiers the world over – complaining about their duties, complaining about their officers, complaining about every last inconvenience of war, both real and imagined.

Jones even spotted a spark of fire, the pair huddling round a flame, lighting up to share a smoke. The match's flare confirmed his suspicions – unlike their battle-hardened compatriots on the front lines, the men of Burhanli were soft, grown lazy with the tedium of garrison duty. Although good news for his current endeavour, Jones bristled at the ill-discipline. Night vision ruined for the sake of a cigarette. He'd had many a Sergeant who'd have handed out a good thumping or two for such stupidity.

Strategy informed by their observation, the infiltrators made for the castle's rear – fewer patrols for a start, and from the look of the tumbledown stonework, hopefully an easier climb.

They reached the base of the wall without incident and slipped their packs from their shoulders to slump against the rock. Jones was grateful for the breather but the breeze blew cold against his sweat-soaked shirt, drawing shivers from goose-bump skin. He wasn't right. He could feel it in his bones – a creeping weakness, a deep-seated ache in his joints. The swim and the hike had taken more out of him than he cared to admit. The prospect of hauling himself up the wall filled him with dread.

Alongside him, Kowalski lifted his head, scanning the cracked and pitted masonry which rose above them. "Looks simple enough," he said. "Plenty of handholds."

"You can bloody go first then," said Jones, unable to keep the irritation from his voice.

"Figure you'll be wanting me to toss down a rope?"

"If you wouldn't mind. And see if you can't take care of those sentries whilst you're up there."

"I'll get moving then..." said Kowalski, pulling himself to his feet. "Seeing as I'm doing all the heavy lifting round here."

The Floridian took a coil of rope from his pack and draped it over his shoulder. Without a backwards glance, he began to climb.

*

Von Gossler rolled his eyes open at the faint sound of voices. He had not been asleep, not exactly – more driven into a waking trance by his lack of feeling and immobility. Unable even to turn his head for a change of view, he lay, imprisoned within his own body, forced to stare up at the same patch of ceiling, at the play of shadows cast on the vaulted stone by a lantern he could not see.

He could move his eyes and work his jaw, indeed had spent an age calling for Falke, for anyone, to come and release him. All for naught. He gave up his shouting when he heard his voice crack and rasp.

He felt nothing though – neither discomfort from his dry throat, nor pain from the injuries Falke said he had received. The woman had catalogued Von Gossler's condition in precise, merciless detail as she worked with her scalpel, employing the same detached tone she used when dictating her observations, almost as if she expected him to note them down in the journals.

Von Gossler recalled the cold narration in numb horror. As if his burns hadn't been enough – now he was destined to live out the remainder of his days a cripple, wheeled here and there by some nurse, a broken remnant of a man, fit only for ridicule and pity. Falke should have let him die. His anger burned inside him and he grabbed hold of the emotion, nursing it, letting it fill him up in the absence other sensation.

The murmurs grew louder and he focused his attention on the sounds, his mind sucking in the new stimulus. Some sort of door scraped open, the deep rumble of moving stone surprising him with its volume. He realised how accustomed he had grown to the silence. The shadows on the ceiling shifted, the flame within the unseen lamp set dancing by an influx of air Von Gossler didn't feel.

Faces appeared over him – his old tutor and the Turkish Minister. They peered down, Falke in calculation, Pasha with horrified fascination. I will have to get used to that, thought Von Gossler.

"And how is the... patient?" asked Falke.

Subject. She had almost said subject.

"Thirsty..." he said, giving faint voice to his most immediate desire.

Falke nodded. "Understandable. I will get you water shortly."

"Untie... me..."

Her head moved once more, from side to side this time. "You are not bound, my boy, rather kept dormant for the moment. It will be some time before you are up and about."

Pasha leaned in. "But when you are..." His eyes shone. "You will be a marvel of the age."

"What... do you mean?"

A new voice interrupted – a Turk, speaking in halting German from beyond Von Gossler's field of view. "Professor, we have new prisoners."

Falke turned her head. "How many?"

"Twenty four," came the reply. "Sailors. From a captured ship."

"I don't care where they came from. But they will be useful." The scientist looked to Pasha. "It appears my stock is replenished."

"Excellent. Captain Kemal was most enthusiastic regarding the usefulness of your pets. You must continue your work."

Falke nodded. "I shall review the quality of these men – separate the strong from the weak."

"Survival of the fittest?" chuckled the old Turk.

"Spare me," snapped Falke. "The famous Mister Darwin is a fool. No matter how celebrated, his philosophy of random chance is a poor substitute for the science of intent." She continued, her hand chopping at the air for emphasis. "The ascent towards perfection is no accident of fate. It is a destiny chosen, a triumph of the will over happenstance."

The Turkish Minister blinked at this lecture but remained silent.

"Man will evolve by design…" Falke's raptor gaze roved across Von Gossler's inert frame, the eyes finally locking on his own. "My design."

*

Anderson raised his head as the door of the cell scraped open. A trio of soldiers trooped in, followed by a woman, her stare reflecting the fire of the men's torches. The flames illuminated the sailors huddled against the walls of the dank dungeon.

The crew stirred, blinking in the light, the first relief from darkness they'd had since their cell door had been locked. How long had they been cooped up in here? Three hours? Four? Anderson had no clue – the Turks had relieved him of his pocket watch along with the rest of his effects. The theft gnawed at him almost as much as the loss of the *Nautica* – the timepiece had been a gift from his wife.

The rustle of movement and conversation prompted by the return of sight fell away as the crew became aware of the carbine muzzles pointed in their direction. Anderson hauled himself to his feet.

"We have injured men here, and we need food and water."

The woman's English matched her look – clipped and hard as iron. "I am not a nurse. Your comforts are not my concern."

She pushed past Anderson and made her way along the line of seated figures, scanning the upturned faces of the crew. She paused before one man, the sailor pale and sweating, nursing a bandaged arm, dark bloodstains mottling the strips of cloth. She pointed and snapped a command to the soldiers. Two of the guards began to haul the wounded sailor away from his fellows.

"Now hold on a bloody moment..." called Anderson, stepping forward, outraged at this none-too-gentle treatment.

The third of the Turks blocked his path, brandishing his carbine. Anderson ignored the warning – he'd be damned if he'd stand for mistreatment of his men. His continued advance bought him a blow to the stomach with the weapon's butt. He collapsed, all breath driven from his lungs, curled up around a knot of agony. The guard followed up with a hefty kick. The boot thumped into Anderson's side bringing another bloom of pain and the audible crunch of a rib. He bit his tongue, salty blood in his mouth as he struggled not to cry out – don't give the bastard the satisfaction, he thought. His pulse thumped in his ears and he hugged his arms around his injured torso, bracing himself for a beating. A long moment dragged past, sick anticipation threatening to overwhelm him. But no further blows came his way and he dared to breathe once again.

He cracked open an eye and peered upwards. The Turkish guard still loomed over him, but the man was frozen, hands held high, his eyes swivelled round almost completely in their sockets, trying to see the pistol pressed against his temple.

Wincing, Anderson lifted his head to see the other soldiers and the woman posed in similar fashion, arms raised in surrender, gazes fixed on the new arrivals and the revolvers they brandished.

A face appeared at the man's shoulder – drawn and pale, but smiling.

"Up you get Captain," said Jones. "Now's not the time for a nap..."

*

Dawn's approach tinted the Eastern horizon a dusky pink. Wilberforce turned away from the lightening sky with a frown.

"Hurry along!" he bellowed. "I don't want to be late."

His exhortations had no effect on the levels of activity around the moored airship. They never did, he thought. No matter the importance of the mission, ground crew the world over appeared to have two operating speeds: dead slow and stop.

The men in overalls continued to amble around the airship's gondola, lugging fuel hoses and tinkering with the gubbins beneath her engine cowlings – all with a distinct lack of urgency. Wilberforce pulled his pipe from his pocket before remembering he was out of tobacco. He gave the bowl a sniff anyway, relishing the faint aroma it still carried. He tucked it away again with a rueful smile.

The hardship he endured for Queen and country – the boys back home would scarcely credit it. Join the Aeronautic Corps, they said. See the world, they said. Well he'd seen enough of this God-forsaken corner of the globe to last him a lifetime, thank you very much. The sooner they were out of this bloody place and back to civilisation the better.

"Come on Johnson," he said, looking to his co-pilot. "Let's see if we can't chivvy them along."

The airmen made their way towards the dirigible, ducking under the mooring cables and into the shadows beneath the curve of the gasbag. They stepped around the fuel truck and the men sweating at its pumps.

"Good work lads," said Wilberforce. "Right to the top mind." He chuckled at the scowls this drew.

"You're very chipper today sir," put in Johnson.

"Of course. Getting to do some proper flying rather than another bloody reconnaissance trip."

Wilberforce was sick to the back teeth of bobbing about, armed with nothing more threatening than a pair of binoculars, his aircraft little more than a floating lookout post. They'd burned away most of their fuel in such activity, and for what? To relay aerial confirmation of what everybody already knew – the Imperial forces were stuck on the beach and the Turks were stuck in the hills.

A mechanic wheeled a trolley beneath the gondola. Wilberforce regarded the stack of fat cylinders, their rounded noses, the sharp fins protruding at their rear. The very sight of the munitions filled him with childish glee – a dozen of the buggers, and the same again already loaded.

He wondered where the quartermaster had kept them squirreled away. The response to Wilberforce's requests had been the same for a month now – no munitions available. Perhaps the miserable old sod had been saving them for a special occasion.

"Look at them Johnson," he said. "Can you think of a finer way to spend the morning than in delivering these delightful little chaps?"

He reached out and rapped his knuckles on the topmost bomb's metal casing. His co-pilot and the mechanic winced in tandem.

"I do wish you wouldn't do that sir," said Johnson.

"Where's your sense of adventure man?" Wilberforce shook his head. "It's not every day you get to blow up a bloody castle."

*

"Remember," said Jones, addressing the *Nautica*'s crew in a low voice. "Keep moving. And every gun you can get is another man armed."

The sailors nodded at their instructions and began to file from the dungeon, those with weapons to the fore, their faces set in grim determination. Jones joined Anderson at the door as the captain ushered his men out into the passageway.

"How is it?"

"Bloody sore." Anderson rolled his shoulder with a grunt of discomfort. "But I can shoot," he said, lifting the pistol. "Seems I owe you one this time Major."

"Makes a change. Get your lads out of here – don't get bogged down in any fighting. We can't have long before Wilberforce gets here."

"And what about you?"

Jones glanced across the chamber. Kowalski and Sullivan were putting the finishing touches to their trussing-up of the Turks.

"We still have a job to do."

"A swift one I hope..."

Jones didn't give voice to his bleak thoughts. He couldn't take his time now, even if he'd wanted to. A blackness gnawed at his insides, the pain rising in regular peaks of cramp, their frequency steadily increasing. Pretty soon he would find it difficult to move, and not long after, he reckoned staying conscious would be beyond him. He pasted a smile into place and directed it towards the submariner.

"We'll be right behind you."

Anderson looked thoroughly unconvinced by Jones' thin veneer of cheeriness, but declined to offer any further comment. He gave Jones a nod and followed the last of his men from the chamber.

Jones pushed the door shut behind the departing sailors and turned the key in the lock. Time for a little privacy with their lady guest. He crossed the damp floor towards the others. Kowalski and Sullivan stood to either side of Falke. Between them, the woman stood proud, revealing nothing but disdain for her captors.

"Good morning Professor," said Jones in German.

"English will suffice," replied the scientist. "My command of your language is better than your mangling of my mother-tongue."

The woman's haughty contempt immediately put Jones in mind of his old housemaster. The man had been possessed of a fearsome intellect, but a narrowness of mind – quick to criticise and quick to punish, altogether too fond of the switch of his cane. The same cruel cleverness glittered in the scientist's glare, yet this woman's crimes stretched far beyond the overenthusiastic beating of schoolboys.

"I'm not here to play linguistic games," he said, stepping closer. "My friends and I each require something from you."

"And in return I will be spared? Such scant imagination." Her mouth twisted. "I am an old woman. I do not fear death."

Jones leaned into her face. "Maybe not. But do you fear suffering?"

Cracks crept into Falke's confidence, her eyes unable to hold Jones' own. He let her stew, caught in his unrelenting regard for a long moment, then he stepped back and gave Kowalski a nod.

The Floridian grabbed the woman and hauled her head back, his hand clamped under her jaw, twisting it up and around, exposing her scrawny neck. Sullivan raised a syringe, blue-black liquid washing around within the glass cylinder. The last vestiges of Falke's composure evaporated. She wriggled in Kowalski's grasp, straining away from the needle as the doctor advanced.

"I am a great admirer of your work Professor," said Sullivan. "Most unfortunate we could only meet under these circumstances."

He pressed the needle against the woman's skin, the puncture making her gasp. He pressed down on the plunger, sending the contents of the syringe bubbling into her veins. The injection complete, he pulled the needle free and stepped back.

"What have you done?" said Falke, voice quivering, robbed of all its previous arrogance.

Sullivan removed his spectacles. He blinked as he rubbed at the lenses with a corner of his shirt.

"I would very much like to see your laboratory, but I rather suspect you'd make an unwilling tour guide." He waved a hand towards Jones. "I've just injected you with the same venom currently working its way through the Major here."

Falke's eyes grew round, flicking towards Jones and then back to Sullivan as the man continued.

"Unless you're happy with the unpleasant departure your own poison promises, I suggest you lead the way..." He popped his glasses back into place and gave the woman an encouraging nod. "Perhaps you already have an antidote, or at least one you can whip up in short order?"

Jones stared at their captive, disturbed at his own reaction to the procedure. He'd expected to feel shame at what they were doing, to experience some sympathy for Falke as the venom entered her system. But in truth, he found himself eager for the poison to work its way into the woman's organs, keen for her to feel the same black ache which growled around Jones' innards.

Kowalski hauled harder on the woman's jaw, threatening to detach her head from its torso. The action drew a frown from Sullivan and he put out a hand to restrain the Floridian. Kowalski shook him off and growled into Falke's ear.

"And when the medical business is done and dusted, it's my turn. You fix up the Major and then you take me to Von Gossler."

*

The tunnels appeared to go on forever – an endless succession of flagstones and spiral stairs.

A burst of cramp clutched at Jones' insides and he stumbled to a halt, bracing himself against the wall. His chest tightened, breath ragged, reduced to short hollow gasps. He closed his eyes, willing the spasm to pass. A hand on his shoulder prompted him to lift his head. Sullivan peered down. He made to wave the doctor off but his knees buckled and only the other man's quick hands stopped him pitching onto the floor.

Sullivan stooped, taking Jones' weight with his arm. Jones grunted his thanks as he regained his breath and his balance. Together the pair shuffled down the corridor after Kowalski and Falke. Jones lurched forwards, eyes fixed on the torch flame. His sight contracted around the flickering point of light, black shadows clouding his peripheral vision.

Eventually they found themselves before a heavy door bound with straps of iron. Kowalski pulled the professor close.

"Any friends in there? You lie to me, I'll put a bullet in you."

"Hardly a threat," sneered Falke. "A quicker end than your poison."

"I didn't say where I'd shoot you lady. Bullet in the gut ain't nobody's idea of quick."

"No guards," she said, tone sullen. "Perhaps an assistant, but they will be unarmed."

"Give them a knock," said Kowalski. He turned to Jones. "Let's go get you some medicine."

Jones stretched his face into something he hoped resembled a smile.

"Any chance of a pretty nurse?"

All the while cramp clawed at his stomach, threatening to drag him to his knees, Sullivan's support the only thing keeping him upright.

*

The door creaked open. The laboratory assistant's eyes went wide at the sight of Kowalski lurking over Falke's shoulder. They went rounder still as Kowalski shoved past the scientist, pushing the man backwards into the chamber, the revolver thrust into the pit of his stomach.

Kowalski scanned the laboratory, eyes fixing on the single figure standing amidst the workbenches and machinery. The old man looked towards the melee at the door, his lined features twisted in surprise beneath a dark red fez.

Kowalski lifted the pistol. "Don't move."

The man ignored the command, instead dropping to the floor and out of sight behind the clutter of equipment. Kowalski gave a grunt of appreciation – decent moves for an old-timer.

He dragged his captive forward, the assistant complaining and wriggling as they went. The man received a snarl for his troubles and fell silent at the look on Kowalski's face. They manoeuvred around a bank of electrical generators and Kowalski bent, peering through the legs of the heavy tables. Where had that old bastard scuttled off to?

A flash of movement caught his eye and he fired. The shot brought a ricochet but no cry of injury. Kowalski cursed and headed for the far side of the chamber, shoving the assistant before him, a human shield in the event of any attack. With a grinding of stone, a section of the far wall swung inward. A figure threw itself into the black gap. Kowalski fired again, the bullet sending up a puff of mortar and chipped rock as the secret doorway swung closed.

Irritation burned through him. He whirled on the scientist. Falke answered his unspoken question, enjoying his frustration.

"I have no idea where it leads, nor how to open it. He knows this place much better than I."

Kowalski scowled at the blank stonework thorough which the old man had vanished. Damned castle was likely riddled with passageways like this – it could take days to search it. He'd had about enough of sneaking around in the dark. And where the hell was Von Gossler?

The man in his grasp babbled something – maybe German, maybe Turkish – Kowalski couldn't tell and didn't care. He brought his knee up sharply between the captive's legs. The man went down with a high-pitched squeal, clutching at himself. Kowalski aimed a kick at his head and the moans came to an abrupt halt.

"Was that entirely necessary?" asked Sullivan as he hauled Jones into the chamber.

Maybe not, acknowledged Kowalski regarding the unconscious figure at his feet. But damned if the burst of violence hadn't made him feel better. He ignored the doctor's disapproving frown and pointed at Falke.

"Antidote. Now."

The woman moved past him, without even a glance at her assistant stretched out on the flagstones. She made for a bench, its top cluttered with bottles and vials. Kowalski took Jones' weight away from Sullivan and nodded after the scientist.

"Watch her," he said. "And she takes the first drink of any potion she comes up with."

Sullivan loped off towards Falke and her chemicals, head twitching this way and that, attention drawn from one piece of scientific apparatus to the next. The doctor's passage across the chamber faltered and he paused at a table piled with books. He lifted an old leather-bound tome and thumbed through the tattered pages, fingers tracing the words and diagrams within, his expression rapt.

"Doc," called Kowalski, his none-too-gentle tone echoing under the vaulted ceiling. "Medicine first. Toys later."

Sullivan coloured and placed the book down. "Yes, of course."

Kowalski shook his head and turned his attention to Jones. He lowered the Englishman to the floor, leaning him back against the wall. Jones was grey, his skin beaded with sweat, bags under bloodshot eyes.

"You don't look too good Major. Hell of a hangover, huh?"

"Seems I missed the night out... to cause it..."

Jones tilted his head back, grimacing at some renewed stab of pain. Kowalski stood, bristling at the sight of Falke and Sullivan locked in conversation. This was no time for a God-damned scientific convention.

"Get a move on," he shouted. "Or I'll shoot the both of you."

Sullivan looked outraged at this statement, but Falke ignored the threat. "I need more light," she snapped, pointing a finger to the bank of generators. "Throw those switches."

Kowalski made for the metal cabinets. He grabbed the wooden handle affixed to the casing and heaved it upwards. The switch thumped into place and the cabinet began to hum, needles flitting across the gauges as a row of ceiling lamps crackled into life. He activated the next two switches in turn, adding further illumination to the laboratory.

"This too?" he asked, indicating a fourth cabinet, separate from the others, connected to a bulky generator, thick rubber cables snaking out from its flanks.

"Yes," nodded Falke. "Definitely that one."

Kowalski threw the switch and the generator burst into activity, a fizz of sparks spouting from its crown as it shook itself into noisy, juddering life. He shied away from the eruption, his hair prickling in the charged air, nose wrinkling at the smell of scorched rubber.

"You trying to kill me?" he called.

Once again Falke ignored the barb, instead raising a bottle containing some clear liquid. She tugged the cork free from its neck and gulped down a mouthful, wincing as she swallowed. She wiped a hand across her lips before resealing the bottle and handing it to Sullivan.

She kept her gaze fixed on Kowalski throughout, her expression twisting from disgust at the taste of the medicine into something else entirely. Kowalski didn't like the look in the woman's eyes. What the hell was she so pleased about?

*

The electrical charge crackled through Von Gossler's frame, jangling his nerves, his mind flooded with joyous agony. He could feel – the fire sparking in his veins, the burning sting of his stitches, the rough grating of bolts against his bones.

From across his body, sensation poured in – an overwhelming torrent of pain. He revelled in it, bucking and twitching on the table as lightning coursed through him.

The initial surge passed and he rose, his limbs his own to command. His arms pulled at the edge of the bench and he swung his feet down to the floor. He pushed himself upright and raised his hand, caught in rapt fascination at its appearance. He flexed his fingers, watching the greased metal rods slide in and out of the puckered holes in his skin, relishing the scrape of steel on raw flesh. Strips of tendon glistened in the candlelight, contracting and shifting across his forearm as he turned his wrist.

He craned forward over his neck collar and looked down to his bare torso. The skin of his chest was studded with rivets and bolts, hexagonal nuts securing patches of gleaming metal plate into flesh puffy and throbbing with inflammation. From the iron socket mounted above his heart a thick cable coiled out, dropping away and snaking across the floor. He grasped this rubber-coated umbilical and hauled it loose. It popped wetly from the hole in a blue burst of electricity.

Like a candle snuffed, the flood of sensation cut off. The delicious agony was severed mid-flow, reduced to the ghost of a tingle in his dead nerves. Disconnected from his pain, he was empty once more, trapped within the hollow unfeeling shell of his own body.

The vacuum in his soul sucked everything in, all his emotions, all his remembered pain – compressing them, hardening them, until it could hold no more. The rage inside him burst, boiling out in a seething storm.

He dived down into his anger, finding its core and feeding it. He poured memories of flames and falls and scalpels and shame into the crucible. Here was his power, here was his strength. With an animal roar, he surrendered himself to fury.

*

The wall beside Kowalski exploded. Shards of stone and brick sprayed across the chamber, an avalanche of dust rolling out as the debris showered down. He stood, frozen in place, gawping at the nightmare form which lurched through the hole in the wall.

The figure shoved its way through the shattered masonry and out into the laboratory proper, dragging a tangle of sparking cable. Its limbs bulged with flesh, tendons anchored to the exposed metal of the skeleton, sinews sliding over steel, rods and pistons expanding and contracting with each movement. Atop the expanse of its shoulders, an iron collar locked around its throat, a base for the criss-cross metal frame which supported the forest of wires sprouting from the hairless skull.

The mass of metal and muscle stomped forward, looming over Kowalski. Recovering his wits, he raised his pistol, only for a heavy limb to snap out, fingers closing around both the weapon and Kowalski's hand. The giant squeezed and Kowalski howled, his bones grinding against one another. The weapon fired, the blast muffled within the creature's fist. The bullet tore its way out though grey skin but the monstrosity didn't even flinch. Instead it hoisted Kowalski aloft. He dangled, legs kicking, fingers crushed in the creature's iron grasp.

Pulled in close, Kowalski's view filled with the thing's leering features. The face was twisted, scarred by fire and hate, but the eyes and the voice were the same as in the airship above the Boston docks months before.

"You..." snarled Von Gossler.

Kowalski was lifted higher, and then suddenly he was flying. He soared across the laboratory, smashing down onto a workbench halfway across the chamber. His momentum sent him sliding across the table's top, dislodging stacks of journals and test tubes and medical instruments. He went over the far edge and thumped to the flagstones in a shower of paper and broken glass.

He lay amidst the wreckage, vision swimming, his body's aches lost in the more immediate agony of his mangled fingers. With his good hand, he pulled at the pistol, prying it free from his crumpled digits. The action brought tears of agony pouring down his cheeks. Gun clutched in his left hand, he forced himself into motion. He scrambled to his feet, pulling himself up to see Von Gossler ploughing across the room towards him.

Sullivan and Falke stood directly in the path of the giant's advance, both gawping at the monstrosity's approach. Even Falke seemed astonished at the spectacle of Von Gossler's mechanical rage. Sullivan was the first to recover his wits. He hauled the woman in close and thrust his pistol against her temple.

"Stop! Don't come any closer."

Von Gossler clomped to a halt, his mass towering over even Sullivan's lanky figure. He glared down at the two scientists, eyes shining with menace from within the steel supports of his headdress.

"Stay back," said Sullivan, flinching beneath the stare. "I'll kill her..."

"No," growled the giant. "You shall not."

He snatched Falke from Sullivan's grasp and swept the doctor aside. The Englishman crashed into a control console and slid to the floor. Von Gossler made for Sullivan, only to be brought up short by a command from the woman wriggling in his grip.

"Viktor, I want this one alive."

Sullivan took advantage of the reprieve and crawled away between the workbenches. Von Gossler ignored the Englishman's attempted escape, attention fixed on the scientist.

"Put me down Viktor."

He did not relax his grip. Instead, he hauled her in, bringing her severe features scant inches from his own scarred and twisted face.

"Why?" he roared.

Falke blanched. "I saved you…"

Von Gossler's eyes blazed. "You call this salvation?"

"Viktor, release me –" Falke's demands were cut off, strangled by tightening fingers. Her eyes bulged, her mouth open, no sound emerging.

Anger and triumph chased one another across Von Gossler's ravaged features. He raised her up and flexed his metallic sinews, pistons compressing, rubber-coated cables quivering with pressure.

A crack echoed across the chamber and Falke flopped still – a marionette with her strings severed, head dangling loose from the rest of her skeleton. Von Gossler stared at the broken corpse, letting the silence stretch out. He gave her a shake, as if checking for any last signs of life, then tossed her body aside like a scrap of rubbish.

Von Gossler scanned the laboratory, his ghastly stare settling on Sullivan and Jones where they huddled together against the wall. He lumbered into motion, heading for the pair. No you don't, thought Kowalski. He hadn't interfered as Von Gossler confronted Falke – if anything he'd been cheering the mechanical monster on. But the Englishmen were another matter entirely. He raised his pistol left-handed, squinting at the unfamiliar aim.

He pulled the trigger and the weapon barked. The bullet flew wide, but had the intended effect. Von Gossler's gaze whipped round, feral rage burning in his look. With a grunt and a surge of hydraulics the German threw himself across the laboratory.

Spurred into motion, Kowalski backed away from the approaching menace. He banged up against a workbench and crabbed his way round it. The table's surface was clustered with specimen jars stuffed with unsavoury items – a gruesome yet entirely insubstantial barrier between himself and Von Gossler. The German smashed his fists down onto the workbench, shattering glass and sending liquid and grisly remains spraying everywhere. Kowalski's head was filled with the acrid reek of chemicals as Von Gossler shoved his way through the wreckage of the table.

Kowalski lifted his pistol once more and snapped off a shot. Von Gossler didn't even flinch, the bullet ricocheting away off his metal frame. But the spark of the impact set tongues of fire licking up the German's arm – spilled formaldehyde from the jars providing fuel for the flames.

In moments Von Gossler's limb was wreathed in flickering orange. He froze in place, Kowalski forgotten for the moment. He lifted his arm, pistons sliding in his blackening flesh. He held his hand before his face and stared at the lick of flames from his fingertips. He swung his burning hand through the air before him, transfixed by the play of fire and the trail of smoke the movement left in the air. His lips curled in a savage smile.

Suddenly he was on the move again. In a single bound the mechanical giant closed the distance between them. His hand shot out and Kowalski was caught, the German's fingers tight at his throat.

Kowalski gasped, coughing air from his lungs – precious breath he couldn't replace. He squirmed, to no avail.

Von Gossler lifted his other arm, the claw at its end cloaked in curls of fire. The flaming fist drew back and Kowalski went limp, exhausted, awaiting the final blow.

And then the air was filled with the lurid snap of lightning, its roar drowning out all else.

*

Jones rocked on his feet, every last ounce of effort spent on holding the cables in place. His muscles ached and he flinched at the fountain of sparks erupting from the contact. He retched, stomach turning somersaults at the awful smell of scorched flesh.

Von Gossler shook, electrical energy pouring into his gargantuan frame from the bundle of wires pressed to his back. Inhuman cries echoed from the vaulted stones, a dreadful counterpoint to the harsh crackle of electricity. The metallic limbs twitched, hydraulics in spasm, pistons expanding and contracting in random spurts. Kowalski tumbled from Von Gossler's grasp and the German slumped forward, as limp as the Floridian, crumpling to the floor, metalwork gouging the stone.

Jones fought a wave of blackness, his own weakness threatening to claim him once more. He panted, chest struggling to take in air. The bitter taste of Falke's antidote burned in the back of his throat. Bloody awful stuff – although complaining about it would be somewhat churlish. Cramp still gnawed at his guts, but its grip had begun to loosen mere moments after Sullivan had poured the liquid between his lips. He felt awful, his whole body shivering, soaked with cold sweat. But he was alive.

He raised a hand and Sullivan turned off the generator, bringing a halt to the flow of sparks. Jones cast the rubber-coated cables aside and staggered forward, dropping to his knees beside the Floridian's prostrate form. He fumbled at Kowalski's neck, then his wrist – seeking a pulse, finding nothing.

Sullivan shoved him aside and leaned over the mercenary. Jones watched, helpless, drained of all energy as the doctor began to pound his fist on the fallen man's chest.

*

The orange orb of the sun still hung low, the dawn painting long fingers of shadow across the ground behind the hills. Wilberforce flicked down the smoked glass shield over the binoculars' lenses and squinted into the sunrise, seeking their objective.

The jagged silhouette of the horizon sprang into sharp relief. He scanned along the line of hills, fixing on the castle's outline. Even from here he could make out the tumbledown nature of its fortifications.

"Puff of wind would probably do it," he said. "Might even save us some munitions eh?"

"Yes sir," answered Johnson, attention fixed on the ranks of gauges rather than the view.

"Mind you, seeing as we're buggering off back to Blighty, maybe we'll just drop the lot. What do you say to that?"

"Yes sir."

The man alongside him was Wilberforce's idea of a perfect co-pilot – capable, reliable and quiet – happy to leave the talking to his commander.

"That's the spirit. How long until we get there?"

Johnson checked the chart and the dials set into the control panel. "The Babbage says fifteen minutes." He opened a notebook and ran his finger down a scribbled list of figures. "I make it sixteen."

"Good chap. Never place too much trust in the clockwork."

"No sir."

"I hear they're working on contraptions that will actually fly. Automatic pilots if you can believe that." Wilberforce shuddered at the thought. "Mark my words, one day they'll have the machines doing everything – flying, navigating, bombing, the lot."

"Safer for us sir," put in Johnson. "We could fly the craft from the ground. Control them from a distance. Radio – that's the secret."

Wilberforce turned a black look on his co-pilot. It was probably the longest speech Johnson had made the entire flight, yet it had been comprised of total drivel.

"Safer?" he snorted. "Where's the bloody fun in that?"

*

The clamour of alarm bells bounced around the passageway, rattling off the masonry, pushing past the men huddled in the cover of the entrance and out, free, into the open space of the courtyard. The sharp reports of gunfire and the smack of bullet on stone offered punctuation to the incessant clang.

Anderson ducked his head around the corner, drawing a flurry of Turkish shots but affording him a glimpse of the courtyard beyond the tunnel. Their situation had not improved. A tantalising vision of the castle gate and the rising sun was obstructed by the upturned cart the garrison soldiers had adopted as a barricade. From behind this makeshift fortification, and from atop the surrounding walls, the Turks maintained a steady suppressing fire, keeping Anderson and his crew kettled up within the confines of the passage.

Over the din of the bell Anderson made out shouts – incomprehensible Turkish babble, but the tone of command crystal clear. That damned old man no doubt – the Turkish grandee who'd appeared from nowhere and whipped the garrison into some semblance of order.

Anderson risked another look, pistol held high, ready to snap off a shot, longing for a glimpse of red fez above white hair. No such luck – nothing but the spark of multiple muzzle flashes, the reports of the gunfire arriving at the same time as the projectiles themselves. Fragments sprayed from the stonework as he threw himself back into the lee of the doorway. This was no good – no bloody good at all.

With a surge of temper he levelled his pistol at the bell mounted above them on the wall. He put two rounds into the mechanism, and then a third for good measure. The ringing in his ears from the shots was as bad as the alarm, but as it faded away it was replaced by relative silence.

"Thank the Lord..." he breathed.

"We could rush 'em sir," said Dixon, nodding towards the courtyard. "Charge out there, screaming and shouting. Like as not the buggers will wet their breeches and scarper."

"Maybe Chief," said Anderson. "The look on your face could prompt incontinence in anyone."

The engineer's frown lifted for a moment, then returned in full force. "Frankly sir, it's been a piss-poor day, if you'll excuse my French. I wouldn't mind taking out a few of these bastards before the end." He lifted his carbine. "Repayment – for the boys in the engine room."

Anderson put his hand on Dixon's shoulder, his grim expression a match for the engineer's. "If it comes to it, we'll repay the debt together."

The exchange was interrupted by movement amongst the men behind them. The crew parted to allow a trio of new arrivals to push through the throng. There was Jones – pale but upright. He limped ahead of the other two, grimacing with every step. He looked like death warmed up, but that was still a damn sight healthier than Anderson might have expected. Kowalski however, was another matter entirely. The Floridian hung limp, feet dragging as Sullivan hauled him along.

The doctor caught Anderson's look. "Don't worry Captain. He'll live."

Sullivan was bent like a half-shut knife between the twin burdens of the unconscious mercenary and the huge battered book he lugged beneath his other arm.

"A little light reading?" said Anderson, nodding at the thick volume.

"Don't bother," put in Jones. "I've told him it's not the time for collecting souvenirs. He's determined to ignore me."

Sullivan scowled. "We all had reasons for coming. This was mine."

Jones acknowledged the point. He nodded over Anderson's shoulder towards the courtyard.

"We need to get moving before Wilberforce arrives..."

"Our hosts appear reluctant for us to depart," said Anderson. "We'll have to wait until your aeronautical friend arrives with our ride home. Some supporting fire from above should sort things out."

Jones and Sullivan shared a look.

"What?" asked Anderson.

"He's not coming to pick us up," said Jones. "He doesn't even know we're here..."

Beyond the doorway, the eerie shriek of falling bombs drowned out the crack of the Turkish guns.

*

Smoke mushroomed up from the castle – sunburst detonations swallowed up in blooming showers of debris. A ragged cluster of explosions shattered the front of the fortress – the walls tumbling inward.

Wilberforce whooped at the sight, craning round in his seat, peering down at the carnage unfolding in their wake.

"Bloody marvellous, eh Johnson?"

"Round for another pass sir?" said the co-pilot, phlegmatic as ever.

Wilberforce turned back to the controls, his fingers twitching on the stick. "Good Lord yes."

He pulled the throttles out to their stops, setting the engines roaring, the props a blur as they chopped at the air with increased vigour. The vibration worked its way up the aircraft, the entire cockpit set rattling with the acceleration.

Wilberforce hauled on the yoke, pushing the rudders into position, forcing the dirigible around in a tight turn. The airship's shuddering went up another notch, the girders of her frame groaning in protest.

"Steady on sir," said Johnson, bracing himself against the control panel as they banked.

Wilberforce flashed his co-pilot a smile. High time the lad enjoyed a bit of proper flying – give him a taste for the real thrill of it.

He held the stick locked in place, the dirigible keeled over, almost horizontal. They approached the desired heading and he jerked the stick back in the opposite direction. His feet danced across the pedals as the gondola swung, the airship's tortured joints redoubling their complaints.

The view through the forward windows steadied – the castle on its crag, smoke and fire surging up from its shattered frontage.

"Don't ever let them tell you an airship's not manoeuvrable..."

Johnson swallowed, face pale. "No sir."

Wilberforce flicked a switch on the console, triggering a rumble from below as the gondola's second set of bay doors swung open. He imagined the shining metal curves of the bombs dangling beneath him – ready to unleash another round of explosive mayhem.

He grinned beneath his moustache and pointed at the fortress ahead.

"Let's finish the job. The place still looks a tad upright for my tastes."

*

Torches flared into life, banishing the dark, clouds of dust swirling in the orange light. Jones spat dirt and regarded the pile of rubble which filled the passage. It looked as if the entire bloody castle had collapsed into the narrow space the men had occupied only moments before.

The whistle of the bombs had sent the *Nautica*'s crew scrabbling back into the depths of the tunnel – escaping the explosions with little more than scrapes and bruises.

"Well, that rather scuppers our exit plans," said Anderson.

"Quite. I had rather hoped Wilberforce would be late," said Jones. "He is for everything else."

A figure pushed through the press of men. Kowalski's features were drawn and haggard beneath a coating of dust. He wiped a bandaged hand across his forehead, scraping a clear stripe through the grime. He squinted in the flickering torchlight.

"What'd I miss?"

"The usual," said Jones. "People trying to blow us up."

The Floridian eyed the wall of broken stone sealing the passage.

"What now Major?"

"I'll be buggered if I know. But one thing I'm sure of – Wilberforce will be back." He looked at the arched stone ceiling above them. "As we haven't been buried alive just yet, I'm assuming at least some of the castle is still standing. Wilberforce won't like that. Airmen and their bombs – he won't be able to help himself."

Dixon shouldered his way into the discussion. "If we're not getting a lift in that balloon, why don't we take the boat?"

Jones and Kowalski spoke together.

"What boat?"

*

A second wave of explosions rumbled through the rock, setting tremors shaking beneath their feet. The growl of collapsing masonry lent desperate haste to their flight down the uneven steps, the men stumbling in the half-light leaking in through the cavern's mouth.

Jones' gaze flicked between his footing and the launch moored below. How it was there, and why it had a Royal Navy flag hanging at its stern remained a complete mystery to him. Not that it mattered. However the boat had wound up in the cave, it was a sight for sore eyes.

A crack rang out from the roof, as loud as a rifle report, drawing Jones' attention upward. One of the hanging stalactites detached from amidst its fellows and dropped, a heavy spear of stone.

"Look out!"

He dived for the scant cover offered by the cliff face. The men around him did the same, all squashing back against the rock, pressing themselves flat, attempting to occupy as little space as possible.

The column thumped down, smashing into the ledge ahead of Jones. The impact cracked a section from the steps, sending three men tumbling in an avalanche of stone and screams.

Jones watched the men fall, their upturned faces twisted, mouths frozen in horrified o's of surprise. Limbs flailing, the trio struck the water, followed by a tonne of rubble. A single man surfaced, but only to float face down and motionless.

More cracks echoed out, more rock breaking free across the cavern roof. Fissures appeared in the stone ceiling, jagged gaps opening up between the stalactites. A steady rain of fragments spattered down, punctuated with the occasional massive boulder.

"Get to the damned boat," called Jones, waving the men forward, ushering them on from their contemplation of their fallen crewmate.

Amidst a clattering hail of broken stone, they scrambled down the stairway. Those in the vanguard had already made it to the jetty far below. They sprinted for the moored launch. The men immediately ahead of Jones moved more slowly, bunched up as they took turns to leap the newly-created gap in the stairs.

Kowalski made the jump. Jones sucked in a breath and followed, launching himself across the crack, stomach lurching at the drop below. He landed, feet skidding on gravel, grateful for Kowalski's steadying hand.

Kowalski beckoned to Sullivan, the only man still to make the leap.

"Come on Doc."

"This first..." replied Sullivan, raising the book.

"Leave the bloody thing," shouted Jones.

Sullivan turned his attention from the chasm to the tome in his hands, then back to the waiting men. He shook his head and lifted the bulky volume, making to throw it across.

But before he could release the book, a dark shape reared up behind him, a twisted claw swinging round out of the gloom. The cruel swipe took Sullivan in the side of the head, sending him reeling.

He staggered, dazed, blinking behind the spider-cracked lenses of his glasses. The book tumbled from his fingers and slipped towards the void. He lunged after his prize, fingers scrabbling desperately at the air. The movement took him over the edge and the man from Porton Down was gone, dropping without a sound.

A monstrous apparition lurched into the space Sullivan had occupied – a groaning, heaving mess of metal. Torn hydraulic hoses flapped and hissed, damaged gears slipped against one another. Suspended within the mangled steel struts hung a lump of blackened flesh. The fire had consumed Von Gossler, leaving him a foul scrap of a man – his skin scorched, twisted and cracked.

The eyes rolled round, red-rimmed in the twice-burnt face. The awful stare fixed on Jones and Kowalski as they backed away. What little remained of Von Gossler opened its jaws wide. The skin cracked wetly at the corners of its mouth, adding a spray of blood into the screech it directed at them.

They hoisted their pistols as one and fired. Kowalski's gun wobbled in his left hand, his shots flying in sporadic pattern, some striking home, most pinging harmlessly from the rock face. Jones' fire was more accurate but had as little effect. Von Gossler shrugged off the impacts and continued his awkward shuffle towards the crack in the stairs.

Kowalski's gun fell silent, its magazine spent. Jones' pistol too hammered down on an empty chamber. He hauled at the Floridian's arm.

"Come on..."

Kowalski turned, eyes hard, his voice cold and flat.

"Get going Major."

"Don't be insane..."

Von Gossler leapt the gap, the effort sending air pressure howling from his joints. He landed in a clumsy crouch, iron feet skidding across the rock in a shower of sparks. His arms flailed and his pistons groaned as he struggled to keep his balance.

Kowalski ripped free from Jones' grasp and charged up the steps.

The Floridian crashed into Von Gossler's steel skeleton. The pair strained against one another – twisted metalwork and leaking hydraulics versus injured bones and aching muscle. The German hissed and Kowalski roared as they lurched back and forth, their hatred a perfect match.

With a crack of stone, the ledge beneath them gave way. Clawing at each other, the pair tumbled and fell, disappearing from Jones' view.

*

The boat heaved and pitched as another chunk of rock plummeted from above, thumping into the water and sending great waves surging across the pool. Anderson cringed at the sound of stones clattering down across the deck. They'd get no warning – one moment they'd be bobbing on the surface, the next, smashed into driftwood.

Anderson cast his gaze towards the stairway, his eyes following the course of the ancient steps up into the gloom. The others hadn't been that far behind, he thought. Where the bloody hell had they got to?

The launch's engine rumbled into life and dirty smoke spewed up from the funnel. A moment later Dixon appeared at his side. Despite their situation, the man appeared to have regained his gruff composure now he had a deck beneath his feet and machinery to fiddle with. The engineer rubbed his oil-stained hands together.

"Ready to go sir," he said.

"We wait. As long as we can."

A crash from behind drew their attention. A lump of stone, as big as Anderson's head, had smacked down into the corner of the wheelhouse roof, caving in the woodwork and shattering half the window panes. A pair of crewmen hunched within the buckled compartment, peering wide-eyed through the cracked glass.

Dixon frowned. "Don't want to lose two boats in one day – we'll get ourselves a reputation..."

Both men clutched at the rail as another wave rolled into the launch, setting the deck pitching and the hull scraping against the quay.

"They got us out of that bloody dungeon," said Anderson. "We wait."

*

Jones dived forward. He slid to the edge of the cliff in time to see Von Gossler strike the water's surface. Gouts of spray shot up at the impact. The German didn't float, not even for an instant. A surge of foam closed over him and he vanished, dragged to oblivion by his metal frame.

"A little help here?" croaked a voice.

Kowalski hung by his good hand, spread-eagled on the jagged incline left by the landslide. His battered face peered up at Jones.

"Any time you're ready —"

Kowalski's half-smile vanished as his handhold gave out. His feet scrabbled for purchase and his fingers clawed at the rock. Jones launched himself out, stretching as far as he could. He clamped his grip around Kowalski's wrist. The Floridian's slide ground to a halt. A cascade of pebbles and fragments of stone skittered past them, beginning the long drop towards the pool.

"I've got you," said Jones through gritted teeth, attempting to ignore the shrieks from his shoulder muscles.

"Swell Major," grunted Kowalski. "But who's got you?"

As if prompted by the question, Jones began to slip. He slithered forward, powerless to resist gravity's pull. Kowalski dangled beneath, unable to find a hold on the rock face.

"Let me go..." said Kowalski. "Done what I came to do."

"Don't be bloody daft," snarled Jones.

He spread his body out flat, pressing himself into the stone, trying to slow the inexorable drag. The sinews popped in his arm and the hard angle of the cliff's lip dug into his chest. Sweat streamed from his brow — the hot salt sting of it in his eyes.

Something closed around his ankle and he kicked out in reflex. The thrash sent him another six inches over the edge. Kowalski's eyes went wide at the lurch.

The grip on Jones' ankle was back, unshakeable this time, and then the other too was grabbed. With a jerk, the awful slide came to an abrupt halt. His joints howled in protest as he stretched out between the pull at his feet and Kowalski's unforgiving heft.

Jones stared down at his fingers, willing strength into his grip. He ignored all else, pouring his focus down his trembling forearm into the burning muscles of his hand.

A cruel eternity of effort dragged out and then the rough stone was scraping against him and he and Kowalski were pulled back from the lip.

Anderson and Dixon dropped Jones' legs and slumped down beside the rescued pair. The four men huddled together against the rock face.

"I think that's us even again..." panted Anderson, clutching at his injured ribs, pale from his exertions.

"Even?" Kowalski rolled over to regard the submariners. "Heh. Not even close. Figure I'll be buying you fellers drinks 'til Judgement Day."

Dixon eyed the cavern roof. "Let's get out of here before we start totting up the bar bill."

Jones hauled himself to his feet, wincing at the complaints from his tortured ankles.

"The Chief's right. Come on – we've a boat to catch."

*

They staggered down the steps, clutching each other for support – dividing their time between watching their footing and keeping a weather eye out for danger from above. The air was thick with dust, clogging their throats with each laboured breath. They limped through the murk, their coughs swallowed up by the rumbles and cracks of the cave's collapse.

A constant rain of fragments pitter-pattered down around them, the occasional larger stone knocking lumps from the steps then bouncing out and down, tumbling to the water. The men scrambled through the downfall, arms curled over their heads – meagre protection from the hail, and no protection at all if they were to find themselves in the path of a descending stalactite.

Jones sent up a silent prayer of gratitude when they finally stumbled onto the jetty. It was a bloody miracle they'd made it down with nothing more serious than new bruises and mouthfuls of grit.

They clambered over the launch's rail, the task costing more effort than Jones could have imagined possible. Dixon was the only one of the quartet who didn't make a meal of this simple obstacle. After helping to haul the others aboard, the engineer bustled off, bellowing orders to get the boat underway. The remaining trio leaned against the railing, too drained to speak.

The engine noise shifted into higher gear and the deck rumbled beneath their feet. The boat pulled away from the dock, foam churning at its stern. The cave mouth beckoned, hints of daylight drawing them forward. Behind, the stalactites dropped with increasing frequency – the stairway now lost from view behind the tumble of stone.

Jones spotted something bobbing amidst the debris, rocking in the swell caused by the falling rocks. He nudged Kowalski and pointed. They regarded Sullivan's book – its red leather cover waterlogged and black.

"We could circle round," said Anderson, following their gaze. "Maybe fish it out." His tone and the way his eyes flicked up to the cavern roof suggested he was anything but keen on the idea.

Jones' mind was filled with images of Sullivan's eager gaze, of Falke's cruel intelligence, and of teeth and iron claws glittering in the night.

"Leave it," he said.

The three men watched the book recede in their wake. Its outline grew smaller and smaller until it was lost from view along with any details of the cave's crumbling interior.

The boat steamed out into the morning sun, her Red Ensign snapping in the breeze.

***

Acknowledgements

Firstly, a massive thanks to YOU. I'm delighted you chose to give these stories a go and I really hope you enjoyed them. If you did, it would be lovely if you could see your way to posting a short review on Amazon or Goodreads. Go on, it'll genuinely make my day!

These books wouldn't have happened without a bunch of people who provided encouragement, advice and much-needed beer or coffee at various stages in the writing. Particular thanks to Alex, Doug, Richard, Chris, Aidan, Suzanne, Gillian, and my Mum, for being brave Beta Readers and dealing with the awfulness of the early drafts.

Thanks to the staff at Orocco Pier in Queensferry for keeping me supplied with coffee and bacon during my Sunday morning writing sessions.

Big thanks to Judy and Toby, in whose beautiful house "Lochside" most of my plot outlines were written.

Thanks also to all my friends at work and on Facebook who took a chance on reading the first one and were then kind enough to say it wasn't dreadful. The continuation of the series was your fault!

Lastly, a massive thank you to Al, for not rolling her eyes back in 2012 when I said for the millionth time I was going to write a book. And, of course, to Danny and Blythe who make me proud every single day.

Rod Gillies, Edinburgh 2015

11354395R00216

Printed in Great Britain
by Amazon.co.uk, Ltd.,
Marston Gate.